"Wonderfully eclectic, impressive . . . a superior feline festschrift for the lasting enjoyment of cat lovers!"
—*Booklist*

"A delightful anthology."   —*Publishers Weekly*

"The cat anthology to top all other cat anthologies . . . a delightful surprise for cat lovers!"   —*Buffalo News*

"Feline fanciers and literature gourmets will enjoy this charming collection."   —*Library Journal*

"Proves that serious literary types—such as W. B. Yeats, Damon Runyon, and Rainer Maria Rilke—are just as batty about their cats as the rest of us!"   —*Princeton Times*

JOYCE CAROL OATES—novelist, short story writer, poet, essayist, and playwright—occupies a unique place among American writers.

DANIEL HALPERN is a poet, editor of the literary magazine *Antaeus*, and editor/publisher of the Ecco Press.

Both live in Princeton, New Jersey, with their cats.

THE
SOPHISTICATED

A WILLIAM ABRAHAMS BOOK
PLUME

CAT *A Gathering of Stories, Poems, and Miscellaneous Writings About Cats*

CHOSEN BY

Joyce Carol Oates

AND

Daniel Halpern

PLUME
Published by the Penguin Group
Penguin Books USA Inc., 375 Hudson Street, New York, New York 10014, U.S.A.
Penguin Books Ltd, 27 Wrights Lane, London W8 5TZ, England
Penguin Books Australia Ltd, Ringwood, Victoria, Australia
Penguin Books Canada Ltd, 10 Alcorn Avenue, Toronto, Ontario, Canada M4V 3B2
Penguin Books (N.Z.) Ltd, 182–190 Wairau Road, Auckland 10, New Zealand

Penguin Books Ltd, Registered Offices: Harmondsworth, Middlesex, England

Published by Plume, an imprint of Dutton Signet, a division of Penguin Books USA Inc.
Previously published in a hardcover edition by Dutton.

First Plume Printing, November, 1993
10 9 8 7 6 5 4 3 2 1

Acknowledgments for permission to reprint appear on pages 393–96.

Ⓟ REGISTERED TRADEMARK—MARCA REGISTRADA

LIBRARY OF CONGRESS CATALOGING-IN-PUBLICATION DATA
The Sophisticated cat : a gathering of stories, poems, and
    miscellaneous writings about cats / chosen by Joyce Carol Oates and
    Daniel Halpern.
        p.   cm.
    ISBN 0-452-27045-6
    1. Cats—Literary collections.   I. Oates, Joyce Carol, 1938–
II. Halpern, Daniel, 1945–
[PN6071.C3S65   1993]
808.8′036—dc20   93–803
                                                                CIP

Printed in the United States of America
Original hardcover design by Eve L. Kirch

PUBLISHER'S NOTE
Some of these stories are works of fiction. Names, characters, places, and incidents
either are the product of the authors' imagination or are used fictitiously, and any
resemblance to actual persons, living or dead, events, or locales is entirely coincidental.

To Muffin & Poppy
Sophisticates Extraordinaire

CONTENTS

3. MORE STORIES ABOUT CATS
FROM THE MASTERS

4. CAT POETRY FROM THE
TWENTIETH CENTURY

5. MORE STORIES ABOUT CATS

6. CAT POETRY IN TRANSLATION

7.   CONTEMPORARY STORYTELLERS ON CATS

8.   CONTEMPORARY POETS ON CATS

9.   WHIMSICAL CAT TALES

10. WHIMSICAL CAT POEMS

11. THE TRUTH ABOUT CATS

PREFACE

by Joyce Carol Oates

It has often been observed that, through the centuries, writers have been drawn to cats above all animals: not simply to loving relationships with them, but to the veneration of them in poetry and prose. Why?

I was watching our new, six-month kitten stalking, with excruciating patience, an invisible prey in the grass and tangled vines outside my study window, observing how, in what must seem to him "the wild," Reynard quivered as if charged with electricity: his eyes tawny yellow, ears stiffly alert, head poised and body in a crouch that would enable his muscular little hindlegs to propel him forward onto his prey. There was something touching and comical in such behavior in so young a cat—unless there was something chilling. For, no mistake about it, little Reynard is a born hunter, a true carnivore, and his small jaws are made to tear, crunch, and chew. Fortunately, as his human owner, I am too large to be his prey.

After some suspenseful moments, during which time Reynard tremulously advanced upon whatever it was that had excited his hunter's instinct, a real or fancied movement triggered a spring, and he leapt—pouncing on some leaves. I tapped against the windowpane, and he immediately trotted over, tail erect, eyes urgently fixed upon me, tiny mouth opening in a mewing appeal. How swift, the transformation from lethal hunter-carnivore to sweet-natured household pet! Is this a dazzling display of virtuoso "adaptive behavior," or is it a brilliant example of animal hypocrisy? Is it both? Which is the "real" Reynard? Where genetically determined behavior and socialized behavior conflict, which would yield to the other?

In the cats with whom many of us live so companionably, the transition from hunter-carnivore to household pet takes place in a matter of seconds; in the history of evolution, it is a matter of millennia. Though it is estimated that dogs first became domesticated approximately twelve thousand years ago, it is estimated that *Felis sylvestris* (the wildcat) evolved into *Felis catus* (the domestic cat) only five thousand years ago; the claim that man "domesticated" the cat for his own purposes is surely a flattering myth propagated by cats, for how much more likely that *Felis sylvestris* "domesticated" man for his purposes. (Can we speculate what those purposes might be?) It is a mystery of evolution that, while all members of the family of Felidae save one are known for their untameability (and their dangerousness), this one member, *Felis sylvestris*, so happily adapted himself to man. How cunning! How farsighted! Unlike dogs, with whom they are obliged to share human households, cats are creatures unwilling (not unable: unwilling) to do anything against the grain of their desire, even for rewards.

Clearly, *Felis sylvestris* domesticated us because he wished to: *because he had a plan.*

As the great variety of poetry and prose pieces in *The Sophisticated Cat* suggests, writers have long been fascinated by cats. Male, female, "romantic," coolly skeptical—we are mesmerized by the beautiful wild creatures who long ago chose to domesticate us, and who condescend to live with us, so wonderfully to their advantage; and, of course, to ours. My theory is that the writer senses a deep and profound kinship with the cat: *Felis sylvestris* in the well-groomed furry cloak and mask of *Felis catus*. The wildcat is the "real" cat, the soul of the domestic cat; unknowable to human beings, he yet exists inside our household pets, who have long ago seduced us with their seemingly civilized ways. (Yes, and with their beauty, grace, independence, willfulness—the model of what a human being should be.) The writer, like any artist, is inhabited by an unknowable and unpredictable core of being which, by custom, we designate "the imagination" or "the unconscious" (as if naming were equivalent to knowing, let alone controlling), and so in the accessibility of *Felis catus* we sense the secret, demonic, wholly inaccessible presence of *Felis sylvestris*.

For like calls out to like, across even the abyss of species.

THE CAT: A PREFACE

by *Daniel Halpern*

It may be that the first living thing with a metabolism of its own that falls into your control and becomes *your* dependent, maintains itself in the imagination like the earliest memories of family. The purpose of compiling an anthology of texts in honor of cats, beyond the obvious nod to literature, is to pay homage to that early memory, that first pet whose well-being was the first true responsibility. My earliest dependent was a seven-toed alley cat we named Dubsie, because she had two double toes, as well as eighteen other normal digits. I found her, won for her a place in our house, and took firm control of her future.

Having divulged this, I must admit that the great love of my life—I'd say "cat love," but I know this would diminish the relationship in the minds of some—is Poppy, my twenty-two-year-old Burmese, whose bag of tricks and lives numbering fewer than nine have made my own twenty-two years in New York City possible, even bearable. There are numerous anecdotes I'd love to share, but it is one in particular that illustrates the personality and wiles of Poppy the cat. For years visitors to my apartment claimed to lose small articles of adornment: rings, earrings, barrettes, small but colorful brooches, and pins of an assorted variety. They were never recovered and it was no doubt assumed that these petty thefts were an aspect my own questionable character. Of course, I was innocent, even if those visitors would have voted to the negative. But a few years after my first and only marriage, adequate time for Poppy to assume this resident was here to stay, the mystery of the missing articles was solved. It was a Sunday morning; my wife and I were pondering the Sunday *New York Times* with a selection of smoked fish from Russ and Daughters on the Lower East Side. Something on the floor caught the early sun and flashed a ricochet of light on to me. I looked up and there, in a small, neat pile, were the missing articles from the Seventies and Eighties, a foot away from our sunning cat, who had (and this part too is true) a wonderful smile spread from one furry ear to the other. As written by Lewis Carroll in these pages, " 'Well! I've often seen a cat without a grin,' thought Alice; 'but a grin without a cat! It's the most curious thing I ever saw in all my life!' "

Cats have a body of mythology built up for themselves that is mostly correct and usually has to do with notions of mystery; this mythology, or feline reputation, addresses their *affect*, the way they move, the way they don't move, the way they respond (or don't), the hours they keep, their eating habits, their interest in the breath of infant humans, and so on. I don't wish to address here the various issues inherent in these notions, but I do want to argue with one belief that runs deeply through much of the body of cat mythology: "Cats are independent." Cats are not independent. They are *cool*, yes, but they are not, as some mistakenly believe, unattached or participants solely in their own world. When you watch a cat carefully you begin to understand that he or she knows, every minute you're in a room together, exactly where you are, especially if you're the primary guardian. Cats don't actually need to look at you to know this. Their ears rotate to find you, they catch the drift of your particular essence, they sense your shadow float over the fine, thin skin of their lightly furred eyelids. But regardless of how they know it, they know. They know and they *care*, notwithstanding William Faulkner's accusation, "But he [the cat] does not love you." Because they do. Oh yes, they love you. And that love is of a high order, or, as Pierre Loti described it, a love "with no docility, but with an unalterable and touching constancy."

If yours is the indoor variety, *you* are what they know of the world, save friends, members of the family, and other loved ones, when appropriate. If they have dual lives, which is to say, if they are allowed out of the house on their own, *you* are what awaits them after a hard bout of nocturnal foraging. You are the nonpareil parent, the provider, the meal ticket, the warm lap where these spiritual animals (if they've been properly raised) go to relax, to forget the suburban game that got away, the sticks and stones that might have broken their bones, as well as the others of their species, now left to the cold of the cold, indifferent world.

Adlai Stevenson, as Governor of Illinois, once vetoed a bill entitled "An Act to Provide Protection to Insectivorous Birds by Restraining Cats." He wrote to the members of his Senate, in a typically subtle but irrefutable rebuke, "It is in the nature of cats to do a certain amount of unescorted roaming. . . . Also consider the owner's dilemma: To escort a cat abroad on a leash is against the nature of the cat, and to permit it to venture forth for exercise unattended into the night of new dangers is against the nature of the owner." And so the bill went down—and so the pragmatic beauty of this anthology, which allows the actual cats of this life to remain safely at home (or well-bedded in memory), and at the same time venture forth into the literary night as *cats represented*, as celebrated objects via the pages that follow, and ultimately into the hearts of readers everywhere.

* * *

The Sophisticated Cat divides into eleven sections—casual groups of particular genres, which aim to flush different aspects of *catness* into the open. The collection begins with stories by the masters, wonderful glimpses into the world of cats by the likes of Chekhov ("Obviously he was born a mouse catcher, a worthy son of his bloodthirsty ancestors"), Balzac, and Wodehouse ("Cats as a class, have never completely got over the snootiness caused by the fact that in Ancient Egypt they were worshipped as gods"). This is followed by a sampling of pre-twentieth-century poetry: "The Canon" begins with Christopher Smart's undeniable cat Jeoffry, who "counteracts the powers of darkness by his electrical skin & glaring eyes," and includes poems by Keats and Shelley, Wordsworth's moving "The Kitten and Falling Leaves," and John Skelton's "The Churlyshe Cat," with its edgy and wacky Skeltonics:

> That cat especyally,
> That slew so cruelly
> My lytell pretty sparowe
> That I brought up at Carowe.
> O cat of churlyshe kynde

Then the early masters of this century, in turn, invoke the subject at hand—Hemingway and Mark Twain, and W. B. Yeats, who writes of his cat Minnaloushe and the moon:

> Minnaloushe creeps through the grass
> Alone, important and wise,
> And lifts to the changing moon
> His changing eyes.

And Hart Crane writes, in one of his most memorable poems, again featuring the moon to further the cat:

> . . . but we have seen
> The moon in lonely alleys make
> A grail of laughter of an empty ash can,
> And through all sound of gaiety and quest
> Have heard a kitten in the wilderness.

There are poems honoring cats in translation by Rilke, Baudelaire, and the great Chilean Nobel Prize–winning poet Pablo Neruda, who is not one to neglect his own invocation:

> His is that peerless
> integrity,
> neither moonlight nor petal
> repeats
> his contexture:
> he is all things in all,
> like the sun or a topaz,
> and the flexible line of his contour
> is subtle and certain
> as the cut of a bowsprit.

There are poems to the favored beast by contemporary fiction writers and poets, followed by a selection of stories and poems that address the more whimsical aspects of the cat personality: Kipling's cat, who walked alone; Lewis Carroll's famous Cheshire; even the fabled cats Aesop employed will be found between these covers.

And to keep honest the cats included herein, the book comes to a close with the section entitled "The Truth About Cats," with contributions by Maupassant, who relates his own encounters with cats

---

("I remember that when I was a child I loved cats, yet I had even then that strange desire to strangle them with my little hands"); Herodotus on the cats of Egypt; Boswell on Dr. Johnson's beloved Hodge, for whom the good doctor purchased oysters; Roy Blount, Jr.'s dogs-versus-cats polemic; and other miscellany by the likes of Sir Walter Scott, Thomas Gray, William Faulkner, Benjamin Franklin, and Adlai Stevenson.

If you the reader enjoy this feline festschrift half as much as we enjoyed assembling it, we will have rewarded each other, and things will have worked out perfectly [*sic*].

Part One

CAT STORIES
BY THE
MASTERS

ANTON CHEKHOV

Who Was to Blame?

As my uncle Pyotr Demyanitch, a lean, bilious collegiate councillor, exceedingly like a stale smoked fish with a stick through it, was getting ready to go to the high school, where he taught Latin, he noticed that the corner of his grammar was nibbled by mice.

"I say, Praskovya," he said, going into the kitchen and addressing the cook, "how is it we have got mice here? Upon my word! yesterday my top hat was nibbled, to-day they have disfigured my Latin grammar. . . . At this rate they will soon begin eating my clothes!"

"What can I do? I did not bring them in!" answered Praskovya.

"We must do something! You had better get a cat, hadn't you?" . . .

"I've got a cat, but what good is it?"

And Praskovya pointed to the corner where a white kitten, thin as a match, lay curled up asleep beside a broom.

"Why is it no good?" asked Pyotr Demyanitch.

"It's young yet, and foolish. It's not two months old yet."

"H'm. . . . Then it must be trained. It had much better be learning instead of lying there."

Saying this, Pyotr Demyanitch sighed with a careworn air and went out of the kitchen. The kitten raised his head, looked lazily after him, and shut his eyes again.

The kitten lay awake thinking. Of what? Unacquainted with real life, having no store of accumulated impressions, his mental processes could only be instinctive, and he could but picture life in accordance with the conceptions that he had inherited, together with his flesh and blood, from his ancestors, the tigers (*vide* Darwin). His thoughts were of the nature of day-dreams. His feline imagination pictured something like the Arabian desert, over which flitted shadows closely resembling Praskovya, the stove, the broom. In the midst of the shadows there suddenly appeared a saucer of milk; the saucer began to grow paws, it began moving and displayed a tendency to run; the kitten made a bound, and with a thrill of bloodthirsty sensuality thrust his claws into it. . . . When the saucer had vanished into obscurity a piece of meat appeared, dropped by Praskovya; the meat ran away with a cowardly squeak, but the kitten made a bound and got his claws into it. . . . Everything that rose before the imagination of the young dreamer had for its starting-point leaps, claws, and teeth. . . . The soul of another is darkness, and a cat's soul more than most, but how near the visions just described are to the truth may be seen from the following fact: under the influence of his day-dreams the kitten suddenly leaped up, looked with flashing eyes at Praskovya, ruffled up his coat, and making one bound, thrust his claws into the cook's skirt. Obviously he was born a mouse catcher, a worthy son of his bloodthirsty ancestors. Fate had destined him to be the terror of cellars, store-rooms and cornbins, and had it not been for education . . . we will not anticipate, however.

On his way home from the high school, Pyotr Demyanitch went into a general shop and bought a mouse-trap for fifteen kopecks. At dinner he fixed a little bit of his rissole on the hook, and set the trap under the sofa, where there were heaps of the pupils' old exercise-books, which Praskovya used for various domestic purposes. At six o'clock in the evening, when the worthy Latin master was sitting at the table correcting his pupils' exercises, there was a sudden "klop!" so loud that my uncle started and dropped his pen. He went at once to the sofa and took out the trap. A neat little mouse, the size of a thimble, was sniffing the wires and trembling with fear.

"Aha," muttered Pyotr Demyanitch, and he looked at the mouse malignantly, as though he were about to give him a bad mark. "You are cau—aught, wretch! Wait a bit! I'll teach you to eat my grammar!"

Having gloated over his victim, Pyotr Demyanitch put the mouse-trap on the floor and called:

"Praskovya, there's a mouse caught! Bring the kitten here!"

"I'm coming," responded Praskovya, and a minute later she came in with the descendant of tigers in her arms.

"Capital!" said Pyotr Demyanitch, rubbing his hands. "We will give him a lesson. . . . Put him down opposite the mouse-trap . . . that's it. . . . Let him sniff it and look at it. . . . That's it. . . ."

The kitten looked wonderingly at my uncle, at his arm-chair, sniffed the mouse-trap in bewilderment, then, frightened probably by the glaring lamplight and the attention directed to him, made a dash and ran in terror to the door.

"Stop!" shouted my uncle, seizing him by the tail, "stop, you rascal! He's afraid of a mouse, the idiot! Look! It's a mouse! Look! Well? Look, I tell you!"

Pyotr Demyanitch took the kitten by the scruff of the neck and pushed him with his nose against the mouse-trap.

"Look, you carrion! Take him and hold him, Praskovya. . . . Hold him opposite the door of the trap. . . . When I let the mouse out, you let him go instantly. . . . Do you hear? . . . Instantly let go! Now!"

My uncle assumed a mysterious expression and lifted the door of the trap. . . . The mouse came out irresolutely, sniffed the air, and flew like an arrow under the sofa. . . . The kitten on being released darted under the table with his tail in the air.

"It has got away! got away!" cried Pyotr Demyanitch, looking ferocious. "Where is he, the scoundrel? Under the table? You wait. . . ."

My uncle dragged the kitten from under the table and shook him in the air.

"Wretched little beast," he muttered, smacking him on the ear. "Take that, take that! Will you shirk it next time? Wr-r-r-etch. . . ."

Next day Praskovya heard again the summons.

"Praskovya, there is a mouse caught! Bring the kitten here!"

After the outrage of the previous day the kitten had taken refuge under the stove and had not come out all night. When Praskovya pulled him out and, carrying him by the scruff of the neck into the study, set him down before the mouse-trap, he trembled all over and mewed piteously.

"Come, let him feel at home first," Pyotr Demyanitch commanded. "Let him look and sniff. Look and learn! Stop, plague take you!" he shouted, noticing that the kitten was backing away from the mouse-trap. "I'll thrash you! Hold him by the ear! That's it. . . . Well now, set him down before the trap. . . ."

My uncle slowly lifted the door of the trap . . . the mouse whisked under the very nose of the kitten, flung itself against Praskovya's hand and fled under the cupboard; the kitten, feeling himself free, took a desperate bound and retreated under the sofa.

"He's let another mouse go!" bawled Pyotr Demyanitch. "Do you call that a cat? Nasty little beast! Thrash him! thrash him by the mouse-trap!"

When the third mouse had been caught, the kitten shivered all over at the sight of the mouse-trap and its inmate, and scratched Praskovya's hand. . . . After the fourth mouse my uncle flew into a rage, kicked the kitten, and said:

"Take the nasty thing away! Get rid of it! Chuck it away! It's no earthly use!"

A year passed, the thin, frail kitten had turned into a solid and sagacious tom-cat. One day he was on his way by the back yards to an amatory interview. He had just reached his destination when he suddenly heard a rustle, and thereupon caught sight of a mouse which ran from a water-trough towards a stable; my hero's hair stood on end, he arched his back, hissed, and trembling all over, took to ignominious flight.

Alas! sometimes I feel myself in the ludicrous position of the flying cat. Like the kitten, I had in my day the honour of being taught Latin by my uncle. Now, whenever I chance to see some work of classical antiquity, instead of being moved to eager enthusiasm, I begin recalling, *ut consecutivum*, the irregular verbs, the sallow grey face of my uncle, the ablative absolute. . . . I turn pale, my hair stands up on my head, and, like the cat, I take to ignominious flight.

—*Translated from the Russian by Constance Garnett*

P. G. WODEHOUSE

The Story of Webster

"Cats are not dogs!"

There is only one place where you can hear good things like that thrown off quite casually in the general run of conversation, and that is the bar parlor of the "Angler's Rest." It was there, as we sat grouped about the fire, that a thoughtful Pint of Bitter had made the statement just recorded.

Although the talk up to this point had been dealing with Einstein's Theory of Relativity, we readily adjusted our minds to cope with the new topic. Regular attendance at the nightly sessions over which Mr. Mulliner presides with such unfailing dignity and geniality tends to produce mental nimbleness. In our little circle I have known an argument on the Final Destination of the Soul to change inside forty seconds into one concerning the best method of preserving the juiciness of bacon fat.

"Cats," proceeded the Pint of Bitter, "are selfish. A man waits on a cat hand and foot for weeks, humoring its lightest whim, and then it goes and leaves him flat because it has found a place down the road where the fish is more frequent."

"What I've got against cats," said a Lemon Sour, speaking feelingly, as one brooding on a private grievance, "is their unreliability. They lack candor and are not square shooters. You get your cat and you call him Thomas or George, as the case may be. So far, so good. Then one morning you wake up and find six kittens in the hat-box and you have to reopen the whole matter, approaching it from an entirely different angle."

"If you want to know what's the trouble with cats," said a red-

7

faced man with glassy eyes, who had been rapping on the table for his fourth whisky, "they've got no tact. That's what's the trouble with them. I remember a friend of mine had a cat. Made quite a pet of that cat, he did. And what occurred? What was the outcome? One night he came home rather late and was feeling for the keyhole with his corkscrew; and, believe me or not, his cat selected that precise moment to jump on the back of his neck out of a tree. No tact."

Mr. Mulliner shook his head.

"I grant you all this," he said, "but still, in my opinion, you have not got to the root of the matter. The real objection to the great majority of cats is their insufferable air of superiority. Cats, as a class, have never completely got over the snootiness caused by the fact that in Ancient Egypt they were worshipped as gods. This makes them too prone to set themselves up as critics and censors of the frail and erring human beings whose lot they share. They stare rebukingly. They view with concern. And on a sensitive man this often has the worst effects, inducing an inferiority complex of the gravest kind. It is odd that the conversation should have taken this turn," said Mr. Mulliner, sipping his hot Scotch and lemon, "for I was thinking only this afternoon of the rather strange case of my cousin Edward's son, Lancelot."

"I knew a cat—" began a Small Bass.

My cousin Edward's son, Lancelot (said Mr. Mulliner) was, at the time of which I speak, a comely youth of some twenty-five summers. Orphaned at an early age, he had been brought up in the home of his Uncle Theodore, the saintly Dean of Bolsover; and it was a great shock to that good man when Lancelot, on attaining his majority, wrote from London to inform him that he had taken a studio in Bott Street, Chelsea, and proposed to remain in the metropolis and become an artist.

The Dean's opinion of artists was low. As a prominent member of the Bolsover Watch Committee, it had recently been his distasteful duty to be present at a private showing of the super-super-film *Palettes of Passion*; and he replied to his nephew's communication with a vibrant letter in which he emphasized the grievous pain it gave him to think that one of his flesh and blood should deliberately be embarking on a career which must inevitably lead sooner or later to the painting of Russian princesses lying on divans in the semi-nude with their arms round tame jaguars. He urged Lancelot to return and become a curate while there was yet time.

But Lancelot was firm. He deplored the rift between himself and a relative whom he had always respected; but he was dashed if he meant to go back to an environment where his individuality had been stifled and his soul confined in chains. And for four years there was silence between uncle and nephew.

During these years Lancelot had made progress in his chosen profession. At the time at which this story opens, his prospects seemed bright. He was painting the portrait of Brenda, only daughter of Mr. and Mrs. B. B. Carberry-Pirbright, of 11 Maxton Square, South Kensington, which meant thirty pounds in his sock on delivery. He had learned to cook eggs and bacon. He had practically mastered the ukulele. And, in addition, he was engaged to be married to a fearless young *vers libre* poetess of the name of Gladys Bingley, better known as The Sweet Singer of Garbridge Mews, Fulham—a charming girl who looked like a pen-wiper.

It seemed to Lancelot that life was very full and beautiful. He lived joyously in the present, giving no thought to the past.

But how true it is that the past is inextricably mixed up with the present and that we can never tell when it may spring some delayed bomb beneath our feet. One afternoon, as he sat making a few small alterations to the portrait of Brenda Carberry-Pirbright, his fiancée entered.

He had been expecting her to call, for today she was going off for a three weeks' holiday to the South of France, and she had promised to look in on her way to the station. He laid down his brush and gazed at her with a yearning affection, thinking for the thousandth time how he worshipped every spot of ink on her nose. Standing there in the doorway with her bobbed hair sticking out in every direction like a golliwog's, she made a picture that seemed to speak to his very depths.

"Hullo, Reptile!" he said lovingly.

"What ho, Worm!" said Gladys, maidenly devotion shining through the monocle which she wore in her left eye. "I can stay just half an hour."

"Oh, well, half an hour soon passes," said Lancelot. "What's that you've got there?"

"A letter, ass. What did you think it was?"

"Where did you get it?"

"I found the postman outside."

Lancelot took the envelope from her and examined it.

"Gosh!" he said.

"What's the matter?"

"It's from my Uncle Theodore."

"I didn't know you had an Uncle Theodore."

"Of course I have. I've had him for years."

"What's he writing to you about?"

"If you'll kindly keep quiet for two seconds, if you know how," said Lancelot, "I'll tell you."

And in a clear voice which, like that of all the Mulliners, however distant from the main branch, was beautifully modulated, he read as follows:

> *The Deanery,*
> *Bolsover,*
> *Wilts.*

My dear Lancelot,

    As you have, no doubt, already learned from your *Church Times*, I have been offered and have accepted the vacant Bishopric of Bongo-Bongo, in West Africa. I sail immediately to take up my new duties, which I trust will be blessed.

    In these circumstances it becomes necessary for me to find a good home for my cat Webster. It is, alas, out of the question that he should accompany me, as the rigors of the climate and the lack of essential comforts might well sap a constitution which has never been robust.

    I am dispatching him, therefore, to your address, my dear boy, in a straw-lined hamper, in the full confidence that you will prove a kindly and conscientious host.

    With cordial good wishes,

    Your affectionate uncle,

THEODORE BONGO-BONGO

For some moments after he had finished reading this communication, a thoughtful silence prevailed in the studio. Finally Gladys spoke.

"Of all the nerve!" she said. "I wouldn't do it."

"Why not?"

"What do you want with a cat?"

Lancelot reflected.

"It is true," he said, "that, given a free hand, I would prefer not to have my studio turned into a cattery or cat-bin. But consider the special circumstances. Relations between Uncle Theodore and self have for the last few years been a bit strained. In fact, you might say we had definitely parted brass-rags. It looks to me as if he were coming round. I should describe this letter as more or less what you might call an olive-branch. If I lush this cat up satisfactorily, shall I not be in a position later on to make a swift touch?"

"He is rich, this bean?" said Gladys, interested.

"Extremely."

"Then," said Gladys, "consider my objections withdrawn. A good stout check from a grateful cat-fancier would undoubtedly come in very handy. We might be able to get married this year."

"Exactly," said Lancelot. "A pretty loathsome prospect, of course; but still, as we've arranged to do it, the sooner we get it over, the better, what?"

"Absolutely."

"Then that's settled. I accept custody of cat."

"It's the only thing to do," said Gladys. "Meanwhile, can you lend me a comb? Have you such a thing in your bedroom?"

"What do you want with a comb?"

"I got some soup in my hair at lunch. I won't be a minute."

She hurried out, and Lancelot, taking up the letter again, found that he had omitted to read a continuation of it on the back page.

It was to the following effect:

> PS. In establishing Webster in your home, I am actuated by another motive than the simple desire to see to it that my faithful friend and companion is adequately provided for.
>
> From both a moral and an educative standpoint, I am convinced that Webster's society will prove of inestimable value to you. His advent, indeed, I venture to hope, will be a turning-point in your life. Thrown, as you must be, incessantly among loose and immoral Bohemians, you will find in this cat an example of upright conduct which cannot but act as an antidote to the poison cup of temptation which is, no doubt, hourly pressed to your lips.
>
> PPS. Cream only at midday, and fish not more than three times a week.

He was reading these words for the second time, when the front doorbell rang and he found a man on the steps with a hamper. A discreet mew from within revealed its contents, and Lancelot, carrying it into the studio, cut the strings.

"Hi!" he bellowed, going to the door.

"What's up?" shrieked his betrothed from above.

"The cat's come."

"All right. I'll be down in a jiffy."

Lancelot returned to the studio.

"What ho, Webster!" he said cheerily. "How's the boy?"

The cat did not reply. It was sitting with bent head, performing that wash and brush up which a journey by rail renders so necessary.

In order to facilitate these toilet operations, it had raised its left leg and was holding it rigidly in the air. And there flashed into Lancelot's mind an old superstition handed on to him, for what it was worth, by one of the nurses of his infancy. If, this woman had said, you creep up to a cat when its leg is in the air and give it a pull, then you make a wish and your wish comes true in thirty days.

It was a pretty fancy, and it seemed to Lancelot that the theory might as well be put to the test. He advanced warily, therefore, and was in the act of extending his fingers for the pull, when Webster, lowering the leg, turned and raised his eyes.

He looked at Lancelot. And suddenly with sickening force there came to Lancelot the realization of the unpardonable liberty he had been about to take.

Until this moment, though the postscript to his uncle's letter should have warned him, Lancelot Mulliner had had no suspicion of what manner of cat this was that he had taken into his home. Now, for the first time, he saw him steadily and saw him whole.

Webster was very large and very black and very composed. He conveyed the impression of being a cat of deep reserves. Descendant of a long line of ecclesiastical ancestors who had conducted their decorous courtships beneath the shadow of cathedrals and on the back walls of bishops' palaces, he had that exquisite poise which one sees in high dignitaries of the Church. His eyes were clear and steady, and seemed to pierce to the very roots of the young man's soul, filling him with a sense of guilt.

Once, long ago, in his hot childhood, Lancelot, spending his summer holidays at the deanery, had been so far carried away by ginger-beer and original sin as to plug a senior canon in the leg with his air-gun—only to discover, on turning, that a visiting archdeacon had been a spectator of the entire incident from his immediate rear. As he had felt then, when meeting the archdeacon's eye, so did he feel now as Webster's gaze played silently upon him.

Webster, it is true, had not actually raised his eyebrows. But this, Lancelot felt, was simply because he hadn't any.

He backed, blushing.

"Sorry!" he muttered.

There was a pause. Webster continued his steady scrutiny. Lancelot edged towards the door.

"Er—excuse me—just a moment . . ." he mumbled. And, sidling from the room, he ran distractedly upstairs.

"I say," said Lancelot.

"Now what?" asked Gladys.

"Have you finished with the mirror?"

"Why?"

"Well, I—er—I thought," said Lancelot, "that I might as well have a shave."

The girl looked at him, astonished.

"Shave? Why, you shaved only the day before yesterday."

"I know. But, all the same . . . I mean to say, it seems only respectful. That cat, I mean."

"What about him?"

"Well, he seems to expect it, somehow. Nothing actually said, don't you know, but you could tell by his manner. I thought a quick shave and perhaps a change into my blue serge suit—"

"He's probably thirsty. Why don't you give him some milk?"

"Could one, do you think?" said Lancelot doubtful. "I mean, I hardly seem to know him well enough." He paused. "I say, old girl," he went on, with a touch of hesitation.

"Hullo?"

"I know you won't mind my mentioning it, but you've got a few spots of ink on your nose."

"Of course I have. I always have spots of ink on my nose."

"Well . . . you don't think . . . a quick scrub with a bit of pumice-stone . . . I mean to say, you know how important first impressions are. . . ."

The girl stared.

"Lancelot Mulliner," she said, "if you think I'm going to skin my nose to the bone just to please a mangy cat—"

"Sh!" cried Lancelot, in agony.

"Here, let me go down and look at him," said Gladys petulantly.

As they re-entered the studio, Webster was gazing with an air of quiet distaste at an illustration from *La Vie Parisienne* which adorned one of the walls. Lancelot tore it down hastily.

Gladys looked at Webster in an unfriendly way.

"So that's the blighter!"

"Sh!"

"If you want to know what I think," said Gladys, "that cat's been living too high. Doing himself a dashed sight too well. You'd better cut his rations down a bit."

In substance, her criticism was not unjustified. Certainly, there was about Webster more than a suspicion of *embonpoint*. He had that air of portly well-being which we associate with those who dwell in cathedral closes. But Lancelot winced uncomfortably. He had so hoped that Gladys would make a good impression, and here she was, starting right off by saying the tactless thing.

He longed to explain to Webster that it was only her way; that in the Bohemian circles of which she was such an ornament genial chaff of a personal order was accepted and, indeed, relished. But it was too late. The mischief had been done. Webster turned in a pointed manner and withdrew silently behind the chesterfield.

Gladys, all unconscious, was making preparations for departure.

"Well, bung-oh," she said lightly. "See you in three weeks. I suppose you and that cat'll both be out on the tiles the moment my back's turned."

"Please! Please!" moaned Lancelot. "Please!"

He had caught sight of the tip of a black tail protruding from behind the chesterfield. It was twitching slightly, and Lancelot could read it like a book. With a sickening sense of dismay, he knew that Webster had formed a snap judgment of his fiancée and condemned her as frivolous and unworthy.

It was some ten days later that Bernard Worple, the neo-Vorticist sculptor, lunching at the Puce Ptarmigan, ran into Rodney Scollop, the powerful young surrealist. And after talking for a while of their art:

"What's all this I hear about Lancelot Mulliner?" asked Worple. "There's a wild story going about that he was seen shaved in the middle of the week. Nothing in it, I suppose?"

Scollop looked grave. He had been on the point of mentioning Lancelot himself, for he loved the lad and was deeply exercised about him.

"It is perfectly true," he said.

"It sounds incredible."

Scollop leaned forward. His fine face was troubled.

"Shall I tell you something, Worple?"

"What?"

"I know for an absolute fact," said Scollop, "that Lancelot Mulliner now shaves every morning."

Worple pushed aside the spaghetti which he was wreathing about him and through the gap stared at this companion.

"Every morning?"

"Every single morning. I looked in on him myself the other day, and there he was, neatly dressed in blue serge and shaved to the core. And, what is more, I got the distinct impression that he had used talcum powder afterwards."

"You don't mean that!"

"I do. And shall I tell you something else? There was a book lying open on the table. He tried to hide it, but he wasn't quick enough. It was one of those etiquette books!"

"An etiquette book!"

"*Polite Behaviour*, by Constance, Lady Bodbank."

Worple unwound a stray tendril of spaghetti from about his left ear. He was deeply agitated. Like Scollop, he loved Lancelot.

"He'll be dressing for dinner next!" he exclaimed.

"I have every reason to believe," said Scollop gravely, "that he does dress for dinner. At any rate, a man closely resembling him was seen furtively buying three stiff collars and a black tie at Hope Brothers in the King's Road last Tuesday."

Worple pushed his chair back, and rose. His manner was determined.

"Scollop," he said, "we are friends of Mulliner's, you and I. It is evident from what you tell me that subversive influences are at work and that never has he needed our friendship more. Shall we not go round and see him immediately?"

"It was what I was about to suggest myself," said Rodney Scollop.

Twenty minutes later they were in Lancelot's studio, and with a significant glance Scollop drew his companion's notice to their host's appearance. Lancelot Mulliner was neatly, even foppishly, dressed in blue serge with creases down the trouser-legs, and his chin, Worple saw with a pang, gleamed smoothly in the afternoon light.

At the sight of his friends' cigars, Lancelot exhibited unmistakable concern.

"You don't mind throwing those away, I'm sure," he said pleadingly.

Rodney Scollop drew himself up a little haughtily.

"And since when," he asked, "have the best fourpenny cigars in Chelsea not been good enough for you?"

Lancelot hastened to soothe him.

"It isn't me," he exclaimed. "It's Webster. My cat. I happen to know he objects to tobacco smoke. I had to give up my pipe in deference to his views."

Bernard Worple snorted.

"Are you trying to tell us," he sneered, "that Lancelot Mulliner allows himself to be dictated to by a blasted cat?"

"Hush!" cried Lancelot, trembling. "If you knew how he disapproves of strong language!"

"Where is this cat?" asked Rodney Scollop. "Is that the animal?" he said, pointing out of the window to where, in the yard, a tough-looking Tom with tattered ears stood mewing in a hard-boiled way out of the corner of its mouth.

"Good heavens, no!" said Lancelot. "That is an alley cat which comes round here from time to time to lunch at the dustbin. Webster is quite different. Webster has a natural dignity and repose of manner. Webster is a cat who prides himself on always being well turned out and whose high principles and lofty ideals shine from his eyes like beacon fires. . . ." And then suddenly, with an abrupt change of manner, Lancelot broke down and in a low voice added: "Curse him! Curse him! Curse him! Curse him!"

Worple looked at Scollop. Scollop looked at Worple.

"Come, old man," said Scollop, laying a gentle hand on Lancelot's bowed shoulder. "We are your friends. Confide in us."

"Tell us all," said Worple. "What's the matter?"

Lancelot uttered a bitter, mirthless laugh.

"You want to know what's the matter? Listen, then. I'm cat-pecked!"

"Cat-pecked?"

"You've heard of men being hen-pecked, haven't you?" said Lancelot with a touch of irritation. "Well, I'm cat-pecked."

And in broken accents he told his story. He sketched the history of his association with Webster from the latter's first entry into the studio. Confident now that the animal was not within earshot, he unbosomed himself without reserve.

"It's something in the beast's eye," he said in a shaking voice. "Something hypnotic. He casts a spell upon me. He gazes at me and disapproves. Little by little, bit by bit, I am degenerating under his influence from a wholesome, self-respecting artist into . . . well, I don't know what you call it. Suffice it to say that I have given up smoking, that I have ceased to wear carpet slippers and go about without a collar, that I never dream of sitting down to my frugal evening meal without dressing, and"—he choked—"I have sold my ukulele."

"Not that!" said Worple, paling.

"Yes," said Lancelot. "I felt he considered it frivolous."

There was a long silence.

"Mulliner," said Scollop, "this is more serious than I had supposed. We must brood upon your case."

"It may be possible," said Worple, "to find a way out."

Lancelot shook his head hopelessly.

"There is no way out. I have explored every avenue. The only thing that could possibly free me from this intolerable bondage would be if once—just once—I could catch that cat unbending. If once—merely once—it would lapse in my presence from its austere dignity for but a single instant, I feel that the spell would be broken. But what hope is there of that?" cried Lancelot passionately. "You were pointing just now to that alley cat in the yard. There stands one who has strained every nerve and spared no effort to break down Webster's inhuman self-control. I have heard that animal say things to him which you would think no cat with red blood in its veins would suffer for an instant. And Webster merely looks at him like a Suffragan Bishop eyeing an erring choirboy and turns his head and falls into a refreshing sleep."

He broke off with a dry sob. Worple, always an optimist, attempted in his kindly way to minimize the tragedy.

"Ah, well," he said. "It's bad, of course, but still, I suppose there is no actual harm in shaving and dressing for dinner and so on. Many great artists . . . Whistler, for example—"

"Wait!" cried Lancelot. "You have not heard the worst."

He rose feverishly, and, going to the easel, disclosed the portrait of Brenda Carberry-Pirbright.

"Take a look at that," he said, "and tell me what you think of her."

His two friends surveyed the face before them in silence. Miss Carberry-Pirbright was a young woman of prim and glacial aspect. One sought in vain for her reasons for wanting to have her portrait painted. It would be a most unpleasant thing to have about any house.

Scollop broke the silence.

"Friend of yours?"

"I can't stand the sight of her," said Lancelot vehemently.

"Then," said Scollop, "I may speak frankly. I think she's a pill."

"A blister," said Worple.

"A boil and a disease," said Scollop, summing up.

Lancelot laughed hackingly.

"You have described her to a nicety. She stands for everything most alien to my artist soul. She gives me a pain in the neck. I'm going to marry her."

"What!" cried Scollop.

"But you're going to marry Gladys Bingley," said Worple.

"Webster thinks not," said Lancelot bitterly. "At their first meeting he weighed Gladys in the balance and found her wanting. And the moment he saw Brenda Carberry-Pirbright he stuck his tail up at right angles, uttered a cordial gargle, and rubbed his head against her leg. Then turning, he looked at me. I could read that glance. I knew what was in his mind. From that moment he has been doing everything in his power to arrange the match."

"But, Mulliner," said Worple, always eager to point out the bright side, "why should this girl want to marry a wretched, scrubby, hard-up footler like you? Have courage, Mulliner. It is simply a question of time before you repel and sicken her."

Lancelot shook his head.

"No," he said. "You speak like a true friend, Worple, but you do not understand. Old Ma Carberry-Pirbright, this exhibit's mother, who chaperones her at the sittings, discovered at an early date my relationship to my Uncle Theodore, who, as you know, has got it in gobs. She knows well enough that some day I shall be a rich man. She used to know my Uncle Theodore when he was Vicar of St. Botolph's in Knightsbridge, and from the very first she assumed towards me the repellent chumminess of an old family friend. She was always trying to lure me to her At Homes, her Sunday luncheons, her little dinners. Once she actually suggested that I should escort her and her beastly daughter to the Royal Academy."

He laughed bitterly. The mordant witticisms of Lancelot Mulliner at the expense of the Royal Academy were quoted from Tite Street in the south to Holland Park in the north and eastward as far as Bloomsbury.

"To all these overtures," resumed Lancelot, "I remained firmly unresponsive. My attitude was from the start one of frigid aloofness. I did not actually say in so many words that I would rather be dead in a ditch than at one of her At Homes, but my manner indicated it. And I was just beginning to think I had choked her off when in crashed Webster and upset everything. Do you know how many times I have been to that infernal house in the last week? Five. Webster seemed to wish it. I tell you, I am a lost man."

He buried his face in his hands. Scollop touched Worple on the arm, and together the two men stole silently out.

"Bad!" said Worple.

"Very bad," said Scollop.

"It seems incredible."

"Oh, no. Cases of this kind are, alas, by no means uncommon among those who, like Mulliner, possess to a marked degree the highly-strung, ultra-sensitive artistic temperament. A friend of mine, a rhythmical interior decorator, once rashly consented to put his aunt's parrot up at his studio while she was away visiting friends in the north of England. She was a woman of strong evangelical views, which the bird had imbibed from her. It had a way of putting its head on one side, making a noise like someone drawing a cork from a bottle, and asking my friend if he was saved. To cut a long story short, I happened to call on him a month later and he had installed a harmonium in his studio and was singing hymns, ancient and modern, in a rich tenor, while the parrot, standing on one leg on its perch, took the bass. A very sad affair. We were all much upset about it."

Worple shuddered.

"You appal me, Scollop! Is there nothing we can do?"

Rodney Scollop considered for a moment.

"We might wire Gladys Bingley to come home at once. She might possibly reason with the unhappy man. A woman's gentle influence . . . Yes, we could do that. Look in at the post office on your way home and send Gladys a telegram. I'll owe you for my half of it."

In the studio they had left, Lancelot Mulliner was staring dumbly at a black shape which had just entered the room. He had the appearance of a man with his back to the wall.

"No!" he was crying. "No! I'm dashed if I do!"

Webster continued to look at him.

"Why should I?" demanded Lancelot weakly.

Webster's gaze did not flicker.

"Oh, all right," said Lancelot sullenly.

He passed from the room with leaden feet, and, proceeding upstairs, changed into morning clothes and a top hat. Then, with a gardenia in his buttonhole, he made his way to 11 Maxton Square, where Mrs. Carberry-Pirbright was giving one of her intimate little teas ("just a few friends") to meet Clara Throckmorton Stooge, authoress of *A Strong Man's Kiss*.

Gladys Bingley was lunching at her hotel in Antibes when Worple's telegram arrived. It occasioned her the gravest concern.

Exactly what it was all about she was unable to gather, for emotion had made Bernard Worple rather incoherent. There were moments, reading it, when she fancied that Lancelot had met with a serious accident; others when the solution seemed to be that he had sprained his brain to such an extent that rival lunatic asylums were competing eagerly for his custom; others, again, when Worple appeared to be suggesting that he had gone into partnership with his cat to start a harem. But one fact emerged clearly. Her loved one was in serious trouble of some kind, and his best friends were agreed that only her immediate return could save him.

Gladys did not hesitate. Within half an hour of the receipt of the telegram she had packed her trunk, removed a piece of asparagus from her right eyebrow, and was negotiating for accommodation on the first train going north.

Arriving in London, her first impulse was to go straight to Lancelot. But a natural feminine curiosity urged her, before doing so, to call upon Bernard Worple and have light thrown on some of the more abstruse passages in the telegram.

Worple, in his capacity of author, may have tended towards obscurity, but, when confining himself to the spoken word, he told a plain story well and clearly. Five minutes of his society enabled Gladys to obtain a firm grasp on the salient facts, and there appeared on her face that grim, tight-lipped expression which is seen only on the faces of fiancées who have come back from a short holiday to discover that their dear one has been straying in their absence from the straight and narrow path.

"Brenda Carberry-Pirbright, eh?" said Gladys, with ominous calm. "I'll give him Brenda Carberry-Pirbright! My gosh, if one can't go off to Antibes for the merest breather without having one's betrothed getting it up his nose and starting to act like a Mormon Elder, it begins to look a pretty tough world for a girl."

Kind-hearted Bernard Worple did his best.

"I blame the cat," he said. "Lancelot, to my mind, is more sinned against than sinning. I consider him to be acting under undue influence or duress."

"How like a man!" said Gladys. "Shoving it all off on to an innocent cat!"

"Lancelot says it has a sort of something in its eye."

"Well, when I meet Lancelot," said Gladys, "he'll find that I have a sort of something in my eye."

She went out, breathing flame quietly through her nostrils. Worple, saddened, heaved a sigh and resumed his neo-Vorticist sculpting.

It was some five minutes later that Gladys, passing through Maxton Square on her way to Bott Street, stopped suddenly in her tracks. The sight she had seen was enough to make any fiancée do so.

Along the pavement leading to No. 11 two figures were advancing. Or three, if you counted a morose-looking dog of a semi-dachshund nature which preceded them, attached to a leash. One of the figures was that of Lancelot Mulliner, natty in grey herringbone tweed and a new Homburg hat. It was he who held the leash. The other Gladys recognized from the portrait which she had seen on Lancelot's easel as that modern Du Barry, that notorious wrecker of homes and breaker-up of love-nests, Brenda Carberry-Pirbright.

The next moment they had mounted the steps of No. 11, and had gone in to tea, possibly with a little music.

It was perhaps an hour and a half later that Lancelot, having wrenched himself with difficulty from the lair of the Philistines, sped homeward in a swift taxi. As always after an extended *tête-à-tête* with Miss Carberry-Pirbright, he felt dazed and bewildered, as if he had been swimming in a sea of glue and had swallowed a great deal of it. All he could think of clearly was that he wanted a drink and that the materials for the drink were in the cupboard behind the chesterfield of his studio.

He paid the cab and charged in with his tongue rattling dryly against his front teeth. And there before him was Gladys Bingley, whom he had supposed far, far away.

"You!" exclaimed Lancelot.

"Yes, me!" said Gladys.

Her long vigil had not helped to restore the girl's equanimity. Since arriving at the studio she had had leisure to tap her foot three thousand, one hundred and forty-two times on the carpet, and the number of bitter smiles which had flitted across her face was nine hundred and eleven. She was about ready for the battle of the century.

She rose and faced him, all the woman in her flashing from her eyes.

"Well, you Casanova!" she said.

"You who?" said Lancelot.

"Don't you say 'Yoo-hoo!' to me!" cried Gladys. "Keep that for your Brenda Carberry-Pirbright. Yes, I know all about it, Lancelot Don Juan Henry the Eighth Mulliner! I saw you with her just now. I hear that you and she are inseparable. Bernard Worple says you said you were going to marry her."

"You mustn't believe everything a neo-Vorticist sculptor tells you," quavered Lancelot.

"I'll bet you're going back to dinner there tonight," said Gladys.

She had spoken at a venture, basing the charge purely on a possessive cock of the head which she had noticed in Brenda Carberry-Pirbright at their recent encounter. There, she had said to herself at the time, had gone a girl who was about to invite—or had just invited—Lancelot Mulliner to dine quietly and take her to the pictures afterwards. But the shot went home. Lancelot hung his head.

"There was some talk of it," he admitted.

"Ah!" exclaimed Gladys.

Lancelot's eyes were haggard.

"I don't want to go," he pleaded. "Honestly, I don't. But Webster insists."

"Webster!"

"Yes, Webster. If I attempt to evade the appointment, he will sit in front of me and look at me."

"Tchah!"

"Well, he will. Ask him for yourself."

Gladys tapped her foot six times in rapid succession on the carpet, bringing the total to three thousand, one hundred and forty-eight. Her manner had changed and was now dangerously calm.

"Lancelot Mulliner," she said, "you have your choice. Me, on the one hand, Brenda Carberry-Pirbright on the other. I offer you a home where you will be able to smoke in bed, spill the ashes on the floor, wear pyjamas and carpet slippers all day and shave only on Sunday mornings. From her, what have you to hope? A house in South Kensington—possibly the Brompton Road—probably with her mother living with you. A life that will be one long round of stiff collars and tight shoes, of morning coats and top hats."

Lancelot quivered, but she went on remorselessly.

"You will be at home on alternate Thursdays, and will be expected to hand the cucumber sandwiches. Every day you will air the dog, till you become a confirmed dog-airer. You will dine out in Bayswater and go for the summer to Bournemouth or Dinard. Choose well, Lancelot Mulliner! I will leave you to think it over. But one last word. If by seven-thirty on the dot you have not presented yourself at 6a Garbidge Mews ready to take me out to dinner at the Ham and Beef, I shall know what to think and shall act accordingly."

And brushing the cigarette ashes from her chin, the girl strode haughtily from the room.

"Gladys!" cried Lancelot.

But she had gone.

For some minutes Lancelot Mulliner remained where he was, stunned. Then, insistently, there came to him the recollection that he had not had that drink. He rushed to the cupboard and produced the bottle. He uncorked it, and was pouring out a lavish stream, when a movement on the floor below him attracted his attention.

Webster was standing there, looking up at him. And in his eyes was that familiar expression of quiet rebuke.

"Scarcely what I have been accustomed to at the Deanery," he seemed to be saying.

Lancelot stood paralysed. The feeling of being bound hand and foot, of being caught in a snare from which there was no escape, had become more poignant than ever. The bottle fell from his nerveless fingers and rolled across the floor, spilling its contents in an amber river, but he was too heavy in spirit to notice it. With a gesture such as Job might have made on discovering a new boil, he crossed to the window and stood looking moodily out.

Then, turning with a sigh, he looked at Webster again—and, looking, stood spellbound.

The spectacle which he beheld was of a kind to stun a stronger man than Lancelot Mulliner. At first, he shrank from believing his eyes. Then, slowly, came the realization that what he saw was no mere figment of a disordered imagination. This unbelievable thing was actually happening.

Webster sat crouched upon the floor beside the widening pool of whisky. But it was not horror and disgust that had caused him to crouch. He was crouched because, crouching, he could get nearer to the stuff and obtain crisper action. His tongue was moving in and out like a piston.

And then abruptly, for one fleeting instant, he stopped lapping and glanced up at Lancelot, and across his face there flitted a quick smile—so genial, so intimate, so full of jovial camaraderie, that the young man found himself automatically smiling back, and not only smiling but winking. And in answer to that wink Webster winked too—a whole-hearted, roguish wink that said as plainly as if he had spoken the words:

"How long has this been going on?"

Then with a slight hiccough he turned back to the task of getting his drink before it soaked into the floor.

Into the murky soul of Lancelot Mulliner there poured a sudden flood of sunshine. It was as if a great burden had been lifted from his shoulders. The intolerable obsession of the last two weeks had ceased to oppress him, and he felt a free man. At the eleventh hour the reprieve had come. Webster, that seeming pillar of austere virtue, was one of the boys, after all. Never again would Lancelot quail beneath his eye. He had the goods on him.

Webster, like the stag at eve, had now drunk his fill. He had left the pool of alcohol and was walking round in slow, meditative circles. From time to time he mewed tentatively, as if he were trying to say "British Constitution." His failure to articulate the syllables appeared to tickle him, for at the end of each attempt he would utter a slow, amused chuckle. It was about this moment that he suddenly broke into a rhythmic dance, not unlike the old Saraband.

It was an interesting spectacle, and at any other time Lancelot would have watched it raptly. But now he was busy at his desk, writing a brief note to Mrs. Carberry-Pirbright, the burden of which was that if she thought he was coming within a mile of her foul house that night or any other night she had vastly underrated the dodging powers of Lancelot Mulliner.

And what of Webster? The Demon Rum now had him in an iron grip. A lifetime of abstinence had rendered him a ready victim to the fatal fluid. He had now reached the stage when geniality gives way to belligerence. The rather foolish smile had gone from his face, and in its stead there lowered a fighting frown. For a few moments he stood on his hind legs, looking about him for a suitable adversary: then, losing all vestiges of self-control, he ran five times round the room at a high rate of speed and, falling foul of a small footstool, attacked it with the utmost ferocity, sparing neither tooth nor claw.

But Lancelot did not see him. Lancelot was not there. Lancelot was out in Bott Street, hailing a cab.

"6a Garbidge Mews, Fulham," said Lancelot to the driver.

ÉMILE ZOLA

The Cat's Paradise

I was then two years old, and was at the same time the fattest and most naive cat in existence. At that tender age I still had all the presumptuousness of an animal who is disdainful of the sweetness of home.

How fortunate I was, indeed, that providence had placed me with your aunt! That good woman adored me. I had at the bottom of a wardrobe a veritable sleeping salon, with feather cushions and triple covers. My food was equally excellent; never just bread, or soup, but always meat, carefully chosen meat.

Well, in the midst of all this opulence, I had only one desire, one dream, and that was to slip out of the upper window and escape on to the roofs. Caresses annoyed me, the softness of my bed nauseated me, and I was so fat that it was disgusting even to myself. In short, I was bored the whole day long just with being happy.

I must tell you that by stretching my neck a bit, I had seen the roof directly in front of my window. That day four cats were playing with each other up there; their fur bristling, their tails high, they were romping around with every indication of joy on the blue roof slates baked by the sun. I had never before watched such an extraordinary spectacle. And from then on I had a definitely fixed belief: out there on that roof was true happiness, out there beyond the window which was always closed so carefully. In proof of that contention I remembered that the doors of the chest in which the meat was kept were also closed, just as carefully!

I resolved to flee. After all there had to be other things in life besides a comfortable bed. Out there was the unknown, the ideal.

And then one day they forgot to close the kitchen window. I jumped out on to the small roof above it.

How beautiful the roofs were! The wide eaves bordering them exuded delicious smells. Carefully I followed those eaves, where my feet sank into fine mud that smelled tepid and infinitely sweet. It felt as if I were walking on velvet. And the sun shone with a good warmth that caressed my plumpness.

I will not hide from you the fact that I was trembling all over. There was something overwhelming in my joy. I remember particularly the tremendous emotional upheaval which actually made me lose my footing on the slates, when three cats rolled down from the ridge of the roof and approached with excited miaows. But when I showed signs of fear, they told me I was a silly fat goose and insisted that their miaowing was only laughter.

I decided to join them in their caterwauling. It was fun, even though the three stalwarts weren't as fat as I was and made fun of me when I rolled like a ball over the roof heated by the sun.

An old tomcat belonging to the gang honoured me particularly with his friendship. He offered to take care of my education, an offer which I accepted with gratitude.

Oh, how far away seemed all the soft things of your aunt! I drank from the gutters, and never did sugared milk taste half as fine! Everything was good and beautiful.

A female cat passed by, a ravishing she, and the very sight of her filled me with strange emotions. Only in my dreams had I up to then seen such an exquisite creature with such a magnificently arched back. We dashed forward to meet the newcomer, my three companions and myself. I was actually ahead of the others in paying the enchanting female my compliments; but then one of my comrades gave me a nasty bite in the neck, and I let out a shriek of pain.

"Pshaw!" said the old tomcat, dragging me away. "You will meet plenty of others."

After a walk that lasted an hour I had a ravenous appetite.

"What does one eat on these roofs?" I asked my friend the tom.

"Whatever one finds," he replied laconically.

This answer embarrassed me somewhat for, hunt as I might, I couldn't find a thing. Finally I looked through a dormer window and saw a young workman preparing his breakfast. On the table, just above the windowsill, lay a chop of a particularly succulent red.

"There is my chance," I thought, rather naively.

So I jumped on to the table and snatched the chop. But the

workingman saw me and gave me a terrific wallop across my back with a broom. I dropped the meat, cursed rather vulgarly and escaped.

"What part of the world do you come from?" asked the tomcat. "Don't you know that meat on tables is meant only to be admired from afar? What we've got to do is look in the gutters."

I have never been able to understand why kitchen meat shouldn't belong to cats. My stomach began to complain quite bitterly. The tom tried to console me by saying it would only be necessary to wait for the night. Then, he said, we would climb down from the roofs into the streets and forage in the garbage heaps.

Wait for the night! Confirmed philosopher that he was, he said it calmly while the very thought of such a protracted fast made me positively faint.

Night came ever so slowly, a misty night that made me shiver. To make things worse, rain began to fall, a thin, penetrating rain whipped up by brisk howling gusts of wind.

How desolate the streets looked to me! There was nothing left of the good warmth, of the big sun, of those roofs where one could play so pleasantly. My paws slipped on the slimy pavement, and I began to think with some longing of my triple covers and my feather pillow.

We had hardly reached the street when my friend, the tom, began to tremble. He made himself small, quite small, and glided surreptitiously along the walls of the houses, warning me under his breath to be quick about it. When we reached the shelter of a house door, he hid behind it and purred with satisfaction. And when I asked him the reason for his strange conduct, he said:

"Did you see that man with the hook and the basket?"

"Yes."

"Well, if he had seen us, we would have been caught, fried on the spit and eaten!"

"Fried on the spit and eaten!" I exclaimed. "Why, then the street is really not for the likes of us. One does not eat, but is eaten instead!"

In the meantime, however, they had begun to put the garbage out on the sidewalks. I inspected it with growing despair. All I found there were two or three dry bones that had obviously been thrown in among the ashes. And then and there I realized how succulent a dish of fresh meat really is!

My friend, the tom, went over the heaps of garbage with consummate artistry. He made me rummage around until morning, inspecting every cobblestone, without the least trace of hurry. But after ten hours of almost incessant rain my whole body was trembling. Damn the street, I thought, damn liberty! And how I longed for my prison!

When day came, the tomcat noticed that I was weakening.

"You've had enough, eh?" he asked in a strange voice.

"Oh, yes," I replied.

"Do you want to go home?"

"I certainly do. But how can I find my house?"

"Come along. Yesterday morning when I saw you come out I knew immediately that a cat as fat as you isn't made for the joys of liberty. I know where you live. I'll take you back to your door."

He said this all simply enough, the good, dignified tom. And when we finally got there, he added, without the slightest show of emotion:

"Goodbye, then."

"No, no!" I protested. "I shall not leave you like this. You come with me! We shall share bed and board. My mistress is a good woman . . ."

He didn't even let me finish.

"Shut up!" he said brusquely. "You are a fool. I'd die in that stuffy softness. Your abundant life is for weaklings. Free cats will never buy your comforts and your featherbeds at the price of being imprisoned. Goodbye!"

With these words he climbed back on to the roof. I saw his proud thin shadow shudder deliciously as it began to feel the warmth of the morning sun.

When I came home your aunt acted the martinet and administered a corrective which I received with profound joy. I revelled in being punished and voluptuously warm. And while she cuffed me, I thought with delight of the meat she would give me directly afterwards.

You see—an afterthought, while stretched out before the embers—true happiness, paradise, my master, is where one is locked up and beaten, wherever there is meat.

I speak for cats.

—*Translated from the French by Edward Vizetelly*

HONORÉ DE BALZAC

The Afflictions of an English Cat

When the report of your first meeting arrived in London, O! French Animals, it caused the hearts of the friends of Animal Reform to beat faster. In my own humble experience, I have so many proofs of the superiority of Beasts over Man that in my character of an English Cat I see the occasion, long awaited, of publishing the story of my life, in order to show how my poor soul has been tortured by the hypocritical laws of England. On two occasions, already, some Mice, whom I have made a vow to respect since the bill passed by your august parliament, have taken me to Colburn's, where, observing old ladies, spinsters of uncertain years, and even young married women, correcting proofs, I have asked myself why, having claws, I should not make use of them in a similar manner. One never knows what women think, especially the women who write, while a Cat, victim of English perfidy, is interested to say more than she thinks, and her profuseness may serve to compensate for what these ladies do not say. I am ambitious to be the Mrs. Inchbald of Cats and I beg you to have consideration for my noble efforts, O! French Cats, among whom has risen the noblest house of our race, that of Puss in Boots, eternal type of Advertiser, whom so many men have imitated but to whom no one has yet erected a monument.

I was born at the home of a parson in Catshire, near the little town of Miaulbury. My mother's fecundity condemned nearly all her infants to a cruel fate, because, as you know, the cause of the maternal intemperance of English Cats, who threaten to populate the whole world, has not yet been decided. Toms and females each insist it is due to their own amiability and respective virtues. But impertinent observers have remarked that Cats in England are required to be so boringly proper that this is their only distraction. Others pretend that herein may lie concealed great questions of commerce and politics, having to do with the English rule of India, but these matters are not for my paws to write of and I leave them to the *Edinburgh-Review*. I was not drowned with the others on account of the whiteness of my robe. Also I was named Beauty. Alas! the parson, who had a wife and eleven daughters, was too poor to keep me. An elderly female noticed that I had an affection for the parson's Bible; I slept on it all the time, not because I was religious, but because it was the only clean spot I could find in the house. She believed, perhaps, that I belonged to the sect of sacred animals which had already furnished the she-ass of Balaam, and took me away with her. I was only two months old at this time. This old woman, who gave evenings for which she sent out cards inscribed *Tea and Bible*, tried to communicate to me the fatal science of the daughters of Eve. Her method, which consisted in delivering long lectures on personal dignity and on the obligations due the world, was a very successful one. In order to avoid these lectures one submitted to martyrdom.

One morning I, a poor little daughter of Nature, attracted by a bowl of cream, covered by a muffin, knocked the muffin off with my paw, and lapped the cream. Then in joy, and perhaps also on account of the weakness of my young organs, I delivered myself on the waxed floor to the imperious need which young Cats feel. Perceiving the proofs of what she called my intemperance and my faults of education, the old woman seized me and whipped me vigorously with a birchrod, protesting that she would make me a lady or she would abandon me.

"Permit me to give you a lesson in gentility," she said. "Understand, Miss Beauty, that English Cats veil natural acts, which are opposed to the laws of English respectability, in the most profound mystery, and banish all that is improper, applying to the creature, as you have heard the Reverend Doctor Simpson say, the laws made by God for the creation. Have you ever seen the Earth behave itself indecently? Learn to suffer a thousand deaths rather than reveal your desires; in this suppression consists the virtue of the saints. The greatest privilege of Cats is to depart with the grace that characterizes your actions, and let no one know where you are going to make your little toilets. Thus you expose yourself only when you are beautiful. Deceived by appearances, everybody will take you for an angel. In the future when such a desire seizes you, look out of the window, give the impression that you desire to go for a walk, then run to a copse or to the gutter."

As a simple Cat of good sense, I found much hypocrisy in this doctrine, but I was so young!

"And when I am in the gutter?" thought I, looking at the old woman.

"Once alone, and sure of not being seen by anybody, well, Beauty, you can sacrifice respectability with much more charm because you have been discreet in public. It is in the observance of this very precept that the perfection of the moral English shines the brightest: they occupy themselves exclusively with appearances, this world being, alas, only illusion and deception."

I admit that these disguises were revolting to all my animal good sense, but on account of the whipping, it seemed preferable to understand that exterior propriety was all that was demanded of an English Cat. From this moment I accustomed myself to conceal the titbits that I loved under the bed. Nobody ever saw me eat, or drink, or make my toilet. I was regarded as the pearl of Cats.

Now I had occasion to observe those stupid men who are called savants. Among the doctors and others who were friends of my mistress, there was this Simpson, a fool, a son of a rich landowner, who was waiting for a bequest, and who, to deserve it, explained all animal actions by religious theories. He saw me one evening lapping milk from a saucer and complimented the old woman on the manner in which I had been bred, seeing me lick first the edges of the saucer and gradually diminish the circle of fluid.

"See," he said, "how in saintly company all becomes perfection: Beauty understands eternity, because she describes the circle which is its emblem in lapping her milk."

Conscience obliges me to state that the aversion of Cats to wetting their fur was the only reason for my fashion of drinking, but we will always be badly understood by the savants who are much more preoccupied in showing their own wit, than in discovering ours.

When the ladies or the gentlemen lifted me to pass their hands over my snowy back to make the sparks fly from my hair, the old woman remarked with pride, "You can hold her without having any fear for your dress; she is admirably well-bred!" Everybody said I was an angel; I was loaded with delicacies, but I assure you that I was profoundly bored. I was well aware of the fact that a young female Cat of the neighbourhood had run away with a Tom. This word, Tom, caused my soul a suffering which nothing could alleviate, not even the compliments I received, or rather that my mistress lavished on herself.

"Beauty is entirely moral; she is a little angel," she said. "Although she is very beautiful she has the air of not knowing it. She never looks at anybody, which is the height of a fine aristocratic education. When she does look at anybody it is with that perfect indifference which we demand of our young girls, but which we obtain only with great difficulty. She never intrudes herself unless you call her; she never jumps on you with familiarity; nobody ever sees her eat, and certainly that monster of a Lord Byron would have adored her. Like a tried and true Englishwoman she loves tea, sits, gravely calm, while the Bible is being explained, and thinks badly of nobody, a fact which permits one to speak freely before her. She is simple, without affectation, and has no desire for jewels. Give her a ring and she will not keep it. Finally, she does not imitate the vulgarity of the hunter. She loves her home and remains there so perfectly tranquil that at times you would believe that she was a mechanical Cat made at Birmingham or Manchester, which is the *ne plus ultra* of the finest education."

What these men and old women call education is the custom of dissimulating natural manners, and when they have completely depraved us they say that we are well-bred. One evening my mistress begged one of the young ladies to sing. When this girl went to the piano and began to sing I recognized at once an Irish melody that I had heard in my youth, and I remembered that I also was a musician. So I merged my voice with hers, but I received some raps on the head while she received compliments. I was revolted by this sovereign injustice and ran away to the garret. Sacred love of country! What a delicious night! I at last knew what the roof was. I heard Toms sing hymns to their mates, and these adorable elegies made me feel ashamed of the hypocrisies my mistress had forced upon me. Soon some of the Cats observed me and appeared to take offence at my presence, when a Tom with shaggy hair, a magnificent beard, and a fine figure, came to look at me and said to the company, "It's only a child!" At these condescending words, I bounded about on the tiles, moving with that agility which distinguishes us; I fell on my paws in that flexible fashion which no other animal knows how to imitate in order to show that I was no child. But these calineries were a pure waste of time. "When will some one serenade me?" I asked myself. The aspect of these haughty Toms, their melodies, that the human voice could never hope to rival, had moved me profoundly, and were the cause of my inventing little lyrics that I sang on the stairs. But an event of tremendous importance was about to occur which tore me violently from this innocent life. I went to London with a niece of my mistress, a rich heiress who adored me, who kissed me, caressed me with a kind of madness, and who pleased me so much that I became attached to her, against all the habits of our race. We were never separated and I was able to observe the great world of London during the season. It was there that I studied the perversity of English manners, which have power even over the beasts, that I became acquainted with that cant which Byron cursed and of which I am the victim as well as he, but without having enjoyed my hours of leisure.

Arabella, my mistress, was a young person like many others in England; she was not sure whom she wanted for a husband. The absolute liberty that is permitted girls in choosing a husband drives them nearly crazy, especially when they recall that English custom does not sanction intimate conversation after marriage. I was far from dreaming that the London Cats had adopted this severity, that the English laws would be cruelly applied to me, and that I would be a victim of the court at the terrible Doctors' Commons. Arabella was charming to all the men she met, and every one of them believed that he was going to marry this beautiful girl, but when an affair threatened to terminate in wedlock, she would find some pretext for a break, conduct which did not seem very respectable to me. "Marry a bow-legged man! Never!" she said of one. "As to that little fellow he is snub-nosed." Men were all so much alike to me that I could not understand this uncertainty founded on purely physical differences.

Finally one day an old English Peer, seeing me, said to her: "You have a beautiful Cat. She resembles you. She is white, she is young, she should have a husband. Let me bring her a magnificent Angora that I have at home."

Three days later the Peer brought in the handsomest Tom of the Peerage. Puff, with a black coat, had the most magnificent eyes, green and yellow, but cold and proud. The long silky hair of his tail, remarkable for its yellow rings, swept the carpet. Perhaps he came from the imperial house of Austria, because, as you see, he wore the colours. His manners were those of a Cat who had seen the court and the great world. His severity, in the matter of carrying himself, was so great that he would not scratch his head were anybody present. Puff had travelled on the continent. To sum up, he was so remarkably handsome that he had been, it was said, caressed by the

Queen of England. Simple and naïve as I was I leaped at his neck to engage him in play, but he refused under the pretext that we were being watched. I then perceived that this English Cat Peer owed this forced and fictitious gravity that in England is called respectability to age and to intemperance at table. His weight, that men admired, interfered with his movements. Such was the true reason for his not responding to my pleasant advances. Calm and cold he sat on his unnamable, agitating his beard, looking at me and at times closing his eyes. In the society world of English Cats, Puff was the richest kind of catch for a Cat born at a parson's. He had two valets in his service; he ate from Chinese porcelain, and he drank only black tea. He drove in a carriage in Hyde Park and had been to parliament.

My mistress kept him. Unknown to me, all the feline population of London learned that Miss Beauty from Catshire had married Puff, marked with the colours of Austria. During the night I heard a concert in the street. Accompanied by my lord, who, according to his taste, walked slowly, I descended. We found the Cats of the Peerage, who had come to congratulate me and to ask me to join their Ratophile Society. They explained that nothing was more common than running after Rats and Mice. The words, shocking, vulgar, were constantly on their lips. To conclude, they had formed, for the glory of the country, a Temperance Society. A few nights later my lord and I went on the roof of Almack's to hear a grey Cat speak on the subject. In his exhortation, which was constantly supported by cries of "Hear! Hear!" he proved that Saint Paul in writing about charity had the Cats of England in mind. It was then the special duty of the English, who could go from one end of the world to the other on their ships without fear of the sea, to spread the principles of the *morale ratophile*. As a matter of fact English Cats were already preaching the doctrines of the Society, based on the hygienic discoveries of science. When Rats and Mice were dissected little distinction could be found between them and Cats; the oppression of one race by the other then was opposed to the Laws of Beasts, which are stronger even than the Laws of Men. "They are our brothers," he continued. And he painted such a vivid picture of the suffering of a Rat in the jaws of a Cat that I burst into tears.

Observing that I was deceived by this speech, Lord Puff confided to me that England expected to do an immense trade in Rats and Mice; that if the Cats would eat no more, Rats would be England's best product; that there was always a practical reason concealed behind English morality; and that the alliance between morality and trade was the only alliance on which England really counted.

Puff appeared to me to be too good a politician ever to make a satisfactory husband.

A country Cat made the observation that on the continent, especially at Paris, near the fortifications, Tom Cats were sacrificed daily by the Catholics. Somebody interrupted with the cry of "Question!" Added to these cruel executions was the frightful slander of passing the brave animals off for Rabbits, a lie and a barbarity which he attributed to an ignorance of the true Anglican religion which did not permit lying and cheating except in the government, foreign affairs, and the cabinet.

He was treated as a radical and a dreamer. "We are here in the interests of the Cats of England, not in those of continental Cats!" cried a fiery Tory Tom. Puff went to sleep. Just as the assembly was breaking up a young Cat from the French embassy, whose accent proclaimed his nationality, addressed me these delicious words:

"Dear Beauty, it will be an eternity before Nature forms another Cat as perfect as you. The cashmere of Persia and the Indies is like camel's hair when it is compared to your fine and brilliant silk. You exhale a perfume which is the concentrated essence of the felicity of the angels, an odour I have detected in the salon of the Prince de Talleyrand, which I left to come to this stupid meeting. The fire of your eyes illuminates the night! Your ears would be entirely perfect if they would listen to my supplications. There is not a rose in England as rose as the rose flesh which borders your little rose mouth. A fisherman would search in vain in the depths of Ormus for pearls of the quality of your teeth. Your dear face, fine and gracious, is the loveliest that England has produced. Near to your celestial robe the snow of the Alps would seem to be red. Ah! those coats which are only to be seen in your fogs! Softly and gracefully your paws bear your body which is the culmination of the miracles of creation, but your tail, the subtle interpreter of the beating of your heart, surpasses it. Yes! never was there such an exquisite curve, more correct roundness. No Cat ever moved more delicately. Come away from this old fool of a Puff, who sleeps like an English Peer in parliament, who besides is a scoundrel who has sold himself to the Whigs, and who, owing to a too long sojourn at Bengal, has lost everything that can please a Cat."

Then, without having the air of looking at him, I took in the appearance of this charming French Tom. He was a careless little rogue and not in any respect like an English Cat. His cavalier manner as well as his way of shaking his ear stamped him as a gay bachelor without a care. I avow that I was weary of the solemnity of English Cats, and of their purely practical propriety. Their respectability, especially, seemed ridiculous to me. The excessive naturalness of this badly groomed Cat surprised me in its violent contrast to all that I had seen in London. Besides my life was so strictly regulated, I knew so well what I had to count on for the rest of my days, that I welcomed the promise of the unexpected in the physiognomy of this French Cat. My whole life appeared insipid to me. I comprehended that I could live on the roofs with an amazing creature who came from that country where the inhabitants consoled themselves for the victories of the greatest English general by these words:

Malbrouk s'en va-t-en guerre,
Mironton, TON, TON, *MIRONTAINE!*

Nevertheless I awakened my lord, told him how late it was, and suggested that we ought to go in. I gave no sign of having listened to this declaration, and my apparent insensibility petrified Brisquet. He remained behind, more surprised than ever because he considered himself handsome. I learned later that it was an easy matter for him to seduce most Cats. I examined him through a corner of my eye: he ran away with little bounds, returned, leaping the width of the street, then jumped back again, like a French Cat in despair. A true Englishman would have been decent enough not to let me see how he felt.

Some days later my lord and I were stopping in the magnificent house of the old Peer; then I went in the carriage for a drive in Hyde Park. We ate only chicken bones, fishbones, cream, milk, and chocolate. However heating this diet might prove to others my so-called husband remained sober. He was respectable even in his treatment of me. Generally he slept from seven in the evening at the whist table on the knees of his Grace. On this account my soul received no satisfaction and I pined away. This condition was aggravated by a little affection of the intestines occasioned by pure herring oil (the Port Wine of English Cats), which Puff used, and which made me very ill. My mistress sent for a physician who had graduated at Edinburgh after having studied a long time in Paris. Having diagnosed my malady he promised my mistress that he would cure me the next day. He returned, as a matter of fact, and took an instrument of French manufacture out of his pocket. I felt a kind of fright on perceiving a barrel of white metal terminating in a slender tube. At the sight of this mechanism, which the doctor exhibited with satisfaction, Their Graces blushed, became irritable, and muttered several fine sentiments about the dignity of the English: for instance that the Catholics of old England were more distinguished for their opinions of this infamous instrument than for their opinions of the Bible. The Duke added that at Paris the French unblushingly made an exhibition of it in their national theatre in a comedy by Molière, but that in London a watchman would not dare pronounce its name.

"Give her some calomel."

"But Your Grace would kill her!" cried the doctor.

"The French can do as they like," replied His Grace. "I do not know, no more do you, what would happen if this degrading instrument were employed, but what I do know is that a true English physician should cure his patients only with the old English remedies."

This physician, who was beginning to make a big reputation, lost all his practice in the great world. Another doctor was called in, who asked me some improper questions about Puff, and who informed me that the real device of the English was: *Dieu et mon droit congugal!*

One night I heard the voice of the French Cat in the street. Nobody could see us; I climbed up the chimney and, appearing on the housetop, cried, "In the raintrough!" This response gave him wings; he was at my side in the twinkling of an eye. Would you believe that this French Cat had the audacity to take advantage of my exclamation. He cried, "Come to my arms," daring to become familiar with me, a Cat of distinction, without knowing me better. I regarded him frigidly and, to give him a lesson, I told him that I belonged to the Temperance Society.

"I see, sir," I said to him, "by your accent and by the looseness of your conversation, that you, like all Catholic Cats, are inclined to laugh and make sport, believing that confession will purge you, but in England we have another standard of morality. We are always respectable, even in our pleasures."

This young Cat, struck by the majesty of English cant, listened to me with a kind of attention which made me hope I could convert him to Protestantism. He then told me in purple words that he would do anything I wished provided I would permit him to adore me. I looked at him without being able to reply because his very beautiful and splendid eyes sparkled like stars; they lighted the night. Made bold by my silence, he cried "Dear Minette!"

"What new indecency is this?" I demanded, being well aware that French Cats are very free in their references.

Brisquet assured me that on the continent everybody, even the King himself, said to his daughter, *Ma petite Minette*, to show his affection, that many of the prettiest and most aristocratic young wives called their husbands, *Mon petit chat*, even when they did not love them. If I wanted to please him I would call him, *Mon petit homme!* Then he raised his paws with infinite grace. Thoroughly frightened I ran away. Brisquet was so happy that he sang *Rule Britannia*, and the next day his dear voice hummed again in my ears.

"Ah! you also are in love, dear Beauty," my mistress said to me, observing me extended on the carpet, the paws flat, the body in soft abandon, bathing in the poetry of my memories.

I was astonished that a woman should show so much intelligence, and so, raising my dorsal spine, I began to rub up against her legs and to purr lovingly with the deepest chords of my contralto voice.

While my mistress was scratching my head and caressing me and while I was looking at her tenderly a scene occurred in Bond Street which had terrible results for me.

Puck, a nephew of Puff's, in line to succeed him and who, for the time being, lived in the barracks of the Life Guards, ran into my dear Brisquet. The sly Captain Puck complimented the *attaché* on his success with me, adding that I had resisted the most charming Toms in England. Brisquet, foolish, vain Frenchman that he was, responded that he would be happy to gain my attention, but that he had a horror of Cats who spoke to him of temperance, the Bible, etc.

"Oh!" said Puck, "she talks to you then?"

Dear French Brisquet thus became a victim of English diplomacy, but later he committed one of these impardonable faults which irritate all well-bred Cats in England. This little idiot was truly very inconsistent. Did he not bow to me in Hyde Park and try to talk with me familiarly as if we were well acquainted? I looked straight through him coldly and severely. The coachman seeing this Frenchman insult me slashed him with his whip. Brisquet was cut but not killed and he received the blow with such nonchalance, continuing to look at me, that I was absolutely fascinated. I loved him for the manner in which he took his punishment, seeing only me, feeling only the favour of my presence, conquering the natural inclination of Cats to flee at the slightest warning of hostility. He could not know that I came near dying, in spite of my apparent coldness. From that moment I made up my mind to elope. That evening, on the roof, I threw myself tremblingly into his arms.

"My dear," I asked him, "have you the capital necessary to pay damages to old Puff?"

"I have no other capital," replied the French Cat, laughing, "than the hairs of my moustache, my four paws, and this tail." Then he swept the gutter with a proud gesture.

"Not any capital," I cried, "but then you are only an adventurer, my dear!"

"I love adventures," he said to me tenderly. "In France it is the custom to fight a duel in the circumstances to which you allude. French Cats have recourse to their claws and not to their gold."

"Poor country," I said to him, "and why does it send beasts so denuded of capital to the foreign embassies?"

"That's simple enough," said Brisquet. "Our new government does not love money—at least it does not love its employees to have money. It only seeks intellectual capacity."

Dear Brisquet answered me so lightly that I began to fear he was conceited.

"Love without money is nonsense," I said. "While you were seeking food you would not occupy yourself with me, my dear."

By way of response this charming Frenchman assured me that he was a direct descendant of Puss in Boots. Besides he had ninety-nine ways of borrowing money and we would have, he said, only a single way of spending it. To conclude, he knew music and could give lessons. In fact, he sang to me, in poignant tones, a national romance of his country, *Au clair de la lune.* . . .

At this inopportune moment, when seduced by his reasoning, I had promised dear Brisquet to run away with him as soon as he could keep a wife comfortably, Puck appeared, followed by several other Cats.

"I am lost!" I cried.

The very next day, indeed, the bench of Doctors' Commons was occupied by a *procès-verbal* in criminal conversation. Puff was deaf; his nephews took advantage of his weakness. Questioned by them, Puff said that at night I had flattered him by calling him, *Mon petit homme!* This was one of the most terrible things against me, because I could not explain where I had learned these words of love. The judge, without knowing it, was prejudiced against me, and I noted that he was in his second childhood. His lordship never suspected the low intrigues of which I was the victim. Many little Cats, who should have defended me against public opinion, swore that Puff was always asking for his angel, the joy of his eyes, his sweet Beauty! My own mother, come to London, refused to see me or to speak to me, saying that an English Cat should always be above suspicion, and that I had embittered her old age. Finally the servants testified against me. I then saw perfectly clearly how everybody lost his head in England. When it is a matter of a criminal conversation, all sentiment is dead; a mother is no longer a mother, a nurse wants to take back her milk, and all the Cats howl in the streets. But the most infamous thing of all was that my old attorney who, in his time, would believe in the innocence of the Queen of England, to whom I had confessed everything to the last detail, who had assured me that there was no reason to whip a Cat, and to whom, to prove my innocence, I avowed that I did not even know the meaning of the words, "criminal conversation" (he told me that the crime was so called precisely because one spoke so little while committing it), this attorney, bribed by Captain Puck, defended me so badly that my case appeared to be lost. Under these circumstances I went on the stand myself.

"My Lords," I said, "I am an English Cat and I am innocent. What would be said of the justice of old England if . . ."

Hardly had I pronounced these words than I was interrupted by a murmur of voices, so strongly had the public been influenced by the *Cat-Chronicle* and by Puck's friends.

"She questions the justice of old England which has created the jury!" cried some one.

"She wishes to explain to you, My Lords," cried my adversary's abominable lawyer, "that she went on the rooftop with a French Cat in order to convert him to the Anglican faith, when, as a matter of fact, she went there to learn how to say, *Mon petit homme*, in French, to her husband, to listen to the abominable principles of papism, and to learn to disregard the laws and customs of old England!"

Such piffle always drives an English audience wild. Therefore the words of Puck's attorney were received with tumultuous applause. I was condemned at the age of twenty-six months, when I could prove that I still was ignorant of the very meaning of the word, Tom. But from all this I gathered that it was on account of such practices that Albion was called Old England.

I fell into a deep miscathropy which was caused less by my divorce than by the death of my dear Brisquet, whom Puck had had killed by a mob, fearing his vengeance. Also nothing made me more furious than to hear the loyalty of English Cats spoken of.

You see, O! French Animals, that in familiarizing ourselves with men, we borrow from them all their vices and bad institutions. Let us return to the wild life where we obey only our instincts, and where we do not find customs in conflict with the sacred wishes of Nature. At this moment I am writing a treatise on the abuse of the working classes of animals, in order to get them to pledge themselves to refrain from turning spits, to refuse to allow themselves to be harnessed to carriages, in order, to sum up, to teach them the means of protecting themselves against the oppression of the grand aristocracy. Although we are celebrated for our scribbling I believe that Miss Martineau would not repudiate me. You know that on the continent literature has become the haven of all Cats who protest against the immoral monopoly of marriage, who resist the tyranny of institutions, and who desire to encourage natural laws. I have omitted to tell you that, although Brisquet's body was slashed with a wound in the back, the coroner, by an infamous hypocrisy, declared that he had poisoned himself with arsenic, as if so gay, so light-headed a Cat could have reflected long enough on the subject of life to conceive so serious an idea, and as if a Cat whom I loved could have the least desire to quit this existence! But with Marsh's apparatus spots have been found on a plate.

—Translated from the French by Carl Van Vechten

SAKI

Tobermory

It was a chill, rain-washed afternoon of a late August day, that indefinite season when partridges are still in security or cold storage, and there is nothing to hunt—unless one is bounded on the north by the Bristol Channel, in which case one may lawfully gallop after fat red stags. Lady Blemley's house-party was not bounded on the north by the Bristol Channel, hence there was a full gathering of her guests round the tea-table on this particular afternoon. And, in spite of the blankness of the season and the triteness of the occasion, there was no trace in the company of that fatigued restlessness which means a dread of the pianola and a subdued hankering for auction bridge. The undisguised open-mouthed attention of the entire party was fixed on the homely negative personality of Mr. Cornelius Appin. Of all her guests, he was the one who had come to Lady Blemley with the vaguest reputation. Some one had said he was "clever," and he had got his invitation in the moderate expectation, on the part of his hostess, that some portion at least of his cleverness would be contributed to the general entertainment. Until tea-time that day she had been unable to discover in what direction, if any, his cleverness lay. He was neither a wit nor a croquet champion, a hypnotic force nor a begetter of amateur theatricals. Neither did his exterior suggest the sort of man in whom women are willing to pardon a generous measure of mental deficiency. He had subsided into mere Mr. Appin, and the Cornelius seemed a piece of transparent baptismal bluff. And now he was claiming to have launched on the world a discovery beside which the invention of gunpowder, of the printing-press, and of steam locomotion were inconsiderable trifles. Science had made bewildering strides in many directions during recent decades, but this thing seemed to belong to the domain of miracle rather than to scientific achievement.

"And do you really ask us to believe," Sir Wilfrid was saying, "that you have discovered a means for instructing animals in the art of human speech, and that dear old Tobermory has proved your first successful pupil?"

"It is a problem at which I have worked for the last seventeen years," said Mr. Appin, "but only during the last eight or nine months have I been rewarded with glimmerings of success. Of course I have experimented with thousands of animals, but latterly only with cats, those wonderful creatures which have assimilated themselves so marvellously with our civilization while retaining all their highly developed feral instincts. Here and there among cats one comes across an outstanding superior intellect, just as one does among the ruck of human beings, and when I made the acquaintance of Tobermory a week ago I saw at once that I was in contact with a 'Beyond-cat' of extraordinary intelligence. I had gone far along the road to success in recent experiments; with Tobermory, as you call him, I have reached the goal."

Mr. Appin concluded his remarkable statement in a voice which he strove to divest of a triumphant inflection. No one said "Rats," though Clovis's lips moved in a monosyllabic contortion which probably invoked those rodents of disbelief.

"And do you mean to say," asked Miss Resker, after a slight pause, "that you have taught Tobermory to say and understand easy sentences of one syllable?"

"My dear Miss Resker," said the wonder-worker patiently, "one teaches little children and savages and backward adults in that piecemeal fashion; when one has once solved the problem of making a beginning with an animal of highly developed intelligence one has no need for those halting methods. Tobermory can speak our language with perfect correctness."

This time Clovis very distinctly said, "Beyond-rats!" Sir Wilfrid was more polite, but equally sceptical.

"Hadn't we better have the cat in and judge for ourselves?" suggested Lady Blemley.

Sir Wilfrid went in search of the animal, and the company settled themselves down to the languid expectation of witnessing some more or less adroit drawing-room ventriloquism.

In a minute Sir Wilfrid was back in the room, his face white beneath its tan and his eyes dilated with excitement.

"By Gad, it's true!"

His agitation was unmistakably genuine, and his hearers started forward in a thrill of awakened interest.

Collapsing into an armchair he continued breathlessly: "I found him dozing in the smoking-room, and called out to him to come for his tea. He blinked at me in his usual way, and I said, 'Come on, Toby; don't keep us waiting'; and, by Gad! he drawled out in a most horribly natural voice that he'd come when he dashed well pleased! I nearly jumped out of my skin!"

Appin had preached to absolutely incredulous hearers; Sir Wilfrid's statement carried instant conviction. A Babel-like chorus of startled exclamation arose, amid which the scientist sat mutely enjoying the first fruit of his stupendous discovery.

In the midst of the clamour Tobermory entered the room and made his way with velvet tread and studied unconcern across to the group seated round the tea-table.

A sudden hush of awkwardness and constraint fell on the company. Somehow there seemed an element of embarrassment in addressing on equal terms a domestic cat of acknowledged dental ability.

"Will you have some milk, Tobermory?" asked Lady Blemley in a rather strained voice.

"I don't mind if I do," was the response, couched in a tone of even indifference. A shiver of suppressed excitement went through the listeners, and Lady Blemley might be excused for pouring out the saucerful of milk rather unsteadily.

"I'm afraid I've spilt a good deal of it," she said apologetically.

"After all, it's not my Axminster," was Tobermory's rejoinder.

Another silence fell on the group, and then Miss Resker, in her best district-visitor manner, asked if the human language had been difficult to learn. Tobermory looked squarely at her for a moment and then fixed his gaze serenely on the middle distance. It was obvious that boring questions lay outside his scheme of life.

"What do you think of human intelligence?" asked Mavis Pellington lamely.

"Of whose intelligence in particular?" asked Tobermory coldly.

"Oh, well, mine for instance," said Mavis, with a feeble laugh.

"You put me in an embarrassing position," said Tobermory, whose tone and attitude certainly did not suggest a shred of embarrassment. "When your inclusion in this house-party was suggested Sir Wilfrid protested that you were the most brainless woman of his acquaintance, and that there was a wide distinction between hospitality and the care of the feeble-minded. Lady Blemley replied that your lack of brain-power was the precise quality which had earned you your invitation, as you were the only person she could think of who might be idiotic enough to buy their old car. You know, the one they call 'The Envy of Sisyphus,' because it goes quite nicely up-hill if you push it."

Lady Blemley's protestations would have had greater effect if she had not casually suggested to Mavis only that morning that the car in question would be just the thing for her down at her Devonshire home.

Major Barfield plunged in heavily to effect a diversion.

"How about your carryings-on with the tortoise-shell puss up at the stables, eh?"

The moment he had said it every one realized the blunder.

"One does not usually discuss these matters in public," said Tobermory frigidly. "From a slight observation of your ways since you've been in this house I should imagine you'd find it inconvenient if I were to shift the conversation on to your own little affairs."

The panic which ensued was not confined to the Major.

"Would you like to go and see if cook has got your dinner ready?" suggested Lady Blemley hurriedly, affecting to ignore the fact that it wanted at least two hours to Tobermory's dinner-time.

"Thanks," said Tobermory, "not quite so soon after my tea. I don't want to die of indigestion."

"Cats have nine lives, you know," said Sir Wilfrid heartily.

"Possibly," answered Tobermory; "but only one liver."

"Adelaide!" said Mrs. Cornett, "do you mean to encourage that cat to go out and gossip about us in the servants' hall?"

The panic had indeed become general. A narrow ornamental balustrade ran in front of most of the bedroom windows at the Towers, and it was recalled with dismay that this had formed a favourite promenade for Tobermory at all hours, whence he could watch the pigeons—and heaven knew what else besides. If he intended to become reminiscent in his present outspoken strain the effect would be something more than disconcerting. Mrs. Cornett, who spent much time at her toilet table, and whose complexion was reputed to be of a nomadic though punctual disposition, looked as ill at ease as the Major. Miss Scrawen, who wrote fiercely sensuous poetry and led a blameless life, merely displayed irritation; if you are methodical and virtuous in private you don't necessarily want every one to know it. Bertie van Tahn, who was so depraved at seventeen that he had long ago given up trying to be any worse, turned a dull shade of gardenia white, but he did not commit the error of dashing out of the room like Odo Finsberry, a young gentleman who was understood to be reading for the Church and who was possibly disturbed at the thought of scandals he might hear concerning other people. Clovis had the presence of mind to maintain a composed exterior; privately he was calculating how long it would take to procure a box of fancy mice through the agency of the *Exchange and Mart* as a species of hush-money.

Even in a delicate situation like the present, Agnes Resker could not endure to remain too long in the background.

"Why did I ever come down here?" she asked dramatically.

Tobermory immediately accepted the opening.

"Judging by what you said to Mrs. Cornett on the croquet-lawn yesterday, you were out for food. You described the Blemleys as the dullest people to stay with that you knew, but said they were clever enough to employ a first-rate cook; otherwise they'd find it difficult to get any one to come down a second time."

"There's not a word of truth in it! I appeal to Mrs. Cornett—" exclaimed the discomfited Agnes.

"Mrs. Cornett repeated your remark afterwards to Bertie van Tahn," continued Tobermory, "and said, 'That woman is a regular Hunger Marcher; she'd go anywhere for four square meals a day,' and Bertie van Tahn said—"

At this point the chronicle mercifully ceased. Tobermory had caught a glimpse of the big yellow Tom from the Rectory working his way through the shrubbery towards the stable wing. In a flash he had vanished through the open French window.

With the disappearance of his too brilliant pupil Cornelius Appin found himself beset by a hurricane of bitter upbraiding, anxious inquiry, and frightened entreaty. The responsibility for the situation lay with him, and he must prevent matters from becoming worse. Could Tobermory impart his dangerous gift to other cats? was the first question he had to answer. It was possible, he replied, that he might have initiated his intimate friend the stable puss into his new accomplishment, but it was unlikely that his teaching could have taken a wider range as yet.

"Then," said Mrs. Cornett, "Tobermory may be a valuable cat

and a great pet; but I'm sure you'll agree, Adelaide, that both he and the stable cat must be done away with without delay."

"You don't suppose I've enjoyed the last quarter of an hour, do you?" said Lady Blemley bitterly. "My husband and I are very fond of Tobermory—at least, we were before this horrible accomplishment was infused into him; but now, of course, the only thing is to have him destroyed as soon as possible."

"We can put some strychnine in the scraps he always gets at dinner-time," said Sir Wilfrid, "and I will go and drown the stable cat myself. The coachman will be very sore at losing his pet, but I'll say a very catching form of mange has broken out in both cats and we're afraid of it spreading to the kennels."

"But my great discovery!" expostulated Mr. Appin; "after all my years of research and experiment—"

"You can go and experiment on the short-horns at the farm, who are under proper control," said Mrs. Cornett, "or the elephants at the Zoological Gardens. They're said to be highly intelligent, and they have this recommendation, that they don't come creeping about our bedrooms and under chairs, and so forth."

An archangel ecstatically proclaiming the Millennium, and then finding that it clashed unpardonably with Henley and would have to be indefinitely postponed, could hardly have felt more crestfallen than Cornelius Appin at the reception of his wonderful achievement. Public opinion, however, was against him—in fact, had the general voice been consulted on the subject it is probable that a strong minority vote would have been in favour of including him in the strychnine diet.

Defective train arrangements and a nervous desire to see matters brought to a finish prevented an immediate dispersal of the party, but dinner that evening was not a social success. Sir Wilfrid had had rather a trying time with the stable cat and subsequently with the coachman. Agnes Resker ostentatiously limited her repast to a morsel of dry toast, which she bit as though it were a personal enemy; while Mavis Pellington maintained a vindictive silence throughout the meal. Lady Blemley kept up a flow of what she hoped was conversation, but her attention was fixed on the doorway. A plateful of carefully dosed fish scraps was in readiness on the sideboard, but sweets and savoury and dessert went their way, and no Tobermory appeared either in the dining-room or kitchen.

The sepulchral dinner was cheerful compared with the subsequent vigil in the smoking-room. Eating and drinking had at least supplied a distraction and cloak to the prevailing embarrassment. Bridge was out of the question in the general tension of nerves and tempers, and after Odo Finsberry had given a lugubrious rendering of "Mélisande in the Wood" to a frigid audience, music was tacitly avoided. At eleven the servants went to bed, announcing that the small window in the pantry had been left open as usual for Tobermory's private use. The guests read steadily through the current batch of magazines, and fell back gradually on the "Badminton Library" and bound volumes of *Punch*. Lady Blemley made periodic visits to the pantry, returning each time with an expression of listless depression which forestalled questioning.

At two o'clock Clovis broke the dominating silence.

"He won't turn up tonight. He's probably in the local newspaper office at the present moment, dictating the first instalment of his reminiscences. Lady What's-her-name's book won't be in it. It will be the event of the day."

Having made this contribution to the general cheerfulness, Clovis went to bed. At long intervals the various members of the house-party followed his example.

The servants taking round the early tea made a uniform announcement in reply to a uniform question. Tobermory had not returned.

Breakfast was, if anything, a more unpleasant function than dinner had been, but before its conclusion the situation was relieved. Tobermory's corpse was brought in from the shrubbery, where a gardener had just discovered it. From the bites on his throat and the yellow fur which coated his claws it was evident that he had fallen in unequal combat with the big Tom from the Rectory.

By midday most of the guests had quitted the Towers, and after lunch Lady Blemley had sufficiently recovered her spirits to write an extremely nasty letter to the Rectory about the loss of her valuable pet.

Tobermory had been Appin's one successful pupil, and he was destined to have no successor. A few weeks later an elephant in the Dresden Zoological Garden, which had shown no previous signs of irritability, broke loose and killed an Englishman who had apparently been teasing it. The victim's name was variously reported in the papers as Oppin and Eppelin, but his front name was faithfully rendered Cornelius.

"If he was trying German irregular verbs on the poor beast," said Clovis, "he deserved all he got."

EDGAR ALLAN POE

The Black Cat

For the most wild, yet most homely narrative which I am about to pen, I neither expect nor solicit belief. Mad indeed would I be to expect it, in a case where my very senses reject their own evidence. Yet, mad am I not—and very surely do I not dream. But to-morrow I die, and to-day I would unburthen my soul. My immediate purpose is to place before the world, plainly, succinctly, and without comments, a series of mere household events. In their consequences, these events have terrified—have tortured—have destroyed me. Yet I will attempt to expound them. To me, they have presented little but Horror—to many they will seem less terrible than *barroques*. Hereafter, perhaps, some intellect may be found which will reduce my phantasm to the common-place—some intellect more calm, more logical, and far less excitable than my own, which will perceive, in the circumstances I detail with awe, nothing more than an ordinary succession of very natural causes and effects.

From my infancy I was noted for the docility and humanity of my disposition. My tenderness of heart was even so conspicuous as to make me the jest of my companions. I was especially fond of animals, and was indulged by my parents with a great variety of pets. With these I spent most of my time, and never was so happy as when feeding and caressing them. This peculiarity of character grew with my growth, and, in my manhood, I derived from it one of my principal sources of pleasure. To those who have cherished an affection for a faithful and sagacious dog, I need hardly be at the trouble of explaining the nature or the intensity of the gratification thus derivable. There is something in the unselfish and self-sacrificing love of a brute, which goes directly to the heart of him who has had frequent occasion to test the paltry friendship and gossamer fidelity of mere *Man*.

I married early, and was happy to find in my wife a disposition not uncongenial with my own. Observing my partiality for domestic pets, she lost no opportunity of procuring those of the most agreeable kind. We had birds, gold-fish, a fine dog, rabbits, a small monkey, and *a cat*.

This latter was a remarkably large and beautiful animal, entirely black, and sagacious to an astonishing degree. In speaking of his intelligence, my wife, who at heart was not a little tinctured with superstition, made frequent allusion to the ancient popular notion, which regarded all black cats as witches in disguise. Not that she was ever *serious* upon this point—and I mention the matter at all for no better reason than that it happens, just now, to be remembered.

Pluto—this was the cat's name—was my favorite pet and playmate. I alone fed him, and he attended me wherever I went about the house. It was even with difficulty that I could prevent him from following me through the streets.

Our friendship lasted, in this manner, for several years, during which my general temperament and character—through the instrumentality of the Fiend Intemperance—had (I blush to confess it) experienced a radical alteration for the worse. I grew, day by day, more moody, more irritable, more regardless of the feelings of others. I suffered myself to use intemperate language to my wife. At length, I even offered her personal violence. My pets, of course, were made to feel the change in my disposition. I not only neglected, but ill-used them. For Pluto, however, I still retained sufficient regard to restrain me from maltreating him, as I made no scruple of maltreating the rabbits, the monkey, or even the dog, when by accident, or through affection, they came in my way. But my disease grew upon me—for what disease is like Alcohol!—and at length even Pluto, who was now becoming old, and consequently somewhat peevish—even Pluto began to experience the effects of my ill temper.

One night, returning home, much intoxicated, from one of my haunts about town, I fancied that the cat avoided my presence. I seized him; when, in his fright at my violence, he inflicted a slight wound upon my hand with his teeth. The fury of a demon instantly possessed me. I knew myself no longer. My original soul seemed, at once, to take its flight from my body; and a more than fiendish malevolence, gin-nurtured, thrilled every fibre of my frame. I took from my waistcoat-pocket a pen-knife, opened it, grasped the poor beast by the throat, and deliberately cut one of its eyes from the socket! I blush, I burn, I shudder, while I pen the damnable atrocity.

When reason returned with the morning—when I had slept off the fumes of the night's debauch—I experienced a sentiment half of horror, half of remorse, for the crime of which I had been guilty; but it was, at best, a feeble and equivocal feeling, and the soul remained untouched. I again plunged into excess, and soon drowned in wine all memory of the deed.

In the meantime the cat slowly recovered. The socket of the lost eye presented, it is true, a frightful appearance, but he no longer appeared to suffer any pain. He went about the house as usual, but, as might be expected, fled in extreme terror at my approach. I had so much of my old heart left, as to be at first grieved by this evident dislike on the part of a creature which had once so loved me. But this feeling soon gave place to irritation. And then came, as if to my final and irrevocable overthrow, the spirit of PERVERSENESS. Of this spirit philosophy takes no account. Yet I am not more sure that my soul lives, than I am that perverseness is one of the primitive impulses of the human heart—one of the indivisible primary faculties, or sentiments, which give direction to the character of Man. Who has not, a hundred times, found himself committing a vile or a silly action, for no other reason than because he knows he should *not?* Have we not a perpetual inclination, in the teeth of our best judgment, to violate that which is *Law*, merely because we understand it to be such? This spirit of perverseness, I say, came to my final overthrow. It was this unfathomable longing of the soul *to vex itself*—to offer violence to its own nature—to do wrong for the wrong's sake only—that urged me to continue and finally to consummate the injury I had inflicted upon the unoffending brute. One morning, in cool blood, I slipped a noose about its neck and hung it to the limb of a tree;—hung it with the tears streaming from my eyes, and with the bitterest remorse at my heart;—hung it *because* I knew that it had loved me, and *because* I felt it had given me no reason of offence;—hung it *because* I knew that in so doing I was committing a sin—a deadly sin that would so jeopardize my immortal soul as to place it—if such a thing were possible—even beyond the reach of the infinite mercy of the Most Merciful and Most Terrible God.

On the night of the day on which this cruel deed was done, I was aroused from sleep by the cry of fire. The curtains of my bed were in flames. The whole house was blazing. It was with great difficulty that my wife, a servant, and myself, made our escape from the conflagration. The destruction was complete. My entire worldly wealth was swallowed up, and I resigned myself thenceforward to despair.

I am above the weakness of seeking to establish a sequence of cause and effect, between the disaster and the atrocity. But I am detailing a chain of facts—and wish not to leave even a possible link imperfect. On the day succeeding the fire, I visited the ruins. The walls, with one exception, had fallen in. This exception was found in a compartment wall, not very thick, which stood about the middle of the house, and against which had rested the head of my bed. The plastering had here, in great measure, resisted the action of the fire—a fact which I attributed to its having been recently spread. About this wall a dense crowd were collected, and many persons seemed to be examining a particular portion of it with very minute and eager attention. The words "strange!" "singular!" and other similar expressions, excited my curiosity. I approached and saw, as if graven in *bas relief* upon the white surface, the figure of a gigantic *cat*. The impression was given with an accuracy truly marvellous. There was a rope about the animal's neck.

When I first beheld this apparition—for I could scarcely regard it as less—my wonder and my terror were extreme. But at length reflection came to my aid. The cat, I remembered, had been hung in a garden adjacent to the house. Upon the alarm of fire, this garden had been immediately filled by the crowd—by some one of whom the animal must have been cut from the tree and thrown, through an open window, into my chamber. This had probably been done with the view of arousing me from sleep. The falling of other walls had compressed the victim of my cruelty into the substance of the freshly-spread plaster; the lime of which, with the flames, and the *ammonia* from the carcass, had then accomplished the portraiture as I saw it.

Although I thus readily accounted to my reason, if not altogether to my conscience, for the startling fact just detailed, it did not the less fail to make a deep impression upon my fancy. For months I could not rid myself of the phantasm of the cat; and, during this period, there came back into my spirit a half-sentiment that seemed, but was not, remorse. I went so far as to regret the loss of the animal, and to look about me, among the vile haunts which I now habitually frequented, for another pet of the same species, and of somewhat similar appearance, with which to supply its place.

One night as I sat, half stupefied, in a den of more than infamy, my attention was suddenly drawn to some black object, reposing upon the head of one of the immense hogsheads of Gin, or of Rum, which constituted the chief furniture of the apartment. I had been looking steadily at the top of this hogshead for some minutes, and what now caused me surprise was the fact that I had not sooner perceived the object thereupon. I approached it, and touched it with my hand. It was a black cat—a very large one—fully as large as Pluto, and closely resembling him in every respect but one. Pluto had not a white hair upon any portion of his body; but this cat had a large, although indefinite splotch of white, covering nearly the whole region of the breast.

Upon my touching him, he immediately arose, purred loudly, rubbed against my hand, and appeared delighted with my notice. This, then, was the very creature of which I was in search. I at once offered to purchase it of the landlord; but this person made no claim to it—knew nothing of it—had never seen it before.

I continued my caresses, and, when I prepared to go home, the animal evinced a disposition to accompany me. I permitted it to do so; occasionally stooping and patting it as I proceeded. When it reached the house it domesticated itself at once, and became immediately a great favorite with my wife.

For my own part, I soon found a dislike to it arising within me. This was just the reverse of what I had anticipated; but—I know not how or why it was—its evident fondness for myself rather disgusted and annoyed. By slow degrees, these feelings of disgust and annoyance rose into the bitterness of hatred. I avoided the creature; a certain sense of shame, and the remembrance of my former deed of cruelty, preventing me from physically abusing it. I did not, for some weeks, strike, or otherwise violently ill use it; but gradually —very gradually—I came to look upon it with unutterable loathing, and to flee silently from its odious presence, as from the breath of a pestilence.

What added, no doubt, to my hatred of the beast, was the discovery, on the morning after I brought it home, that, like Pluto, it also had been deprived of one of its eyes. This circumstance, however, only endeared it to my wife, who, as I have already said, possessed, in a high degree, that humanity of feeling which had once been my distinguishing trait, and the source of many of my simplest and purest pleasures.

With my aversion to this cat, however, its partiality for myself seemed to increase. It followed my footsteps with a pertinacity which it would be difficult to make the reader comprehend. Whenever I sat, it would crouch beneath my chair, or spring upon my knees, covering me with its loathsome caresses. If I arose to walk it would get between my feet and thus nearly throw me down, or, fastening its long and sharp claws in my dress, clamber, in this manner, to my breast. At such times, although I longed to destroy it with a blow, I was yet withheld from so doing, partly by a memory of my former crime, but chiefly—let me confess it at once—by absolute *dread* of the beast.

This dread was not exactly a dread of physical evil—and yet I should be at a loss how otherwise to define it. I am almost ashamed to own—yes, even in this felon's cell, I am almost ashamed to own —that the terror and horror with which the animal inspired me, had been heightened by one of the merest chimaeras it would be possible to conceive. My wife had called my attention, more than once, to the character of the mark of white hair, of which I have spoken, and which constituted the sole visible difference between the strange beast and the one I had destroyed. The reader will remember that this mark, although large, had been originally very indefinite; but, by slow degrees—degrees nearly imperceptible, and which for a long time my Reason struggled to reject as fanciful—it had, at length, assumed a rigorous distinctness of outline. It was now the representation of an object that I shudder to name—and for this, above all, I loathed, and dreaded, and would have rid myself of the monster *had I dared*—it was now, I say, the image of a hideous—of a ghastly thing—of the GALLOWS!—oh, mournful and terrible engine of Horror and of Crime—of Agony and of Death!

And now was I indeed wretched beyond the wretchedness of mere Humanity. And *a brute beast*—whose fellow I had contemptuously destroyed—*a brute beast* to work out for *me*—for me a man, fashioned in the image of the High God—so much of insufferable wo! Alas! neither by day nor by night knew I the blessing of Rest any more! During the former the creature left me no moment alone; and, in the latter, I started, hourly, from dreams of unutterable fear, to find the hot breath of *the thing* upon my face, and its vast weight—

an incarnate Night-Mare that I had no power to shake off—incumbent eternally upon my *heart!*

Beneath the pressure of torments such as these, the feeble remnant of the good within me succumbed. Evil thoughts became my sole intimates—the darkest and most evil of thoughts. The moodiness of my usual temper increased to hatred of all things and of all mankind; while, from the sudden, frequent, and ungovernable outbursts of a fury to which I now blindly abandoned myself, my uncomplaining wife, alas! was the most usual and the most patient of sufferers.

One day she accompanied me, upon some household errand, into the cellar of the old building which our poverty compelled us to inhabit. The cat followed me down the steep stairs, and, nearly throwing me headlong, exasperated me to madness. Uplifting an axe, and forgetting, in my wrath, the childish dread which had hitherto stayed my hand, I aimed a blow at the animal which, of course, would have proved instantly fatal had it descended as I wished. But this blow was arrested by the hand of my wife. Goaded, by the interference, into a rage more than demoniacal, I withdrew my arm from her grasp and buried the axe in her brain. She fell dead upon the spot, without a groan.

This hideous murder accomplished, I set myself forthwith, and with entire deliberation, to the task of concealing the body. I knew that I could not remove it from the house, either by day or by night, without the risk of being observed by the neighbors. Many projects entered my mind. At one period I thought of cutting the corpse into minute fragments and destroying them by fire. At another, I resolved to dig a grave for it in the floor of the cellar. Again, I deliberated about casting it in the well in the yard—about packing it in a box, as if merchandize, with the usual arrangements, and so getting a porter to take it from the house. Finally I hit upon what I considered a far better expedient than either of these. I determined to wall it up in the cellar—as the monks of the middle ages are recorded to have walled up their victims.

For a purpose such as this the cellar was well adapted. Its walls were loosely constructed, and had lately been plastered throughout with a rough plaster, which the dampness of the atmosphere had prevented from hardening. Moreover, in one of the walls was a projection, caused by a false chimney, or fireplace, that had been filled up, and made to resemble the rest of the cellar. I made no doubt that I could readily displace the bricks at this point, insert the corpse, and wall the whole up as before, so that no eye could detect anything suspicious.

And in this calculation I was not deceived. By means of a crow-bar I easily dislodged the bricks, and, having carefully deposited the body against the inner wall, I propped it in that position, while, with little trouble, I re-laid the whole structure as it originally stood. Having procured mortar, sand, and hair, with every possible pre-caution, I prepared a plaster which could not be distinguished from the old, and with this I very carefully went over the new brick-work. When I had finished, I felt satisfied that all was right. The wall did not present the slightest appearance of having been disturbed. The rubbish on the floor was picked up with the minutest care. I looked around triumphantly, and said to myself—"Here at least, then, my labor has not been in vain."

My next step was to look for the beast which had been the cause of so much wretchedness; for I had, at length, firmly resolved to put it to death. Had I been able to meet with it, at the moment, there could have been no doubt of its fate; but it appeared that the crafty animal had been alarmed at the violence of my previous anger, and forebore to present itself in my present mood. It is impossible to describe, or to imagine, the deep, the blissful sense of relief which the absence of the detested creature occasioned in my bosom. It did not make its appearance during the night—and thus for one night at least, since its introduction into the house, I soundly and tranquilly slept; aye, *slept* even with the burden of murder upon my soul!

The second and the third day passed, and still my tormentor came not. Once again I breathed as a freeman. The monster, in terror, had fled the premises forever! I should behold it no more! My hap-piness was supreme! The guilt of my dark deed disturbed me but little. Some few inquiries had been made, but these had been readily answered. Even a search had been instituted—but of course nothing was to be discovered. I looked upon my future felicity as secured.

Upon the fourth day of the assassination, a party of the police came, very unexpectedly, into the house, and proceeded again to make rigorous investigation of the premises. Secure, however, in the inscrutability of my place of concealment, I felt no embarrass-ment whatever. The officers bade me accompany them in their search. They left no nook or corner unexplored. At length, for the third or fourth time, they descended into the cellar. I quivered not in a muscle. My heart beat calmly as that of one who slumbers in innocence. I walked the cellar from end to end. I folded my arms upon my bosom, and roamed easily to and fro. The police were thoroughly satisfied and prepared to depart. The glee at my heart was too strong to be restrained. I burned to say if but one word, by way of triumph, and to render doubly sure their assurance of my guiltlessness.

"Gentlemen," I said at last, as the party ascended the steps, "I delight to have allayed your suspicions. I wish you all health, and a little more courtesy. By the bye, gentlemen, this—this is a very well constructed house." [In the rabid desire to say something easily, I scarcely knew what I uttered at all.]—"I may say an *excellently* well constructed house. These walls—are you going, gentlemen?— these walls are solidly put together"; and here, through the mere phrenzy of bravado, I rapped heavily, with a cane which I held in my hand, upon that very portion of the brick-work behind which stood the corpse of the wife of my bosom.

But may God shield and deliver me from the fangs of the Arch-Fiend! No sooner had the reverberation of my blows sunk into silence, than I was answered by a voice from within the tomb!—by a cry, at first muffled and broken, like the sobbing of a child, and then quickly swelling into one long, loud, and continuous scream, utterly anomalous and inhuman—a howl—a wailing shriek, half of horror and half of triumph, such as might have arisen only out of hell, conjointly from the throats of the damned in their agony and of the demons that exult in the damnation.

Of my own thoughts it is folly to speak. Swooning, I staggered to the opposite wall. For one instant the party upon the stairs remained motionless, through extremity of terror and of awe. In the next, a dozen stout arms were toiling at the wall. It fell bodily. The corpse, already greatly decayed and clotted with gore, stood erect before the eyes of the spectators. Upon its head, with red extended mouth and solitary eye of fire, sat the hideous beast whose craft had seduced me into murder, and whose informing voice had consigned me to the hangman. I had walled the monster up within the tomb!

Part Two

CAT POETRY
FROM THE
CANON

CHRISTOPHER SMART

My Cat Jeoffry

For I will consider my Cat Jeoffry.

For he is the servant of the Living God duly and daily serving him.

For at the first glance of the glory of God in the East he worships in his way.

For is this done by wreathing his body seven times round with elegant quickness.

For then he leaps up to catch the musk, which is the blessing of God upon his prayer.

For he rolls upon prank to work it in.

For having done duty and received blessing he begins to consider himself.

For this he performs in ten degrees.

For first he looks upon his fore-paws to see if they are clean.

For secondly he kicks up behind to clear away there.

For thirdly he works it upon stretch with the fore-paws extended.

For fourthly he sharpens his paws by wood.

For fifthly he washes himself.

For sixthly he rolls upon wash.

For seventhly he fleas himself, that he may not be interrupted upon the beat.

For eighthly he rubs himself against a post.

For ninthly he looks up for his instructions.

For tenthly he goes in quest of food.

For having considered God and himself he will consider his neighbour.

For if he meets another cat he will kiss her in kindness.

For when he takes his prey he plays with it to give it a chance.

For one mouse in seven escapes by his dallying.

For when his day's work is done his business more properly begins.

For he keeps the Lord's watch in the night against the adversary.

For he counteracts the powers of darkness by his electrical skin and glaring eyes.

For he counteracts the Devil, who is death, by brisking about the life.

For in his morning orisons he loves the sun and the sun loves him.

For he is of the tribe of Tiger.

For the Cherub Cat is a term of the Angel Tiger.

For he has the subtlety and hissing of a serpent, which in goodness he suppresses.

For he will not do destruction if he is well-fed, neither will he spit without provocation.

For he purrs in thankfulness, when God tells him he's a good Cat.

For he is an instrument for the children to learn benevolence upon.

For every house is incomplete without him and a blessing is lacking in the spirit.

For the Lord commanded Moses concerning the cats at the departure of the Children of Israel from Egypt.

For every family had one cat at least in the bag.

For the English Cats are the best in Europe.

For he is the cleanest in the use of his fore-paws of any quadruped.

For the dexterity of his defence is an instance of the love of God to him exceedingly.

For he is the quickest to his mark of any creature.

For he is tenacious of his point.

For he is a mixture of gravity and waggery.

For he knows that God is his Saviour.

For there is nothing sweeter than his peace when at rest.

For there is nothing brisker than his life when in motion.

For he is of the Lord's poor and so indeed is he called by benevolence perpetually—Poor Jeoffry! poor Jeoffry! the rat has bit thy throat.

For I bless the name of the Lord Jesus that Jeoffry is better.

For the divine spirit comes about his body to sustain it in complete cat.

For his tongue is exceeding pure so that it has in purity what it wants in music.

For he is docile and can learn certain things.

For he can set up with gravity which is patience upon approbation.

For he can fetch and carry, which is patience in employment.

For he can jump over a stick which is patience upon proof positive.

For he can spraggle upon waggle at the word of command.

For he can jump from an eminence into his master's bosom.

For he can catch the cork and toss it again.

For he is hated by the hypocrite and miser.

For the former is afraid of detection.

For the latter refuses the charge.

For he camels his back to bear the first notion of business.

For he is good to think on, if a man would express himself neatly.

For he made a great figure in Egypt for his signal services.

For he killed the Icneumon-rat very pernicious by land.

For his ears are so acute that they sting again.

For from this proceeds the passing quickness of his attention.

For by stroking of him I have found out electricity.

For I perceived God's light about him both wax and fire.

For the electrical fire is the spiritual substance, which God sends
  from heaven to sustain the bodies both of man and beast.

For God has blessed him in the variety of his movements.

For, though he cannot fly, he is an excellent clamberer.

For his motions upon the face of the earth are more than any other
  quadruped.

For he can tread to all the measures upon the music.

For he can swim for life.

For he can creep.

THOMAS GRAY

Ode

ON THE DEATH OF A FAVORITE CAT,
DROWNED IN A TUB OF GOLDFISHES

'Twas on a lofty vase's side,
Where China's gayest art had dyed
   The azure flowers that blow;
Demurest of the tabby kind,
The pensive Selima, reclined,
   Gazed on the lake below.

Her conscious tail her joy declared;
The fair round face, the snowy beard,
   The velvet of her paws,
Her coat, that with the tortoise vies,

Her ears of jet, and emerald eyes,
  She saw, and purred applause.

Still had she gazed; but 'midst the tide
Two angel forms were seen to glide,
  The genii of the stream:
Their scaly armor's Tyrian hue
Through richest purple to the view
  Betrayed a golden gleam.

The hapless nymph with wonder saw:
A whisker first and then a claw,
  With many an ardent wish,
She stretched in vain to reach the prize.
What female heart can gold despise?
  What cat's averse to fish?

Presumptuous maid! with looks intent
Again she stretched, again she bent,
  Nor knew the gulf between.
(Malignant Fate sat by and smiled)
The slippery verge her feet beguiled,
  She tumbled headlong in.

Eight times emerging from the flood
She mewed to every watery god,
  Some speedy aid to send.
No dolphin came, no Nereid stirred;
Nor cruel Tom, nor Susan heard;
  A favorite has no friend!

From hence, ye beauties, undeceived,
Know, one false step is ne'er retrieved,
  And be with caution bold.
Not all that tempts your wandering eyes
And heedless hearts, is lawful prize;
  Nor all that glisters, gold.

JOHN KEATS

To a Cat

Cat! who hast pass'd thy grand climacteric,
  How many mice and rats hast in thy days
  Destroy'd? How many tit-bits stolen? Gaze
With those bright languid segments green, and
    prick
Those velvet ears—but prythee do not stick
  Thy latent talons in me—and tell me all thy frays,
Of fish and mice, and rats and tender chick;
Nay, look not down, nor lick thy dainty wrists,—
  For all the wheezy asthma—and for all
Thy tail's tip is nick'd off—and though the fists
  Of many a maid have given thee many a maul,
Still is thy fur as when the lists
  In youth thou enter'dst on glass-bottled wall.

PERCY BYSSHE SHELLEY

Verses on a Cat

  A cat in distress,
    Nothing more, nor less;
  Good folks, I must faithfully tell ye,
    As I am a sinner,
    It waits for some dinner,
  To stuff out its own little belly.

    You would not easily guess
    All the modes of distress

Which torture the tenants of earth;
   And the various evils,
   Which, like so many devils,
Attend the poor souls from their birth.

   Some living require,
   And others desire
An old fellow out of the way;
   And which is best
   I leave to be guessed,
For I cannot pretend to say.

   One wants society,
   Another variety,
Others a tranquil life;
   Some want food,
   Others, as good,
Only want a wife.

   But this poor little cat
   Only wanted a rat,
To stuff out its own little maw;
   And it were as good
   Some people had such food,
To make them *hold their jaw!*

EMILY DICKINSON

She Sights a Bird

She sights a Bird—she chuckles—
She flattens—then she crawls—
She runs without the look of feet—
Her eyes increase to Balls—

Her Jaws stir—twitching—hungry—
Her Teeth can hardly stand—

She leaps, but Robin leaped the first—
Ah, Pussy, of the Sand,

The Hopes so juicy ripening—
You almost bathed your Tongue—
When Bliss disclosed a hundred Toes—
And fled with every one—

ALGERNON CHARLES SWINBURNE

To a Cat

Stately, kindly, lordly friend,
      Condescend
Here to sit by me, and turn
Glorious eyes that smile and burn,
Golden eyes, love's lustrous meed,
On the golden page I read.

All your wondrous wealth of hair,
      Dark and fair,
Silken-shaggy, soft and bright
As the clouds and beams of night,
Pays my reverent hand's caress
Back with friendlier gentleness.

Dogs may fawn on all and some,
      As they come;
You, a friend of loftier mind,
Answer friends alone in kind;
Just your foot upon my hand
Softly bids it understand.

.   .   .   .

Wild on woodland ways, your sires
      Flashed like fires;

Fair as flame, and fierce, and fleet,
As with wings on wingless feet,
Shone and sprang your mother, free,
Bright and brave as wind or sea.

Free, and proud, and glad as they,
       Here to-day
Rests or roams their radiant child,
Vanquished not, but reconciled;
Free from curb of aught above
Save the lovely curb of love.

Love, through dreams of souls divine,
       Fain would shine
Round a dawn whose light and song
Then should right our mutual wrong,—
Speak, and seal the love-lit law,
Sweet Assisi's seer foresaw.

Dreams were theirs; yet haply may
       Dawn a day
When such friends and fellows born,
Seeing our earth as fair at morn,
May, for wiser love's sake, see
More of heaven's deep heart than we.

JONATHAN SWIFT

A Fable of the Widow and Her Cat

A widow kept a favourite cat.
  At first a gentle creature;
But when he was grown sleek and fat,

With many a mouse, and many a rat,
   He soon disclosed his nature.

The fox and he were friends of old,
   Nor could they now be parted;
They nightly slunk to rob the fold,
Devoured the lambs, the fleeces sold,
   And puss grew lion-hearted.

He scratched her maid, he stole the cream,
   He tore her best laced pinner;
Nor Chanticleer upon the beam,
Nor chick, nor duckling 'scapes, when Grim
   Invites the fox to dinner.

The dame full wisely did decree,
   For fear he should dispatch more,
That the false wretch should worried be:
But in a saucy manner he
   Thus speeched it like a Lechmere.

"Must I, against all right and law,
   Like pole-cat vile be treated?
I! who so long with tooth and claw
Have kept domestic mice in awe,
   And foreign foes defeated!

"Your golden pippins, and your pies,
   How oft have I defended?
'Tis true, the pinner which you prize
I tore in frolic; to your eyes
   I never harm intended.

"I am a cat of honour—" "Stay,"
   Quoth she, "no longer parley;
Whate'er you did in battle slay,
By law of arms become your prey,
   I hope you won it fairly.

"Of this, we'll grant you stand acquit,
   But not of your outrages:

Tell me, perfidious! was it fit
To make my cream a *perquisite*,
  And steal to mend your wages!

"So flagrant is thy insolence,
  So vile thy breach of trust is;
That longer with thee to dispense,
Were want of power, or want of sense:
  Here, Towser!—Do him justice."

CHRISTINA ROSSETTI

On the Death of a Cat, a Friend of Mine Aged Ten Years and a Half

Who shall tell the lady's grief
When her cat was past relief?
Who shall number the hot tears
Shed o'er her, belov'd for years?
Who shall say the dark dismay
Which her dying caused that day?

Come ye Muses, one and all,
Come obedient to my call;
Come and mourn with tuneful breath
Each one for a separate death;
And, while you in numbers sigh,
I will sing her elegy.

Of a noble race she came,
And Grimalkin was her name.

Young and old full many a mouse
Felt the prowess of her house;
Weak and strong full many a rat
Cowered beneath her crushing pat;
And the birds around the place
Shrank from her too-close embrace.
But one night, reft of her strength,
She lay down and died at length:
Lay a kitten by her side
In whose life the mother died.
Spare her life and lineage,
Guard her kitten's tender age,
And that kitten's name as wide
Shall be known as hers that died.
And whoever passes by
The poor grave where Puss doth lie,
Softly, softly let him tread,
Nor disturb her narrow bed.

AMY LOWELL

To Winky

Cat,
Cat,
What are you?
Son, through a thousand generations, of the black leopards
Padding among the sprigs of young bamboo;
Descendant of many removals from the white panthers
Who crouch by night under the loquat-trees?
You crouch under the orange begonias,
And your eyes are green
With the violence of murder,
Or half-closed and stealthy
Like your sheathed claws.

Slowly, slowly,
You rise and stretch
In a glossiness of beautiful curves,
Of muscles fluctuating under black, glazed hair.

Cat,
You are a strange creature.
You sit on your haunches
And yawn,
But when you leap
I can almost hear the whine
Of a released string,
And I look to see its flaccid shaking
In the place whence you sprang.

You carry your tail as a banner,
Slowly it passes my chair,
But when I look for you, you are on the table
Moving easily among the most delicate porcelains.
Your food is a matter of importance
And you are insistent on having
Your wants attended to,
And yet you will eat a bird and its feathers
Apparently without injury.

In the night, I hear you crying,
But if I try to find you
There are only the shadows of rhododendron leaves
Brushing the ground.
When you come in out of the rain,
All wet and with your tail full of burrs,
You fawn upon me in coils and subtleties;
But once you are dry
You leave me with a gesture of inconceivable impudence,
Conveyed by the vanishing quirk of your tail
As you slide through the open door.

You walk as a king scorning his subjects;
You flirt with me as a concubine in robes of silk.
Cat,
I am afraid of your poisonous beauty,

I have seen you torturing a mouse.
Yet when you lie purring in my lap
I forget everything but how soft you are,
And it is only when I feel your claws open upon my hand
That I remember—

Remember a puma lying out on a branch above my head
Years ago.

Shall I choke you, Cat,
Or kiss you?
Really I do not know.

WILLIAM WORDSWORTH

The Kitten and Falling Leaves

That way look, my Infant, lo!
What a pretty baby-show!
See the Kitten on the wall,
Sporting with the leaves that fall,
Withered leaves—one—two—and three—
From the lofty elder-tree!
Through the calm and frosty air
Of this morning bright and fair,
Eddying round and round they sink
Softly, slowly: one might think,
From the motions that are made,
Every little leaf conveyed
Sylph or Faery hither tending,—
To this lower world descending,
Each invisible and mute,
In his wavering parachute.

——But the Kitten, how she starts,
Crouches, stretches, paws, and darts!
First at one, and then its fellow,
Just as light and just as yellow;
There are many now—now one—
Now they stop and there are none:
What intenseness of desire
In her upward eye of fire!
With a tiger-leap half-way
Now she meets the coming prey,
Lets it go as fast, and then
Has it in her power again:
Now she works with three or four,
Like an Indian conjurer;
Quick as he in feats of art,
Far beyond in joy of heart.
Were her antics played in the eye
Of a thousand standers-by,
Clapping hands with shout and stare,
What would little Tabby care
For the plaudits of the crowd?
Over happy to be proud,
Over wealthy in the treasure
Of her own exceeding pleasure!

'Tis a pretty baby-treat;
Nor, I deem, for me unmeet;
Here, for neither Babe nor me,
Other playmate can I see.
Of the countless living things,
That with stir of feet and wings
(In the sun or under shade,
Upon bough or grassy blade)
And with busy revellings,
Chirp and song, and murmurings,
Made this orchard's narrow space,
And this vale, so blithe a place;
Multitudes are swept away
Never more to breathe the day:
Some are sleeping; some in bands
Travelled into distant lands;

Others slunk to moor and wood,
Far from human neighborhood;
And among the Kinds that keep
With us closer fellowship,
With us openly abide,
All have laid their mirth aside.

Where is he that giddy Sprite,
Blue-cap, with his colours bright,
Who was blest as bird could be,
Feeding in the apple-tree;
Made such wanton spoil and rout,
Turning blossoms inside out;
Hung—head pointing towards the ground—
Fluttered, perched, into a round
Bound himself, and then unbound;
Lithest, gaudiest Harlequin!
Prettiest Tumbler ever seen!
Light of heart and light of limb;
What is now become of Him?
Lambs, that through the mountains went
Frisking, bleating merriment,
When the year was in its prime,
They are sobered by this time.
If you look to vale or hill,
If you listen, all is still,
Save a little neighbouring rill,
That from out the rocky ground
Strikes a solitary sound.
Vainly glitter hill and plain,
And the air is calm in vain;
Vainly Morning spreads the lure
Of a sky serene and pure;
Creature none can she decoy
Into open sign of joy:
Is it that they have a fear
Of the dreary season near?
Or that other pleasures be
Sweeter even than gaiety?

Yet, whate'er enjoyments dwell
In the impenetrable cell
Of the silent heart which Nature
Furnishes to every creature;
Whatsoe'er we feel and know
Too sedate for outward show,
Such a light of gladness breaks,
Pretty Kitten! from thy freaks—
Spreads with such a living grace
O'er my little Dora's face;
Yes, the sight so stirs and charms
Thee, Baby, laughing in my arms,
That almost I could repine
That your transports are not mine,
That I do not wholly fare
Even as ye do, thoughtless pair!
And I will have my careless season
Spite of melancholy reason,
Will walk through life in such a way
That, when time brings on decay,
Now and then I may possess
Hours of perfect gladsomeness.
—Pleased by any random toy;
By a kitten's busy joy,
Or an infant's laughing eye
Sharing in the ecstasy;
I would fare like that or this,
Find my wisdom in my bliss;
Keep the sprightly soul awake,
And have faculties to take,
Even from things by sorrow wrought,
Matter for a jocund thought,
Spite of care, and spite of grief,
To gambol with Life's falling Leaf.

ALFRED, LORD TENNYSON

The Spinster's Sweet-Arts

I

Milk for my sweet-arts, Bess! fur it mun be the time about now
When Molly cooms in fro' the far-end close wi' her paäils fro' the
    cow.
Eh! tha be new to the plaäce—thou 'rt gaäpin'—does n't tha see
I calls 'em arter the fellers es once was sweet upo' me?

II

Naäy, to be sewer, it be past 'er time.
What maäkes 'er sa laäte?
Goä to the laäne at the back, an' looök thruf Maddison's gaäte!

III

Sweet-arts! Molly belike may 'a lighted to-night upo' one.
Sweet-arts! thanks to the Lord that I niver not listen'd to noän!
So I sits i' my oän armchair wi' my oän kettle theere o' the hob,
An' Tommy the fust, an' Tommy the second, an' Steevie an' Rob.

IV

Rob, coom oop 'ere o' my knee. Thou sees that i' spite o' the men
I 'a kep' thruf thick an' thin my two 'oonderd a-year to mysen;
Yis! thaw tha call'd me es pretty es ony lass i' the Shere;
An' thou be es pretty a tabby, but Robby I seed thruf ya theere.

V

Feyther 'ud saäy I wur ugly es sin, an' I beänt not vaäin,
But I niver wur downright hugly, thaw soom 'ud 'a thowt ma plaäin,
An' I was n't sa plaäin i' pink ribbons—ye said I wur pretty i' pinks,
An' I liked to 'ear it I did, but I beänt sich a fool as ye thinks;

Ye was stroäkin' ma down wi' the 'air, as I be a-stroäkin' o' you,
But whiniver I looöked i' the glass I wur sewer that it could n't be true;
Niver wur pretty, not I, but ye knaw'd it wur pleasant to 'ear,
Thaw it warn't not me es wur pretty, but my two 'oonderd a-year.

VI

D' ya mind the murnin' when we was a-walkin' togither, an' stood
By the claäy'd-oop pond, that the foälk be sa scared at, i' Gigglesby wood,
Wheer the poor wench drowndid hersen, black Sal, es 'ed been disgraäced?
An' I feel'd thy arm es I stood wur a-creeäpin' about my waäist;
An' me es wur allus afear'd of a man's gittin' ower fond,
I sidled awaäy an' awaäy till I plumpt foot fust i' the pond;
And, Robby, I niver 'a liked tha sa well, as I did that daäy,
Fur tha joompt in thysen, an' tha hoickt my feet wi' a flop fro' the claäy.
Ay, stick oop thy back, an' set oop thy taäil, tha may gie ma a kiss,
Fur I walk'd wi' tha all the way hoäm an' wur niver sa nigh saäyin' Yis.
But wa boäth was i' sich a clat we was shaämed to cross Gigglesby Greeän,
Fur a cat may looök at a king, thou knaws, but the cat mun be cleän.
Sa we boäth on us kep' out o' sight o' the winders o' Gigglesby Hinn—
Naäy, but the claws o' tha! quiet! they pricks cleän thruf to the skin—
An' wa boäth slinkt 'oäm by the brokken shed i' the laäne at the back,
Wheer the poodle runn'd at tha once, an' thou runn'd oop o' the thack;
An' tha squeedg'd my 'and i' the shed, fur theere we was forced to 'ide,
Fur I seed that Steevie wur coomin', and one o' the Tommies beside.

VII

Theere now, what art 'a mewin' at, Steevie? for owt I can tell—
Robby wur fust, to be sewer, or I mowt 'a liked tha as well.

VIII

But, Robby, I thowt o' tha all the while I wur chaängin' my gown,
An' I thowt, shall I chaänge my staäte? but, O Lord, upo' coomin'
  down—
My bran-new carpet es fresh es a midder o' flowers i' Maäy—
Why 'ed n't tha wiped thy shoes? it wur clatted all ower wi' claäy.
An' I could 'a cried ammost, fur I seed that it could n't be,
An', Robby, I gied tha a raätin' that sattled thy coortin' o' me.
An' Molly an' me was agreed, as we was a-cleänin' the floor,
That a man be a durty thing an' a trouble an' plague wi' indoor.
But I rued it arter a bit, fur I stuck to tha moor na the rest,
But I could n't 'a lived wi' a man, an' I knaws it be all fur the best.

IX

Naäy—let ma stroäk tha down till I maäkes tha es smooth es silk,
But if I 'ed married tha, Robby, thou'd not 'a been worth thy milk,
Thou'd niver 'a cotch'd ony mice but 'a left me the work to do.
And 'a taäen to the bottle beside, so es all that I 'ears be true;
But I loovs tha to maäke thysen 'appy, an' soä purr awaäy, my dear,
Thou 'ed wellnigh purr'd ma awaäy fro' my oän two 'oonderd a-year.

X

Sweärin' ageän, you Toms, as ye used to do twelve year sin'!
Ye niver eärd Steevie sweär 'cep' it wur at a dog coomin' in,
An' boäth o' ye mun be fools to be hallus a-shawin' your claws,
Fur I niver cared nothink for neither—an' one o' ye deäd, ye knaws!
Coom, give hoäver then, weänt ye? I warrant ye soom fine daäy—
Theere, lig down—I shall hev to gie one or tother awaäy.
Can't ye taäke pattern by Steevie? ye shan't hev a drop fro' the paäil.
Steevie be right good manners bang thruf to the tip o' the taäil.

XI

Robby, git down wi' tha, wilt tha? let Steevie coom oop o' my knee.
Steevie, my lad, thou 'ed very nigh been the Steevie fur me!
Robby wur fust, to be sewer, 'e wur burn an' bred i' the 'ouse,
But thou be es 'ansom a tabby es iver patted a mouse.

XII

An' I beänt not vaäin, but I knaws I 'ed led tha a quieter life
Nor her wi' the hepitaph yonder! "A faäithful an' loovin' wife!"
An' 'cos o' thy farm by the beck, an' thy windmill oop o' the croft,
Tha thowt tha would marry ma, did tha? but that wur a bit ower
   soft,
Thaw thou was es soäber es daäy, wi' a niced red faäce, an' es cleän
Es a shillin' fresh fro' the mint wi' a bran-new 'eäd o' the Queeän,
An' thy farmin' es cleän es thysen, fur, Steevie, tha kep' it sa neät
That I niver not spied sa much es a poppy along wi' the wheät,
An' the wool of a thistle a-flyin' an' seeädin' tha haäted to see;
'T wur es bad es a battle-twig 'ere i' my oän blue chaumber to me.
Ay, roob thy whiskers ageän ma, fur I could 'a taäen to tha well,
But fur thy bairns, poor Steevie, a bouncin' boy an' a gell.

XIII

An' thou was es fond o' thy bairns es I be mysen o' my cats,
But I niver not wish'd fur childer, I hev n't naw likin' fur brats;
Pretty anew when ya dresses 'em oop, an' they goäs fur a walk,
Or sits wi' their 'ands afoor 'em, an' does n't not 'inder the talk!
But their bottles o' pap, an' their mucky bibs, an' the clats an' the
   clouts,
An' their mashin' their toys to pieäces an' maäkin' ma deäf wi' their
   shouts,
An' hallus a-joompin' about ma as if they was set upo' springs,
An' a haxin' ma hawkard questions, an' saäyin' ondecent things,
An' a-callin' ma 'hugly' mayhap to my faäce, or a-teärin' my gown—
Dear! dear! dear! I mun part them Tommies—Steevie, git down.

XIV

Ye be wuss nor the men-tommies, you. I tell'd ya, na moor o' that!
Tom, lig theere o' the cushion, an' tother Tom 'ere o' the mat.

XV

Theere! I ha' master'd *them!* Hed I married the Tommies—O Lord,
To loove an' obaäy the Tommies! I could n't 'a stuck by my word.
To be horder'd about, an' waäked, when Molly 'd put out the light,

By a man coomin' in wi' a hiccup at ony hour o' the night!
An' the taäble staäin'd wi' 'is aäle, an' the mud o' 'is boots o' the
    stairs,
An' the stink o' 'is pipe i' the 'ouse, an' the mark o' 'is 'eäd o' the
    chairs!
An' noän o' my four sweet-arts 'ud 'a let me 'a hed my oän waäy,
Sa I likes 'em best wi' taäils when they 'ev n't a word to saäy.

XVI

An' I sits i' my oän little parlor, an' sarved by my oän little lass,
Wi' my oän little garden outside, an' my oän bed o' sparrow-grass,
An' my oän door-poorch wi' the woodbine an' jessmine a-dressin' it
    greeän,
An' my oän fine Jackman i' purple a roäbin' the 'ouse like a queeän.

XVII

An' the little gells bobs to ma hoffens es I be abroad i' the laänes,
When I goäs fur to coomfut the poor es be down wi' their haäches
    an' their paäins:
An' a haäf-pot o' jam, or a mossel o' meät when it beänt too dear,
They maäkes ma a graäter lady nor 'er i' the mansion theer,
Hes 'es hallus to hax of a man how much to spare or to spend;
An' a spinster I be an' I will be, if soä pleäse God, to the hend.

XVIII

Mew! mew!—Bess wi' the milk! what ha maäde our Molly sa laäte?
It should 'a been 'ere by seven, an' theere—it be strikin' height—
"Cushie wur craäzed fur 'er cauf," well—I 'eärd 'er a-maäkin' 'er
    moän,
An' I thowt to mysen, "thank God that I hev n't naw cauf o' my
    oän."
Theere!
      Set it down!
           Now, Robby!
     You Tommies shall waäit to-night
Till Robby an' Steevie 'es 'ed their lap—an' it sarves ye right.

JOHN SKELTON

[The Churlyshe Cat]

That vengeaunce I aske and crye,
By way of exclamacyon,
Of all the whole nacyon
Of cattes wylde and tame;
God send them sorowe and shame!
That cat especyally
That slew so cruelly
My lytell pretty sparowe,
That I brought up at Carowe.
  O cat of churlyshe kynde,
The Fynde was in thy minde
When thou my byrde untwynde!
I would thou haddest ben blynde!
The leopardes savage,
The lyons in theyr rage,
Myght catche thee in theyr pawes!
And gnawe thee in theyr jawes!
The serpentes of Lybany
Myght stynge thee venymously!
The dragones with theyr tonges
Myght poyson thy lyver and longes!
The mantycors of the montaynes
Myght fede them on thy braynes!
Melanchates, that hounde
That plucked Actæon to the grounde,
Gave hym his mortall wounde,
Chaunged to a dere,
The story doth appere,
Was chaunged to an harte:
So thou, foule cat that thou arte,
The selfesame hounde
Myght thee confounde,
That his owne lord bote,

Myght byte asondre thy throte!
  Of Inde the gredy grypes
Myght tere out all thy trypes!
Of Arcady the beares
Myght plucke awaye thyne eares!
The wylde wolfe Lycaon
Byte asondre thy backe bone!
Of Ethna the brennynge hyll,
That day and nyghte brenneth styl,
Set in thy tayle a blase,
That all the world may gase
And wonder upon thee!
From Ocyan the greate sea
Unto the Isles of Orchady;
From Tyllbery ferry
To the playne of Salysbery!
So trayterously my byrde to kyll,
That never wrought thee evyll wyll!

Part Three

More Stories About Cats from the Masters

ERNEST HEMINGWAY

Cat in the Rain

There were only two Americans stopping at the hotel. They did not know any of the people they passed on the stairs on their way to and from their room. Their room was on the second floor facing the sea. It also faced the public garden and the war monument. There were big palms and green benches in the public garden. In the good weather there was always an artist with his easel. Artists liked the way the palms grew and the bright colors of the hotels facing the gardens and the sea. Italians came from a long way off to look up at the war monument. It was made of bronze and glistened in the rain. It was raining. The rain dripped from the palm trees. Water stood in pools on the gravel paths. The sea broke in a long line in the rain and slipped back down the beach to come up and break again in a long line in the rain. The motor cars were gone from the square by the war monument. Across the square in the doorway of the café a waiter stood looking out at the empty square.

The American wife stood at the window looking out. Outside right under their window a cat was crouched under one of the dripping green tables. The cat was trying to make herself so compact that she would not be dripped on.

"I'm going down and get that kitty," the American wife said.

"I'll do it," her husband offered from the bed.

"No, I'll get it. The poor kitty out trying to keep dry under a table."

The husband went on reading, lying propped up with the two pillows at the foot of the bed.

"Don't get wet," he said.

The wife went downstairs and the hotel owner stood up and bowed to her as she passed the office. His desk was at the far end of the office. He was an old man and very tall.

"Il piove," the wife said. She liked the hotel-keeper.

"Si, si, Signora, brutto tempo. It's very bad weather."

He stood behind his desk in the far end of the dim room. The wife liked him. She liked the deadly serious way he received any complaints. She liked his dignity. She liked the way he wanted to serve her. She liked the way he felt about being a hotel-keeper. She liked his old, heavy face and big hands.

Liking him she opened the door and looked out. It was raining harder. A man in a rubber cape was crossing the empty square to the café. The cat would be around to the right. Perhaps she could go along under the eaves. As she stood in the doorway an umbrella opened behind her. It was the maid who looked after their room.

"You must not get wet," she smiled, speaking Italian. Of course, the hotel-keeper had sent her.

With the maid holding the umbrella over her, she walked along the gravel path until she was under their window. The table was there, washed bright green in the rain, but the cat was gone. She was suddenly disappointed. The maid looked up at her.

"Ha perduto qualque cosa, Signora?"

"There was a cat," said the American girl.

"A cat?"

"Si, il gatto."

"A cat?" the maid laughed. "A cat in the rain?"

"Yes," she said, "under the table." Then, "Oh, I wanted it so much. I wanted a kitty."

When she talked English the maid's face tightened.

"Come, Signora," she said. "We must get back inside. You will be wet."

"I suppose so," said the American girl.

They went back along the gravel path and passed in the door. The maid stayed outside to close the umbrella. As the American girl passed the office, the padrone bowed from his desk. Something felt very small and tight inside the girl. The padrone made her feel very small and at the same time really important. She had a momentary feeling of being of supreme importance. She went on up the stairs. She opened the door of the room. George was on the bed, reading.

"Did you get the cat?" he asked, putting the book down.

"It was gone."

"Wonder where it went to," he said, resting his eyes from reading.

She sat down on the bed.

"I wanted it so much," she said. "I don't know why I wanted it so much. I wanted that poor kitty. It isn't any fun to be a poor kitty out in the rain."

George was reading again.

She went over and sat in front of the mirror of the dressing table looking at herself with the hand glass. She studied her profile, first one side and then the other. Then she studied the back of her head and her neck.

"Don't you think it would be a good idea if I let my hair grow out?" she asked, looking at her profile again.

George looked up and saw the back of her neck, clipped close like a boy's.

"I like it the way it is."

"I get so tired of it," she said. "I get so tired of looking like a boy."

George shifted his position in the bed. He hadn't looked away from her since she started to speak.

"You look pretty darn nice," he said.

She laid the mirror down on the dresser and went over to the window and looked out. It was getting dark.

"I want to pull my hair back tight and smooth and make a big knot at the back that I can feel," she said. "I want to have a kitty to sit on my lap and purr when I stroke her."

"Yeah?" George said from the bed.

"And I want to eat at a table with my own silver and I want candles. And I want it to be spring and I want to brush my hair out in front of a mirror and I want a kitty and I want some new clothes."

"Oh, shut up and get something to read," George said. He was reading again.

His wife was looking out of the window. It was quite dark now and still raining in the palm trees.

"Anyway, I want a cat," she said, "I want a cat. I want a cat now. If I can't have long hair or any fun, I can have a cat."

George was not listening. He was reading his book. His wife looked out of the window where the light had come on in the square.

Someone knocked at the door.

"Avanti," George said. He looked up from his book.

In the doorway stood the maid. She held a big tortoise-shell cat pressed tight against her and swung down against her body.

"Excuse me," she said, "the padrone asked me to bring this for the Signora."

MARK TWAIN

Dick Baker's Cat

One of my comrades there—another of those victims of eighteen years of unrequited toil and blighted hopes—was one of the gentlest spirits that ever bore its patient cross in a weary exile: grave and simple Dick Baker, pocket-miner of Dead-Horse Gulch. He was forty-six, grey as a rat, earnest, thoughtful, slenderly educated, slouchily dressed and clay-soiled, but his heart was finer metal than any gold his shovel ever brought to light—than any, indeed, that ever was mined or minted.

Whenever he was out of luck and a little downhearted, he would fall to mourning over the loss of a wonderful cat he used to own (for where women and children are not, men of kindly impulses take up with pets, for they must love something). And he always spoke of the strange sagacity of that cat with the air of a man who believed in his secret heart that there was something human about it—maybe even supernatural.

I heard him talking about this animal once. He said:

"Gentlemen, I used to have a cat here, by the name of Tom Quartz, which you'd 'a' took an interest in, I reckon—'most anybody would. I had him here eight year—and he was the remarkablest cat *I* ever see. He was a large grey one of the Tom specie, an' he had more hard, natchral sense than any man in this camp—'n' a *power* of dignity—he wouldn't let the Gov'ner of Californy be familiar with him. He never ketched a rat in his life—'peared to be above it. He never cared for nothing but mining. He knowed more about mining, that cat did, than any man *I* ever, ever see. You couldn't tell *him* noth'n' 'bout placer-diggin's—'n' as for pocket-mining, why he was just born for it. He would dig out after me an' Jim when we went over the hills prospect'n', and he would trot along behind us for as much as five mile, if we went so fur. An' he had the best judgment about mining-ground—why you never see anything like it. When we went to work, he'd scatter a glance around, 'n' if he didn't think much of the indications, he would give a look as much as to say, 'Well, I'll have to get you to excuse *me*,' 'n' without another word he'd hyste his nose into the air 'n' shove for home. But if the ground suited him, he would lay low 'n' keep dark till the first pan was washed, 'n' then he would sidle up 'n' take a look, an' if there was about six or seven grains of gold *he* was satisfied—he didn't want no better prospect 'n' that—'n' then he would lay down on our coats and snore like a steamboat till we'd struck the pocket, an' then get up 'n' superintend. He was nearly lightnin' on superintending.

"Well, by an' by, up comes this yer quartz excitement. Everybody was into it—everybody was pick'n' 'n' blast'n' instead of shovelin' dirt on the hillside—everybody was putt'n' down a shaft instead of scrapin' the surface. Noth'n' would do Jim, but *we* must tackle the ledges, too, 'n' so we did. We commenced putt'n' down a shaft, 'n' Tom Quartz he begin to wonder what in the Dickens it was all about. *He* hadn't ever seen any mining like that before, 'n' he was all upset, as you may say—he couldn't come to a right understanding of it no way—it was too many for *him*. He was down on it too, you bet you—he was down on it powerful—'n' always appeared to consider it the cussedest foolishness out. But that cat, you know, was *always* agin newfangled arrangements—somehow he never could abide 'em. *You* know how it is with old habits. But by an' by Tom Quartz begin to git sort of reconciled a little, though he never *could* altogether understand that eternal sinkin' of a shaft an' never pannin' out anything. At last he got to comin' down in the shaft, hisself, to try to cipher it out. An' when he'd git the blues, 'n' feel kind o' scruffy, 'n' aggravated 'n' disgusted—knowin' as he did, that the bills was runnin' up all the time an' we warn't makin' a cent—he would curl up on a gunnysack in the corner an' go to sleep. Well, one day when the shaft was down about eight foot, the rock got so hard that we had to put in a blast—the first blast'n' we'd ever done since Tom Quartz was born. An' then we lit the fuse 'n' clumb out 'n' got off 'bout fifty yards—'n' forgot 'n' left Tom Quartz sound asleep on the gunnysack. In 'bout a minute we seen a puff of smoke bust up out of the hole, 'n' then everything let go with an awful crash, 'n' about four million ton of rocks 'n' dirt 'n' smoke 'n' splinters shot up 'bout a mile an' a half into the air, an' by George, right in the dead centre of it was old Tom Quartz a-goin' end over end, an' a-snortin' an' a-sneez'n, an' a-clawin' an' a-reach'n' for things like all possessed. But it warn't no use, you know, it warn't no use. An' that was the last we see of *him* for about two minutes 'n' a half, an' then all of a sudden it begin to rain rocks and rubbage an' directly he come down ker-whoop about ten foot off f'm where we stood. Well, I reckon he was p'raps the orneriest-lookin' beast you ever see. One ear was sot back on his neck, 'n' his tail was stove up, 'n' his eyewinkers was singed off, 'n' he was all blacked up with powder an' smoke, an' all sloppy with mud 'n' slush f'm one end to the other. Well, sir, it warn't no use to try to apologize—we couldn't say a word. He took a sort of a disgusted look at hisself, 'n' then he looked at us—an' it was just exactly the same as if he had said—'Gents, maybe *you* think it's smart to take advantage of a cat that ain't had no experience of quartz-minin', but *I* think *different*'—an' then he turned on his heel 'n' marched off home without ever saying another word.

"That was jest his style. An' maybe you won't believe it, but after that you never see a cat so prejudiced agin quartz-mining as what he was. An' by an' by when he *did* get to goin' down in the shaft ag'in, you'd 'a' been astonished at his sagacity. The minute we'd tetch off a blast 'n' the fuse'd begin to sizzle, he'd give a look as much as to say, 'Well, I'll have to git you to excuse *me*,' an' it was supris'n' the way he'd shin out of that hole 'n' go f'r a tree. Sagacity? It ain't no name for it. 'Twas *inspiration!*"

I said, "Well, Mr. Baker, his prejudice against quartz-mining *was* remarkable, considering how he came by it. Couldn't you ever cure him of it?"

"*Cure him!* No! When Tom Quartz was sot once, he was *always* sot—and you might 'a' blowed him up as much as three million times 'n' you'd never 'a' broken him of his cussed prejudice ag'in quartz-mining."

DAMON RUNYON

Lillian

What I always say is that Wilbur Willard is nothing but a very lucky guy, because what is it but luck that has him teetering along Forty-ninth Street one cold snowy morning when Lillian is mer-owing around the sidewalk looking for her mamma?

And what is it but luck that has Wilbur Willard all mulled up to a million, what with him having been sitting out a few glasses of Scotch with a friend by the name of Haggerty in an apartment over in Fifty-ninth Street? Because if Wilbur Willard is not mulled up he will see Lillian is nothing but a little black cat, and give her plenty of room, for everybody knows that black cats are terribly bad luck, even when they are only kittens.

But being mulled up like I tell you, things look very different to Wilbur Willard, and he does not see Lillian as a little black kitten scrabbling around in the snow. He sees a beautiful leopard; because a copper by the name of O'Hara, who is walking past about then, and who knows Wilbur Willard, hears him say:

"Oh, you beautiful leopard!"

The copper takes a quick peek himself, because he does not wish any leopards running around his beat, it being against the law, but all he sees, as he tells me afterwards, is this rumpot ham, Wilbur Willard, picking up a scrawny little black kitten and shoving it in his overcoat pocket, and he also hears Wilbur say:

"Your name is Lillian."

Then Wilbur teeters on up to his room on the top floor of an old fleabag in Eighth Avenue that is called the Hotel de Brussels, where he lives quite a while, because the management does not mind actors, the management of the Hotel de Brussels being very broadminded, indeed.

There is some complaint this same morning from one of Wilbur's neighbours, an old burlesque doll by the name of Minnie Madigan, who is not working since Abraham Lincoln is assassinated, because she hears Wilbur going on in his room about a beautiful leopard, and calls up the clerk to say that a hotel which allows wild animals is not respectable. But the clerk looks in on Wilbur and finds him playing with nothing but a harmless-looking little black kitten, and nothing comes of the old doll's grouse, especially as nobody ever claims the Hotel de Brussels is respectable anyway, or at least not much.

Of course when Wilbur comes out from under the ether next afternoon he can see Lillian is not a leopard, and in fact Wilbur is quite astonished to find himself in bed with a little black kitten, because it seems Lillian is sleeping on Wilbur's chest to keep warm. At first Wilbur does not believe what he sees, and puts it down to Haggerty's Scotch, but finally he is convinced, and so he puts Lillian in his pocket, and takes her over to the Hot Box night club and gives her some milk, of which it seems Lillian is very fond.

Now where Lillian comes from in the first place of course nobody knows. The chances are somebody chucks her out of a window into the snow, because people are always chucking kittens, and one thing and another, out of windows in New York. In fact, if there is one thing this town has plenty of, it is kittens, which finally grow up to be cats, and go snooping around ash cans, and mer-owing on roofs, and keeping people from sleeping well.

Personally, I have no use for cats, including kittens, because I never seen one that has any too much sense, although I know a guy by the name of Pussy McGuire who makes a first-rate living doing nothing but stealing cats, and sometimes dogs, and selling them to old dolls who like such things for company. But Pussy only steals Persian and Angora cats, which are very fine cats, and of course Lillian is no such cat as this. Lillian is nothing but a black cat, and nobody will give you a dime a dozen for black cats in this town, as they are generally regarded as very bad jinxes.

Furthermore, it comes out in a few weeks that Wilbur Willard can just as well name her Herman, or Sidney, as not, but Wilbur sticks to Lillian, because this is the name of his partner when he is in vaudeville years ago. He often tells me about Lillian Withington when he is mulled up, which is more often than somewhat, for Wilbur is a great hand for drinking Scotch, or rye, or bourbon, or gin, or whatever else there is around for drinking, except water. In fact, Wilbur Willard is a high-class drinking man, and it does no good telling him it is against the law to drink in this country, because it only makes him mad, and he says to the dickens with the law, only Wilbur Willard uses a much rougher word than dickens.

"She is like a beautiful leopard," Wilbur says to me about Lillian Withington. "Black-haired, and black-eyed, and all ripply, like a leopard I see in an animal act on the same bill at the Palace with us once. We are headliners then," he says, "Willard and Withington, the best singing and dancing act in the country.

"I pick her up in San Antonio, which is a spot in Texas," Wilbur says. "She is not long out of a convent, and I just lose my old partner, Mary McGee, who ups and dies on me of pneumonia down there. Lillian wishes to go on the stage, and joins out with me. A natural-born actress with a great voice. But like a leopard," Wilbur says. "Like a leopard. There is cat in her, no doubt of this, and cats and women are both ungrateful. I love Lillian Withington. I wish to marry her. But she is cold to me. She says she is not going to follow the stage all her life. She says she wishes money, and luxury, and a fine home, and of course a guy like me cannot give a doll such things.

"I wait on her hand and foot," Wilbur says. "I am her slave. There is nothing I will not do for her. Then one day she walks in on me in Boston very cool and says she is quitting me. She says she is marrying a rich guy there. Well, naturally it busts up the act and I never have the heart to look for another partner, and then I get to belting that old black bottle around, and now what am I but a cabaret performer?"

Then sometimes he will bust out crying, and sometimes I will cry with him, although the way I look at it, Wilbur gets a pretty fair break, at that, in getting rid of a doll who wishes things he cannot give her. Many a guy in this town is tangled up with a doll who wishes things he cannot give her, but who keeps him tangled up just the same and busting himself trying to keep her quiet.

Wilbur makes pretty fair money as an entertainer in the Hot Box, though he spends most of it for Scotch, and he is not a bad entertainer, either. I often go to the Hot Box when I am feeling blue to hear him sing Melancholy Baby, and Moonshine Valley, and other sad songs which break my heart. Personally, I do not see why any doll cannot love Wilbur, especially if they listen to him sing such songs as Melancholy Baby when he is mulled up well, because he is a tall, nice-looking guy with long eyelashes, and sleepy brown eyes, and his voice has a low moaning sound that usually goes very big with the dolls. In fact, many a doll does do some pitching to Wilbur when he is singing in the Hot Box, but somehow Wilbur never gives them a tumble, which I suppose is because he is thinking only of Lillian Withington.

Well, after he gets Lillian, the black kitten, Wilbur seems to find a new interest in life, and Lillian turns out to be right cute, and not bad-looking after Wilbur gets her fed up well. She is blacker than a yard up a chimney, with not a white spot on her, and she grows so fast that by and by Wilbur cannot carry her in his pocket any more, so he puts a collar on her and leads her around. So Lillian becomes very well known on Broadway, what with Wilbur taking her to many places, and finally she does not even have to be led around by Willard, but follows him like a pooch. And in all the Roaring Forties there is no pooch that cares to have any truck with Lillian, for she will leap aboard them quicker than you can say scat, and scratch and bite them until they are very glad indeed to get away from her.

But of course the pooches in the Forties are mainly nothing but Chows, and Pekes, and Poms, or little woolly white poodles, which are led around by blonde dolls, and are not fit to take their own part against a smart cat. In fact, Wilbur Willard is finally not on speaking terms with any doll that owns a pooch between Times Square and Columbus Circle, and they are all hoping that both Wilbur and Lillian will go lay down and die somewhere. Furthermore, Wilbur has a couple of battles with guys who also belong to the dolls, but Wilbur is no boob in a battle if he is not mulled up too much and leg-weary.

After he is through entertaining people in the Hot Box, Wilbur generally goes around to any speakeasies which may still be open, and does a little off-hand drinking on top of what he already drinks down in the Hot Box, which is plenty, and although it is considered very risky in this town to mix Hot Box liquor with any other, it never seems to bother Wilbur. Along toward daylight he takes a couple of bottles of Scotch over to his room in the Hotel de Brussels and uses them for a nightcap, so by the time Wilbur Willard is ready to slide off to sleep he has plenty of liquor of one kind and another inside him, and he sleeps pretty good.

Of course nobody on Broadway blames Wilbur so very much for being such a rumpot, because they know about him loving Lillian Withington, and losing her, and it is considered a reasonable excuse in this town for a guy to do some drinking when he loses a doll, which is why there is so much drinking here, but it is a mystery to one and all how Wilbur stands all this liquor without croaking. The cemeteries are full of guys who do a lot less drinking than Wilbur, but he never even seems to feel extra tough, or if he does he keeps it to himself and does not go around saying it is the kind of liquor you get nowadays.

He costs some of the boys around Mindy's plenty of dough one winter, because he starts in doing most of his drinking after hours in Good Time Charley's speakeasy, and the boys lay a price of four to one against him lasting until spring, never figuring a guy can drink very much of Good Time Charley's liquor and keep on living. But Wilbur Willard does it just the same, so everybody says the guy is just naturally superhuman, and lets it go at that.

Sometimes Wilbur drops into Mindy's with Lillian following him on the look-out for pooches, or riding on his shoulder if the weather is bad, and the two of them will sit with us for hours chewing the rag about one thing and another. At such times Wilbur generally has a bottle on his hip and takes a shot now and then, but of course this does not come under the head of serious drinking with him. When Lillian is with Wilbur she always lies as close to him as she can get and anybody can see that she seems to be very fond of Wilbur, and that he is very fond of her, although he sometimes forgets himself and speaks of her as a beautiful leopard. But of course this is only a slip of the tongue, and anyway if Wilbur gets any pleasure out of thinking Lillian is a leopard, it is nobody's business but his own.

"I suppose she will run away from me some day," Wilbur says, running his hand over Lillian's back until her fur crackles. "Yes, although I give her plenty of liver and catnip, and one thing and another, and all my affection, she will probably give me the go-by. Cats are like women, and women are like cats. They are both very ungrateful."

"They are both generally bad luck," Big Nip, the crap shooter, says. "Especially cats, and most especially black cats."

Many other guys tell Wilbur about black cats being bad luck, and advise him to slip Lillian into the North River some night with a sinker on her, but Wilbur claims he already has all the bad luck in the world when he loses Lillian Withington, and that Lillian, the cat, cannot make it any worse, so he goes on taking extra good care of her, and Lillian goes on getting bigger and bigger until I commence thinking maybe there is some St. Bernard in her.

Finally I commence to notice something funny about Lillian.

Sometimes she will be acting very loving towards Wilbur, and then again she will be very unfriendly to him, and will spit at him, and snatch at him with her claws, very hostile. It seems to me that she is all right when Wilbur is mulled up, but is as sad and fretful as he is himself when he is only a little bit mulled. And when Lillian is sad and fretful she makes it very tough indeed on the pooches in the neighborhood of the Brussels.

In fact, Lillian takes to pooch-hunting, sneaking off when Wilbur is getting his rest, and running pooches bow-legged, especially when she finds one that is not on a leash. A loose pooch is just naturally cherry pie for Lillian.

Well, of course this causes great indignation among the dolls who own the pooches, particularly when Lillian comes home one day carrying a Peke as big as she is herself by the scruff of the neck, and with a very excited blonde doll following her and yelling bloody murder outside Wilbur Willard's door when Lillian pops into Wilbur's room through a hole he cuts in the door for her, still lugging the Peke. But it seems that instead of being mad at Lillian and giving her a pasting for such goings on, Wilbur is somewhat pleased, because he happens to be still in a fog when Lillian arrives with the Peke, and is thinking of Lillian as a beautiful leopard.

"Why," Wilbur says, "this is devotion, indeed. My beautiful leopard goes off into the jungle and fetches me an antelope for dinner."

Now of course there is no sense whatever to this, because a Peke is certainly not anything like an antelope, but the blonde doll outside Wilbur's door hears Wilbur mumble, and gets the idea that he is going to eat her Peke for dinner and the squawk she puts up is very terrible. There is plenty of trouble around the Brussels in cooling the blonde doll's rage over Lillian snagging her Peke, and what is more the blonde doll's ever-loving guy, who turns out to be a tough Ginney bootlegger by the name of Gregorio, shows up at the Hot Box the next night and wishes to put the slug on Wilbur Willard.

But Wilbur rounds him up with a few drinks and by singing Melancholy Baby to him, and before he leaves the Ginney gets very sentimental towards Wilbur, and Lillian, too, and wishes to give Wilbur five bucks to let Lillian grab the Peke again, if Lillian will promise not to bring it back. It seems Gregorio does not really care for the Peke, and is only acting quarrelsome to please the blonde doll and make her think he loves her dearly.

But I can see Lillian is having different moods, and finally I ask Wilbur if he notices it.

"Yes," he says, very sad, "I do not seem to be holding her love. She is getting very fickle. A guy moves on to my floor at the Brussels the other day with a little boy, and Lillian becomes very fond of this kid at once. In fact, they are great friends. Ah, well," Wilbur says, "cats are like women. Their affection does not last."

I happen to go over to the Brussels a few days later to explain to a guy by the name of Crutchy, who lives on the same floor as Wilbur Willard, that some of our citizens do not like his face and that it may be a good idea for him to leave town, especially if he insists on bringing ale into their territory, and I see Lillian out in the hall with a youngster which I judge is the kid Wilbur is talking about. This kid is maybe three years old, and very cute, what with black hair and black eyes, and he is mauling Lillian around the hall in a way that is most surprising, for Lillian is not such a cat as will stand for much mauling around, not even from Wilbur Willard.

I am wondering how anybody comes to take such a kid to a place like the Brussels, but I figure it is some actor's kid, and that maybe there is no mamma for it. Later I am talking to Wilbur about this, and he says:

"Well, if the kid's old man is an actor, he is not working at it. He sticks close to his room all the time, and he does not allow the kid to go anywhere but in the hall, and I feel sorry for the little guy, which is why I allow Lillian to play with him."

Now it comes on a very cold spell, and a bunch of us are sitting in Mindy's along towards five o'clock in the morning when we hear fire engines going past. By and by in comes a guy by the name of Kansas, who is named Kansas because he comes from Kansas, and who is a gambler by trade.

"The old Brussels is on fire," this guy Kansas says.

"She is always on fire," Big Nig says, meaning there is always plenty of hot stuff going on around the Brussels.

About this time who walks in but Wilbur Willard, and anybody can see he is just naturally floating. The chances are he comes from Good Time Charley's, and is certainly carrying plenty of pressure. I never see Wilbur Willard mulled up more. He does not have Lillian with him, but then he never takes Lillian to Good Time Charley's because Charley hates cats.

"Hey, Wilbur," Big Nig says, "your joint, the Brussels, is on fire."

"Well," Wilbur says, "I am a little firefly, and I need a light. Let us go where there is a fire."

The Brussels is only a few blocks from Mindy's and there is nothing else to do just then, so some of us walk over to Eighth Avenue with Wilbur teetering along ahead of us. The old shack is certainly roaring away when we get in sight of it, and the firemen are tossing water into it, and the coppers have the fire lines out to keep the crowd back, although there is not much of a crowd at such an hour in the morning.

"Is it not beautiful?" Wilbur Willard says, looking up at the flames. "Is it not like a fairy palace all lighted up this way?"

You see, Wilbur does not realize the place is on fire, although guys and dolls are running out of it every which way, most of them half dressed, or not dressed at all, and the firemen are getting out the life nets in case anybody wishes to hop out of the windows.

"It is certainly beautiful," Wilbur says, "I must get Lillian so she can see this."

And before anybody has time to think, there is Wilbur Willard walking into the front door of the Brussels as if nothing happens. The firemen and the coppers are so astonished all they can do is holler at Wilbur, but he pays no attention whatever. Well, naturally everybody figures Wilbur is a gone gosling, but in about ten minutes he comes walking out of this same door through the fire and smoke as cool as you please, and he has Lillian in his arms.

"You know," Wilbur says, coming over to where we are standing with our eyes popping out, "I have to walk all the way up to my floor because the elevators seem to be out of commission. The service is getting terrible in this hotel. I will certainly make a strong complaint to the management about it as soon as I pay something on my account."

Then what happens but Lillian lets out a big mer-row, and hops out of Wilbur's arms and skips past the coppers and the firemen with her back all humped up, and the next thing anybody knows she is tearing through the front door of the old hotel and making plenty of speed.

"Well, well," Wilbur says, looking much surprised, "there goes Lillian."

And what does this daffy Wilbur Willard do but turn and go marching back into the Brussels again, and by this time the smoke is pouring out of the front doors so thick he is out of sight in a second. Naturally he takes the coppers and firemen by surprise, because they are not used to guys walking in and out of fires on them.

This time anybody standing around will lay you plenty of odds

—two and a half and maybe three to one that Wilbur never shows up again, because the old Brussels is now just popping with fire and smoke from the lower windows, although there does not seem to be quite so much fire in the upper storey. Everybody seems to be out of the building, and even the firemen are fighting the blaze from the outside because the Brussels is so old and ramshackly there is no sense in them risking the floors.

I mean everybody is out of the place except Wilbur Willard and Lillian, and we figure they are getting a good frying somewhere inside, although Feet Samuels is around offering to take thirteen to five for a few small bets that Lillian comes out okay, because Feet claims that a cat has nine lives and that is a fair bet at the price.

Well, up comes a swell-looking doll all heated up about something and pushing and clawing her way through the crowd up to the ropes and screaming until you can hardly hear yourself think, and about this same minute everybody hears a voice going ai-lee-hi-hee-hoo, like a Swiss yodeller, which comes from the roof of the Brussels, and looking up what do we see but Wilbur Willard standing up there on the edge of the roof, high above the fire and smoke, and yodelling very loud.

Under one arm he has a big bundle of some kind, and under the other he has the little kid I see playing in the hall with Lillian. As he stands up there going ai-lee-hi-hee-hoo, the swell-dressed doll near us begins screaming louder than Wilbur is yodelling, and the firemen rush over under him with a life net.

Wilbur lets go another ai-lee-hi-hee-hoo, and down he comes all spraddled out, with the bundle and the kid, but he hits the net sitting down and bounces up and back again for a couple of minutes before he finally settles. In fact, Wilbur is enjoying the bouncing, and the chances are he will be bouncing yet if the firemen do not drop their hold on the net and let him fall to the ground.

Then Wilbur steps out of the net, and I can see the bundle is a rolled-up blanket with Lillian's eyes peeking out of one end. He still has the kid under the other arm with his head stuck out in front, and his legs stuck out behind, and it does not seem to be that Wilbur is handling the kid as careful as he is handling Lillian. He stands there looking at the firemen with a very sneering look, and finally he says:

"Do not think you can catch me in your net unless I wish to be caught. I am a butterfly, and very hard to overtake."

Then all of a sudden the swell-dressed doll who is doing so much hollering, piles on top of Wilbur and grabs the kid from him and begins hugging and kissing it.

"Wilbur," she says, "God bless you, Wilbur, for saving my baby! Oh, thank you, Wilbur, thank you! My wretched husband kidnaps and runs away with him, and it is only a few hours ago that my detectives find out where he is."

Wilbur gives the doll a funny look for about half a minute and starts to walk away, but Lillian comes wiggling out of the blanket, looking and smelling pretty much singed up, and the kid sees Lillian and begins hollering for her, so Wilbur finally hands Lillian over to the kid. And not wishing to leave Lillian, Wilbur stands around somewhat confused, and the doll gets talking to him, and finally they go away together, and as they go Wilbur is carrying the kid, and the kid is carrying Lillian, and Lillian is not feeling so good from her burns.

Furthermore, Wilbur is probably more sober than he ever is before in years at this hour in the morning, but before they go I get a chance to talk some to Wilbur when he is still rambling somewhat, and I make out from what he says that the first time he goes to get Lillian he finds her in his room and does not see hide or hair of the little kid and does not even think of him, because he does not know what room the kid is in, anyway, having never noticed such a thing.

But the second time he goes up, Lillian is sniffing at the crack under the door of a room down the hall from Wilbur's and Wilbur says he seems to remember seeing a trickle of something like water coming out of the crack.

"And," Wilbur says, "as I am looking for a blanket for Lillian, and it will be a bother to go back to my room, I figure I will get one out of this room. I try the knob but the door is locked, so I kick it in, and walk in to find the room is full of smoke, and fire is shooting through the windows very lovely, and when I grab a blanket off the bed for Lillian, what is under the blanket but the kid?

"Well," Wilbur says, "the kid is squawking, and Lillian is merowing, and there is so much confusion generally that it makes me nervous, so I figure we better go up on the roof and let the stink blow off us, and look at the fire from there. It seems there is a guy stretched out on the floor of the room alongside an upset table between the door and the bed. He has a bottle in one hand, and he is dead. Well, naturally there is nothing to be gained by lugging a dead guy along, so I take Lillian and the kid and go up on the roof, and we just naturally fly off like humming birds. Now I must get a drink," Wilbur says. "I wonder if anybody has anything on their hip?"

Well, the papers are certainly full of Wilbur and Lillian the next day, especially Lillian, and they are both great heroes.

But Wilbur cannot stand publicity very long, because he never has no time to himself for his drinking, what with the scribes and the photographers hopping on him every few minutes wishing to hear his story, and to take more pictures of him and Lillian, so one night he disappears, and Lillian disappears with him.

About a year later it comes out that he marries his old doll, Lillian Withington-Harmon, and falls into a lot of dough, and what is more he cuts out the liquor and becomes quite a useful citizen one way and another. So everybody has to admit that black cats are not always bad luck, although I say Wilbur's case is a little exceptional because he does not start out knowing Lillian is a black cat, but thinking she is a leopard.

I happen to run into Wilbur one day all dressed up in good clothes and jewellery and cutting quite a swell.

"Wilbur," I say to him, "I often think how remarkable it is the way Lillian suddenly gets such an attachment for the little kid and remembers about him being in the hotel and leads you back there a second time to the right room. If I do not see this come off with my own eyes, I will never believe a cat has brains enough to do such a thing, because I consider cats are extra dumb."

"Brains nothing," Wilbur says. "Lillian does not have brains enough to grease a gimlet. And what is more she has no more attachment for the kid than a jack rabbit. The time has come," Wilbur says, "to expose Lillian. She gets a lot of credit which is never coming to her. I will now tell you about Lillian, and nobody knows this but me.

"You see," Wilbur says, "when Lillian is a little kitten I always put a little Scotch in her milk, partly to help make her good and strong, and partly because I am never no hand to drink alone, unless there is nobody with me. Well, at first Lillian does not care so much for this Scotch in her milk, but finally she takes a liking to it, and I keep making her toddy stronger until in the end she will lap up a good big snort without any milk for a chaser, and yell for more. In fact, I suddenly realize that Lillian becomes a rumpot, just like I am in those days, and simply must have her grog, and it is when she is good and rummed up that Lillian goes off snatching Pekes, and acting tough generally.

"Now," Wilbur says, "the time of the fire is about the time I get home every morning and give Lillian her schnapps. But when I go into the hotel and get her the first time I forget to Scotch her up, and the reason she runs back into the hotel is because she is looking for her shot. And the reason she is sniffing at the kid's door is not because the kid is in there but because the trickle that is coming through the crack under the door is nothing but Scotch running out of the bottle in the dead guy's hand. I never mention this before because I figure it may be a knock to a dead guy's memory," Wilbur says. "Drinking is certainly a disgusting thing, especially secret drinking."

"But how is Lillian getting along these days?" I ask Wilbur Willard.

"I am greatly disappointed in Lillian," he says. "She refuses to reform when I do and the last I hear of her she takes up with Gregorio, the Ginney bootlegger, who keeps her well Scotched up all the time so she will lead his blonde doll's Peke a dog's life."

COLETTE

from *La Chatte*
Saha

One July evening, as they were both waiting for Alain to come home, Camille and the cat sat quietly at the same railing, the cat sitting on her elbows, the girl leaning over, her arms crossed. Camille did not like this balcony, reserved for the cat, and shut in by two cement walls which protected it from the wind and from all communication with the front terrace.

Each gave the other a quick, searching glance and Camille said nothing to Saha. On her elbows, she leaned out as though to count the flights of yellow, slackened awnings, from the top to the bottom of the dizzying façade of the apartment house; stroked the cat, who got up, drew away, and lay down again a little farther along on the railing.

The moment Camille was alone she always looked very much like the little girl who would not say "how-do-you-do." Her face took on its childlike expression of merciless innocence, that hard perfection which gives children's faces the look of angels. With an expression impartially severe, which could have no reproach in it, she was gazing on Paris, from whose sky the light was dying earlier each day. She yawned nervously, got up, took several aimless steps, leaned over the railing again, obliging the cat to jump down to the floor. Saha drew off, preferring to go back into the bedroom. But the door of the three-cornered room had been closed and so Saha sat down in front of it, patiently. A moment later she had to yield the entrance to Camille, who began to walk back and forth from one wall to the other with long, quick strides; and the cat jumped back on the railing.

As though teasing her, Camille dislodged her again as she leaned on her elbows and gazed across Paris. Once again Saha drew back and took up her station before the closed door.

Her eye on the horizon, her back to the cat, Camille stood motionless as a statue. But as Saha stared at that back, her breath came faster and faster. She got up, turned around two or three times, sniffed inquiringly at the closed door. . . . Camille had not stirred. The cat distended her nostrils; she had that distressed look which accompanies nausea. A long-drawn-out, desolate "Meow," the plaintive reaction to a menacing and unexpressed design, escaped her; and Camille wheeled squarely around.

She was a little pale; that is, her rouge outlined two oval moons on her cheeks. She feigned the preoccupied air she would have had under the glance of a human being. At the same time she began to hum, her mouth tightly closed. Then she resumed her walk from one wall to the opposite one, back and forth, moving to the rhythm of the tune after her voice could no longer carry it. She drove the cat first to regain with one leap her narrow place of observation on the railing, and next to sit tightly pressed against the bedroom door.

Saha did not lose her composure; she would have died rather than utter a second cry. Closing in on the cat but pretending not to see her, Camille walked back and forth in complete silence. Saha did not jump on to the railing until she saw Camille's feet coming close; and when she jumped down on the balcony floor, it was only to avoid the arm which, if extended, would have thrown her down from a height of five stories.

She was not confused. She fled with design, jumped carefully, kept her eyes fixed on the enemy; and she stooped neither to anger nor to pleading. Extreme emotion, the fear of death, moistened her paws with sweat; they stamped flowerlike imprints on the cement balcony floor.

Camille seemed to be the first to weaken, to dissipate her murderous power. She made the mistake of noticing that the sun was setting; glanced at her wristwatch; listened to the tinkling of glasses inside the apartment. A few seconds more, and her resolution, slipping from her as sleep does from a sleepwalker, would have left her guiltless and exhausted. . . . Sensing her enemy's wavering strength of purpose, Saha hesitated a second on the railing; and Camille, spreading her arms wide apart, pushed the cat off into space.

She had time to hear the scratching of the claws on the cement, to see Saha's blue body, curved into an **S**, clutch at the air with the upward leap of a trout. Then the girl drew back and leaned against the wall.

She showed no desire to look below into the little garden outlined in fresh pebbles. Back in the bedroom, she put her hands over her ears, withdrew them again, shook her head as though troubled by the buzzing of mosquitoes, sat down, and nearly fell asleep. But the oncoming night roused her, and she chased away the twilight by lighting squares of glass, shining grooves, blinding, mushroom-shaped crystals, and also the chromium bar which threw an opaline light across the bed.

She moved lithely from place to place, and as she passed them, touched each object lightly, dexterously, dreamily.

"I feel as though I had grown thin," she said aloud.

She changed her clothes, dressed herself all in white.

"My fly in the ointment," she said, imitating the voice in which Alain had said it to her. Color returned to her cheeks again at a sensual memory which brought her back to reality, and she looked forward to Alain's homecoming.

She bent her head toward the buzzing of the elevator and trembled at every sound—the irritating squeaks, the metallic scrapings of a ship at anchor, strangled music—all the discordant sounds which a new house emits. But an expression of fright came into her face only when the sepulchral tinkling of the bell in the entrance hall followed the fumbling of a key in the door. She ran, and opened it herself.

"Shut the door," Alain ordered. "If only I were sure that she's not hurt! Come, turn on some light."

He was carrying the still breathing Saha in his arms. He went straight to the bedroom, pushed aside the trinkets on the disguised dressing table, and carefully put the cat down on its glass top. She managed to stand on her feet and kept her balance, but her deep-set eyes glanced around the room as if she were in some unfamiliar house.

"Saha!" Alain called to her in a low tone. "If she's not hurt it's a miracle . . . Saha!"

She lifted her head as though to reassure her friend, and leaned her cheek against his hand.

"Take a step or two for me, Saha. . . . She's walking! Ah, good. . . . A fall of five stories! . . . It was the awnings on the second floor that broke her fall. . . . From there she bounced off onto the caretaker's little grass patch. He saw her dropping. He said to me, 'I thought it was an umbrella falling!' . . . What's that in her ear? . . . No, it's just something white from the wall. Wait a moment till I listen to her heart."

He laid the cat down on her side and examined the heaving ribs; the irregular, faint movement of the mechanism. His fair hair pushed back, his eyes shut, he seemed to be sleeping on Saha's fur. Then he opened his eyes and noticed Camille standing by, silent, looking down on the impervious pair.

"Can you believe it? She hasn't any . . . at least, I can't find anything but a heart terribly excited; still a cat's heart is normally excited. But how could this have happened to her? I'm asking you as though you could know, my poor little Camille. She fell from this side here," he said, looking at the wide-open French window. "Jump down, Saha, if you can."

She hesitated, then jumped, but lay down again on the rug. She was breathing quickly and still had that lost expression in her eyes as she looked around the room.

"I've a mind to telephone Chéron. . . . And still, look . . . she's cleaning herself. She wouldn't be stirring as much as that if she had hurt herself inside, somewhere. . . . Ah, thank heaven . . ."

He withdrew, threw his waistcoat on the bed, and went over to Camille.

"What a scare! . . . There you are, very pretty, all in white. . . . Give me a kiss, my little fly in the ointment."

She gave herself up to the arms that had at last become aware of her; but she could not hold back the sobs that shook her.

"Why . . . you're crying?"

He himself became upset and buried his face in her thick black hair.

"I did not realize you were so tender-hearted . . . Imagine . . ."

She had the courage not to release herself at that word. Alain, moreover, turned quickly back to Saha, to take her out into the cool air of the balcony. But the cat resisted; she preferred to lie down near the window sill and look into the sky, as blue as herself. From time to time she shivered slightly and turned to question the depths of the triangular bedroom.

"It's the shock," Alain explained. "I would like to make her comfortable outside."

"Let her alone," answered Camille feebly, "if she doesn't want to."

"Her whims are my commands. Especially today. Can there possibly be anything left fit to eat at this hour? Half past nine!"

Buque rolled the table out on to the terrace and they dined looking out on East Paris, the Paris most thickly dotted with lights. Alain talked a good deal, drank reddened water, accused Saha of awkwardness, of imprudence, of what he called "cat mistakes."

"Cat mistakes are the kind of 'accidental' errors, biological 'setbacks' chargeable to civilization and to domestication. They have nothing in common with clumsy, blunt actions that are almost intentional . . ."

But Camille did not ask, "How do you know that?"

Dinner over, he carried Saha and led Camille into the studio where the cat consented to drink the milk she had refused before. As she drank she shivered all through her body as cats do when they are drenched with cold water.

"The shock," Alain said again. "Even so, I'll ask Chéron to look at her tomorrow morning. Oh, I forgot," he said gaily. "Please telephone the superintendent. I forgot to bring up the roll that Massart, our accursed decorator, left for me there."

Camille obeyed, while Alain fell exhausted into one of the armchairs, relaxed, and closed his eyes.

"Hello," Camille said into the telephone. "Yes, that must be it . . . a large roll . . . thank you."

His eyes closed, he grinned. She had come back near him and saw him smiling.

"That tiny voice of yours! What's this new little voice? 'A large roll . . . thank you,' " he mimicked. "Do you keep such a thin small voice just for the superintendent? Come on, the two of us are not too many to tackle Massart's latest creations."

He spread a large sheet of water-color paper on the ebony table. Immediately Saha, enamored of everything made of paper, leapt onto the design.

"Isn't she good?" Alain exclaimed. "She wants to show me that she isn't really hurt anywhere. . . . Isn't that a swelling on her head, though? Camille, feel her head. . . . No, it isn't. Still, just feel her head anyway, Camille."

A miserable little murderess, obedient, she tried to pull herself out of the exile into which she had been sinking. She put out her hand with a meek sort of hatred, and gently touched the cat's forehead.

The most savage scream, a snarl, an epileptic spasm responded to her touch. Camille said "Oh!" as if she had been burned. Standing on the spread-out paper, the cat glowered at the young woman with flaming accusation, stiffened the fur on her back, showed her teeth and the dry red of her jaw.

Alain had risen, ready to protect the one from the other—Saha and Camille.

"Careful. She is . . . perhaps she's mad. Saha!"

She stared at him fiercely, yet the lucid look in her eyes proved that she had her reason.

"What's the matter with her? Where did you touch her?"

"I didn't touch her."

They spoke in low tones, the words coming from the edges of their lips.

"Now that I don't understand," Alain said. "Put out your hand again."

"No, I don't want to," Camille protested. "Perhaps she is mad," she added.

Alain took the risk of caressing Saha, who stopped bristling, shaped herself to her friend's palm, but still glared at Camille.

"So, that's it," Alain said slowly. "Wait a moment. She has a scratch on her nose; I hadn't seen that. And that's dried blood. Quiet, Saha, quiet," he said, noticing the fury gathering in her yellow eyes. The puffing out of her cheeks, the huntress-like stiffness of the whiskers brought forward, made the infuriated cat look as though she were laughing. The conflicts within her, coming one after the other in such quick succession, drew down the mauve corners of her jaw, stiffened her trembling chin; and all her feline face was straining itself toward a universal language, toward a word forgotten of men. . . .

"What's that?" asked Alain sharply.

"What's what?"

The cat's glare brought back Camille's bravado and her instinct of defense. Bending over the drawing, Alain deciphered some moist pink spots in groups of four around a central irregular spot.

"Her paws . . . moist?" he said, very low.

He turned towards his wife.

"She must have stepped in some water," Camille said. "You exaggerate every little thing so."

Alain lifted up his head toward the dry, blue night.

"In water? In what water?"

His round, staring eyes made him look singularly ugly as he turned toward his wife.

"Don't you know what those marks are?" he said bitterly. "No, you don't know anything about it. That's fear, you understand, the sweat that comes from fright—a cat's sweat, the only moisture a cat has. That means she's been through some terrible fright. . . ."

Delicately he took one of Saha's front paws, and with his fingers wiped off the fleshy sole of the foot. Then he pushed back the living white tissue covering her retractive claws.

"All her claws are broken. . . ." he said, talking to himself. "She caught herself . . . tried to stop herself . . . tried to cling to the stone. She—"

He stopped suddenly, took the cat under his arm, and carried her into the kitchen.

Alone, perfectly still, Camille listened. She clasped her hands tightly together and, though free, looked as if bound by shackles.

"Buque," said Alain, "have you any milk?"

"Yes, sir, in the icebox."

"Then it's cold?"

"But I can heat it on the stove. . . . I can heat it in a jiffy. It's for the cat? Nothing the matter with her, I hope?"

"No, she's . . ."

Alain stopped himself, and changed to: "Some food must have disagreed with her in this hot weather. Thank you, Buque. Yes, you may leave now."

Camille heard her husband turning on a faucet, and knew that he was giving the cat food and fresh water. A diffused shadow above a metal lamp shade showed the slow movement of her big eyeballs.

Alain came back, automatically tightened his leather belt, and sat down at the black table. But he was oblivious of Camille's presence, and it was she who had to speak first.

"You told Buque she could go?"

"Yes. Shouldn't I have?"

He lighted a cigarette and blinked above the flames of the lighter.

"I was going to ask her if she would bring . . . Oh, it's not important; don't excuse yourself."

"But I wasn't excusing myself. Perhaps I should."

Lured by the blue depth of the night, he went to the open French window. He noted in himself an agitation which did not have its birth in this recent emotion, a trembling comparable to the quavering of an orchestra, deafening, prophetic. A skyrocket shot up from the Folie-Sainte-James, burst into shimmering petals which faded out, one by one, as they fell, and peace came back into the powdery depth of the blue night. In the park of the Folie, a rocky grotto, a colonnade, and a cascade were illuminated with incandescent white. Camille drew near.

"Is this a gala night? Let's watch the fireworks. Do you hear the guitars?"

Absorbed in his own nervous trembling, he did not answer her. His wrists, his tingling hands, his tired backbone prickled with a thousand torments. It all brought back to him a hated feeling of fatigue, the fatigue of the athletic competitions in his high-school days—foot races, boat races—from which he emerged vindictive, despising both his victory and his defeat, breathless and stumbling with exhaustion. He was not at peace, except about one thing: he no longer felt any anxiety for Saha. A long moment ago—or a very short moment ago—since the discovery of the broken claws, since Saha's burning fright, he had not exactly been aware of time.

"It's not fireworks," he said. "More likely dancing."

By the movement Camille made near him in the shadow, he gathered that she wasn't expecting him to answer. But she grew bolder and came nearer still; he felt no dread at her coming. Out of the corner of his eye he saw the white dress; one bare arm; one half of her face tinged with yellow from the lamps indoors, the other half blue, absorbed from the clear night; two half-faces divided by the same straight nose, each one endowed with one big eye which blinked very little.

"Yes, dancing, of course," she agreed. "Those are mandolins, not guitars. Listen. '*Les donneurs . . . de . . . sé-é-réna . . . des. Et les bel-les é-écouteu . . .*' "

Her voice stumbled on the highest note and fell, and she coughed to cover her defeat.

"What a thin voice!" Alain marveled. "What has she done with her voice, as big as her eyes? She sings like a little girl, and she's hoarse."

The mandolins stopped playing, the breeze brought a faint murmur of human pleasure and applause. In a moment a rocket went up, and broke like an umbrella of violet rays from which dropped tears of living fire.

"Oh!" Camille exclaimed.

Both of them had emerged from the darkness like two statues:

Camille like lilac marble; Alain white, his hair greenish, his pupils faded. When the rocket burst, Camille sighed.

"They never last long enough," she said plaintively.

The distant music started up again. But the capricious wind transformed the sound of the instruments to a sharp resonance, and the lingering glare of one of the accompanying brasses, on two notes, rose discordantly up to the balcony where the two were watching.

"That's too bad," Camille said. "Probably they play the best jazz. . . . That's 'Love in the Night' they're playing. . . ."

She tried to hum the tune, but her voice—it seemed to come in the wake of tears—was too high and trembling. . . . This new voice redoubled Alain's uneasiness; it engendered in him a necessity for revelation, a desire to break through the thing which—a long moment ago or a very short moment—was being built up between Camille and himself; a thing which as yet had no name, but was growing quickly; the thing which kept him from taking Camille by the neck as though she were a small boy; the thing which held him immovable, vigilant, leaning against the wall, warm still with the day's heat. He became impatient, and said:

"Sing some more. . . ."

A long, three-cornered shower dropping in sprays like boughs of weeping willow lit up the sky above the park, and revealed to Alain a Camille surprised, already defiant.

"Sing what?"

" 'Love in the Night' or . . . anything."

She hesitated a moment; then refused.

"Let me listen to the jazz . . . even from where we are you can hear how mellow it is."

He did not urge her, but restrained his impatience and tried to control the tingling that went through his entire body.

When night closed down, he hesitated no longer, and slipped his bare arm under Camille's. In touching it he seemed to see it quite white, hardly tinted by the summer sun, covered with fine soft hairs, reddish brown on the forearm, paler near the shoulder. . . .

"You're cold," he murmured. "You're not ill?"

She wept softly, but so immediately that Alain suspected her of having had her tears in readiness.

"No . . . it's you. It's you . . . you don't love me."

He backed up to the wall and pressed Camille against his hip. He could feel her shaking and cold from her shoulder to her knees, bare above the rolled stockings. She did not hold back; she yielded her whole body to him, faithfully.

"Ah, ah! I don't love you. So that's it! Another jealous scene on account of Saha?"

He could feel that whole body, pressed against his, stiffen—Camille recapturing her self-defence, her resistance; and he went on, encouraged by the moment and the opportunity.

"Instead of loving that charming animal the way I do. . . . Are we the only young married couple to bring up a cat or a dog? Would you like a parrot, a marmoset, a pair of lovebirds to make me jealous?"

She shook her shoulders and protested by making a peevish sound in her closed mouth. His head high, Alain controlled his own voice and spurred himself on.

"Come now, come on. One or two more childish bickerings, and we'll get somewhere." She's like a jar I have to turn upside down in order to empty it completely. But come on. . . .

"Would you like a little lion, a baby crocodile, say, fifty years old or so? You'd do better to adopt Saha. If you'll just take the trouble, you'll see. . . ."

Camille wrenched herself from his arms so furiously that he tottered.

"No," she cried. "That? Never. You hear what I say? Never!"

She drew a long sigh of rage and repeated in a lower tone:

"No. . . . never!"

"That's that," he said to himself delightedly.

He pushed her into the bedroom, lowered the blinds, turned on the square ceiling lights, closed the window. With a quick movement Camille went to the window, which Alain reopened.

"On the condition that you don't scream," he said.

He rolled up the single armchair for Camille; he himself straddled the one small chair at the foot of the wide, turned-down, freshly sheeted bed. The glazed chintz curtains, drawn for the night, cast a shade of green over Camille's pallor and her crumpled white dress.

"So?" Alain began. "Impossible to settle? Horrible situation? Either she or you?"

An abrupt shake of the head was her answer and Alain was made to realize that he had better drop his bantering manner.

"What do you want me to tell you?" he began, after a silence. "The only thing I can't say? You know very well I won't give up that cat. I'd be ashamed to. Ashamed for my own sake, ashamed for her. . . ."

"I know," Camille said.

"And ashamed in your eyes," he finished.

"Oh, as for me . . ." Camille said, raising her hand.

"You count too," he went on severely. "When all is said and done, I'm the one you're really angry with. The only grudge you've got against Saha is that she loves me."

Her sole answer was a troubled and hesitant expression, and it annoyed him to have to go on putting questions to her. He had thought that one short, decisive scene would force the entire issue, he was relying on that easy disposal of the matter. Not at all. After the first cry had been uttered, Camille recoiled; she did nothing to feed the flames. He resorted to patience.

"Tell me, my dear . . . What's that? I mustn't call you 'my dear'? Tell me . . . if it were a matter of another cat than Saha, would you be less intolerant?"

"Naturally; of course I would," she replied very quickly. "You wouldn't love it as you do this one."

"That's true," he agreed, with studied loyalty.

"Even a woman," Camille went on, indignantly, "even a woman, you would probably not love so much."

"That's true."

"You're not like people who love animals . . . you . . . Take Pat, now, he loves animals. He grabs big dogs by the neck, tumbles them over; imitates cats to see the faces they'll make; whistles to birds . . ."

"Yes, but he's not hard to please," Alain answered.

"But with you, it's not the same thing. You love Saha . . ."

"I've never hidden it from you, but neither did I lie when I told you that Saha is not your rival."

He stopped and lowered his lids upon his secret, that secret concerning purity.

"There are rivals and rivals," Camille said sarcastically.

She reddened suddenly, inflamed with sharp rage.

"I've seen you," she cried. "In the morning after you had spent the night on your little cot. Before daybreak, I've seen you both . . ."

She stretched her trembling arm out toward the balcony.

"Sitting there, both of you. You didn't even hear me. . . . You were like this, your cheeks against each other . . ."

She went to the window, took a breath of air, and came back to Alain.

"It's for you to say, honestly, if I'm wrong in disliking that cat . . . wrong in suffering . . ."

He kept silent so long that she was angry again.

"Go on, say something. What are you waiting for?"

"The sequel," Alain said. "The end of the story."

He got up deliberately, bent over his wife, and lowered his voice as he indicated the French window.

"It was you, wasn't it? You pushed her off?"

She made a swift movement and put the bed between them, but she denied nothing.

With a kind of indulgent smile, he watched her flee.

"You threw her," he said dreamily. "I felt that you had changed everything between us. You pushed her. She broke her claws trying to catch hold of the wall . . ."

He lowered his head, seeming to picture the crime. "But how did you throw her? By clutching her by the skin of her neck? By taking advantage of her sleeping on the balcony? Have you been planning the attack for a long time? Did you two quarrel beforehand?"

He raised his head, looked at Camille's hands and arms.

"No, you haven't any marks. It was she who accused you when I asked you to touch her. She was magnificent."

He turned from Camille to look at the night, the burnt-out stars, the tops of the three poplars with the bedroom lights shining upon them.

"Well," he said simply, "I'm leaving."

"Oh, listen . . . listen . . ." Camille begged in a low voice.

But she did not hinder him from leaving the bedroom. He opened closet doors, talked to the cat in the bathroom, and from the sound of his footsteps Camille knew that he had just put on his street shoes. Mechanically she looked at the clock. He came back into the room, carrying Saha in a wide basket which Buque used when she went to market. Hastily dressed, his hair hardly combed, a handkerchief around his neck, he had the look of a lover after a quarrel. Wide eyed, Camille stared at him. But she heard Saha move in the basket and her lips tightened.

"There you are; I'm leaving," Alain said again.

He lowered his eyes, raised the basket slightly and, with designed cruelty, corrected himself:

"We're leaving."

—*Translated from the French by Morris Bentinck*

THÉOPHILE GAUTIER

The White and Black Dynasties

A cat brought from Havana by Mademoiselle Aïta de la Penuela, a young Spanish artist whose studies of white angoras may still be seen gracing the printsellers' windows, produced the daintiest little kitten imaginable. It was just like a swan's-down powder-puff, and on account of its immaculate whiteness it received the name of Pierrot. When it grew big this was lengthened to Don Pierrot de Navarre as being more grandiose and majestic.

Don Pierrot, like all animals which are spoilt and made much of, developed a charming amiability of character. He shared the life of the household with all the pleasure which cats find in the intimacy of the domestic hearth. Seated in his usual place near the fire, he really appeared to understand what was being said, and to take an interest in it.

His eyes followed the speakers, and from time to time he would utter little sounds, as though he too wanted to make remarks and give his opinion on literature, which was our usual topic of conversation. He was very fond of books, and when he found one open on a table he would lie on it, look at the page attentively, and turn over the leaves with his paw; then he would end by going to sleep, for all the world as if he were reading a fashionable novel.

Directly I took up a pen he would jump on my writing-desk and with deep attention watch the steel nib tracing black spider-legs on the expanse of white paper, and his head would turn each time I began a new line. Sometimes he tried to take part in the work, and would attempt to pull the pen out of my hand, no doubt in order to write himself, for he was an aesthetic cat, like Hoffman's Murr, and I strongly suspect him of having scribbled his memoirs at night on some house-top by the light of his phosphorescent eyes. Unfortunately these lucubrations have been lost.

Don Pierrot never went to bed until I came in. He waited for me inside the door, and as I entered the hall he would rub himself against my legs and arch his back, purring joyfully all the time. Then he proceeded to walk in front of me like a page, and if I had asked him, he would certainly have carried the candle for me. In this fashion he escorted me to my room and waited while I undressed; then he would jump on the bed, put his paws round my neck, rub noses with me, and lick me with his rasping little pink tongue, while giving vent to soft inarticulate cries, which clearly expressed how pleased he was to see me again. Then when his transports of affection had subsided, and the hour for repose had come, he would balance himself on the rail of the bedstead and sleep there like a bird perched on a bough. When I woke in the morning he would come and lie near me until it was time to get up. Twelve o'clock was the hour at which I was supposed to come in. On this subject Pierrot had all the notions of a concierge.

At that time we had instituted little evening gatherings among a few friends, and had formed a small society, which we called the Four Candles Club, the room in which we met being, as it happened, lit by four candles in silver candlesticks, which were placed at the corners of the table.

Sometimes the conversation became so lively that I forgot the time, at the risk of finding, like Cinderella, my carriage turned into a pumpkin and my coachman into a rat.

Pierrot waited for me several times until two o'clock in the morning, but in the end my conduct displeased him, and he went to bed without me. This mute protest against my innocent dissipation touched me so much that ever after I came home regularly at midnight. But it was a long time before Pierrot forgave me. He wanted to be sure that it was not a sham repentance; but when he was convinced of the sincerity of my conversion, he deigned to take me into favour again, and he resumed his nightly post in the entrance-hall.

To gain the friendship of a cat is not an easy thing. It is a philosophic, well-regulated, tranquil animal, a creature of habit and a lover of order and cleanliness. It does not give its affections indiscriminately. It will consent to be your friend if you are worthy of the honour, but it will not be your slave. With all its affection, it preserves its freedom of judgment, and it will not do anything for you which it considers unreasonable; but once it has given its love, what absolute confidence, what fidelity of affection! It will make itself the companion of your hours of work, of loneliness, or of sadness. It will lie the whole evening on your knee, purring and happy in your society, and leaving the company of creatures of its own kind to be with you. In vain the sound of caterwauling reverberates from the house-tops, inviting it to one of those cats' evening parties where essence of red-herring takes the place of tea. It will not be tempted, but continues to keep its vigil with you. If you put it down it climbs up again quickly, with a sort of crooning noise, which is like a gentle reproach. Sometimes, when seated in front of you, it gazes at you with such soft, melting eyes, such a human and caressing look, that you are almost awed, for it seems impossible that reason can be absent from it.

Don Pierrot had a companion of the same race as himself, and no less white. All the imaginable snowy comparisons it were possible to pile up would not suffice to give an idea of that immaculate fur, which would have made ermine look yellow.

I called her Seraphita, in memory of Balzac's Swedenborgian romance. The heroine of that wonderful story, when she climbed the snow peaks of the Falberg with Minna, never shone with a more pure white radiance. Seraphita had a dreamy and pensive character. She would lie motionless on a cushion for hours, not asleep, but with eyes fixed in rapt attention on scenes invisible to ordinary mortals.

Caresses were agreeable to her, but she responded to them with great reserve, and only to those of people whom she favoured with her esteem, which it was not easy to gain. She liked luxury, and it was always in the newest armchair or on the piece of furniture best calculated to show off her swan-like beauty, that she was to be found. Her toilette took an immense time. She would carefully smooth her entire coat every morning, and wash her face with her paw, and every hair on her body shone like new silver when brushed by her pink tongue. If anyone touched her she would immediately efface all traces of the contact, for she could not endure being ruffled. Her elegance and distinction gave one an idea of aristocratic birth, and among her own kind she must have been at least a duchess. She had a passion for scents. She would plunge her nose into bouquets, and nibble a perfumed handkerchief with little paroxysms of delight. She would walk about on the dressing-table sniffling the stoppers of the scent-bottles, and she would have loved to use the violet powder if she had been allowed.

Such was Seraphita, and never was a cat more worthy of a poetic name.

Don Pierrot de Navarre, being a native of Havana, needed a hot-house temperature. This he found indoors, but the house was surrounded by large gardens, divided up by palings through which a cat could easily slip, and planted with big trees in which hosts of birds twittered and sang; and sometimes Pierrot, taking advantage of an open door, would go out hunting of an evening and run over the dewy grass and flowers. He would then have to wait till morning to be let in again, for although he might come mewing under the windows, his appeal did not always wake the sleepers inside.

He had a delicate chest, and one colder night than usual he took a chill which soon developed into consumption. Poor Pierrot, after a year of coughing, became wasted and thin, and his coat, which formerly boasted such a snowy gloss, now put one in mind of the lustreless white of a shroud. His great limpid eyes looked enormous in his attenuated face. His pink nose had grown pale, and he would walk sadly along the sunny wall with slow steps, and watch the yellow autumn leaves whirling up in spirals. He looked as though he were reciting Millevoye's elegy.

There is nothing more touching than a sick animal; it submits to suffering with such gentle, pathetic resignation.

Everything possible was done to try and save Pierrot. He had a very clever doctor who sounded him and felt his pulse. He ordered him asses' milk, which the poor creature drank willingly enough out of his little china saucer. He lay for hours on my knee like the ghost of a sphinx, and I could feel the bones of his spine like the beads of a rosary under my fingers. He tried to respond to my caresses with a feeble purr which was like a death rattle.

When he was dying he lay panting on his side, but with a supreme effort he raised himself and came to me with dilated eyes in which there was a look of intense supplication. This look seemed to say: "Cannot you save me, you who are a man?" Then he staggered a short way with eyes already glazing, and fell down with such a lamentable cry, so full of despair and anguish, that I was pierced with silent horror.

He was buried at the bottom of the garden under a white rosebush which still marks his grave.

Seraphita died two or three years later of diphtheria, against which no science could prevail.

She rests not far from Pierrot. With her the white dynasty became extinct, but not the family. To this snow-white pair were born three kittens as black as ink.

Let him explain this mystery who can.

Just at that time Victor Hugo's *Misérables* was in great vogue, and the names of the characters in the novel were on everyone's lips. I called the two male kittens Enjolras and Gavroche, while the little female received the name of Eponine.

They were perfectly charming in their youth. I trained them like dogs to fetch and carry a bit of paper crumpled into a ball, which I threw for them. In time they learnt to fetch it from the tops of cupboards, from behind chests or from the bottom of tall vases, out of which they would pull it very cleverly with their paws. When they grew up they disdained such frivolous games, and acquired that calm philosophic temperament which is the true nature of cats.

To people landing in America in a slave colony all negroes are negroes, and indistinguishable from one another. In the same way, to careless eyes, three black cats are three black cats; but attentive observers make no such mistake. Animal physiognomy varies as much as that of men, and I could distinguish perfectly between those faces, all three as black as Harlequin's mask, and illuminated by emerald disks shot with gold.

Enjolras was by far the handsomest of the three. He was remarkable for his great leonine head and big ruff, his powerful shoulders, long back and splendid feathery tail. There was something theatrical about him, and he seemed to be always posing like a popular actor who knows he is being admired. His movements were slow, undulating and majestic. He put each foot down with as much circumspection as if he were walking on a table covered with Chinese bric-à-brac or Venetian glass. As to his character, he was by no means a stoic, and he showed a love of eating which that virtuous and sober young man, his namesake, would certainly have disapproved. Enjolras would undoubtedly have said to him, like the angel to Swedenborg: "You eat too much."

I humoured this gluttony, which was as amusing as a gastronomic monkey's, and Enjolras attained a size and weight seldom reached by the domestic cat. It occurred to me to have him shaved poodle-fashion, so as to give the finishing touch to his resemblance to a lion. We left him his mane and a big tuft at the end of his tail, and I would not swear that we did not give him mutton-chop whiskers on his haunches like those Munito wore. Thus tricked out, it must be confessed he was much more like a Japanese monster than an African lion. Never was a more fantastic whim carved out of a living animal. His shaven skin took odd blue tints, which contrasted strangely with his black mane.

Gavroche, as though desirous of calling to mind his namesake in the novel, was a cat with an arch and crafty expression of countenance. He was smaller than Enjolras, and his movements were comically quick and brusque. In him absurd capers and ludicrous postures took the place of the banter and slang of the Parisian gamin. It must be confessed that Gavroche had vulgar tastes. He seized every possible occasion to leave the drawing-room in order to go and make up parties in the backyard, or even in the street, with stray cats,

"De naissance quelconque et de sang peu prouvé,"

in which doubtful company he completely forgot his dignity as cat of Havana, son of Don Pierrot de Navarre, grandee of Spain of the first order, and of the aristocratic and haughty Doña Seraphita.

Sometimes in his truant wanderings he picked up emaciated comrades, lean with hunger, and brought them to his plate of food to give them a treat in his good-natured, lordly way. The poor creatures, with ears laid back and watchful side-glances, in fear of being interrupted in their free meal by the broom of the housemaid, swallowed double, triple, and quadruple mouthfuls, and, like the famous dog, Siete-Aguas (seven waters) of Spanish *posadas* (inns), they licked the plate as clean as if it had been washed and polished by one of Gerard Dow's or Mieris's Dutch housewives.

Seeing Gavroche's friends reminded me of a phrase which illustrates one of Gavarni's drawings, "Ils sont jolis les amis dont vous êtes susceptible d'aller avec!" ("Pretty kind of friends you like to associate with!")

But that only proved what a good heart Gavroche had, for he could easily have eaten all the food himself.

The cat named after the interesting Eponine was more delicate and slender than her brothers. Her nose was rather long, and her eyes slightly oblique, and green as those of Pallas Athene, to whom Homer always applied the epithet of γλαυχωπιζ. Her nose was of velvety black, with the grain of a fine Périgord truffle; her whiskers were in a perpetual state of agitation, all of which gave her a peculiarly expressive countenance. Her superb black coat was always in motion, and was watered and shot with shadowy markings. Never was there a more sensitive, nervous, electric animal. If one stroked her two or three times in the dark, blue sparks would fly crackling out of her fur.

Eponine attached herself particularly to me, like the Eponine of the novel to Marius, but I, being less taken up with Cosette than that handsome young man, could accept the affection of this gentle and devoted cat, who still shares the pleasure of my suburban retreat and is the inseparable companion of my hours of work.

She comes running up when she hears the front-door bell, receives the visitors, conducts them to the drawing-room, talks to them—yes, talks to them—with little chirruping sounds, that do not in the least resemble the language cats use in talking to their own kind, but which simulate the articulate speech of man. What does she say? She says in the clearest way, "Will you be good enough to wait till monsieur comes down? Please look at the pictures, or chat with me in the meantime, if that will amuse you." Then when I come in she discreetly retires to an armchair or a corner of the piano, like a well-bred animal who knows what is correct in good society. Pretty little Eponine gave so many proofs of intelligence, good disposition and sociability, that by common consent she was raised to the dignity of a *person*, for it was quite evident that she was possessed of higher reasoning power than mere instinct. This dignity conferred on her the privilege of eating at table like a person instead of out of a saucer in a corner of the room like an animal.

So Eponine had a chair next to me at breakfast and dinner, but on account of her small size she was allowed to rest her two front paws on the edge of the table. Her place was laid, without spoon or fork, but she had her glass. She went right through dinner dish by dish, from soup to dessert, waiting for her turn to be helped, and behaving with such propriety and nice manners as one would like to see in many children. She made her appearance at the first sound of the bell, and on going into the dining-room one found her already in her place, sitting up in her chair with her paws resting on the edge of the tablecloth, and seeming to offer you her little face to kiss, like a well-brought-up little girl who is affectionately polite towards her parents and elders.

As one finds flaws in diamonds, spots on the sun, and shadows on perfection itself, so Eponine, it must be confessed, had a passion for fish. She shared this in common with all other cats. Contrary to the Latin proverb,

"Catus amat pisces, sed non vult tingere plantas,"

she would willingly have dipped her paw into the water if by so doing she could have pulled out a trout or a young carp. She became nearly frantic over fish, and, like a child who is filled with the expectation of dessert, she sometimes rebelled at her soup when she knew (from previous investigations in the kitchen) that fish was coming. When this happened she was not helped, and I would say to her coldly: "Mademoiselle, a person who is not hungry for soup cannot be hungry for fish," and the dish would be pitilessly carried away from under her nose. Convinced that matters were serious, greedy Eponine would swallow her soup in all haste, down to the last drop, polishing off the last crumb of bread or bit of macaroni, and would then turn round and look at me with pride, like someone who has conscientiously done his duty. She was then given her portion, which she consumed with great satisfaction, and after tasting of every dish in turn, she would finish up by drinking a third of a glass of water.

When I am expecting friends to dinner Eponine knows there is going to be a party before she sees the guests. She looks at her place, and if she sees a knife and fork by her plate she decamps at once and seats herself on a music-stool, which is her refuge on these occasions.

Let those who deny reasoning powers to animals explain if they can this little fact, apparently so simple, but which contains a whole series of inductions. From the presence near her plate of those implements which man alone can use, this observant and reflective cat concludes that she will have to give up her place for that day to a guest, and promptly proceeds to do so. She never makes a mistake; but when she knows the visitor well she climbs on his knee and tries to coax a tit-bit out of him by her pretty caressing ways.

Part Four

FROM THE

W. B. YEATS

The Cat and the Moon

The cat went here and there
And the moon spun round like a top,
And the nearest kin of the moon,
The creeping cat, looked up.
Black Minnaloushe stared at the moon,
For, wander and wail as he would,
The pure cold light in the sky
Troubled his animal blood.
Minnaloushe runs in the grass
Lifting his delicate feet.
Do you dance, Minnaloushe, do you dance?
When two close kindred meet,
What better than call a dance?
Maybe the moon may learn,
Tired of that courtly fashion,
A new dance turn.
Minnaloushe creeps through the grass
From moonlit place to place,
The sacred moon overhead
Has taken a new phase.
Does Minnaloushe know that his pupils
Will pass from change to change,
And that from round to crescent,
From crescent to round they range?
Minnaloushe creeps through the grass
Alone, important and wise,
And lifts to the changing moon
His changing eyes.

THOMAS HARDY

Last Words to a Dumb Friend

Pet was never mourned as you,
Purrer of the spotless hue,
Plumy tail, and wistful gaze
While you humoured our queer ways,
Or outshrilled your morning call
Up the stairs and through the hall—
Foot suspended in its fall—
While, expectant, you would stand
Arched, to meet the stroking hand;
Till your way you chose to wend
Yonder, to your tragic end.

Never another pet for me!
Let your place all vacant be;
Better blankness day by day
Than companion torn away.
Better bid his memory fade,
Better blot each mark he made,
Selfishly escape distress
By contrived forgetfulness,
Than preserve his prints to make
Every morn and eve an ache.

From the chair whereon he sat
Sweep his fur, nor wince thereat;
Rake his little pathways out
Mid the bushes roundabout;
Smooth away his talons' mark

From the claw-worn pine-tree bark,
Where he climbed as dusk embrowned,
Waiting us who loitered round.

Strange it is this speechless thing,
Subject to our mastering,
Subject for his life and food
To our gift, and time, and mood;
Timid pensioner of us Powers,
His existence ruled by ours,
Should—by crossing at a breath
Into save and shielded death,
By the merely taking hence
Of his insignificance—
Loom as largened to the sense,
Shape as part, above man's will,
Of the Imperturbable.

As a prisoner, flight debarred,
Exercising in a yard,
Still retain I, troubled, shaken,
Mean estate, by him forsaken;
And this home, which scarcely took
Impress from his little look,
By his faring to the Dim
Grows all eloquent of him.

Housemate, I can think you still
Bounding to the window-sill,
Over which I vaguely see
Your small mound beneath the tree,
Showing in the autumn shade
That you moulder where you played.

HART CRANE

Chaplinesque

We make our meek adjustments,
Contented with such random consolations
As the wind deposits
In slithered and too ample pockets.

For we can still love the world, who find
A famished kitten on the step, and know
Recesses for it from the fury of the street,
Or warm torn elbow coverts.

We will sidestep, and to the final smirk
Dally the doom of that inevitable thumb
That slowly chafes its puckered index toward us,
Facing the dull squint with what innocence
And what surprise!

And yet these fine collapses are not lies
More than the pirouettes of any pliant cane;
Our obsequies are, in a way, no enterprise.
We can evade you, and all else but the heart:
What blame to us if the heart live on.

The game enforces smirks; but we have seen
The moon in lonely alleys make
A grail of laughter of an empty ash can,
And through all sound of gaiety and quest
Have heard a kitten in the wilderness.

WALLACE STEVENS

A Rabbit as King of the Ghosts

The difficulty to think at the end of day,
When the shapeless shadow covers the sun
And nothing is left except light on your fur—

There was the cat slopping its milk all day,
Fat cat, red tongue, green mind, white milk
And August the most peaceful month.

To be, in the grass, in the peacefullest time,
Without that monument of cat,
The cat forgotten in the moon;

And to feel that the light is a rabbit-light,
In which everything is meant for you
And nothing need be explained;

Then there is nothing to think of. It comes of itself;
And east rushes west and west rushes down,
No matter. The grass is full

And full of yourself. The trees around are for you,
The whole of the wideness of night is for you,
A self that touches all edges,

You become a self that fills the four corners of night.
The red cat hides away in the fur-light
And there you are humped high, humped up,

You are humped higher and higher, black as stone—
You sit with your head like a carving in space
And the little green cat is a bug in the grass.

ROBERT GRAVES

Frightened Men

We were not ever of their feline race,
Never had hidden claws so sharp as theirs
In any half-remembered incarnation;
Have only the least knowledge of their minds
Through a grace on their part in thinking aloud;
And we remain mouse-quiet when they begin
Suddenly in their unpredictable way
To weave an allegory of their lives,
Making each point by walking round it—
Then off again, as interest is warmed.
What have they said? Or unsaid? What?
We understood the general drift only.

They are punctilious as implacable,
Most neighbourly to those who love them least.
A shout will scare them. When they spring, they seize.
The worst is when they hide from us and change
To something altogether other:
We meet them at the door, as who returns
After a one-hour-seeming century
To a house not his own.

T. S. ELIOT

The Naming of Cats

The Naming of Cats is a difficult matter,
    It isn't just one of your holiday games;
You may think at first I'm as mad as a hatter
When I tell you, a cat must have THREE DIFFERENT NAMES.
First of all, there's the name that the family use daily,
    Such as Peter, Augustus, Alonzo or James,
Such as Victor or Jonathan, George or Bill Bailey—
    All of them sensible everyday names.
There are fancier names if you think they sound sweeter,
    Some for the gentlemen, some for the dames:
Such as Plato, Admetus, Electra, Demeter—
    But all of them sensible everyday names.
But I tell you, a cat needs a name that's particular,
    A name that's peculiar, and more dignified,
Else how can he keep up his tail perpendicular,
    Or spread out his whiskers, or cherish his pride?
Of names of this kind, I can give you a quorum,
    Such as Munkustrap, Quaxo, or Coricopat,
Such as Bombalurina, or else Jellylorum—
    Names that never belong to more than one cat.
But above and beyond there's still one name left over,
    And that is the name that you never will guess;
The name that no human research can discover—
    But THE CAT HIMSELF KNOWS, and will never confess.
When you notice a cat in profound meditation,
    The reason, I tell you, is always the same:
His mind is engaged in a rapt contemplation
    Of the thought, of the thought, of the thought of his name:
        His ineffable effable
        Effanineffable
Deep and inscrutable singular Name.

WALTER DE LA MARE

The China Cat

You never stir, and heaven forbid,
Since, mutest companion, if you did—
A creature formed of clay and glaze—
Nature herself would stand at gaze,
Albeit it with an intent to flatter:
Man would have conjured life from matter—
If from your bowels there should befall
A low protracted caterwaul,
Those slanting eyes should open and pause,
Those pads eject their hidden claws.
No nightlong vigil I know well
Would consummate that miracle;
Yet even that passive attitude
Once did a questing dog delude.

MARIANNE MOORE

Peter

    Strong and slippery,
built for the midnight grass-party
confronted by four cats, he sleeps his time away—
the detached first claw on the foreleg corresponding
to the thumb, retracted to its tip; the small tuft of
    fronds
or katydid-legs above each eye numbering all units
in each group; the shadbones regularly set about
    the mouth

to droop or rise in unison like porcupine-quills.
He lets himself be flattened out by gravity,
as seaweed is tamed and weakened by the sun,
compelled when extended, to lie stationary.
Sleep is the result of his delusion that one must
do as well as one can for oneself,
sleep—epitome of what is to him the end of life.
Demonstrate on him how the lady placed a forked
    stick
on the innocuous neck-sides of the dangerous southern snake.
One need not try to stir him up; his prune-shaped head
and alligator-eyes are not party to the joke.
Lifted and handled, he may be dangled like an eel
or set up on the forearm like a mouse;
his eyes bisected by pupils of a pin's width,
are flickeringly exhibited, then covered up.
May be? I should have said might have been;
when he has been got the better of in a dream—
as in a fight with nature or with cats, we all know it.
Profound sleep is not with him a fixed illusion.
Springing about with froglike accuracy, with jerky
    cries
when taken in hand, he is himself again;
to sit caged by the rungs of a domestic chair
would be unprofitable—human. What is the good
    of hypocrisy?
It is permissable to choose one's employment,
to abandon the nail, or roly-poly,
when it shows signs of being no longer a pleasure,
to score the nearby magazine with a double line of
    strokes.
He can talk but insolently says nothing. What of it?
When one is frank, one's very presence is a
    compliment.
It is clear that he can see the virtue of naturalness,
that he does not regard the published fact as a
    surrender.
As for the disposition invariably to affront,
an animal with claws should have an opportunity to use them.
The eel-like extension of trunk into tail is not an
    accident.

To leap, to lengthen out, divide the air, to purloin,
    to pursue.
To tell the hen: fly over the fence, go in the wrong
    way
in your perturbation—this is life;
to do less would be nothing but dishonesty.

CHARLES CALVERLY

Sad Memories

They tell me I am beautiful: they praise my silken hair,
My little feet that silently slip on from stair to stair:
They praise my pretty trustful face and innocent grey eye;
Fond hands caress me oftentimes, yet would that I might die!

Why was I born to be abhorred of man and bird and beast?
The bullfinch marks me stealing by, and straight his song hath
    ceased;
The shrewmouse eyes me shudderingly, then flees; and, worse than
    that,
The housedog he flees after me—why was I born a cat?

Men prize the heartless hound who quits dry-eyed his native land;
Who wags a mercenary tail and licks a tyrant hand.
The leal true cat they prize not, that if e'er compelled to roam
Still flies, when let out of the bag, precipitately home.

They call me cruel. Do I know if mouse or song-bird feels?
I only know they make me light and salutary meals:
And if, as 'tis my nature to, ere I devour I tease 'em,
Why should a low-bred gardener's boy pursue me with a besom?

Should china fall or chandeliers, or anything but stocks—
Nay stocks, when they're in flowerpots—the cat expects hard
  knocks:
Should ever anything be missed—milk, coals, umbrellas, brandy—
The cat's pitched into with a boot or any thing that's handy.

"I remember, I remember," how one night I "fleeted by,"
And gained the blessed tiles and gazed into the cold clear sky.
"I remember, I remember, how my little lovers came;"
And there, beneath the crescent moon, played many a little game.

They fought—by good St. Catharine, 'twas a fearsome sight to see
The coal-black crest, the glowering orbs, of one gigantic He.
Like bow by some tall bowman bent at Hastings or Poietiers,
His huge back curved, till none observed a vestige of his ears:

He stood, an ebon crescent, flouting that ivory moon;
Then raised the pibroch of his race, the Song without a Tune;
Gleamed his white teeth, his mammoth tail waved darkly to and fro,
As with one complex yell he burst, all claws, upon the foe.

It thrills me now, that final Miaow—that weird unearthly din:
Lone maidens heard it far away, and leaped out of their skin.
A potboy from his den o'erhead peeped with a scared wan face;
Then sent a random brickbat down, which knocked me into space.

Nine days I fell, or thereabouts: and, had we not nine lives,
I wis I ne'er had seen again thy sausage-shop, St. Ives!
Had I, as some cats have, nine tails, how gladly I would lick
The hand, and person generally, of him who heaved that brick!

For me they fill the milkbowl up, and cull the choice sardine:
But ah! I nevermore shall be the cat I once have been!
The memories of that fatal night they haunt me even now:
In dreams I see that rampant He, and tremble at that Miaow.

ELIZABETH BISHOP

Lullaby for the Cat

Minnow, go to sleep and dream,
  Close your great big eyes;
Round your bed Events prepare
  The pleasantest surprise.

Darling Minnow, drop that frown,
  Just cooperate,
Not a kitten shall be drowned
In the Marxist State.

Joy and Love will both be yours,
  Minnow, don't be glum.
Happy days are coming soon—
  Sleep, and let them come . . .

WELDON KEES

The Cats

What the cats do
To amuse themselves
When we are gone
I do not know.
They have the yard
And the fences
Of the neighbors,
And, occasionally,
May arrive at the door, miaowing,

With drops of milk
On their chins,
Waving their shining tails
And exhibiting signs of alarm
When the light inside
The refrigerator
Goes on. But what
They do all day
Remains a mystery.
It is a dull neighborhood.
Children scream
From the playground.
The cars go by in a bluish light.
At six o'clock the cats run out
When we come home from work
To greet us, crying, dancing,
After the long day.

RANDALL JARRELL

The Happy Cat

The cat's asleep; I whisper *kitten*
Till he stirs a little and begins to purr—
He doesn't wake. Today out on the limb
(The limb he thinks he can't climb down from)
He mewed until I heard him in the house.
I climbed up to get him down: he mewed.
What he says and what he sees are limited.
My own response is even more constricted.
I think, "It's lucky; what you have is too."
What do you have except—well, me?
I joke about it but it's not a joke:
The house and I are all he remembers.
Next month how will he guess that it is winter

And not just entropy, the universe
Plunging at last into its cold decline?
I cannot think of him without a pang.
Poor rumpled thing, why don't you see
That you have no more, really, than a man?
Men aren't happy: why are you?

WILLIAM CARLOS WILLIAMS

Poem

As the cat
climbed over
the top of

the jamcloset
first the right
forefoot

carefully
then the hind
stepped down

into the pit of
the empty
flowerpot

Part Five

MORE STORIES
ABOUT CATS

JAMES HERRIOT

Mrs. Bond's Cats

"I work for cats."

That was how Mrs. Bond introduced herself on my first visit, gripping my hand firmly and thrusting out her jaw defiantly as though challenging me to make something of it. She was a big woman with a strong, high-cheekboned face and a commanding presence and I wouldn't have argued with her anyway, so I nodded gravely as though I fully understood and agreed, and allowed her to lead me into the house.

I saw at once what she meant. The big kitchen-living room had been completely given over to cats. There were cats on the sofas and chairs and spilling in cascades on to the floor, cats sitting in rows along the window sills and, right in the middle of it all, little Mr. Bond, pallid, wispy-moustached, in his shirt sleeves reading a newspaper.

It was a scene which was going to become very familiar. A lot of the cats were obviously uncastrated Toms because the atmosphere was vibrant with their distinctive smell—a fierce pungency which overwhelmed even the sickly wisps from the big saucepans of nameless cat food bubbling on the stove. And Mr. Bond was always there, always in his shirt sleeves and reading his paper, a lonely little island in a sea of cats.

I had heard of the Bonds, of course. They were Londoners who for some obscure reason had picked on North Yorkshire for their retirement. People said they had a "bit o' brass" and they had bought an old house on the outskirts of Darrowby where they kept themselves to themselves—and the cats. I had heard that Mrs. Bond was in the habit of taking in strays and feeding them and giving them a home if they wanted it and this had predisposed me in her favour, because in my experience the unfortunate feline species seemed to be fair game for every kind of cruelty and neglect. They shot cats, threw things at them, starved them and set their dogs on them for fun. It was good to see somebody taking their side.

My patient on this first visit was no more than a big kitten, a terrified little blob of black and white crouching in a corner.

"He's one of the outside cats," Mrs. Bond boomed.

"Outside cats?"

"Yes. All these you see here are the inside cats. The others are the really wild ones who simply refuse to enter the house. I feed them of course but the only time they come indoors is when they are ill."

"I see."

"I've had frightful trouble catching this one. I'm worried about his eyes—there seemed to be a skin growing over them, and I do hope you can do something for him. His name, by the way, is Alfred."

"Alfred? Ah yes, quite." I advanced cautiously on the little half-grown animal and was greeted by a waving set of claws and a series of open-mouthed spittings. He was trapped in his corner or he would have been off with the speed of light.

Examining him was going to be a problem. I turned to Mrs. Bond. "Could you let me have a sheet of some kind? An old ironing sheet would do. I'm going to have to wrap him up."

"Wrap him up?" Mrs. Bond looked very doubtful but she disappeared into another room and returned with a tattered sheet of cotton which looked just right.

I cleared the table of an amazing variety of cat feeding dishes, cat books, cat medicines and spread out the sheet, then I approached my patient again. You can't be in a hurry in a situation like this and it took me perhaps five minutes of wheedling and "Puss-pussing" while I brought my hand nearer and nearer. When I got as far as being able to stroke his cheek I made a quick grab at the scruff of his neck and finally bore Alfred, protesting bitterly and lashing out in all directions, over to the table. There, still holding tightly to his scruff, I laid him on the sheet and started the wrapping operation.

This is something which has to be done quite often with obstreperous felines and, although I say it, I am rather good at it. The idea is to make a neat, tight roll, leaving the relevant piece of cat exposed; it may be an injured paw, perhaps the tail, and in this case of course the head. I think it was the beginning of Mrs. Bond's unquestioning faith in me when she saw me quickly enveloping that cat till all you could see of him was a small black and white head protruding from an immovable cocoon of cloth. He and I were now facing each other, more or less eyeball to eyeball, and Alfred couldn't do a thing about it.

As I say, I rather pride myself on this little expertise and even today my veterinary colleagues have been known to remark: "Old Herriot may be limited in many respects but by God he can wrap a cat."

As it turned out, there wasn't a skin growing over Alfred's eyes. There never is.

"He's got a paralysis of the third eyelid, Mrs. Bond. Animals have this membrane which flicks across the eye to protect it. In this case it hasn't gone back, probably because the cat is in low condition— maybe had a touch of cat flu or something else which has weakened him. I'll give him an injection of vitamins and leave you some powder to put in his food if you could keep him in for a few days. I think he'll be all right in a week or two."

The injection presented no problems with Alfred furious but helpless inside his sheet and I had come to the end of my first visit to Mrs. Bond's.

It was the first of many. The lady and I established an immediate rapport which was strengthened by the fact that I was always prepared to spend time over her assorted charges; crawling on my stomach under piles of logs in the outhouses to reach the outside cats, coaxing them down from trees, stalking them endlessly through the shrubbery. But from my point of view it was rewarding in many ways.

For instance there was the diversity of names she had for her cats. True to her London upbringing she had named many of the Toms after the great Arsenal team of those days. There was Eddie Hapgood, Cliff Bastin, Ted Drake, Wilf Copping, but she did slip up in one case because Alex James had kittens three times a year with unfailing regularity.

Then there was her way of calling them home. The first time I saw her at this was on a still summer evening. The two cats she wanted me to see were out in the garden somewhere and I walked with her to the back door where she halted, clasped her hands across her bosom, closed her eyes and gave tongue in a mellifluous contralto.

"Bates, Bates, Bates, Ba-hates." She actually sang out the words in a reverent monotone except for a delightful little lilt on the "Ba-hates." Then once more she inflated her ample rib cage like an operatic prima donna and out it came again, delivered with the utmost feeling.

"Bates, Bates, Bates, Ba-hates."

Anyway it worked, because Bates the cat came trotting from behind a clump of laurel. There remained the other patient and I watched Mrs. Bond with interest.

She took up the same stance, breathed in, closed her eyes, composed her features into a sweet half-smile and started again.

"Seven-times-three, Seven-times-three, Seven-times-three-hee." It was set to the same melody as Bates with the same dulcet rise and fall at the end. She didn't get the quick response this time, though, and had to go through the performance again and again, and as the notes lingered on the still evening air the effect was startlingly like a muezzin calling the faithful to prayer.

At length she was successful and a fat tortoiseshell slunk apologetically along the wall-side into the house.

"By the way, Mrs. Bond," I asked, making my voice casual. "I didn't quite catch the name of that last cat."

"Oh, Seven-times-three?" She smiled reminiscently. "Yes, she is a dear. She's had three kittens seven times running, you see, so I thought it rather a good name for her, don't you?"

"Yes, yes, I do indeed. Splendid name, splendid."

Another thing which warmed me towards Mrs. Bond was her concern for my safety. I appreciated this because it is a rare trait among animal owners. I can think of the trainer after one of his racehorses had kicked me clean out of a loose box examining the animal anxiously to see if it had damaged its foot; the little old lady dwarfed by the bristling, teeth-bared Alsatian saying: "You'll be gentle with him won't you and I hope you won't hurt him—he's very nervous"; the farmer, after an exhausting calving which I feel certain has knocked about two years off my life expectancy, grunting morosely: "I doubt you've tired that cow out, young man."

Mrs. Bond was different. She used to meet me at the door with an enormous pair of gauntlets to protect my hands against scratches and it was an inexpressible relief to find that somebody cared. It became part of the pattern of my life; walking up the garden path among the innumerable slinking, wild-eyed little creatures which were the outside cats, the ceremonial acceptance of the gloves at the door, then the entry into the charged atmosphere of the kitchen with little Mr. Bond and his newspaper just visible among the milling furry bodies of the inside cats. I was never able to ascertain Mr. Bond's attitude to cats—come to think of it he hardly ever said anything—but I had the impression he could take them or leave them.

The gauntlets were a big help and at times they were a veritable godsend. As in the case of Boris. Boris was an enormous blue-black member of the outside cats and my bête noire in more senses than one. I always cherished a private conviction that he had escaped from a zoo; I had never seen a domestic cat with such sleek, writhing muscles, such dedicated ferocity. I'm sure there was a bit of puma in Boris somewhere.

It had been a sad day for the cat colony when he turned up. I have always found it difficult to dislike any animal; most of the ones which try to do us a mischief are activated by fear, but Boris was different; he was a malevolent bully and after his arrival the frequency of my visits increased because of his habit of regularly beating up his colleagues. I was forever stitching up tattered ears, dressing gnawed limbs.

We had one trial of strength fairly early. Mrs. Bond wanted me to give him a worm dose and I had the little tablet all ready held in forceps. How I ever got hold of him I don't quite know, but I hustled him on to the table and did my wrapping act at lightning speed, swathing him in roll upon roll of stout material. Just for a few seconds I thought I had him as he stared up at me, his great brilliant eyes full of hate. But as I pushed my loaded forceps into his mouth he clamped his teeth viciously down on them and I could feel claws of amazing power tearing inside the sheet. It was all over in moments. A long leg shot out and ripped its way down my wrist, I let go my tight hold of the neck and in a flash Boris sank his teeth through the gauntlet into the ball of my thumb and was away. I was left standing there stupidly, holding the fragmented worm tablet in a bleeding hand and looking at the bunch of ribbons which had once been my wrapping sheet. From then on Boris loathed the very sight of me and the feeling was mutual.

But this was one of the few clouds in a serene sky. I continued to enjoy my visits there and life proceeded on a tranquil course except, perhaps, for some legpulling from my colleagues. They could never understand my willingness to spend so much time over a lot of cats. And of course this fitted in with the general attitude because Siegfried didn't believe in people keeping pets of any kind. He just couldn't understand their mentality and propounded his views to anybody who cared to listen. He himself, of course, kept five dogs and two cats. The dogs, all of them, travelled everywhere with him in the car and he fed dogs and cats every day with his own hands— wouldn't allow anybody else to do the job. In the evening all seven animals would pile themselves round his feet as he sat in his chair by the fire. To this day he is still as vehemently anti-pet as ever, though another generation of waving dogs' tails almost obscures him as he drives around and he also has several cats, a few tanks of tropical fish and a couple of snakes.

Tristan saw me in action at Mrs. Bond's on only one occasion. I was collecting some long forceps from the instrument cupboard when he came into the room.

"Anything interesting, Jim?" he asked.

"No, not really. I'm just off to see one of the Bond cats. It's got a bone stuck between its teeth."

The young man eyed me ruminatively for a moment. "Think I'll come with you. I haven't seen much small animal stuff lately."

As we went down the garden at the cat establishment I felt a twinge of embarrassment. One of the things which had built up my happy relationship with Mrs. Bond was my tender concern for her charges. Even with the wildest and the fiercest I exhibited only gentleness, patience and solicitude; it wasn't really an act, it came quite naturally to me. However, I couldn't help wondering what Tristan would think of my cat bedside manner.

Mrs. Bond in the doorway had summed up the situation in a flash and had two pairs of gauntlets waiting. Tristan looked a little surprised as he received his pair but thanked the lady with typical charm. He looked still more surprised when he entered the kitchen, sniffed the rich atmosphere and surveyed the masses of furry creatures occupying almost every available inch of space.

"Mr. Herriot, I'm afraid it's Boris who has the bone in his teeth," Mrs. Bond said.

"Boris!" My stomach lurched. "How on earth are we going to catch him?"

"Oh I've been rather clever," she replied. "I've managed to entice him with some of his favourite food into a cat basket."

Tristan put his hand on a big wicker cage on the table. "In here, is he?" he asked casually. He slipped back the catch and opened the lid. For something like a third of a second the coiled creature within and Tristan regarded each other tensely, then a sleek black body exploded silently from the basket past the young man's left ear on to the top of a tall cupboard.

"Christ!" said Tristan. "What the hell was that?"

"That," I said, "was Boris, and now we've got to get hold of him again." I climbed on to a chair, reached slowly on to the cupboard top and started "Puss-puss-puss"ing in my most beguiling tone.

After about a minute Tristan appeared to think he had a better idea; he made a sudden leap and grabbed Boris's tail. But only briefly, because the big cat freed himself in an instant and set off on a whirlwind circuit of the room; along the tops of cupboards and dressers, across the curtains, careering round and round like a wall-of-death rider.

Tristan stationed himself at a strategic point and as Boris shot past he swiped at him with one of the gauntlets.

"Missed the bloody thing!" he shouted in chagrin. "But here he comes again . . . take that, you black sod! Damn it, I can't nail him!"

The docile little inside cats, startled by the scattering of plates and tins and pans and by Tristan's cries and arm wavings, began to run around in their turn, knocking over whatever Boris had missed. The noise and confusion even got through to Mr. Bond because just for a moment he raised his head and looked around him in mild surprise at the hurtling bodies before returning to his newspaper.

Tristan, flushed with the excitement of the chase, had really begun to enjoy himself. I cringed inwardly as he shouted over to me happily.

"Send him on, Jim, I'll get the bugger next time round!"

We never did catch Boris. We just had to leave the piece of bone to work its own way out, so it wasn't a successful veterinary visit. But Tristan as we got back into the car smiled contentedly.

"That was great, Jim. I didn't realize you had such fun with your pussies."

Mrs. Bond on the other hand, when I next saw her, was rather tight-lipped over the whole thing.

"Mr. Herriot," she said, "I hope you aren't going to bring that young man with you again."

J. F. POWERS

Death of a Favorite

I had spent most of the afternoon mousing—a matter of sport with me and certainly not of diet—in the sunburnt fields that begin at our back door and continue hundreds of miles into the Dakotas. I gradually gave up the idea of hunting, the grasshoppers convincing me that there was no percentage in stealth. Even to doze was difficult, under such conditions, but I must have managed it. At least I was late coming to dinner, and so my introduction to the two missionaries took place at table. They were surprised, as most visitors are, to see me take the chair at Father Malt's right.

Father Malt, breaking off the conversation (if it could be called that), was his usual dear old self. "Fathers," he said, "meet Fritz."

I gave the newcomers the first good look that invariably tells me whether or not a person cares for cats. The mean old buck in charge of the team did not like me, I could see, and would bear watching. The other one obviously did like me, but he did not appear to be long enough from the seminary to matter. I felt that I had broken something less than even here.

"My assistant," said Father Malt, meaning me, and thus unconsciously dealing out our fat friend at the other end of the table. Poor Burner! There was a time when, thinking of him, as I did now, as the enemy, I could have convinced myself I meant something else. But he *is* the enemy, and I was right from the beginning, when it could only have been instinct that told me how much he hated me even while trying (in his fashion!) to be friendly. (I believe his prejudice to be acquired rather than congenital, and very likely, at this stage, confined to me, not to cats as a class—there *is* that in his favor. I intend to be fair about this if it kills me.)

My observations of humanity incline me to believe that one of us—Burner or I—must ultimately prevail over the other. For myself, I should not fear if this were a battle to be won on the solid ground of Father Malt's affections. But the old man grows older, the grave beckons to him ahead, and with Burner pushing him from behind, how long can he last? Which is to say: How long can *I* last? Unfortunately, it is naked power that counts most in any rectory, and as things stand now, I am safe only so long as Father Malt retains it here. Could I—this impossible thought is often with me now—could I effect a reconciliation and alliance with Father Burner? Impossible! Yes, doubtless. But the question better asked is: *How* impossible? (Lord knows I would not inflict this line of reasoning upon myself if I did not hold with the rumors that Father Burner will be the one to succeed to the pastorate.) For I do like it here. It is not at all in my nature to forgive and forget, certainly not as regards Father Burner, but it is in my nature to come to terms (much as nations do) when necessary, and in this solution there need not be a drop of good will. No dog can make that statement, or take the consequences, which I understand are most serious, in the world to come. Shifts and ententes. There is something fatal about the vocation of favorite, but it is the only one that suits me, and, all things considered—to dig I am not able, to beg I am ashamed—the rewards are adequate.

"We go through Chicago all the time," said the boss missionary, who seemed to be returning to a point he had reached when I entered. I knew Father Malt would be off that evening for a convention in Chicago. The missionaries, who would fill in for him and conduct a forty hours' devotion on the side, belonged to an order just getting started in the diocese and were anxious to make a good impression. For the present, at least, as a kind of special introductory offer, they could be had dirt-cheap. Thanks to them, pastors who'd never been able to get away had got a taste of Florida last winter.

"Sometimes we stay over in Chicago," bubbled the young missionary. He was like a rookie ballplayer who hasn't made many road trips.

"We've got a house there," said the first, whose name in religion, as they say, was—so help me—Philbert. Later, Father Burner would get around it by calling him by his surname. Father Malt was the sort who wouldn't see anything funny about "Philbert," but it would be too much to expect him to remember such a name.

"What kind of a house?" asked Father Malt. He held up his hearing aid and waited for clarification.

Father Philbert replied in a shout, "The Order owns *a house* there!"

Father Malt fingered his hearing aid.

Father Burner sought to interpret for Father Philbert. "I think, Father, he wants to know what it's made out of."

"Red brick—it's red brick," bellowed Father Philbert.

"*My* house is red brick," said Father Malt.

"I *noticed* that," said Father Philbert.

Father Malt shoved the hearing aid at him.

"I know it," said Father Philbert, shouting again.

Father Malt nodded and fed me a morsel of fish. Even for a Friday, it wasn't much of a meal. I would not have been sorry to see this housekeeper go.

"All right, all right," said Father Burner to the figure lurking behind the door and waiting for him, always the last one, to finish. "She stands and looks in at you through the crack," he beefed. "Makes you feel like a condemned man." The housekeeper came into the room, and he addressed the young missionary (Burner was a great one for questioning the young): "Ever read any books by this fella Koestler, Father?"

"The Jesuit?" the young one asked.

"Hell, no, he's some kind of a writer. I know the man you mean, though. Spells his name different. Wrote a book—apologetics."

"That's the one. Very—"

"Dull."

"Well . . ."

"This other fella's not bad. He's a writer who's ahead of his time—about fifteen minutes. Good on jails and concentration camps. You'd think he was born in one if you ever read his books." Father Burner regarded the young missionary with absolute indifference. "But you didn't."

"No. Is he a Catholic?" inquired the young one.

"He's an Austrian or something."

"Oh."

The housekeeper removed the plates and passed the dessert around. When she came to Father Burner, he asked her privately, "What is it?"

"Pudding," she said, not whispering, as he would have liked.

"*Bread* pudding?" Now he was threatening her.

"Yes, Father."

Father Burner shuddered and announced to everybody, "No dessert for me." When the housekeeper had retired into the kitchen, he said, "Sometimes I think he got her from a hospital and sometimes, Father, I think she came from one of *your* fine institutions"—this to the young missionary.

Father Philbert, however, was the one to see the joke, and he laughed.

"My God," said Father Burner, growing bolder. "I'll never forget the time I stayed at your house in Louisville. If I hadn't been there for just a day—for the Derby, in fact—I'd have gone to Rome about it. I think I've had better meals here."

At the other end of the table, Father Malt, who could not have heard a word, suddenly blinked and smiled; the missionaries looked to him for some comment, in vain.

"He doesn't hear me," said Father Burner. "Besides, I think he's listening to the news."

"I didn't realize it was a radio too," said the young missionary.

"Oh, hell, yes."

"I think he's pulling your leg," said Father Philbert.

"Well, I thought so," said the young missionary ruefully.

"It's an idea," said Father Burner. Then in earnest to Father Philbert, whom he'd really been working around to all the time—the young one was decidedly not his type—"You the one drivin' that new Olds, Father?"

"It's not mine, Father," said Father Philbert with a meekness that would have been hard to take if he'd meant it. Father Burner understood him perfectly, however, and I thought they were two persons who would get to know each other a lot better.

"Nice job. They say it compares with the Cad in power. What do you call that color—oxford or clerical gray?"

"I really couldn't say, Father. It's my brother's. He's a layman in Minneapolis—St. Stephen's parish. He loaned it to me for this little trip."

Father Burner grinned. He could have been thinking, as I was, that Father Philbert protested too much. "Thought I saw you go by earlier," he said. "What's the matter—didn't you want to come in when you saw the place?"

Father Philbert, who was learning to ignore Father Malt, laughed discreetly. "Couldn't be sure this was it. That house on the *other* side of the church, now—"

Father Burner nodded. "Like that, huh? Belongs to a Mason."

Father Philbert sighed and said, "It would."

"Not at all," said Father Burner. "I like 'em better than K.C.s." If he could get the audience for it, Father Burner enjoyed being broad-minded. Gazing off in the direction of the Mason's big house, he said, "I've played golf with him."

The young missionary looked at Father Burner in horror. Father Philbert merely smiled. Father Burner, toying with a large crumb, propelled it in my direction.

"Did a bell ring?" asked Father Malt.

"His P.A. system," Father Burner explained. "Better tell him," he said to the young missionary. "You're closer. He can't bring me in on those batteries he uses."

"No bell," said the young missionary, lapsing into basic English and gestures.

Father Malt nodded, as though he hadn't really thought so.

"How do you like it?" said Father Burner.

Father Philbert hesitated, and then he said, "Here you mean?"

"I wouldn't ask you that," said Father Burner, laughing. "Talkin' about that Olds. Like it? Like the Hydramatic?"

"No kiddin', Father. It's not mine," Father Philbert protested.

"All right, all right," said Father Burner, who obviously did not believe him. "Just so you don't bring up your vow of poverty." He looked at Father Philbert's uneaten bread pudding—"Had enough?"—and rose from the table blessing himself. The other two followed when Father Malt, who was feeding me cheese, waved them away. Father Burner came around to us, bumping my chair—intentionally, I know. He stood behind Father Malt and yelled into his ear, "Any calls for me this aft?" He'd been out somewhere, as usual. I often thought he expected too much to happen in his absence.

"There was something . . ." said Father Malt, straining his memory, which was poor.

"*Yes?*"

"Now I remember—they had the wrong number."

Father Burner, looking annoyed and downhearted, left the room.

"They said they'd call back," said Father Malt, sensing Father Burner's disappointment.

I left Father Malt at the table reading his Office under the orange light of the chandelier. I went to the living room, to my spot in the window from which I could observe Father Burner and the missionaries on the front porch, the young one in the swing with his breviary—the mosquitoes, I judged, were about to join him—and the other two just smoking and standing around, like pool players waiting for a table. I heard Father Philbert say, "Like to take a look at it, Father?"

"Say, that's an idea," said Father Burner.

I saw them go down the front walk to the gray Olds parked at the curb. With Father Burner at the wheel they drove away. In a minute they were back, the car moving uncertainly—this I noted with considerable pleasure until I realized that Father Burner was simply testing the brakes. Then they were gone, and after a bit, when they did not return, I supposed they were out killing poultry on the open road.

That evening, when the ushers dropped in at the rectory, there was not the same air about them as when they came for pinochle. Without fanfare, Mr. Bauman, their leader, who had never worked any but the center aisle, presented Father Malt with a travelling bag. It was nice of him, I thought, when he said, "It's from all of us" for it could not have come from all equally. Mr. Bauman, in hardware, and Mr. Keller, the druggist, were the only ones well off, and must have forked out plenty for such a fine piece of luggage, even after the discount.

Father Malt thanked all six ushers with little nods in which there was no hint of favoritism. "Ha," he kept saying. "You shouldn'a done it."

The ushers bobbed and ducked, dodging his flattery, and kept up a mumble to the effect that Father Malt deserved everything they'd ever done for him and more. Mr. Keller came forward to instruct Father Malt in the use of the various clasps and zippers. Inside the bag was another gift, a set of military brushes, which I could see they were afraid he would not discover for himself. But he unsnapped a brush, and, like the veteran crowd-pleaser he was, swiped once or twice at his head with it after spitting into the bristles. The ushers all laughed.

"Pretty snazzy," said the newest usher—the only young blood among them. Mr. Keller had made him a clerk at the store, had pushed through his appointment as alternate usher in the church, and was gradually weaning him away from his motorcycle. With Mr. Keller, the lad formed a block to Mr. Bauman's power, but he was perhaps worse than no ally at all. Most of the older men, though they pretended a willingness to help him meet the problems of an usher, were secretly pleased when he bungled at collection time and skipped a row or overlapped one.

Mr. Keller produced a box of ten-cent cigars, which, as a *personal* gift from him, came as a bitter surprise to the others. He was not big enough, either, to attribute it to them too. He had anticipated their resentment, however, and now produced a bottle of milk of magnesia. No one could deny the comic effect, for Father Malt had been known to recommend the blue bottle from the confessional.

"Ha!" said Father Malt, and everybody laughed.

"In case you get upset on the trip," said the druggist.

"You know it's the best thing," said Father Malt in all seriousness, and then even he remembered he'd said it too often before. He passed the cigars. The box went from hand to hand, but, except for the druggist's clerk, nobody would have one.

Father Malt, seeing this, wisely renewed his thanks for the bag, insisting upon his indebtedness until it was actually in keeping with the idea the ushers had of their own generosity. Certainly none of them had ever owned a bag like that. Father Malt went to the housekeeper with it and asked her to transfer his clothes from the old bag, already packed, to the new one. When he returned, the ushers were still standing around feeling good about the bag and not so good about the cigars. They'd discuss that later. Father Malt urged them to sit down. He seemed to want them near him as long as possible. They *were* his friends, but I could not blame Father Burner for avoiding them. He was absent now, as he usually managed to be when the ushers called. If he ever succeeded Father Malt, who let them have the run of the place, they would be the first to suffer—after me! As Father Malt was the heart, they were the substance of a parish that remained rural while becoming increasingly suburban. They dressed up occasionally and dropped into St. Paul and Minneapolis, "the Cities," as visiting firemen into Hell, though it would be difficult to imagine any other place as graceless and far-gone as our own hard little highway town—called Sherwood but about as sylvan as a tennis court.

They were regular fellows—not so priestly as their urban colleagues—loud, heavy of foot, wearers of long underwear in wintertime and iron-gray business suits the year round. Their idea of a good time (pilsner beer, cheap cigars smoked with the bands left on, and pinochle) coincided nicely with their understanding of "doing good" (a percentage of every pot went to the parish building fund). Their wives, also active, played cards in the church basement and sold vanilla extract and chances—mostly to each other, it appeared—with all revenue over cost going to what was known as "the missions." This evening I could be grateful that time was not going to permit the usual pinochle game. (In the midst of all their pounding—almost as hard on me as it was on the dining-room table—I often felt they should have played on a meat block.)

The ushers, settling down all over the living room, started to talk about Father Malt's trip to Chicago. The housekeeper brought in a round of beer.

"How long you be gone, Father—three days?" one of them asked.

Father Malt said that he'd be gone about three days.

"Three days! This is Friday. Tomorrow's Saturday. Sunday. Monday." Everything stopped while the youngest usher counted on his fingers. "Back on Tuesday?"

Father Malt nodded.

"Who's takin' over on Sunday?"

Mr. Keller answered for Father Malt. "He's got some missionary fathers in."

"Missionaries!"

The youngest usher then began to repeat himself on one of his two or three topics. "Hey, Father, don't forget to drop in the U.S.O. if it's still there. I was in Chi during the war," he said, but nobody would listen to him.

Mr. Bauman had cornered Father Malt and was trying to tell him where that place was—that place where he'd eaten his meals during the World's Fair; one of the waitresses was from Minnesota. I'd had enough of this—the next thing would be a diagram on the back of an envelope—and I'd heard Father Burner come in earlier. I went upstairs to check on him. For a minute or two I stood outside his room listening. He had Father Philbert with him, and, just as I'd expected, he was talking against Father Malt, leading up to the famous question with which Father Malt, years ago, had received the Sherwood appointment from the Archbishop: "Have dey got dere a goot meat shop?"

Father Philbert laughed, and I could hear him sip from his glass and place it on the floor beside his chair. I entered the room, staying close to the baseboard, in the shadows, curious to know what they were drinking. I maneuvered myself into position to sniff Father Philbert's glass. To my surprise, Scotch. Here was proof that Father

Burner considered Father Philbert a friend. At that moment I could not think what it was he expected to get out of a lowly missionary. My mistake, not realizing then how correct and prophetic I'd been earlier in thinking of them as two of a kind. It seldom happened that Father Burner got out the real Scotch for company, or for himself *in* company. For most guests he had nothing—a safe policy, since a surprising number of temperance cranks passed through the rectory—and for unwelcome guests who would like a drink he kept a bottle of "Scotch-type" whiskey, which was a smooth, smoky blend of furniture polish that came in a fancy bottle, was offensive even when watered, and cheap, though rather hard to get since the end of the war. He had a charming way of plucking the rare bottle from a bureau drawer, as if this were indeed an occasion for him; even so, he would not touch the stuff, presenting himself as a chap of simple tastes, of no taste at all for the things of this world, who would prefer, if anything, the rude wine made from our own grapes—if we'd had any grapes. Quite an act and one he thoroughly enjoyed, holding his glass of pure water and asking, "How's your drink, Father? Strong enough?"

The housekeeper, appearing at the door, said there'd been a change of plans and some of the ushers were driving Father Malt to the train.

"Has he gone yet?" asked Father Burner.

"Not yet, Father."

"Well, tell him goodbye for me."

"Yes, Father."

When she had gone, he said, "I'd tell him myself, but I don't want to run into that bunch."

Father Philbert smiled. "What's he up to in Chicago?"

"They've got one of those pastors' and builders' conventions going on at the Stevens Hotel."

"Is he building?"

"No, but he's a pastor and he'll get a lot of free samples. He won't buy anything."

"Not much has been done around here, huh?" said Father Philbert.

He had fed Father Burner the question he wanted. "He built that fish pond in the back yard—for his minnows. That's the extent of the building program in his time. Of course he's only been here a while."

"How long?"

"Fourteen years," said Father Burner. *He* would be the greatest builder of them all—if he ever got the chance. He lit a cigarette and smiled. "What he's really going to Chicago for is to see a couple of ball games."

Father Philbert did not smile. "Who's playing there now?" he said.

A little irritated at this interest, Father Burner said, "I believe it's the Red Sox—or is it the Reds? Hell, how do I know?"

"Couldn't be the Reds," said Father Philbert. "The boy and I were in Cincinnati last week and it was the start of a long home stand for them."

"Very likely," said Father Burner.

While the missionary, a Cardinal fan, analyzed the pennant race in the National League, Father Burner sulked. "What's the best train out of Chicago for Washington?" he suddenly inquired.

Father Philbert told him what he could, but admitted that his information dated from some years back. "We don't make the run to Washington any more."

"That's right," said Father Burner. "Washington's in the American League."

Father Philbert laughed, turning aside the point that he traveled with the Cardinals. "I thought you didn't know about these things," he said.

"About these things it's impossible to stay ignorant," said Father Burner. "Here, and the last place, and the place before that, and in the seminary—a ball, a bat, and God. I'll be damned, Father, if I'll do as the Romans do."

"What price glory?" inquired Father Philbert as if he smelt heresy.

"I know," said Father Burner. "And it'll probably cost me the red hat." A brave comment, perhaps, from a man not yet a country pastor, and it showed me where his thoughts were again. He did not disguise his humble ambition by speaking lightly of an impossible one. "Scratch a prelate and you'll find a second baseman," he fumed.

Father Philbert tried to change the subject. "Somebody told me Father Malt's the exorcist for the diocese."

"Used to be." Father Burner's eyes flickered balefully.

"Overdid it, huh?" asked Father Philbert—as if he hadn't heard!

"Some." I expected Father Burner to say more. He could have told some pretty wild stories, the gist of them all that Father Malt, as an exorcist, was perhaps a little quick on the trigger. He had stuck pretty much to livestock, however, which was to his credit in the human view.

"Much scandal?"

"Some."

"Nothing serious, though?"

"No."

"Suppose it depends on what you call serious."

Father Burner did not reply. He had become oddly morose. Perhaps he felt that he was being catered to out of pity, or that Father Philbert, in giving him so many opportunities to talk against Father Malt, was tempting him.

"Who plays the accordion?" inquired Father Philbert, hearing it downstairs.

"He does."

"Go on!"

"Sure."

"How can he hear what he's playing?"

"What's the difference—if he plays an accordion?"

Father Philbert laughed. He removed the cellophane from a cigar, and then he saw me. And at that moment I made no attempt to hide. "There's that damn cat."

"His assistant!" said Father Burner with surprising bitterness. "Coadjutor with right of succession."

Father Philbert balled up the cellophane and tossed it at the wastebasket, missing.

"Get it," he said to me, fatuously.

I ignored him, walking slowly toward the door.

Father Burner made a quick movement with his feet, which were something to behold, but I knew he wouldn't get up, and took my sweet time.

Father Philbert inquired, "Will she catch mice?"

She! Since coming to live at the rectory, I've been celibate, it's true, but I daresay I'm as manly as the next one. And Father Burner, who might have done me the favor of putting him straight, said nothing.

"She looks pretty fat to be much of a mouser."

I just stared at the poor man then, as much as to say that I'd think one so interested in catching mice would have heard of a little thing called the mousetrap. After one last dirty look, I left them to themselves—to punish each other with their company.

I strolled down the hall, trying to remember when I'd last had a mouse. Going past the room occupied by the young missionary, I smiled upon his door, which was shut, confident that he was inside hard at his prayers.

The next morning, shortly after breakfast, which I took, as usual, in the kitchen, I headed for the cool orchard to which I often repaired on just such a day as this one promised to be. I had no appetite for the sparrows hopping from tree to tree above me, but there seemed no way to convince them of that. Each one, so great is his vanity, thinks himself eminently edible. Peace, peace, they cry, and there is no peace. Finally, tired of their noise, I got up from the matted grass and left, levelling my ears and flailing my tail, in a fake dudgeon that inspired the males to feats of stunt flying and terrorized the young females most delightfully.

I went then to another favorite spot of mine, that bosky strip of green between the church and the brick sidewalk. Here, however, the horseflies found me, and as if that were not enough, visions of stray dogs and children came between me and the kind of sleep I badly needed after an uncommonly restless night.

When afternoon came, I remembered that it was Saturday, and that I could have the rectory to myself. Father Burner and the missionaries would be busy with confessions. By this time the temperature had reached its peak, and though I felt sorry for the young missionary, I must admit the thought of the other two sweltering in the confessionals refreshed me. The rest of the afternoon I must have slept something approaching the sleep of the just.

I suppose it was the sound of dishes that roused me. I rushed into the dining room, not bothering to wash up, and took my customary place at the table. Only then did I consider the empty chair next to me—the utter void. This, I thought, is a foreshadowing of what I must someday face—this, and Father Burner munching away at the other end of the table. And there was the immediate problem: no one to serve me. The young missionary smiled at me, but how can you eat a smile? The other two, looking rather wilted—to their hot boxes I wished them swift return—talked in expiring tones of reserved sins and did not appear to notice me. Our first meal together without Father Malt did not pass without incident, however. It all came about when the young missionary extended a thin sliver of meat to me.

"Hey, don't do that!" said Father Philbert. "You'll never make a mouser out of her that way."

Father Burner, too, regarded the young missionary with disapproval.

"Just this one piece," said the young missionary. The meat was already in my mouth.

"Well, watch it in the future," said Father Philbert. It was the word "future" that worried me. Did it mean that he had arranged to cut off my sustenance in the kitchen too? Did it mean that until Father Malt returned I had to choose between mousing and fasting?

I continued to think along these melancholy lines until the repast, which had never begun for me, ended for them. Then I whisked into the kitchen, where I received the usual bowl of milk. But whether the housekeeper, accustomed as she was to having me eat my main course at table, assumed there had been no change in my life, or was now acting under instructions from these villains, I don't know. I was too sickened by their meanness to have any appetite. When the pastor's away, the curates will play, I thought. On the whole I was feeling pretty glum.

It was our custom to have the main meal at noon on Sundays. I arrived early, before the others, hungrier than I'd been for as long as I could remember, and still I had little or no expectation of food at this table. I was there for one purpose—to assert myself—and possibly, where the young missionary was concerned, to incite sympathy for myself and contempt for my persecutors. By this time I knew that to be the name for them.

They entered the dining room, just the two of them.

"Where's the kid?" asked Father Burner.

"He's not feeling well," said Father Philbert.

I was not surprised. They'd arranged between the two of them to have him say the six- and eleven-o'clock Masses, which meant, of course, that he'd fasted in the interval. I had not thought of him as the hardy type, either.

"I'll have the housekeeper take him some beef broth," said Father Burner. He suddenly whirled and swept me off my chair. Then he picked it up and placed it against the wall. Then he went to the lower end of the table, removed his plate and silverware, and brought them to Father Malt's place. Talking and fuming to himself, he sat down in Father Malt's chair. I did not appear very brave, I fear, cowering under mine.

Father Philbert, who had been watching with interest, now greeted the new order with a cheer. "Attaboy, Ernest!"

Father Burner began to justify himself. "More light here," he said, and added, "Cats kill birds," and for some reason he was puffing.

"If they'd just kill mice," said Father Philbert, "they wouldn't be so bad." He had a one-track mind if I ever saw one.

"Wonder how many that black devil's caught in his time?" said Father Burner, airing a common prejudice against cats of my shade (though I do have a white collar). He looked over at me. "Sssssss," he said. But I held my ground.

"I'll take a dog any day," said the platitudinous Father Philbert.

"Me, too."

After a bit, during which time they played hard with the roast, Father Philbert said, "How about taking her for a ride in the country?"

"Hell," said Father Burner. "He'd just come back."

"Not if we did it right, she wouldn't."

"Look," said Father Burner. "Some friends of mine dropped a cat off the high bridge in St. Paul. They saw him go under in mid-channel. I'm talking about the Mississippi, understand. Thought they'd never lay eyes on that animal again. That's what they thought. He was back at the house before they were." Father Burner paused—he could see that he was not convincing Father Philbert—and then he tried again. "That's a fact, Father. They might've played a quick round of golf before they got back. Cat didn't even look damp, they said. He's still there. Case a lot like this. Except now they're afraid of *him*."

To Father Burner's displeasure, Father Philbert refused to be awed or even puzzled. He simply inquired: "But did they use a bag? Weights?"

"Millstones," snapped Father Burner. "Don't quibble."

Then they fell to discussing the burial customs of gangsters—poured concrete and the rest—and became so engrossed in the matter that they forgot all about me.

Over against the wall, I was quietly working up the courage to act against them. When I felt sufficiently lionhearted, I leaped up and occupied my chair. Expecting blows and vilification, I encountered only indifference. I saw then how far I'd come down in their estimation. Already the remembrance of things past—the disease of noble politicals in exile—was too strong in me, the hope of restoration unwarrantably faint.

At the end of the meal, returning to me, Father Philbert remarked, "I think I know a better way." Rising, he snatched the crucifix off the wall, passed it to a bewildered Father Burner, and, saying "Nice Kitty," grabbed me behind the ears. "Hold it up to her," said Father Philbert. Father Burner held the crucifix up to me. "See that?" said Father Philbert to my face. I miaowed. "Take that!" said Father Philbert, cuffing me. He pushed my face into the crucifix again. "See that?" he said again, but I knew what to expect next, and when he cuffed me, I went for his hand with my mouth, pinking him nicely on the wrist. Evidently Father Burner had begun to understand and appreciate the proceedings. Although I was in a good position to observe everything, I could not say as much for myself. "Association," said Father Burner with mysterious satisfaction, almost with zest. He poked the crucifix at me. "If he's just smart enough to react properly," he said. "Oh, she's plenty smart," said Father Philbert, sucking his wrist and giving himself, I hoped, hydrophobia. He scuffed off one of his sandals for a paddle. Father Burner, fingering the crucifix nervously, inquired, "Sure it's all right to go on with this thing?" "It's the intention that counts in these things," said Father Philbert. "Our motive is clear enough." And they went at me again.

After that first taste of the sandal in the dining room, I foolishly believed I would be safe as long as I stayed away from the table; there was something about my presence there, I thought, that brought out the beast in them—which is to say very nearly all that was in them. But they caught me in the upstairs hall the same evening, one brute thundering down upon me, the other sealing off my only avenue of escape. And this beating was worse than the first—preceded as it was by a short delay that I mistook for a reprieve until Father Burner, who had gone downstairs muttering something about "leaving no margin for error," returned with the crucifix from the dining room, although we had them hanging all over the house. The young missionary, coming upon them while they were at me, turned away. "I wash my hands of it," he said. I thought he might have done more.

Out of mind, bruised of body, sick at heart, for two days and nights I held on, I know not how or why—unless I lived in hope of vengeance. I wanted simple justice, a large order in itself, but I would never have settled for that alone. I wanted nothing less than my revenge.

I kept to the neighborhood, but avoided the rectory. I believed, of course, that their only strategy was to drive me away. I derived some little satisfaction from making myself scarce, for it was thus I deceived them into thinking their plan to banish me successful. But this was my single comfort during this hard time, and it was as nothing against their crimes.

I spent the nights in the open fields. I reeled, dizzy with hunger, until I bagged an aged field mouse. It tasted bitter to me, this stale provender, and seemed, as I swallowed it, an ironic concession to the enemy. I vowed I'd starve before I ate another mouse. By way of retribution to myself, I stalked sparrows in the orchard—hating myself for it but persisting all the more when I thought of those bird-lovers, my persecutors, before whom I could stand and say in self-redemption, "You made me what I am now. You thrust the killer's part upon me." Fortunately, I did not flush a single sparrow. Since *my* motive was clear enough, however, I'd had the pleasure of sinning against them and their ideals, the pleasure without the feathers and mess.

On Tuesday, the third day, all caution, I took up my post in the lilac bush beside the garage. Not until Father Malt returned, I knew, would I be safe in daylight. He arrived along about dinnertime, and I must say the very sight of him aroused a sentiment in me akin to human affection. The youngest usher, who must have had the afternoon off to meet him at the station in St. Paul, carried the new bag before him into the rectory. It was for me an act symbolic of the counter-revolution to come. I did not rush out from my hiding place, however. I had suffered too much to play the fool now. Instead I slipped into the kitchen by way of the flap in the screen door, which they had not thought to barricade. I waited under the stove for my moment, like an actor in the wings.

Presently I heard them tramping into the dining room and seating themselves, and Father Malt's voice saying, "I had a long talk with the Archbishop." (I could almost hear Father Burner praying, Did he say anything about *me*?) And then, "Where's Fritz?"

"He hasn't been around lately," said Father Burner cunningly. He would not tell the truth and he would not tell a lie.

"You know, there's something mighty funny about that cat," said Father Philbert. "We think she's possessed."

I was astonished, and would have liked a moment to think it over, but by now I was already entering the room.

"*Possessed!*" said Father Malt. "Aw, no!"

"Ah, yes," said Father Burner, going for the meat right away. "And good riddance."

And then I miaowed and they saw me.

"Quick!" said Father Philbert, who made a nice recovery after involuntarily reaching for me and his sandal at the same time. Father Burner ran to the wall for the crucifix, which had been, until now, a mysterious and possibly blasphemous feature of my beatings—the crucifix held up to me by the one not scourging at the moment, as if it were the will behind my punishment. They had schooled me well, for even now, at the sight of the crucifix, an undeniable fear was rising in me. Father Burner handed it to Father Malt.

"Now you'll see," said Father Philbert.

"We'll leave it up to you," said Father Burner.

I found now that I could not help myself. What followed was hidden from them—from human eyes. I gave myself over entirely to the fear they'd beaten into me, and in a moment, according to their plan, I was fleeing the crucifix as one truly possessed, out of the dining room and into the kitchen, and from there, blindly, along the house and through the shrubbery, ending in the street, where a powerful gray car ran over me—and where I gave up the old ghost for a new one.

Simultaneously, reborn, redeemed from my previous fear, identical with my former self, so far as they could see, and still in their midst, I padded up to Father Malt—he still sat gripping the crucifix—and jumped into his lap. I heard the young missionary arriving from an errand in Father Philbert's *brother's* car, late for dinner he thought, but just in time to see the stricken look I saw coming into the eyes of my persecutors. This look alone made up for everything I'd suffered at their hands. Purring now, I was rubbing up against the crucifix, myself effecting my utter revenge.

"What have we done?" cried Father Philbert. He was basically an emotional dolt and would have voted then for my canonization.

"I ran over a cat!" said the young missionary excitedly. "I'd swear it was this one. When I looked, there was nothing there!"

"Better go upstairs and rest," growled Father Burner. He sat down—it was good to see him in his proper spot at the low end of the table—as if to wait a long time, or so it seemed to me. I found myself wondering if I could possibly bring about his transfer to another parish—one where they had a devil for a pastor and several assistants, where he would be able to start at the bottom again.

But first things first, I always say, and all in good season, for now Father Malt himself was drawing my chair up to the table, restoring me to my rightful place.

SYLVIA TOWNSEND WARNER

The Best Bed

The cat had known many winters, but none like this. Through two slow darkening months it had rained, and now, on the eve of Christmas, the wind had gone round to the east, and instead of rain, sleet and hail fell.

The hard pellets hit his drenched sides and bruised them. He ran faster. When boys threw stones at him he could escape by running; but from this heavenly lapidation there was no escape. He was hungry, for he had had no food since he had happened upon a dead sparrow, dead of cold, three days ago. It had not been the cat's habit to eat dead meat, but having fallen upon evil days he had been thankful even for that unhealthy-tasting flesh. Thirst tormented him, worse than hunger. Every now and then he would stop, and scrape the frozen gutters with his tongue. He had given up all hope now, he had forgotten all his wiles. He despaired, and ran on.

The lights, the footsteps on the pavements, the crashing buses, the swift cars like monster cats whose eyes could outstare his own, daunted him. Though a Londoner, he was not used to these things, for he was born by Thames' side, and had spent his days among the docks, a modest useful life of rat-catching and secure slumbers upon flour sacks. But one night the wharf where he lived had caught fire; and terrified by flames, and smoke, and uproar, he had begun to run, till by the morning he was far from the river, and homeless, and too unversed in the ways of the world to find himself another home.

A street door opened, and he flinched aside, and turned a corner. But in that street, doors were opening too, every door letting out horror. For it was closing-time. Once, earlier in his wanderings, he had crouched in by such a door, thinking that any shelter would be better than the rainy street. Before he had time to escape a hand snatched him up and a voice shouted above his head. "Gorblime if the cat hasn't come in for a drink," the voice said. And the cat felt his nose thrust into a puddle of something fiery and stinking, that burned on in his nostrils and eyes for hours afterwards.

He flattened himself against the wall, and lay motionless until the last door should have swung open for the last time. Only when someone walked by, bearing that smell with him, did the cat stir. Then his nose quivered with invincible disgust, his large ears pressed back upon his head, and the tip of his tail beat stiffly upon the pavement. A dog, with its faculty of conscious despair, would have abandoned itself, and lain down to await death; but when the streets were quiet once more the cat ran on.

There had been a time when he ran and leaped for the pleasure of the thing, rejoicing in his strength like an athlete. The resources of that lean, sinewy body, disciplined in the hunting days of his youth, had served him well in the first days of his wandering; then, speeding before some barking terrier, he had hugged amidst his terrors a compact and haughty joy in the knowledge that he could so surely outstrip the pursuer; but now his strength would only serve to prolong his torment. Though an accumulated fatigue smouldered in every nerve, the obdurate limbs carried him on, and would carry him on still, a captive to himself, meekly trotting to the place of his death.

He ran as the wind directed, turning this way and that to avoid the gusts, spiked with hail, that ravened through the streets. His eyes were closed, but suddenly at a familiar sound he stopped, and stiffened with fear. It was the sound of a door swinging on its hinges. He snuffed apprehensively. There was a smell, puffed out with every swinging-to of the door, but it was not the smell he abhorred; and though he waited in the shadow of a buttress, no sounds of jangling voices came to confirm his fears, and though the door continued to open and shut, no footsteps came from it. He stepped cautiously from his buttress into a porch. The smell was stronger here. It was aromatic, rich and a little smoky. It tickled his nose and made him sneeze.

The door was swinging with the wind. The aperture was small, too small for anything to be seen through it, save only a darkness that was not quite dark. With a sudden determination the cat flitted through.

Of his first sensations, one overpowered all the others. Warmth! It poured over him, it penetrated his being, and confused his angular physical consciousness of cold and hunger and fatigue into something rounded and indistinct. Half-swooning, he sank down on the stone flags.

Another sneezing fit roused him. He jumped up, and began to explore.

The building he was in reminded him of home. Often, hunting the river-side, he had strayed into places like this—lofty and dusky, stone-floored and securely uninhabited. But they had smelt of corn, of linseed, of tallow, of sugar: none of them had smelt as this did, smokily sweet. They had been cold. Here it was warm. They had been dark; and here the dusk was mellowed with one red star, burning in mid-air, and with the glimmer of a few tapers, that added to the smoky sweetness their smell of warm wax.

His curiosity growing with his confidence, the cat ran eagerly about the church. He rubbed his back against the font, he examined into the varying smell of the hassocks, he trotted up the pulpit stairs, sprang on to the ledge, and sharpened his claws in the cushion. Outside the wind boomed, and the hail clattered against the windows, but within the air was warm and still, and the red star burned mildly on. Over against the pulpit the cat came on something that reminded him even more of home—a wisp of hay, lying on the flags. He had often seen hay; sometimes borne towering above the greasy tide on barges, sometimes fallen from the nosebags of the great draught horses who waited so peacefully in the wharfingers' yard.

The hay seemed to have fallen from a box on trestles, cut out of unstained wood. The cat stood on his hind legs, and tried to look in, but it was too high for him. He turned about, but his curiosity brought him back again; and poising himself on his clustered paws he rocked slightly, gauging his spring, and then jumped, alighting softly in a bed of hay. He landed so delicately that though the two kneeling figures at either end of the crib swayed forward for a moment, they did not topple over. The cat sniffed them, a trifle suspiciously, but they did not hold his attention long. It was the hay that interested him. A drowsy scent rose out of the deep, warm bed as he kneaded and shuffled it with his forepaws. This, this, promised him what he had so long yearned for: sound sleep, an enfolding in warmth and softness, a nourishing forgetfulness. He paced round in a small circle, burrowing himself a close nest, purring with a harsh note of joy. As he turned he brushed against a third figure in the crib; but he scarcely noticed it. Already a rapture of sleepiness was overcoming him; the two kneeling figures had done him no harm, nor would this reposing one. Soon the bed was made to his measure. Bowing his head upon his paws, he abandoned himself.

Another onslaught of hail dashed against the windows, the door creaked, and at a gust of wind entering the church the candle flames wavered, as though they were nodding their heads in assent; but though the cat's ears flicked once or twice against the feet of the plaster Jesus, he was too securely asleep to know or heed.

SOSEKI NATSUME

from
I Am a Cat

I am a cat but as yet I have no name.

I haven't the faintest idea of where I was born. The first thing I do remember is that I was crying "meow, meow," somewhere in a gloomy damp place. It was there that I met a human being for the first time in my life. Though I found this all out at a later date, I learned that this human being was called a Student, one of the most ferocious of the human race. I also understand that these Students sometimes catch us, cook us and then take to eating us. But at that time, I did not have the slightest idea of all this so I wasn't frightened a bit. When this Student placed me on the palm of his hand and lifted me up lightly, I only had the feeling of floating around. After a while, I got used to this position and looked around. This was probably the first time I had a good look at a so-called "human being." What impressed me as being most strange still remains deeply imbedded in my mind: the face which should have been covered with hair was a slippery thing similar to what I now know to be a teakettle. I have since come across many other cats but none of them are such freaks. Moreover, the center of the Student's face protruded to a great extent, and from the two holes located there, he would often emit smoke. I was extremely annoyed by being choked by this. That this was what they term as tobacco, I came to know only recently.

I was snuggled up comfortably in the palm of this Student's hand when, after a while, I started to travel around at a terrific speed. I was unable to find out if the Student was moving or if it was just myself that was in motion, but in any case I became terribly dizzy and a little sick. Just as I was thinking that I couldn't last much longer at this rate, I heard a thud and saw sparks. I remember everything up till that moment but think as hard as I can, I can't recall what took place immediately after this.

When I came to, I could not find the Student anywhere. Nor could I find the many cats that had been with me either. Moreover, my dear mother had also disappeared. And the extraordinary thing was that this place, when compared to where I had been before, was extremely bright—ever so bright. I could hardly keep my eyes open. This was because I had been removed from my straw bed and thrown into a bamboo bush.

Finally, mustering up my strength, I crawled out from this bamboo grove and found myself before a large pond. I sat on my haunches and tried to take in the situation. I didn't know what to do but suddenly I had an idea. If I could attract some attention by meowing, the Student might come back for me. I commenced but this was to no avail; nobody came.

By this time, the wind had picked up and came blowing across the pond. Night was falling. I sensed terrible pangs of hunger. Try as I would, my voice failed me and I felt as if all hope were lost. In any case, I resolved to get myself to a place where there was food and so, with this decision in mind, I commenced to circle the water by going around to the left.

This was very difficult but at any rate, I forced myself along and eventually came to a locality where I sensed Man. Finding a hole in a broken bamboo fence, I crawled through, having confidence that it was worth the try, and lo! I found myself within somebody's estate. Fate is strange; if that hole had not been there, I might have starved to death by the roadside. It is well said that every tree may offer shelter. For a long time afterwards, I often used this hole for my trips to call on Mi-ke, the tomcat living next door.

Having sneaked into the estate, I was at a loss as to what the next step should be. Darkness had come and my belly cried for food. The cold was bitter and it started to rain. I had no time to fool around any longer so I went in to a room that looked bright and cozy. Coming to think of it now, I had entered somebody's home for the first time. It was there that I was to confront other humans.

The first person I met was the maid Osan. This was a human much worse than the Student. As soon as she saw me, she grabbed me by the neck and threw me outdoors. I sensed I had no chance against her sudden action so I shut my eyes and let things take their course. But I couldn't endure the hunger and the cold any longer. I don't know how many times I was thrown out but because of this, I came to dislike Osan all through. That's one reason why I stole the fish the other day and why I felt so proud of myself.

When the maid was about to throw me out for the last time, the master of the house made his appearance and asked what all the row was about. The maid turned to him with me hanging limp from her hand, and told him that she had repeatedly tried throwing this stray cat out but that it always kept sneaking into the kitchen again—and that she didn't like it at all. The master, twisting his moustache, looked at me for a while and then told the maid to let me in. He then left the room. I took it that the master was a man of few words. The maid, still mad at me, threw me down on the kitchen floor. In such a way, I was able to establish this place as my home. . . .

At one time, I went in for sports. Some of you, upon hearing this, will surely laugh at me because even some of you humans don't enjoy them. Many of you think that your only mission in life is to eat and sleep. There was once a time when noblemen, with their hands folded at their bosoms and their buttocks rotting on cushions, claimed that they were in a state of ecstacy; they felt they were assuming the honors and the wealth of their superiors. Only recently have we heard that we should take exercise, drink milk, dash cold water over ourselves, dive into the sea, seclude ourselves in the mountains, and eat mist for the good of our health. These are all recent maladies which have infected this divine land from Western countries, and these suggestions should be classified as being as dangerous as the pest, tuberculosis, and neurasthenia. I myself was born only last year so I am only one year old now. Therefore, I did not witness the time that men were first infected by this sickness but it must have been before I began floating around in the wind of this world. But we may say that a year of a cat's life is equal to ten years of a man's. The span of my life is only a fraction of a human's, but during that short interval, I will manage to accomplish what all cats should do. It would be wrong to calculate the days of cats as the same as the days of humans. . . .

I myself thought up many games. One was trying to leap from the edge of the kitchen eaves to the roof of the main house; another was to stand on all four legs on the plum-blossom-shaped tile ends of the roof. I also tried to walk along the bamboo laundry pole (this I could not do because it is so slippery), and to jump suddenly up on a child's back from behind. This last-mentioned game was more fun than any other sport but I usually received a terrible scolding so I try it only about three times a month at the most. At times, a paper bag is put over my head but this game is only agonizing for me. Moreover, as it requires human participation, it isn't much of a success.

Ranking next as my favorite sport is to claw at book covers. This has the disadvantage of being too risky, because when my master catches me in the act he beats me unmercifully. Besides, it only offers exercise for my paws and does not benefit the rest of my body. I like to classify such a sport as old-fashioned.

Of my new sports, the first on the list is to hunt praying mantises. Mantis hunting is not as strenuous as rat hunting, but neither does it involve so many hazards. The best season for this game is from middle summer till early autumn.

As to the method of this game, first of all I go out to the yard and find a mantis. Although it depends on the weather, it's generally quite simple to find one or two. After seeing one, I rush it as fast as the wind. The mantis, sensing danger, will raise its head and get ready to protect itself. Mantises are rather bold, even when they don't know the strength of their foe. They're harmless but they put up a good fight so it's great fun. . . .

The wings of a mantis are like its neck in that they are extremely narrow. According to my understanding, the wings are only there for ornamental purposes—in other words, like the study of English, French, and German for humans. They are not at all practical. When a mantis spreads its good-for-nothing wings, it is doing no good as far as its escape is concerned. Having wings sounds wonderful but actually those of the mantis only drag the owner along the ground as it walks. I often feel sorry for my prey but as it is essential for my exercise, I simply beg its pardon and run after it all the more.

The mantis cannot turn around easily so it usually keeps going straight ahead in its attempt to escape. I give it a tap on its nose, and the mantis spreads its wings and lies prostrate. Then I hold it flat against the ground with my forepaws and take a little rest. Suddenly I let go again, but not for long. I'm quick to press it flat once more. This is the strategy employed by the Chinese warlord K'ungming, who let his foe escape seven times but then captured his adversary seven times.

After about thirty minutes of this, the mantis is exhausted so I pick it up in my mouth and shake it. After I let go, it lies on the ground unable to move. I give it a shove with my paw, and as it again tries to fly, I pounce on it once more. Being a little bored by the game by now, I simply commence to eat it. For those of you who haven't eaten mantises yet, I may as well admit that they're not very tasty. Nor are they especially nutritious, either.

Beside mantises, there are also cicadas to hunt. Not all the cicadas are the same. Just as there are the greasy, the arrogant, and the loud types among humans, you find the same peculiarities among cicadas. The greasy cicadas are literally very rich in oil. The arrogant cicadas are too proud and haughty, and are therefore a nuisance. The species that's most fun to catch is the *oshii-tsuku-tsuku* cicadas, the noisy kind.

I have to wait until late summer before they arrive. When the autumn wind begins to steal through your kimono sleeves and makes you start sneezing, that is the time these insects commence to sing by moving their tails up and down. And when it comes to singing, they really make a lot of noise! They seem to have no other object in life than to sing and to be caught by cats.

So in early autumn, I go about catching cicadas. It is here that I should explain that you won't find cicadas lying around on the ground. The only ones not in trees are those that ants have attacked. But the cicada that is the object of my game is certainly not the kind lying within the jurisdiction of ants! My prey is the cicada that clings to a branch of a high tree, singing out for all it is worth *"Oshii-tsuku-tsuku!"* By the way, I would like to ask you learned humans this question: how do cicadas really sing? Is it *"Oshii-tsuku-tsuku"* or *"Tsuku-tsuku-oshii"*? I believe there is still much research to be done on this insect. The reason humans consider themselves so superior to cats may lie in the fact that man supposedly knows all about such matters. But if you can give no immediate reply to this question, you'd better begin worrying more about your superiority. Considering cicadas as insects to be hunted, however, it really doesn't make much difference how they happen to sing. The trick is to climb a tree, track the cicada down by its song, and to catch one when it is in the middle of a shrill chorus. This may sound easy but actually it's quite difficult to accomplish.

I use all my four feet when traversing the good earth, so I do not feel inferior to any other animal. Considering the number of legs I possess, I know that I'm better off than humans—they have only two. But when it comes to climbing trees, there are many animals better equipped than I am. Monkeys are professional tree climbers but there are many descendants of monkeys and apes—humans—who still retain this skill. As climbing is against the law of gravity, not to be able to accomplish it should not cause anyone shame. But cicada hunting, even considered as an exercise, does have its inconveniences.

Fortunately, I have been given those sharp implements called claws so I can climb trees, one way or the other. But frankly speaking, it's not as easy as it may look and, besides, cicadas can fly. Different from mantises, once cicadas take wing, they make it impossible for me to follow. I often find myself in a sad plight, thinking that it would have been better if I hadn't bothered to climb the tree in the first place. Then, last but not least, there is the danger of being urinated on, and it almost seems that cicadas aim at my eyes. Of course, I understand their wanting to fly away, but I'd like to ask them not to make water when doing so. What is the psychological factor that affects a cicada's physiological organs and induces it to urinate when flying away? It is, most probably, caused by some pain. Or is it a way of gaining time, surprising its foes before its flight? If that is so, it would be the same as a squid which squirts black ink when in danger, or as a quick-tempered bully showing off his tattoos before coming to blows, or the same as my master who speaks in Latin when angered. This again, is another problem for researchers to deal with when studying the cicada. It might even win somebody a doctor's degree. But now let's get back to the main subject.

Cicadas concentrate—if you think my use of the word "concentrate" sounds funny, I could say "gather" but "gather" doesn't seem right so I'll stick to my first term—cicadas concentrate mostly on green paulownia trees. This might be a little technical but the green paulownia tree is called *wu t'ung* in Chinese. Its many leaves are as large as fans. When the leaves are thick, it's impossible to see the branches of the tree. This is naturally a great obstacle in cicada hunting. There's a song now popular that goes "Though the voice is heard, the figure doesn't appear." It is as if this had been especially written for cicadas, I'm afraid. Therefore, I can only track the insect by listening to its song.

All paulownia trees have a crotch in the main trunk, about six feet above the ground. After climbing this far, I generally rest and then commence searching. I must be careful because if one cicada takes flight, I am out of luck. The rest also fly away.

When it comes to imitating others, cicadas are not inferior to humans—they love to play "follow the leader." Sometimes when I've established myself in the crotch of a tree, I often find the entire paulownia enveloped in silence; and hard as I may look and listen, I don't find a single cicada around. I hardly ever feel like going down to repeat the whole performance after climbing this far, so I generally decide to stay where I am and wait for a second chance. Eventually I become sleepy and take a nap then and there. But, upon waking up, I usually find myself on a stepping stone at the base of the tree.

Yet I must average at least one cicada to each climb. The reason I prefer mantis hunting is that I have to grasp a cicada between my teeth in the tree, so by the time I reach the ground to play with the insect, it is dead.

But cicada hunting is not without its exciting moments. I stealthily creep up to one as it feverishly sings by drawing its tail in and out, and just as I pounce on it, the *tsuku-tsuku* cicada lets out a squeal and flutters its thin transparent wings in all directions. The speed at which all this happens is incredible, something that must be experienced to appreciate. The moribund flutter is indeed the most beautiful sight in the cicada world; and every time I trap one of these *tsuku-tsuku* cicadas, I thrill at this aesthetic performance. After witnessing this spectacle, I ask forgiveness and throw the insect into my mouth. At times, some of them continue to perform this aesthetic act even after they are inside.

The game that I like best next to cicada hunting is pine sliding. There's no need to make a lengthy explanation of this so I'll make it as simple as possible. When I say "pine sliding," you'll naturally presume I take slides down a pine tree, but actually it's more like tree "climbing." In cicada hunting, I climb trees mainly to catch insects but in pine sliding I climb trees with no other purpose beyond the ascent. This is the main difference between the two sports. It is said that Genzaemon Tsuneyo Sano once prepared a meal for a lay priest by the name of Saimyoji in the days of Tokiyori Hojo (1226–1263). He cooked it using a treasured pine tree as fuel so it is said that this evergreen tree became extremely knotty. There's no tree that is so rough surfaced as a pine, and, therefore, there's no tree that's more clawable. In other words, there's no tree easier to climb.

In this game, I dash straight up the trunk and then come dashing down again. In descending, there are two methods. One is to return headfirst, facing the ground; the other is to go down in the same position as climbing up, or backwards.

Now I'd like to ask you humans another question: which do you think would be the more difficult of the two? Like most shallow-brained humans, you will probably say that it would be much easier to descend headfirst. Well, that's where you're wrong. You're probably thinking of Yoshitsune instead of cats. Yoshitsune was the famous warrior who drove his horse over Hiyodorigoe Cliff to win a battle. Do you really think that it would be proper for cats to go headfirst, too? Nothing could be more insulting!

You may already know how the claws of a cat grow, but I'll tell you anyway: they grow with the points curving backwards. That's why we can pull objects towards us so easily, like using a fireman's hook; but when it comes to pushing, we are often quite clumsy.

Let's imagine now that I've just dashed up the trunk of a pine tree. As a cat is an animal born to walk on the ground, it is only natural that I cannot maintain my perch long. If I don't take any action, I will begin to slide down. If I didn't try to break the fall, I would be sure to get hurt. Therefore I must do something to reach the ground safely.

There is a great difference between falling down and going down, but not always as great as it may sound at first. If the descent is slow, it's "going down," but if the "going down" is too fast, it's "falling." The difference lies in a wee bit of reasoning. As I don't like falling down from a pine tree, I try to descend by slackening my speed. In other words, I try to do something to check the downward motion.

As I have already mentioned, all of my claws turn backwards so when I place my paws skyward and stick the claws out, I can slacken the speed. And thus "falling" becomes "going down." This is comprehensive reasoning.

But if I took the opposite position and tried going down the trunk in the Yoshitsune style, or headfirst, the claws would be useless. I'd slip with nothing to check the speed of my heavy body. In any case, I sometimes go down headfirst intentionally so therefore I am literally falling down. It is quite difficult to go down headfirst, as Yoshitsune must have found out on Hiyodorigoe Cliff. I believe that of all cats, I'm the only one that can accomplish this feat. I have therefore named this sport as I please: pine sliding.

I'd also like to say a few words about "going around the fence," one more form of taking exercise. The fence all around my master's house is made of bamboo and it forms a rectangle. The sides parallel to the veranda are probably between forty-eight and fifty-four feet long, while the other sides only measure about twenty-one feet. What I term as the "going-around-the-fence" sport is to circle the whole fence without falling off. It is true that I often fall off, but when I'm able to make a complete trek, I feel satisfied to the utmost.

There are several cryptomeria stakes supporting the bamboo lattice work of the fence. The lower halves of the poles have been burnt so as to prevent their rotting, but on top they are convenient places to take rests.

The other day I was in exceptionally good form so I was able to repeat my trek three times before noon. The more I practiced, the better I became. And the better I got, the more interesting I found the sport. I was halfway around on my fourth trip when three crows came flying from the roof of the neighboring house and settled in a neat row about three yards ahead of me.

Rather unexpected visitors, and great obstacles to my game! They had no right to come perching on somebody else's fence, so I hissed at them: "I'm coming. You'd better get out of my way."

The crow nearest me just looked my way and grinned; the one in the middle simply stared into my master's yard; and the third bird only continued to sharpen its beak on the bamboo fence. It most probably had some food in its mouth.

I gave them three minutes to leave and stood there waiting. I have always known that crows possess very bad memories, but this was the first time to find this theory true. They had no memory at all! I waited for a long time but the crows didn't speak to me or fly away. So I started walking ahead again.

The crow right in front of me spread its wings just a little. "Haa! Now he's afraid and is going to fly!" Or so I thought. Instead, it just hopped up and round-about-faced itself.

Stupid! If this had happened on the ground, I wouldn't have let it get away with such impudence. Unfortunately, however, just plain walking on a fence is difficult enough—chasing birds would be almost impossible. Still, I didn't feel like waiting until the three crows decided to take flight. In the first place, my legs wouldn't have lasted much longer. The three creatures in front of me, however, had wings so they are used to perching on such places and can stay put as long as they want.

As this was my fourth trip around the fence I felt pretty nearly all in. I was doing something similar to tightrope walking besides exercising. It was difficult to stay on the fence even with nothing hindering me, so having these three black-cloaked feathered idiots come to obstruct my path was too much. I was afraid I'd have to quit exercising and get down from the fence.

To avoid trouble, I wondered if it might be better to simply give up. The enemy had me outnumbered and, moreover, they do not come here often. The beak of a crow is rather pointed so these birds seemed as if they had been sent by Tengu, the goblin with a long nose. They would naturally be dangerous in a fight.

Retreat was the wisest action to take. To start a fight and then accidentally fall off would be terribly embarrassing. While I was pondering on what I should do, the one nearest me burst out: "Aho!"* The next one imitated the first, repeating, "Aho!" The other crow even took the trouble to shriek two times: "Aho, aho!"

Even a gentle cat such as I could not stand this! To be insulted by these crows in my own yard was unforgivable and it affected my very honor. You might say that this couldn't hurt me since I don't have any other name in the first place. But my honor and dignity were involved. Now I would never retreat!

When my master talks about "a flock of crows," he is referring to "a disorderly crowd" or "mere rabble," so I decided these three birds might be less dangerous than I had thought. Determined to protect my good name, I commenced walking slowly forward. It seemed as if the crows were talking among themselves because they didn't even glance at me. It was extremely irritating. If the fence had only been five or six inches wider, I'd have been able to give them a good fight. Unfortunately, however, I could only creep along at a slow pace no matter how angry I was. When I was about five or six inches from them, all the crows suddenly flapped their wings and flew up one or two feet in the air, as if by previous arrangement.

The force of the wind from their wings suddenly caught me in the face and a moment later I lost my foothold and fell to the ground. Looking up from the foot of the fence, I saw the three crows still on their perch looking down at me with their beaks in a neat row.

The brutes! I glared at them but it did not have any effect. I bristled my back and snarled, but that didn't work either. Just as symbolical poems are not understood by laymen, neither were my gestures of anger understood by the crows—they showed no re-action.

Well, perhaps it was my own fault. I had been thinking of them

* "Aho," the cry of a crow, means "fool" in Japanese.

as cats but that was wrong. If they had been cats, the crows would have naturally understood—but they were only crows. It was like a businessman trying to impress my master, Mr. Kushami, or like Shogun Yoritomo presenting Bonze Saigyo with a silver cat. It was also like crows letting their droppings fall on the statue of Takamori Saigo. I at last realized that it was to my disadvantage to persist so without more ado, I retreated to the veranda.

It was almost suppertime. Exercise is good but it shouldn't be overdone. I now felt weak and anxious to rest. Besides, my encounter with the crows took place in early autumn and, as I had been in the sun for a long time, my fur coat had absorbed too much heat from the westbound sun. It was unbearably hot. I kept wishing that the sweat that came out of my pores would run, but no! It only stuck to the roots of my fur like grease. My back felt itchy. This itchiness is quite different from the irritation I have when fleas are crawling around. I can bite at the parts that can be reached with my mouth and I can scratch the places I can reach with my paws, but when the center of my spine becomes itchy, it is beyond the limits of my power to do much about it myself. When it becomes unbearable, I seek out a human and furiously rub myself against him, or I go to a pine tree and give myself a good rubdown; if I don't find relief, I feel uncomfortable and cannot sleep.

Humans are fools. When I purr—now wait, this is the expression humans use. I prefer to say that they are being purred at. In any case, humans are such fools that when they are purred at by me, they mistakenly think that I love them dearly and they do whatever I want them to do. At times, they stroke my head.

But last summer, those little pests called fleas began to inhabit me. They multiplied in my fur so much that when I went close to a human, I was generally grabbed by the neck and flung away. I was avoided only because of these fleas, so little that they can hardly be seen. By this, it would not be altogether wrong to say that the sentiments of humans are only skin deep and tend to change abruptly according to the circumstances. Though there were just a measly one or two thousand of these fleas on my back, it was amazing how calculating humans acted. The first article in the law of love as practiced by them is: love others only when it brings personal benefit. . . .

It is now more than two years since I began living with humans. I once thought that my insight was unique but the other day I happened to meet one of my own kind. His name was Kater Murr. I had never seen him before, but he talked so impressively that I was somewhat amazed. Upon investigation, however, I found that Kater Murr had actually died one hundred years ago but, due to a sudden spirit of curiosity, had become a ghost and left Hades in order to surprise me.

This cat is now in Hell because he was once carrying a fish in his mouth for his mother, and he proved to be such an undutiful son that he couldn't endure the temptation and ate the fish himself. It is said that Kater Murr had a talent not unequal to that of a man. At one time he even composed a poem to surprise his master. Because a no-good cat like me can never hope to realize such achievements, I ought to say goodbye to this world and go to Hell myself.

My master will die, sooner or later, from his stomach ailment. Old Kaneda is already as good as dead because of his greed. The autumn leaves have fallen and most of the trees are bare. All living creatures are destined to die so if you can't make much use of yourself while living, it might be just as well to die right away.

According to Meitei's theory, man is destined to become suicidal. If we are not careful, even cats might become influenced by this cramped world. That would be terrible.

That evening, such talk had made me feel so depressed that I decided to drink some of the beer that Sampei had brought. Perhaps it would brighten me up.

I went around to the kitchen. The lamp had most probably been blown out by the autumn wind which came in from the door left ajar. It was dark but some moonbeams filtered through the window.

I could see three glasses on a tray, and two of them were still half filled with the brownish liquid. The glasses, shining bright in the moonlight, stood beside the charcoal extinguisher and looked cool; but even hot water looks cool in a glass. I didn't really feel like drinking the beer any more but there is nothing like trying. When Sampei drank, he became red in the face and commenced to breathe heavily. Would a cat become gay by drinking beer, too? Well, I am bound to die some time so it is best to do all things while still alive. After I'm dead, I don't want to feel regret so I made up my mind to drink some of it anyway.

I stuck my tongue out fast, and quickly lapped up some beer in one glass—and I was greatly surprised. I felt the tip of my tongue prickle as if needles were being stuck into it. I could not fathom for what freakish reason humans like to drink such bitter liquid. Any way you looked at it, beer and cats do not go hand in hand. It was terrible!

I retracted my tongue but then had a second thought. Humans often say that the best medicine is the most bitter to the taste. When they catch cold, I have often seen them take some obscure medicine while making a sour face. I was never sure whether they got well because of the medicine or in spite of it, but this was a good chance to find out. If my stomach became bitter after drinking the beer, that would be that. But if I became joyful, forgetting everything like Sampei, it would be an epoch-making discovery, and I'd tell all the cats in Japan about my experience. I felt I had to see what would happen so, leaving everything to fate, I stuck my tongue out again. It was difficult to drink with my eyes open so I shut them tight and began lapping up the beer again.

With great effort, I was finally able to drink a little more and then I felt a queer sensation. At first, my tongue burned and it seemed as if my cheeks were being pressed from outside. It was somewhat painful but, as I drank more, this feeling eased off. And when I had finished the glass, there was nothing painful about it any more. I knew it was safe now, so I drank the second glassful very easily. Then, just for good measure, I lapped up all the beer that had been spilled on the tray.

Then, in order to find out how I felt, I stayed in a crouched position for a while. Gradually, my body became warm. My eyelids began to swell. My ears became hot. I suddenly wanted to sing. I felt like dancing to the old folksong *E'en Though You Say 'Twas a Cat, 'Twas a Cat*. I felt like telling my master, Meitei, and Dokusen to go to hell. I wanted to scratch old man Kaneda; I wanted to bite off Mrs. Kaneda's nose; I wanted to do a lot of things. Finally, I wanted to stand up. And when I stood up I wanted to walk with a sway. Finding this great fun, I went outside. There I wanted to greet the moon good evening—*"Hai! Konban-wa!"* This was wonderful!

Realizing that this was what is called being gloriously drunk, I went aimlessly around as if taking a walk. Then again, it was as if I wasn't taking a walk. I took a few unsteady steps and became somewhat sleepy. I don't know myself whether I was sleeping or walking. I meant to keep my eyes open but they were extremely heavy. But I wasn't afraid of anything! I limply made one more step and then heard a splash.

Suddenly I was floating on some water. It was terribly disagreeable so I began to struggle but I could only claw at the water. I kicked with my hind feet and clawed with my forepaws. There was a grating sound. I had touched a solid object. My head only barely floated above the water but it was enough to see where I was. I had fallen into a clay rainbarrel. Now, this barrel had been filled with some water-shield plants during the summertime, but in early autumn, Kanko the crow came along and ate them all up. Afterwards he took a bath in the barrel. Since Kanko's first bath, much water had evaporated so the crow stopped coming. But I never dreamed that I would be taking a bath in the barrel instead of crow.

The water in the barrel was about five inches below the rim. No matter how far I stretched my paws I could not reach the top. Nor did jumping do any good. If I did nothing, I would sink. When I struggled, my claws would scratch the sides of the barrel and I'd feel for a moment as if I were floating a little. But right away I'd sink again. Going under water was a terrible feeling so I'd begin clawing again. Presently my body began to tire. I became bewildered and my paws would not work the way I wanted them to. Finally I didn't know whether I was clawing to sink or if I was sinking to claw.

The reason I was undergoing such terrible torment was only because I had wanted to climb on top of the barrel. Of course I now know it was impossible. My paws are less than three inches long. If I could have floated on the water and stretched my front paws as far as possible, I would have still been about two inches away from the rim. Since my claws could not hook onto the rim of the barrel, it would have made no difference whether I clawed, or if I became bewildered, or whether I simply worked myself to death—I couldn't make it. Knowing that I couldn't get out but still trying, I was attempting the impossible. And when attempting the impossible, the anguish is horrible. What nonsense! I was only prolonging my agony.

"I'm going to quit. Don't care what happens now." I then let my front paws relax, and then my hind legs, my head and my tail. I didn't resist any more.

Gradually I felt uncommonly comfortable. Could this feeling of thankfulness be agony? Was I still in the water or in the middle of a room? But of course it didn't make much difference where I was, or what I was doing. The only thing that counted was that I felt comfortable. Then I could hardly even feel this comfort. I'll cut the sun and the moon down from the sky. I'll pulverize the heaven and the earth. I am entering the mysterious but wonderful realm of peace!

I die.
I die and receive peace.
Peace cannot be had without dying.
Save us, merciful Buddha!
Save us, merciful Buddha!
Gracious blessings,
Gracious blessings.

—Translated from the Japanese by
Katsue Shibata and Motonari Kai

Part Six

CAT POETRY
IN
TRANSLATION

RAINER MARIA RILKE

Black Cat

A ghost, though invisible, still is like a place
your sight can knock on, echoing; but here
within this thick black pelt, your strongest gaze
will be absorbed and utterly disappear:

just as a raving madman, when nothing else
can ease him, charges into his dark night
howling, pounds on the padded wall, and feels
the rage being taken in and pacified.

She seems to hide all looks that have ever fallen
into her, so that, like an audience,
she can look them over, menacing and sullen,
and curl to sleep with them. But all at once

as if awakened, she turns her face to yours;
and with a shock, you see yourself, tiny,
inside the golden amber of her eyeballs
suspended, like a prehistoric fly.

—Translated from the German by Stephen Mitchell

CHARLES BAUDELAIRE

Cat

As if he owned the place, a cat
meanders through my mind,

sleek and proud, yet so discreet
    in making known his will

that I hear music when he mews,
    and even when he purrs
a tender timbre in the sound
    compels my consciousness—

a secret rhythm penetrates
    to unsuspected depths,
obsessive as a line of verse
    and potent as a drug:

all woes are spirited away,
    I hear ecstatic news—
it seems a telling language has
    no need of words at all.

My heart, assenting instrument,
    is masterfully played;
no other bow across its strings
    can draw such music out

the way this cat's uncanny voice
    —seraphic, alien—
can reconcile discordant strains
    into close harmony!

One night his brindled fur gave off
    a perfume so intense
I seemed to be embalmed because
    (just once!) I fondled him . . .

Familiar spirit, genius, judge,
    the cat presides—inspires
events that he appears to spurn,
    half goblin and half god!

and when my spellbound eyes at last
    relinquish worship of

this cat they love to contemplate
and look inside myself,

I find to my astonishment
like living opals there
his fiery pupils, embers which
observe me fixedly.

—Translated from the French by Richard Howard

CHARLES BAUDELAIRE

The Cat

Come here, kitty—sheathe your claws!
Lie on my loving heart
and let me sink into your eyes
of agate fused with steel.

When my fingers freely caress
your head and supple spine,
and my hand thrills to the touch
of your electric fur,

my mistress comes to mind. Her gaze—
cold and deep as yours,
my pet—is like a stab of pain,

and from head to heels
a subtle scent, a dangerous perfume,
rises from her brown flesh.

—Translated from the French by Richard Howard

CHARLES BAUDELAIRE

Cats

Lovers, scholars—the fervent, the austere—
grow equally fond of cats, their household pride.
As sensitive as either to the cold,
as sedentary, though so strong and sleek,

your cat, a friend to learning and to love,
seeks out both silence and the awesome dark . . .
Hell would have made the cat its courier
could it have controverted feline pride!

Dozing, all cats assume the svelte design
of desert sphinxes sprawled in solitude,
apparently transfixed by endless dreams;

their teeming loins are rich in magic sparks,
and golden specks like infinitesimal sand
glisten in those enigmatic eyes.

—Translated from the French by Richard Howard

PAUL VERLAINE

Woman and Cat

She was playing with her cat,
and it was marvelous to see
white hand and white paw, pitty-pat,
spar in the evening sportively.

The little wretch hid in her paws,
those black silk mittens, murderously,
the deadly agate of her claws,
keen as a razor's edge can be.

Her steel drawn in, the other seemed
all sugar, the sly hypocrite,
but the devil didn't lose a bit . . .

and in the room where, sonorous,
her airy laughter rang, there gleamed
four sharp points of phosphorous.

—Translated from the French by C. F. MacIntyre

PAUL VALÉRY

White Cats

To Albert Dugrip

In the clear gold of sunlight, stretching their backs,
—White as snow—see the voluptuous cats,
Closing eyes jealous of their inner glooms,
Slumbering in the tepid warmth of their illumined fur.

Their coats have the dazzle of dawn-bathed glaciers.
Inside them, their bodies, frail, sinewy, and slender,
Feel the shiverings of a girl inside her dress,
And their beauty refines itself in endless languors.

No question but their Soul of old has animated
The flesh of a philosopher, or a woman's body,
For since then their dazzling and inestimable whiteness

Holding the mingled splendor of a grand premiere,
Ennobles them to a rank of calm contempt,
Indifferent to everything but *Light* itself!

—Translated from the French by David Paul

HEINRICH HEINE

[Beware of Kittens]

Beware, my friend, of fiends and their grimaces;
  Of little angels' wiles yet more beware thee;
  Just such a one to kiss her did ensnare me,
But coming, I got wounds and not embraces.
Beware of black old cats, with evil faces;
  Yet more, of kittens white and soft be wary;
  My sweetheart was just such a little fairy,
And yet she well-nigh scratched my heart to pieces.
Oh child! oh sweet love, dear beyond all measure,
  How could those eyes, so bright and clear, deceive me?
  That little paw so sore a heart-wound give me?—
My kitten's tender paw, thou soft, small treasure—
  Oh! could I to my burning lips but press thee,
  My heart the while might bleed to death and bless thee.

—Translated from the German by Alma Strettell

HEINRICH HEINE

Young Tomcats' Society for Poetic Music

The Philharmonic Society
Of tomcats met tonight
Upon the roof—but not in heat,
And not to rut or fight.

No summer-night dreams of honeymoons,
No serenades will do
In wintertime when snow and ice
Freeze all the gutters through.

A newborn spirit's lately seized
The race of cats—ah, yes,
Young tomcats now are all agog
For Lofty Earnestness.

The old generation's flippancy
Dies out; new aims are rife—
A springtide of cat-poetry
Is stirring in art and life.

The Philharmonic Society
Of tomcats now believe
In artless music—primitive,
Self-sprouting, and naive.

They want poetic music now—
Roulades, not trills that pall,
Poetic instrument and voice—
Which isn't music at all.

They want the reign of genius, though
It may botch things outright,
But in the arts, oft unawares,
It soars to the greatest height.

They honor genius that stays close
To nature as its king,
That does not boast great learning, since
It hasn't learned a thing.

Such is the tomcats' program now,
Such are the aims they nursed;
And on the roof tonight they had
Their winter concert, the first.

Their aims were badly carried out,
Those grandiose views of theirs—
Go hang yourself, dear Berlioz,
For missing such affairs!

It was a loud uproar as if
Three dozen bagpipes played
A brandy-soaked fandango fling
Or a barnyard gallopade,

A jumbled din as if the beasts
On Noah's Ark had begun
To serenade the rising flood,
And all in unison.

What croaks and bawls and caterwauls,
What bellows of all sorts!
The drafty chimneys joined right in
With church chorales in snorts.

One voice rang clear above them all,
Somehow both shrill and wan,
Just like the voice that Sontag had
By the time her voice was gone.

Wild concert! A great paean sung
In utter impudence
To celebrate the victory
Of madness over sense.

Perhaps they were rehearsing there
An opera to beguile 'em
By Hungary's greatest pianist
For Charenton Asylum.

This witches' sabbath ended when
Day dawned on these domains;
It made a pregnant cook bed down
With premature labor pains.

This poor befuddled woman had
No memory any more;
She did not know the father of
The baby that she bore.

Say, Lisa, was it Peter? Paul?
The father—tell us that!—
She smiles, and beams, and then she says:
"O Liszt, divine tomcat!"

——Translated from the German by Alma Stettell

GEORGE SEFERIS

The Cats of Saint Nicholas

> But deep inside me sings
> the Fury's lyreless threnody;
> my heart, self-taught, has lost
> the precious confidence of hope . . .
> —Aeschylus, *Agamemnon*

"That's the Cape of Cats ahead," the captain said to me,
pointing through the mist to a low stretch of shore,
the beach deserted; it was Christmas day—
". . . and there, in the distance to the west, is where Aphrodite rose
   out of the waves;
they call the place 'Greek's Rock.'
Left ten degrees rudder!"
She had Salome's eyes, the cat I lost a year ago;
and old Ramazan, how he would look death square in the eyes,
whole days long in the snow of the East,
under the frozen sun,
days long square in the eyes: the young hearth god.
Don't stop, traveler.
"Left ten degrees rudder," muttered the helmsman.

. . . my friend, though, might well have stopped short,
now between ships,
shut up in a small house with pictures,
searching for windows behind the frames.
The ship's bell struck
like a coin from some vanished city
that brings to mind, as it falls,
alms from another time.
"It's strange," the captain said.
"That bell—given what day it is—
reminded me of another one, the monastery bell.

A monk told me the story,
a half-mad monk, a kind of dreamer.

"It was during the great drought,
forty years without rain,
the whole island devastated,
people dying and snakes giving birth.
This cape had millions of snakes
fat as a man's leg
and full of poison.
In those days the monastery of St. Nicholas
was held by the monks of St. Basil,
and they couldn't go out to work their fields,
couldn't put their flocks to pasture.
In the end they were saved by the cats they raised.
Every day at dawn a bell would strike
and an army of cats would move into battle.
They'd fight the day long,
until the bell sounded for the evening feed.
Supper done, the bell would sound again
and out they'd go to battle through the night.
They say it was a marvelous sight to see them,
some lame, some blind, others missing
a nose, an ear, their hides in shreds.
So to the sound of four bells a day
months went by, years, season after season.
Wildly obstinate, always wounded,
they annihilated the snakes; but in the end they disappeared;
they just couldn't take in that much poison.
Like a sunken ship
they left no trace on the surface:
not a meow, not even a bell.
Steady as you go!
Poor devils, what could they do,
fighting like that day and night, drinking
the poisonous blood of those snakes?
Generations of poison, centuries of poison."
"Steady as you go," indifferently echoed the helmsman.

—Translated from the Greek by Edmund Keeley

PABLO NERUDA

Cat

The animal kingdom came
faultily:
too wide in the rump or too
sad-headed.
Little by little they disposed
their proportions,
invented their landscape,
collected their graces and satellites, and took to the air.
Only the cat
issued
wholly a cat,
intact and vainglorious:
he came forth a consummate identity,
knew what he wanted, and walked tall.

Men wish they were fishes or birds;
the worm would be winged,
the dog is a dispossessed lion;
engineers would be poets;
flies ponder the swallow's prerogative
and pets impersonate flies—
but the cat
intends nothing but cat:
he is cat
from his tail to his chin whiskers:
from his living presumption of mouse
and the darkness, to the gold of his irises.

His is that peerless
integrity,
neither moonlight nor petal
repeats
his contexture:

he is all things in all,
like the sun or a topaz,
and the flexible line of his contour
is subtle and certain
as the cut of a bowsprit.
The gold of his pupils
leaves a singular
slash
and coins tumble out of the night.

Unorbed
little emperor,
landless conquistador,
minimal drawing-room tiger and conjugal
khan in a heaven
of aphrodisiacal rooftops:
you command
all the crosswinds of lust
in a hurricane,
you poise
your four delicate paws
on the ground
when you pass,
nosing the wind
and mistrusting
the universe,
as if
all were too gross
for a cat's incorruptible tread.

Wayward and proud
in the houses, a brazen
remainder of darkness,
torpid, gymnastic,
remote,
an unfathomed profundity,
secret police
of the tenements,
and emblem
of vanishing velvets,
your kind

need not puzzle us, surely—
you, the least of
the mysteries
abroad in the world, known to us all, the pawn
of the lowliest householder—
or they think so!—
for each calls himself master,
proprietor, playfellow,
cat's uncle,
colleague,
the pupils of cats
or their cronies.

Not I:
I reckon things otherwise.
I shall never unriddle the cat.
I take note of the other things: life's archipelagoes,
the sea, the incalculable city,
botanical matters,
the pistil, the pistil's mutations,
plus-and-minus arithmetic,
volcanoes that funnel the earth
the improbable rind of the crocodile,
the fireman's unheeded benevolence,
the atavist blue of the clergyman—
but never the cat!
We do not concern him: our reasoning boggles,
and his eyes give their numbers in gold.

—Translated from the Spanish by Ben Belitt

Part Seven

Contemporary Storytellers on Cats

JOYCE CAROL OATES

The White Cat

There was a gentleman of independent means who, at about the age of fifty-six, conceived of a passionate hatred for his much-younger wife's white Persian cat.

His hatred for the cat was all the more ironic, and puzzling, in that he himself had given the cat to his wife as a kitten, years ago, when they were first married. And he himself had named her— Miranda—after his favorite Shakespearean heroine.

It was ironic, too, in that he was hardly a man given to irrational sweeps of emotion. Except for his wife (whom he'd married late— his first marriage, her second) he did not love anyone very much, and would have thought it beneath his dignity to hate anyone. For whom should he take that seriously? Being a gentleman of independent means allowed him that independence of spirit unknown to the majority of men.

Julius Muir was of slender build, with deep-set somber eyes of no distinctive color; thinning, graying, baby-fine hair; and a narrow, lined face to which the adjective *lapidary* had once been applied, with no vulgar intention of mere flattery. Being of old American stock he was susceptible to none of the fashionable tugs and sways of "identity": He knew who he was, who his ancestors were, and thought the subject of no great interest. His studies both in America and abroad had been undertaken with a dilettante's rather than a scholar's pleasure, but he would not have wished to make too much of them. Life, after all, is a man's primary study.

Fluent in several languages, Mr. Muir had a habit of phrasing his words with inordinate care, as if he were translating them into a common vernacular. He carried himself with an air of discreet self-consciousness that had nothing in it of vanity, or pride, yet did not bespeak a pointless humility. He was a collector (primarily of rare books and coins), but he was certainly not an obsessive collector; he looked upon the fanaticism of certain of his fellows with a bemused disdain. So his quickly blossoming hatred for his wife's beautiful white cat surprised him, and for a time amused him. Or did it frighten him? Certainly he didn't know what to make of it!

The animosity began as an innocent sort of domestic irritation, a half-conscious sense that being so respected in public—so recognized as the person of quality and importance he assuredly was—he should warrant that sort of treatment at home. Not that he was naively ignorant of the fact that cats have a way of making their preferences known that lacks the subtlety and tact devised by human beings. But as the cat grew older and more spoiled and ever more choosy it became evident that she did not, for affection, choose *him*. Alissa was her favorite, of course; then one or another of the help; but it was not uncommon for a stranger, visiting the Muirs for the first time, to win or to appear to win Miranda's capricious heart. "Miranda! Come here!" Mr. Muir might call—gently enough, yet forcibly, treating the animal in fact with a silly sort of deference—but at such times Miranda was likely to regard him with indifferent, unblinking eyes and make no move in his direction. What a fool, she seemed to be saying, to court someone who cares so little for you!

If he tried to lift her in his arms—if he tried, with a show of playfulness, to subdue her—in true cat fashion she struggled to get down with as much violence as if a stranger had seized her. Once as she squirmed out of his grasp, she accidentally raked the back of his hand and drew blood that left a faint stain on the sleeve of his dinner jacket. "Julius, dear, are you hurt?" Alissa asked. "Not at all," Mr. Muir said, dabbing at the scratches with a handkerchief. "I think Miranda is excited because of the company," Alissa said. "You know how sensitive she is." "Indeed I do," Mr. Muir said mildly, winking at their guests. But a pulse beat hard in his head and he was thinking he would like to strangle the cat with his bare hands—were he the kind of man who was capable of such an act.

More annoying still was the routine nature of the cat's aversion to him. When he and Alissa sat together in the evening, reading, each at an end of their sofa, Miranda would frequently leap unbidden into Alissa's lap—but shrink fastidiously from Mr. Muir's very touch. He professed to be hurt. He professed to be amused. "I'm afraid

Miranda doesn't like me any longer," he said sadly. (Though in truth he could no longer remember if there'd been a time the creature *had* liked him. When she'd been a kitten, perhaps, and utterly indiscriminate in her affections?) Alissa laughed and said apologetically, "Of course she likes you, Julius," as the cat purred loudly and sensuously in her lap. "But—you know how cats are."

"Indeed, I am learning," Mr. Muir said with a stiff little smile.

And he felt he *was* learning—something to which he could give no name.

What first gave him the idea—the fancy, really—of killing Miranda, he could not have afterward said. One day, watching her rubbing about the ankles of a director-friend of his wife's, observing how wantonly she presented herself to an admiring little circle of guests (even people with a general aversion to cats could not resist exclaiming over Miranda—petting her, scratching her behind the ears, cooing over her like idiots), Mr. Muir found himself thinking that, as he had brought the cat into his household of his own volition and had paid a fair amount of money for her, she was his to dispose of as he wished. It was true that the full-blooded Persian was one of the prize possessions of the household—a household in which possessions were not acquired casually or cheaply—and it was true that Alissa adored her. But ultimately she belonged to Mr. Muir. And he alone had the power of life or death over her, did he not?

"What a beautiful animal! Is it a male or a female?"

Mr. Muir was being addressed by one of his guests (in truth, one of Alissa's guests; since returning to her theatrical career she had a new, wide, rather promiscuous circle of acquaintances) and for a moment he could not think how to answer. The question lodged deep in him as if it were a riddle: *Is it a male or a female?*

"Female, of course," Mr. Muir said pleasantly. "Its name after all is Miranda."

He wondered: Should he wait until Alissa began rehearsals for her new play—or should he act quickly, before his resolution faded? (Alissa, a minor but well-regarded actress, was to be an understudy for the female lead in a Broadway play opening in September.) And how should he do it? He could not strangle the cat—could not bring himself to act with such direct and unmitigated brutality—nor was it likely that he could run over her, as if accidentally, with the car. (Though *that* would have been fortuitous, indeed.) One midsummer evening when sly, silky Miranda insinuated herself onto the lap of Alissa's new friend Alban (actor, writer, director; his talents were evidently lavish) the conversation turned to notorious murder cases—to poisons—and Mr. Muir thought simply, *Of course. Poison.*

Next morning he poked about in the gardener's shed and found the remains of a ten-pound sack of grainy white "rodent" poison. The previous autumn they'd had a serious problem with mice, and their gardener had set out poison traps in the attic and basement of the house. (With excellent results, Mr. Muir surmised. At any rate, the mice had certainly disappeared.) What was ingenious about the poison was that it induced extreme thirst—so that after having devoured the bait the poisoned creature was driven to seek water, leaving the house and dying outside. Whether the poison was "merciful" or not, Mr. Muir did not know.

He was able to take advantage of the servants' Sunday night off—for as it turned out, though rehearsals for her play had not yet begun, Alissa was spending several days in the city. So Mr. Muir himself fed Miranda in a corner of the kitchen where she customarily ate—having mashed a generous teaspoon of the poison in with her usual food. (How spoiled the creature was! From the very first, when she was a seven-weeks' kitten, Miranda had been fed a special high-protein, high-vitamin cat food, supplemented by raw chopped liver, chicken giblets, and God knows what all else. Though as he ruefully had to admit, Mr. Muir had had a hand in spoiling her, too.)

Miranda ate the food with her usual finicky greed, not at all conscious of, or grateful for, her master's presence. He might have been one of the servants; he might have been no one at all. If she sensed something out of the ordinary—the fact that her water dish was taken away and not returned, for instance—like a true aristocrat she gave no sign. Had there ever been any creature of his acquaintance, human or otherwise, so supremely complacent as this white Persian cat?

Mr. Muir watched Miranda methodically poison herself with an air not of elation as he'd anticipated, not even with a sense of satisfaction in a wrong being righted, in justice being (however ambiguously) exacted—but with an air of profound regret. That the spoiled creature deserved to die he did not doubt; for after all, what incalculable cruelties, over a lifetime, must a cat afflict on birds, mice, rabbits! But it struck him as a melancholy thing, that *he*, Julius Muir—who had paid so much for her, and who in fact had shared in the pride of her—should find himself out of necessity in the role of executioner. But it was something that had to be done, and though he had perhaps forgotten why it had to be done, he knew that he and he alone was destined to do it.

The other evening a number of guests had come to dinner, and as they were seated on the terrace Miranda leapt whitely up out of nowhere to make her way along the garden wall—plumelike tail erect, silky ruff floating about her high-held head, golden eyes gleaming—quite as if on cue, as Alissa said. "This is Miranda, come to say hello to you! *Isn't* she beautiful!" Alissa happily exclaimed. (For she seemed never to tire of remarking upon her cat's beauty —an innocent sort of narcissism, Mr. Muir supposed.) The usual praise, or flattery, was aired; the cat preened herself—fully conscious of being the center of attention—then leapt away with a violent sort of grace and disappeared down the steep stone steps to the river embankment. Mr. Muir thought then that he understood why Miranda was so uncannily *interesting* as a phenomenon: She represented a beauty that was both purposeless and necessary; a beauty that was (considering her pedigree) completely an artifice, and yet (considering she *was* a thing of flesh and blood) completely natural: Nature.

Though was Nature always and invariably—*natural*?

Now, as the white cat finished her meal (leaving a good quarter of it in the dish, as usual), Mr. Muir said aloud, in a tone in which infinite regret and satisfaction were commingled, "But beauty won't save you."

The cat paused to look up at him with her flat, unblinking gaze. He felt an instant's terror: Did she know? Did she know—already? It seemed to him that she had never looked more splendid: fur so purely, silkily white; ruff full as if recently brushed; the petulant pug face; wide, stiff whiskers; finely shaped ears so intelligently erect. And, of course, the eyes . . .

He'd always been fascinated by Miranda's eyes, which were a tawny golden hue, for they had the mysterious capacity to flare up, as if at will. Seen at night, of course—by way of the moon's reflection, or the headlights of the Muirs' own homebound car—they were lustrous as small beams of light. "Is that Miranda, do you think?" Alissa would ask, seeing the twin flashes of light in the tall grass bordering the road. "Possibly," Mr. Muir would say. "Ah, she's waiting for us! Isn't that sweet! She's waiting for us to come home!" Alissa would exclaim with childlike excitement. Mr. Muir—who doubted that the cat had even been aware of their absence, let alone eagerly awaited their return—said nothing.

Another thing about the cat's eyes that had always seemed to Mr. Muir somehow perverse was the fact that, while the human eyeball is uniformly white and the iris colored, a cat eyeball is colored and the iris purely black. Green, yellow, gray, even blue—the entire eyeball! And the iris so magically responsive to gradations of light or excitation, contracting to razor-thin slits, dilating blackly to fill almost the entire eye . . . As she stared up at him now her eyes were so dilated their color was nearly eclipsed.

"No, beauty can't save you. It isn't enough," Mr. Muir said quietly. With trembling fingers he opened the screen door to let the cat out into the night. As she passed him—perverse creature, indeed! —she rubbed lightly against his leg as she had not done for many months. Or had it been years?

Alissa was twenty years Mr. Muir's junior but looked even younger: a petite woman with very large, very pretty brown eyes; shoulder-length blond hair; the upbeat if sometimes rather frenetic manner of a well-practiced ingenue. She was a minor actress with a minor ambition—as she freely acknowledged—for after all, serious professional acting is brutally hard work, even if one somehow manages to survive the competition.

"And then, of course, Julius takes such good care of me," she would say, linking her arm through his or resting her head for a moment against his shoulder. "I have everything I want, really, right here . . ." By which she meant the country place Mr. Muir had bought for her when they were married. (Of course they also kept an apartment in Manhattan, two hours to the south. But Mr. Muir had grown to dislike the city—it abraded his nerves like a cat's claws raking against a screen—and rarely made the journey in any longer.) Under her maiden name, Howth, Alissa had been employed intermittently for eight years before marrying Mr. Muir; her first marriage— contracted at the age of nineteen to a well-known (and notorious) Hollywood actor, since deceased—had been a disaster of which she cared not to speak in any detail. (Nor did Mr. Muir care to question her about those years. It was as if, for him, they had not existed.)

At the time of their meeting Alissa was in temporary retreat, as she called it, from her career. She'd had a small success on Broadway but the success had not taken hold. And was it worth it, really, to keep going, to keep trying? Season after season, the grinding round of auditions, the competition with new faces, "promising" new talents . . . Her first marriage had ended badly and she'd had a number of love affairs of varying degrees of worth (precisely how many Mr. Muir was never to learn), and now perhaps it was time to ease into private life. And there was Julius Muir: not young, not particularly charming, but well-to-do, and well-bred, and besotted with love for her, and—*there*.

Of course Mr. Muir was dazzled by her; and he had the time and the resources to court her more assiduously than any man had ever courted her. He seemed to see in her qualities no one else saw; his imagination, for so reticent and subdued a man, was rich, lively to the point of fever, immensely flattering. And he did not mind, he extravagantly insisted, that he loved her more than she loved him —even as Alissa protested she *did* love him—would she consent to marry him otherwise?

For a few years they spoke vaguely of "starting a family," but nothing came of it. Alissa was too busy, or wasn't in ideal health; or they were traveling; or Mr. Muir worried about the unknown effect a child would have upon their marriage. (Alissa would have less time for him, surely?) As time passed he vexed himself with the thought that he'd have no heir when he died—that is, no child of his own— but there was nothing to be done.

They had a rich social life; they were wonderfully *busy* people. And they had, after all, their gorgeous white Persian cat. "Miranda would be traumatized if there was a baby in the household," Alissa said. "We really couldn't do that to her."

"Indeed we couldn't," Mr. Muir agreed.

And then, abruptly, Alissa decided to return to acting. To her "career" as she gravely called it—as if it were a phenomenon apart from her, a force not to be resisted. And Mr. Muir was happy for her—very happy for her. He took pride in his wife's professionalism, and he wasn't at all jealous of her ever-widening circle of friends, acquaintances, associates. He wasn't jealous of her fellow actors and actresses—Rikka, Mario, Robin, Sibyl, Emile, each in turn—and now Alban of the damp dark shiny eyes and quick sweet smile; nor was he jealous of the time she spent away from home; nor, if home, of the time she spent sequestered away in the room they called her studio, deeply absorbed in her work. In her maturity Alissa Howth had acquired a robust sort of good-heartedness that gave her more stage presence even as it relegated her to certain sorts of roles—

the roles inevitable, in any case, for older actresses, regardless of their physical beauty. And she'd become a far better, far more subtle actress—as everyone said.

Indeed, Mr. Muir *was* proud of her, and happy for her. And if he felt, now and then, a faint resentment—or, if not quite resentment, a tinge of regret at the way their life had diverged into lives—he was too much a gentleman to show it.

"Where is Miranda? Have you seen Miranda today?"

It was noon, it was four o'clock, it was nearly dusk, and Miranda had not returned. For much of the day Alissa had been preoccupied with telephone calls—the phone seemed always to be ringing—and only gradually had she become aware of the cat's prolonged absence. She went outside to call her; she sent the servants out to look for her. And Mr. Muir, of course, gave his assistance, wandering about the grounds and for some distance into the woods, his hands cupped to his mouth and his voice high-pitched and tremulous: "*Kitty-kitty-kitty-kitty-kitty! Kitty-kitty-kitty*—" How pathetic, how foolish—how futile! Yet it had to be performed since it was what, in innocent circumstances, *would* be performed. Julius Muir, that most solicitous of husbands, tramping through the underbrush looking for his wife's Persian cat . . .

Poor Alissa! he thought. She'll be heartbroken for days—or would it be weeks?

And he, too, would miss Miranda—as a household presence at the very least. They would have had her, after all, for ten years this autumn.

Dinner that night was subdued, rather leaden. Not simply because Miranda was missing (and Alissa did seem inordinately and genuinely worried), but because Mr. Muir and his wife were dining alone; the table, set for two, seemed almost aesthetically wrong. And how unnatural, the quiet . . . Mr. Muir tried to make conversation but his voice soon trailed off into a guilty silence. Midmeal Alissa rose to accept a telephone call (from Manhattan, of course—her agent, or her director, or Alban, or a female friend—an urgent call, for otherwise Mrs. Muir did not accept calls at this intimate hour) and Mr. Muir—crestfallen, hurt—finished his solitary meal in a kind of trance, tasting nothing. He recalled the night before—the pungent-smelling cat food, the grainy white poison, the way the shrewd animal had looked up at him, and the way she'd brushed against his leg in a belated gesture of . . . was it affection? Reproach?

Mockery? He felt a renewed stab of guilt, and an even more powerful stab of visceral satisfaction. Then, glancing up, he chanced to see something white making its careful way along the top of the garden wall . . .

Of course it was Miranda come home.

He stared, appalled. He stared, speechless—waiting for the apparition to vanish.

Slowly, in a daze, he rose to his feet. In a voice meant to be jubilant he called out the news to Alissa in the adjoining room: "Miranda's come home!"

He called out: "Alissa! Darling! Miranda's come home!"

And there Miranda was, indeed; indeed it *was* Miranda, peering into the dining room from the terrace, her eyes glowing tawny gold. Mr. Muir was trembling, but his brain worked swiftly to absorb the fact, and to construe a logic to accommodate it. She'd vomited up the poison, no doubt. Ah, no doubt! Or, after a cold, damp winter in the gardener's shed, the poison had lost its efficacy.

He had yet to bestir himself, to hurry to unlatch the sliding door and let the white cat in, but his voice fairly quavered with excitement: "Alissa! Good news! Miranda's come home!"

Alissa's joy was so extreme and his own initial relief so genuine that Mr. Muir—stroking Miranda's plume of a tail as Alissa hugged the cat ecstatically in her arms—thought he'd acted cruelly, selfishly—certainly he'd acted out of character—and decided that Miranda, having escaped death at her master's hands, should be granted life. He would *not* try another time.

Before his marriage at the age of forty-six Julius Muir, like most never-married men and women of a certain temperament—introverted, self-conscious; observers of life rather than participants—had believed that the marital state was unconditionally *marital*; he'd thought that husband and wife were one flesh in more than merely the metaphorical sense of that term. Yet it happened that his own marriage was a marriage of a decidedly diminished sort. Marital relations had all but ceased, and there seemed little likelihood of their being resumed. He would shortly be fifty-seven years old, after all. (Though sometimes he wondered: Was that truly *old*?)

During the first two or three years of their marriage (when Alissa's theatrical career was, as she called it, in eclipse), they had shared a double bed like any married couple—or so Mr. Muir assumed. (For his own marriage had not enlightened him to what "marriage" in a generic sense meant.) With the passage of time, however, Alissa began to complain gently of being unable to sleep because of Mr. Muir's nocturnal "agitation"—twitching, kicking, thrashing about, exclaiming aloud, sometimes even shouting in terror. Wakened by her he would scarcely know, for a moment or two, where he was; he would then apologize profusely and shamefully, and creep away into another bedroom to sleep, if he could, for the rest of the night. Though unhappy with the situation, Mr. Muir was fully sympathetic with Alissa; he even had reason to believe that the poor woman (whose nerves were unusually sensitive) had suffered many a sleepless night on his account without telling him. It was like her to be so considerate; so loath to hurt another's feelings.

As a consequence they developed a cozy routine in which Mr. Muir spent a half-hour or so with Alissa when they first retired for the night; then, taking care not to disturb her, he would tiptoe quietly away into another room, where he might sleep undisturbed. (If, indeed, his occasional nightmares allowed him undisturbed sleep. He rather thought the worst ones, however, were the ones that failed to wake him.)

Yet a further consequence had developed in recent years: Alissa had acquired the habit of staying awake late—reading in bed, or watching television, or even, from time to time, chatting on the telephone—so it was most practical for Mr. Muir simply to kiss her good-night without getting in bed beside her, and then to go off to his own bedroom. Sometimes in his sleep he imagined Alissa was calling him back—awakened, he would hurry out into the darkened corridor to stand by her door for a minute or two, eager and hopeful. At such times he dared not raise his voice above a whisper: "Alissa? Alissa, dearest? Did you call me?"

Just as unpredictable and capricious as Mr. Muir's bad dreams were the nighttime habits of Miranda, who at times would cozily curl up at the foot of Alissa's bed and sleep peacefully through to dawn, but at other times would insist upon being let outside, no matter that Alissa loved her to sleep on the bed. There was comfort of a kind—childish, Alissa granted—in knowing the white Persian was there through the night, and feeling at her feet the cat's warm, solid weight atop the satin coverlet.

But of course, as Alissa acknowledged, a cat can't be forced to do anything against her will. "It seems almost to be a law of nature," she said solemnly.

———

A few days after the abortive poisoning Mr. Muir was driving home in the early dusk when, perhaps a mile from his estate, he caught sight of the white cat in the road ahead—motionless in the other lane, as if frozen by the car's headlights. Unbidden, the thought came to him: *This is just to frighten her*—and he turned his wheel and headed in her direction. The golden eyes flared up in a blaze of blank surprise—or perhaps it was terror, or recognition—*This is just to redress the balance*, Mr. Muir thought as he pressed down harder on the accelerator and drove directly at the white Persian— and struck her, just as she started to bolt toward the ditch, with the front left wheel of his car. There was a thud and a cat's yowling, incredulous scream—and it was done.

My God! It *was* done!

Dry mouthed, shaking, Mr. Muir saw in his rearview mirror the broken white form in the road; saw a patch of liquid crimson blossoming out around it. He had not meant to kill Miranda, and yet he had actually done it this time—without premeditation, and therefore without guilt.

And now the deed was done forever.

"And no amount of remorse can undo it," he said in a slow, wondering voice.

Mr. Muir had driven to the village to pick up a prescription for Alissa at the drugstore—she'd been in the city on theater matters; had returned home late on a crowded commuter train and gone at once to lie down with what threatened to be a migraine headache. Now he felt rather a hypocrite, a brute, presenting headache tablets to his wife with the guilty knowledge that if she knew what he'd done, the severity of her migraine would be tenfold. Yet how could he have explained to her that he had not meant to kill Miranda this time, but the steering wheel of his car had seemed to act of its own volition, wresting itself from his grip? For so Mr. Muir—speeding home, still trembling and excited as though he himself had come close to violent death—remembered the incident.

He remembered too the cat's hideous scream, cut off almost at once by the impact of the collision—but not quite at once.

And was there a dent in the fender of the handsome, English-built car? There was not.

And were there bloodstains on the left front tire? There were not.

Was there in fact any sign of a mishap, even of the mildest, most innocent sort? There was not.

"No proof! No proof!" Mr. Muir told himself happily, taking the stairs to Alissa's room two at a time. It was a matter of some relief as well when he raised his hand to knock at the door to hear that Alissa was evidently feeling better. She was on the telephone, talking animatedly with someone; even laughing in her light, silvery way that reminded him of nothing so much as wind chimes on a mild summer's night. His heart swelled with love and gratitude. "Dear Alissa—we will be so happy from now on!"

Then it happened, incredibly, that at about bedtime the white cat showed up again. *She had not died after all.*

Mr. Muir, who was sharing a late-night brandy with Alissa in her bedroom, was the first to see Miranda: She had climbed up onto the roof—by way, probably, of a rose trellis she often climbed for that purpose—and now her pug face appeared at one of the windows in a hideous repetition of the scene some nights ago. Mr. Muir sat paralyzed with shock, and it was Alissa who jumped out of bed to let the cat in.

"Miranda! What a trick! What *are* you up to?"

Certainly the cat had not been missing for any worrisome period of time, yet Alissa greeted her with as much enthusiasm as if she had. And Mr. Muir—his heart pounding in his chest and his very soul convulsed with loathing—was obliged to go along with the charade. He hoped Alissa would not notice the sick terror that surely shone in his eyes.

The cat he'd struck with his car must have been another cat, not Miranda . . . Obviously it had not been Miranda. Another white Persian with tawny eyes, and not his own.

Alissa cooed over the creature, and petted her, and encouraged her to settle down on the bed for the night, but after a few minutes Miranda jumped down and scratched to be let out the door: She'd missed her supper; she was hungry; she'd had enough of her mistress's affection. Not so much as a glance had she given her master, who was staring at her with revulsion. He knew now that he *must* kill her—if only to prove he could do it.

Following this episode the cat shrewdly avoided Mr. Muir—not out of lazy indifference, as in the past, but out of a sharp sense of their altered relations. She could not be conscious, he knew, of the fact that he had tried to kill her—but she must have been able to sense it. Perhaps she had been hiding in the bushes by the road and had seen him aim his car at her unfortunate doppelgänger, and run it down . . .

This was unlikely, Mr. Muir knew. Indeed, it was highly improbable. But how otherwise to account for the creature's behavior in his presence—her demonstration, or simulation, of animal fear? Leaping atop a cabinet when he entered a room, as if to get out of his way; leaping atop a fireplace mantel (and sending, it seemed deliberately, one of his carved jade figurines to the hearth, where it shattered into a dozen pieces); skittering gracelessly through a doorway, her sharp toenails clicking against the hardwood floor. When, without intending to, he approached her out-of-doors, she was likely to scamper noisily up one of the rose trellises, or the grape arbor, or a tree; or run off into the shrubbery like a wild creature. If Alissa happened to be present she was invariably astonished, for the cat's behavior *was* senseless. "Do you think Miranda is ill?" she asked. "Should we take her to the veterinarian?" Mr. Muir said uneasily that he doubted they would be able to catch her for such a purpose—at least, he doubted *he* could.

He had an impulse to confess his crime, or his attempted crime, to Alissa. He had killed the hateful creature—*and she had not died.*

One night at the very end of August Mr. Muir dreamt of glaring, disembodied eyes. And in their centers those black, black irises like old-fashioned keyholes: slots opening into the Void. He could not move to protect himself. A warm, furry weight settled luxuriantly upon his chest . . . upon his very face! The cat's whiskery white muzzle pressed against his mouth in a hellish kiss and in an instant the breath was being sucked from him . . .

"Oh, no! Save me! Dear God—"

The damp muzzle against his mouth, sucking his life's breath from him, and he could not move to tear it away—his arms, leaden at his sides; his entire body struck dumb, paralyzed . . .

"Save me . . . *save me!*"

His shouting, his panicked thrashing about in the bedclothes, woke him. Though he realized at once it had been only a dream, his breath still came in rapid, shallow gasps, and his heart hammered so violently he was in terror of dying: Had not his doctor only the other week spoken gravely to him of imminent heart disease, the possibility of heart failure? And how mysterious it was, his blood pressure being so very much higher than ever before in his life . . .

Mr. Muir threw himself out of the damp, tangled bedclothes and switched on a lamp with trembling fingers. Thank God he was alone and Alissa had not witnessed this latest display of nerves!

"Miranda?" he whispered. "Are you in here?"

He switched on an overhead light. The bedroom shimmered with shadows and did not seem, for an instant, any room he knew.

"Miranda . . . ?"

The sly, wicked creature! The malevolent beast! To think that cat's muzzle had touched his very lips, the muzzle of an animal that devoured mice, rats—any sort of foul filthy thing out in the woods! Mr. Muir went into his bathroom and rinsed out his mouth even as he told himself calmly that the dream had been only a dream, and the cat only a phantasm, and that of course Miranda was *not* in his room.

Still, she had settled her warm, furry, unmistakable weight on his chest. She had attempted to suck his breath from him, to choke him, suffocate him, stop his poor heart. *It was within her power.* "Only a dream," Mr. Muir said aloud, smiling shakily at his reflection in the mirror. (Oh! To think that pale, haggard apparition was indeed *his* . . .) Mr. Muir raised his voice with scholarly precision. "A foolish dream. A child's dream. A woman's dream."

Back in his room he had the fleeting sense that something—a vague white shape—had just now scampered beneath his bed. But when he got down on his hands and knees to look, of course there was nothing.

He did, however, discover in the deep-pile carpet a number of cat hairs. White, rather stiff—quite clearly Miranda's. Ah, quite clearly. "Here's the evidence!" he said excitedly. He found a light scattering of them on the carpet near the door and, nearer his bed, a good deal more—as if the creature had lain there for a while and had even rolled over (as Miranda commonly did out on the terrace in the sun) and stretched her graceful limbs in an attitude of utterly pleasurable abandon. Mr. Muir had often been struck by the cat's remarkable *luxuriance* at such times: a joy of flesh (and fur) he could not begin to imagine. Even before relations between them had deteriorated, he had felt the impulse to hurry to the cat and bring the heel of his shoe down hard on that tender, exposed, pinkish-pale belly . . .

"Miranda? Where are you? Are you still in here?" Mr. Muir said. He was breathless, excited. He'd been squatting on his haunches for some minutes, and when he tried to straighten up his legs ached.

Mr. Muir searched the room, but it was clear that the white cat had gone. He went out onto his balcony, leaned against the railing, blinked into the dimly moonlit darkness, but could see nothing—in his fright he'd forgotten to put on his glasses. For some minutes he breathed in the humid, sluggish night air in an attempt to calm himself, but it soon became apparent that something was wrong. Some vague murmurous undertone of—was it a voice? Voices?

Then he saw it: the ghostly white shape down in the shrubbery. Mr. Muir blinked and stared, but his vision was unreliable. "Miranda . . . ?" A scuttling noise rustled above him and he turned to see another white shape on the sharp-slanted roof making its rapid way over the top. He stood absolutely motionless—whether out of terror or cunning, he could not have said. That there was more than one white cat, more than one white Persian—more, in fact, than *merely one Miranda*—was a possibility he had not considered! "Yet perhaps that explains it," he said. He was badly frightened, but his brain functioned as clearly as ever.

It was not so very late, scarcely 1:00 A.M. The undertone Mr. Muir heard was Alissa's voice, punctuated now and then by her light, silvery laughter. One might almost think there was someone in the bedroom with her—but of course she was merely having a late-night telephone conversation, very likely with Alban—they would be chatting companionably, with an innocent sort of malice, about their co-actors and -actresses, mutual friends and acquaintances. Alissa's balcony opened out onto the same side of the house that Mr. Muir's did, which accounted for her voice (or *was* it voices? Mr. Muir listened, bemused) carrying so clearly. No light irradiated from her room; she must have been having her telephone conversation in the dark.

Mr. Muir waited another few minutes, but the white shape down in the shrubbery had vanished. And the slate-covered roof overhead was empty, reflecting moonlight in dull, uneven patches. He was alone. He decided to go back to bed but before doing so he checked carefully to see that he *was* alone. He locked all the windows, and the door, and slept with the lights on—but so deeply and with such grateful abandon that in the morning, it was Alissa's rapping on the door that woke him. "Julius? Julius? Is something wrong, dear?" she cried. He saw with astonishment that it was *nearly noon*: He'd slept four hours past his usual rising time!

Alissa said good-bye to him hurriedly. A limousine was coming to carry her to the city; she was to be away for several nights in succession; she was concerned about him, about his health, and hoped there was nothing wrong . . . "Of course there is nothing wrong," Mr. Muir said irritably. Having slept so late in the day left him feeling sluggish and confused; it had not at all refreshed him. When Alissa kissed him good-bye he seemed rather to suffer the kiss than to participate in it, and after she had gone he had to resist an impulse to wipe his mouth with the back of his hand.

"God help us!" he whispered.

By degrees, as a consequence of his troubled mind, Mr. Muir had lost interest in collecting. When an antiquarian bookdealer offered him a rare octavo edition of the *Directorium Inquisitorum* he felt only the mildest tinge of excitement, and allowed the treasure to be snatched up by a rival collector. Only a few days afterward he responded with even less enthusiasm when offered the chance to bid on a quarto Gothic edition of Machiavelli's *Belfagor*. "Is something wrong, Mr. Muir?" the dealer asked him. (They had been doing business together for a quarter of a century.) Mr. Muir said ironically, "*Is* something wrong?" and broke off the telephone connection. He was never to speak to the man again.

Yet more decisively, Mr. Muir had lost interest in financial affairs. He would not accept telephone calls from the various Wall Street gentlemen who managed his money; it was quite enough for him to know that the money was there and would always be there. Details regarding it struck him as tiresome and vulgar.

In the third week of September the play in which Alissa was an understudy opened to superlative reviews, which meant a good, long run. Though the female lead was in excellent health and showed little likelihood of ever missing a performance, Alissa felt obliged to remain in the city a good deal, sometimes for a full week at a time. (What she did there, how she busied herself day after day, evening after evening, Mr. Muir did not know and was too proud to ask.) When she invited him to join her for a weekend (why didn't he visit some of his antiquarian dealers, as he used to do with such pleasure?) Mr. Muir said simply, "But why, when I have all I require for happiness here in the country?"

Since the night of the attempted suffocation Mr. Muir and Miranda were yet more keenly aware of each other. No longer did the white cat flee his presence; rather, as if in mockery of him, she held her ground when he entered a room. If he approached her she eluded him only at the last possible instant, often flattening herself close against the floor and scampering, snakelike, away. He cursed her;

she bared her teeth and hissed. He laughed loudly to show her how very little he cared; she leapt atop a cabinet, out of his reach, and settled into a cat's blissful sleep. Each evening Alissa called at an appointed hour; each evening she inquired after Miranda, and Mr. Muir would say, "Beautiful and healthy as ever! A pity you can't see her!"

With the passage of time Miranda grew bolder and more reckless—misjudging, perhaps, the quickness of her master's reflexes. She sometimes appeared underfoot, nearly tripping him on the stairs or as he left the house; she dared approach him as he stood with a potential weapon in hand—a carving knife, a poker, a heavy, leatherbound book. Once or twice, as Mr. Muir sat dreaming through one of his solitary meals, she even leapt onto his lap and scampered across the dining room table, upsetting dishes and glasses. "Devil!" he shrieked, swiping in her wake with his fists. "What do you want of me!"

He wondered what tales the servants told of him, whispered backstairs. He wondered if any were being relayed to Alissa in the city.

One night, however, Miranda made a tactical error, and Mr. Muir did catch hold of her. She had slipped into his study—where he sat examining some of his rarest and most valuable coins (Mesopotamian, Etruscan) by lamplight—having calculated, evidently, on making her escape by way of the door. But Mr. Muir, leaping from his chair with extraordinary, almost feline swiftness, managed to kick the door shut. And now what a chase! What a struggle! What a mad frolic! Mr. Muir caught hold of the animal, lost her, caught hold of her again, lost her; she raked him viciously on the backs of both hands and on his face; he managed to catch hold of her again, slamming her against the wall and closing his bleeding fingers around her throat. He squeezed, he squeezed! He had her now and no force on earth could make him release her! As the cat screamed and clawed and kicked and thrashed and seemed to be suffering the convulsions of death, Mr. Muir crouched over her with eyes bulging and mad as her own. The arteries in his forehead visibly throbbed. "Now! Now I have you! Now!" he cried. And at that very moment when, surely, the white Persian was on the verge of extinction, the door to Mr. Muir's study was flung open and one of the servants appeared, white faced and incredulous: "Mr. Muir? What is it? We heard such—" the fool was saying; and of course Miranda slipped from Mr. Muir's loosened grasp and bolted from the room.

After that incident Mr. Muir seemed resigned to the knowledge that he would never have such an opportunity again. The end was swiftly approaching.

It happened quite suddenly, in the second week of November, that Alissa returned home.

She had quit the play; she had quit the "professional stage"; she did not even intend, as she told her husband vehemently, to visit New York City for a long time.

He saw to his astonishment that she'd been crying. Her eyes were unnaturally bright and seemed smaller than he recalled. And her prettiness looked worn, as if another face—harder, of smaller dimensions—were pushing through. Poor Alissa! She had gone away with such hope! When Mr. Muir moved to embrace her, however, meaning to comfort her, she drew away from him; her very nostrils pinched as if she found the smell of him offensive. "Please," she said, not looking him in the eye. "I don't feel well. What I want most is to be alone . . . just to be alone."

She retired to her room, to her bed. For several days she remained sequestered there, admitting only one of the female servants and, of course, her beloved Miranda, when Miranda condescended to visit the house. (To his immense relief Mr. Muir observed that the white cat showed no sign of their recent struggle. His lacerated hands and face were slow to heal, but in her own grief and self-absorption, Alissa seemed not to have noticed.)

In her room, behind her locked door, Alissa made a number of telephone calls to New York City. Often she seemed to be weeping over the phone. But so far as Mr. Muir could determine—being forced, under these special circumstances, to eavesdrop on the line —none of her conversations were with Alban.

Which meant . . . ? He had to confess he had no idea; nor could he ask Alissa. For that would give away the fact that he'd been eavesdropping, and she would be deeply shocked.

Mr. Muir sent small bouquets of autumn flowers to Alissa's sick-room; bought her chocolates and bonbons, slender volumes of poetry, a new diamond bracelet. Several times he presented himself at her door, ever the eager suitor, but she explained that she was not prepared to see him just yet—not just yet. Her voice was shrill and edged with a metallic tone Mr. Muir had not heard before.

"Don't you love me, Alissa?" he cried suddenly.

There was a moment's embarrassed silence. Then: "Of course I do. But please go away and leave me alone."

So worried was Mr. Muir about Alissa that he could no longer sleep for more than an hour or two at a time, and these hours were characterized by tumultuous dreams. The white cat! The hideous smothering weight! Fur in his very mouth! Yet awake he thought only of Alissa and of how, though she had come home to him, it was not in fact to *him*.

He lay alone in his solitary bed, amidst the tangled bedclothes, weeping hoarsely. One morning he stroked his chin and touched bristles: He'd neglected to shave for several days.

From his balcony he chanced to see the white cat preening atop the garden wall, a larger creature than he recalled. She had fully recovered from his attack. (If, indeed, she had been injured by it. If, indeed, the cat on the garden wall was the selfsame cat that had blundered into his study.) Her white fur very nearly blazed in the sun; her eyes were miniature golden-glowing coals set deep in her skull. Mr. Muir felt a mild shock seeing her: What a beautiful creature!

Though in the next instant, of course, he realized what she was.

One rainy, gusty evening in late November Mr. Muir was driving on the narrow blacktop road above the river, Alissa silent at his side—stubbornly silent, he thought. She wore a black cashmere cloak and a hat of soft black felt that fitted her head tightly, covering most of her hair. These were items of clothing Mr. Muir had not seen before, and in their stylish austerity they suggested the growing distance between them. When he had helped her into the car she'd murmured "thank you" in a tone that indicated "Oh! Must you touch me?" And Mr. Muir had made a mocking little bow, standing bareheaded in the rain.

And I had loved you so much.

Now she did not speak. Sat with her lovely profile turned from him. As if she were fascinated by the lashing rain, the river pocked and heaving below, the gusts of wind that rocked the English-built car as Mr. Muir pressed his foot ever harder on the gas pedal. "It will be better this way, my dear wife," Mr. Muir said quietly. "Even if you love no other man, it is painfully clear that you do not love me." At these solemn words Alissa started guiltily, but still would not face him. "My dear? Do you understand? It will be better this way—do not be frightened." As Mr. Muir drove faster, as the car rocked more violently in the wind, Alissa pressed her hands against her mouth as if to stifle any protest; she was staring transfixed—as Mr. Muir stared transfixed—at the rushing pavement.

Only when Mr. Muir bravely turned the car's front wheels in the direction of a guardrail did her resolve break: She emitted a series of breathless little screams, shrinking back against the seat, but made no effort to seize his arm or the wheel. And in an instant all was over, in any case—the car crashed through the railing, seemed to spin in midair, dropped to the rock-strewn hillside and bursting into flame, turned end over end . . .

He was seated in a chair with wheels—a wheeled chair! It seemed to him a remarkable invention and he wondered whose ingenuity lay behind it.

Though he had not the capacity, being almost totally paralyzed, to propel it of his own volition.

And, being blind, he had no volition in any case! He was quite content to stay where he was, so long as it was out of the draft. (The invisible room in which he now resided was, for the most part, cozily heated—his wife had seen to that—but there yet remained unpredictable currents of cold air that assailed him from time to time. His bodily temperature, he feared, could not maintain its integrity against any sustained onslaught.)

He had forgotten the names for many things and felt no great grief. Indeed, not knowing *names* relaxes one's desire for the *things* that, ghostlike, forever unattainable, dwell behind them. And of course his blindness had much to do with this—for which he was grateful! Quite grateful!

Blind, yet not wholly blind: for he could see (indeed, could not *not* see) washes of white, gradations of white, astonishing subtleties of white like rivulets in a stream perpetually breaking and falling about his head, not distinguished by any form or outline or vulgar suggestion of an object in space . . .

He had had, evidently, a number of operations. How many he did not know; nor did he care to know. In recent weeks they had spoken earnestly to him of the possibility of yet another operation on his brain, the (hypothetical) object being, if he understood correctly, the restoration of his ability to move some of the toes on his left foot. Had he the capacity to laugh he would have laughed, but perhaps his dignified silence was preferable.

Alissa's sweet voice joined with the others in a chorus of bleak enthusiasm, but so far as he knew the operation had never taken place. Or if it had, it had not been a conspicuous success. The toes of his left foot were as remote and lost to him as all the other parts of his body.

"How lucky you were, Julius, that another car came along! Why, you might have *died*!"

It seemed that Julius Muir had been driving alone in a violent thunderstorm on the narrow River Road, high above the embankment; uncharacteristically, he'd been driving at a high speed; he'd lost control of his car, crashed through the inadequate guardrail, and over the side . . . "miraculously" thrown clear of the burning wreckage. Two-thirds of the bones in his slender body broken, skull severely fractured, spinal column smashed, a lung pierced . . . So the story of how Julius had come to this place, his final resting place, this place of milk-white peace, emerged, in fragments shattered and haphazard as those of a smashed windshield.

"Julius, dear? Are you awake, or—?" The familiar, resolutely cheerful voice came to him out of the mist, and he tried to attach a name to it, *Alissa*? or, no, *Miranda*?—which?

There was talk (sometimes in his very hearing) that, one day, some degree of his vision might be restored. But Julius Muir scarcely heard, or cared. He lived for those days when, waking from a doze, he would feel a certain furry, warm weight lowered into his lap— "Julius, dear, someone very special has come to visit!"—soft, yet surprisingly heavy; heated, yet not disagreeably so; initially a bit restless (as a cat must circle fussily about, trying to determine the ideal position before she settles herself down), yet within a few minutes quite wonderfully relaxed, kneading her claws gently against his limbs and purring as she drifted into a companionable sleep. He would have liked to see, beyond the shimmering watery whiteness of his vision, her particular whiteness; certainly he would have liked to feel once again the softness, the astonishing silkiness, of that fur. But he could hear the deep-throated melodic purring. He could feel, to a degree, her warmly pulsing weight, the wonder of her mysterious *livingness* against his—for which he was infinitely grateful.

"My love!"

ALICE ADAMS

The Islands

What does it mean to love an animal, a pet, in my case a cat, in the
fierce, entire and unambivalent way that some of us do? I really want
to know this. Does the cat (did the cat) represent some person, a
parent or a child? some part of one's self? I don't think so—and
none of the words or phrases that one uses for human connections
sounds quite right: "crazy about," "really liked," "very fond of"—
none of those describes how I felt and still feel about my cat. Many
years ago, soon after we got the cat (her name was Pink), I went to
Rome with my husband, Andrew, whom I really liked; I was crazy
about Andrew, and very fond of him too. And I have a most vivid
memory of lying awake in Rome, in the pretty bed in its deep alcove,
in the nice small hotel near the Borghese Gardens—lying there, so
fortunate to be in Rome, with Andrew, and missing Pink, a small
striped cat with no tail—missing Pink unbearably. Even blaming
Andrew for having brought me there, although he loved her too,
almost as much as I did. And now Pink has died, and I cannot accept
or believe in her death, any more than I could believe in Rome.
(Andrew also died, three years ago, but this is not his story.)

A couple of days after Pink died (this has all been recent), I went
to Hawaii with a new friend, Slater. It had not been planned that
way; I had known for months that Pink was slowly failing (she was
nineteen), but I did not expect her to die. She just suddenly did,
and then I went off to "the islands," as my old friend Zoe Pinkerton
used to call them, in her nasal, moneyed voice. I went to Hawaii as
planned, which interfered with my proper mourning for Pink. I feel
as though those islands interposed themselves between her death
and me. When I needed to be alone, to absorb her death, I was over
there with Slater.

Slater is a developer; malls and condominium complexes all over the world. Andrew would not have approved of Slater, and sometimes I don't think that I do either. Slater is tall and lean, red-haired, a little younger than I am, and very attractive, I suppose, although on first meeting Slater I was not at all drawn to him (which I have come to think is one of the reasons he found me so attractive, calling me the next day, insisting on dinner that night; he was probably used to women who found him terrific, right off). But I thought Slater talked too much about money, or just talked too much, period.

Later on, when I began to like him a little better (I was flattered by all that attention, is the truth), I thought that Slater's very differences from Andrew should be a good sign. You're supposed to look for opposites, not reproductions, I read somewhere.

Andrew and I had acquired Pink from Zoe, a very rich alcoholic, at that time a new neighbor of ours in Berkeley. Having met Andrew down in his bookstore, she invited us to what turned out to be a very long Sunday lunch party, in her splendidly decked and viewed new Berkeley hills house. "Getting to know some of the least offensive neighbors," is how she probably thought of it. Her style was harsh, abrasive; anything-for-a-laugh was surely one of her mottoes, but she was pretty funny, fairly often. We saw her around when she first moved to Berkeley (from Ireland: a brief experiment that had not worked out too well). And then she met Andrew in his store, and found that we were neighbors, and she invited us to her party, and Andrew fell in love with a beautiful cat. "The most beautiful cat I ever saw," he told Zoe, and she was, soft and silver, with great blue eyes. The mother of Pink.

"Well, you're in luck," Zoe told us. "That's Molly Bloom, and she just had five kittens. They're all in a box downstairs, in my bedroom, and you get to choose any one you want. It's your doorprize for being such a handsome couple."

Andrew went off to look at the kittens, and then came back up to me. "There's one that's really great," he said. "A tailless wonder. Must be part Manx."

As in several Berkeley hills houses, Zoe's great sprawl of a bedroom was downstairs, with its own narrow deck, its view of the bay and the bridge, and of San Francisco. The room was the most appalling mess I had ever seen. Clothes, papers, books, dirty glasses, spilled powder, more clothes dumped everywhere. I was surprised

that my tidy, somewhat censorious husband even entered, and that
he was able to find the big wicker basket (filled with what looked to
be discarded silk underthings, presumably clean) in which five very
tiny kittens mewed and tried to rise and stalk about, on thin, uncertain legs.

The one that Andrew had picked was gray striped, a tabby, with
a stub of a tail, very large eyes and tall ears. I agreed that she was
darling, how great it would be to have a cat again; our last cat, Lily,
who was sweet and pretty but undistinguished, had died some years
ago. And so Andrew and I went back upstairs and told Zoe, who
was almost very drunk, that we wanted the one with no tail.

"Oh, Stubs," she rasped. "You don't have to take that one. What
are you guys, some kind of Berkeley bleeding hearts? You can have
a whole cat." And she laughed, delighted as always with her own
wit.

No, we told her. We wanted that particular cat. We liked her
best.

Aside from seeing the cats—our first sight of Pink!—the best
part of Zoe's lunch was her daughter, Lucy, a shy, pretty and very
gentle young woman—as opposed to the other guests, a rowdy, oil-
rich group, old friends of Zoe's from Texas.

"What a curious litter," I remarked to Andrew, walking home,
up Marin to our considerably smaller house. "All different. Five
different patterns of cat."

"Five fathers." Andrew had read a book about this, I could tell.
Andrew read everything. "It's called multiple insemination, and occurs fairly often in cats. It's theoretically possible in humans, but
they haven't come across any instances." He laughed, really pleased
with this lore.

"It's sure something to think about."

"Just don't."

Andrew. An extremely smart, passionate, selfish and generous
man, a medium-successful bookstore owner. A former academic: he
left teaching in order to have more time to read, he said. Also (I
thought) he much preferred being alone in his store to the company
of students or, worse, of other professors—a loner, Andrew. Small
and almost handsome, competitive, a gifted tennis player, mediocre
pianist. Gray hair and gray-green eyes. As I have said, I was crazy

about Andrew (usually). I found him funny and interestingly observant, sexy and smart. His death was more grievous to me than I
can (or will) say.

"You guys don't have to take Stubs, you can have a whole cat all
your own." Zoe Pinkerton on the phone, a few days later. Like many
alcoholics, she tended to repeat herself, although in Zoe's case some
vast Texan store of self-confidence may have fueled her repetitions.

And we in our turn repeated: we wanted the little one with no
tail.

Zoe told us that she would bring "Stubs" over in a week or so;
then the kittens would be old enough to leave Molly Bloom.

Andrew: "Molly Bloom indeed."

I: "No wonder she got multiply inseminated."

Andrew: "Exactly."

We both, though somewhat warily, liked Zoe. Or, we were both
somewhat charmed by her. For one thing, she made it clear that she
thought we were great. For another, she was smart, she had read
even more than Andrew had.

A very small woman, she walked with a swagger; her laugh was
loud, and liberal. I sometimes felt that Pink was a little like Zoe—
a tiny cat with a high, proud walk; a cat with a lot to say.

In a couple of weeks, then, Zoe called, and she came over with
this tiny tailless kitten under her arm. A Saturday afternoon. Andrew was at home, puttering in the garden like the good Berkeley
husband that he did not intend to be.

Zoe arrived in her purple suede pants and a vivid orange sweater
(this picture is a little poignant; fairly soon after that the booze began
to get the better of her legs, and she stopped taking walks at all).
She held out a tiny kitten, all huge gray eyes and pointed ears. A
kitten who took one look at us and began to purr; she purred for
several days, it seemed, as she walked all over our house and made
it her own. This is absolutely the best place I've ever been, she
seemed to say, and you are the greatest people—you are my people.

From the beginning, then, our connection with Pink seemed like
a privilege; automatically we accorded her rights that poor Lily would
never have aspired to.

She decided to sleep with us. In the middle of the night there
came a light soft plop on our bed, which was low and wide, and then

a small sound, *mmrrr*, a little announcement of her presence. "Littlest announcer," said Andrew, and we called her that, among her other names. Neither of us ever mentioned locking her out.

Several times in the night she would leave us and then return, each time with the same small sound, the littlest announcement.

In those days, the early days of Pink, I was doing a lot of free-lance editing, for local small presses, which is to say that I spent many waking hours at my desk. Pink assessed my habits early on, and decided to make them her own; or perhaps she decided that she too was an editor. In any case she would come up to my lap, where she would sit, often looking up with something to say. She was in fact the only cat I have ever known with whom a sort of conversation was possible; we made sounds back and forth at each other, very politely, and though mine were mostly nonsense syllables, Pink seemed pleased.

Pink was her main name, about which Zoe Pinkerton was very happy. "Lordy, no one's ever named a cat for me before." But Andrew and I used many other names for her. I had an idea that Pink liked a new name occasionally: maybe we all would? In any case we called her a lot of other, mostly P-starting names: Peppercorn, Pipsy Doodler, Poipu Beach. This last was a favorite place of Zoe's, when she went out to "the islands." Pink seemed to like all these names; she regarded us both with her great gray eyes—especially me; she was always mostly my cat.

I find that this is very hard, describing a long relationship with a cat. For one thing, there is not much change of feeling, on either side. The cat gets a little bigger, and you get older. Things happen to both of you, but mostly there is just continuation.

Worried about raccoons and Berkeley free-roaming dogs, we decided early on that Pink was to be a house cat, for good. She was not expendable. But Andrew and I liked to take weekend trips, and after she came to live with us we often took Pink along. She liked car travel right away; settled on the seat between us, she would join right in whenever we broke what had been a silence—not interrupting, just adding her own small voice, a sort of soft clear mew.

This must have been in the early 70s; we talked a lot about Nixon and Watergate. "Mew if you think he's guilty," Andrew would say to Pink, who always responded satisfactorily.

Sometimes, especially on summer trips, we would take Pink out for a semi-walk; our following Pink is what it usually amounted to, as she bounded into some meadow grass, with miniature leaps. Once, before I could stop her, she suddenly raced ahead—to a chipmunk. I was horrified. But then she raced back to me with the chipmunk in her mouth, and after a tiny shake she let him go, and the chipmunk ran off, unscathed. (Pink had what hunters call a soft mouth. Of course she did.)

We went to Rome and I missed her, very much; and we went off to the Piazza Argentina and gave a lot of lire to the very old woman there who was feeding all those mangy, half-blind cats. In honor of Pink.

I hope that I am not describing some idealized "perfect" adorable cat, because Pink was never that. She was entirely herself, sometimes cross and always independent. On the few occasions when I swatted her (very gently), she would hit me right back, a return swat on the hand—though always with sheathed claws.

I like to think that her long life with us, and then just with me, was a very happy one. Her version, though, would undoubtedly state that she was perfectly happy until Black and Brown moved in.

Another Berkeley lunch. A weekday, and all the women present work, and have very little time, and so this getting together seems a rare treat. Our hostess, a diminutive and brilliant art historian, announces that her cat, Parsley, is extremely pregnant. "Honestly, any minute," she laughs, and this is clearly true; the poor burdened cat, a brown Burmese, comes into the room, heavy and uncomfortable and restless. Searching.

A little later, in the midst of serving our many-salad lunch, the hostess says that the cat is actually having her kittens now, in the kitchen closet. We all troop out into the kitchen to watch.

The first tiny sac-enclosed kitten to barrel out is a black one, instantly vigorous, eager to stand up and get on with her life. Then three more come at intervals; it is hard to make out their colors.

"More multiple insemination," I told Andrew that night.

"It must be rife in Berkeley, like everyone says."

"It was fascinating, watching them being born."

"I guess, if you like obstetrics."

A month or so later the art historian friend called with a very sad story: she had just been diagnosed as being very clearly allergic to cats. "I thought I wasn't feeling too well, but I never thought it could be the cats. I know you already have that marvelous Pink, but do you think—until I find someone to take them? Just the two that are left?"

Surprisingly, Andrew, when consulted, said, "Well, why not? Be entertainment for old Pink, she must be getting pretty bored with just us."

We did not consult Pink, who hated those cats on sight. But Andrew was right away crazy about them, especially the black one (maybe he had wanted a cat of his own?). We called them, of course, Black and Brown. They were two Burmese females, or semi-Burmese, soon established in our house and seeming to believe that they lived there.

Black was (she is) the more interesting and aggressive of the two. And from the first she truly took to Pink, exhibiting the sort of clear affection that admits of no rebuff.

We had had Pink spayed as soon as she was old enough, after one quite miserable heat. And now Black and Brown seemed to come into heat consecutively, and to look to Pink for relief. She raged and scratched at them, as they, alternatively, squirmed and rubbed toward her. Especially Brown, who gave all the signs of a major passion for Pink. Furious, Pink seemed to be saying, Even if I were the tom cat that you long for, I would never look at you.

Black and Brown were spayed, and relations among the cats settled down to a much less luridly sexual pattern. Black and Brown both liked Pink and wished to be close to her, which she would almost never permit. She refused to eat with them, haughtily waiting at mealtimes until they were through.

It is easy for me to imagine Black and Brown as people, as women. Black would be a sculptor, I think, very strong, moving freely and widely through the world. Unmarried, no children. Whereas Brown would be a very sweet and pretty, rather silly woman, adored by her husband and sons.

But I do not imagine Pink as a person at all. I only see her as herself. A cat.

Zoe was going to move to Hawaii, she suddenly said. "Somewhere on Kauai, natch, and probably Poipu, if those grubby developers have kept their hands off anything there." Her hatchet laugh. "But I like the idea of living on the islands, away from it all. And so does

Gordon. You guys will have to come and visit us there. Bring Pink, but not those other two strays."

"Gordon" was a new beau, just turned up from somewhere in Zoe's complex Dallas childhood. With misgivings, but I think mostly good will, we went over to meet him, to hear about all these new plans.

Gordon was dark and pale and puffy, great black blotches under his narrow, dishonest eyes, a practiced laugh. Meeting him, I right off thought, They're not going to Hawaii, they're not going anywhere together.

Gordon did not drink at all, that day, although I later heard that he was a famous drunk. But occasionally he chided Zoe, who as usual was belting down vodka on ice. "Now, Baby," he kept saying. (Strident, striding Zoe—Baby?) "Let's go easy on the sauce. Remember what we promised." (We?)

At which Zoe laughed long and loud, as though her drinking were a good joke that we all shared.

A week or so after that Zoe called and said she was just out of the hospital. "I'm not in the greatest shape in the world," she said —and after that there was no more mention of Gordon, nor of a move to Hawaii.

And not very long after that Zoe moved down to Santa Barbara. She had friends there, she said.

Pink by now was in some cat equivalent to middle age. Still quite small, still playful, at times, she was almost always talkative. She disliked Black and Brown, but sometimes I would find her nestled against one of them, usually Black, in sleep. I had a clear sense that I was not supposed to know about this occasional rapport, or whatever. Pink still came up to my lap as I worked, and she slept on our bed at night, which we had always forbidden Black and Brown to do.

We bought a new, somewhat larger house, further up in the hills. It had stairs, and the cats ran happily up and down, and they seemed to thrive, like elderly people who benefit from a new program of exercise.

Andrew got sick, a terrible swift-moving cancer that killed him within a year, and for a long time I did very little but grieve. I sometimes saw friends, and I tried to work. There was a lot to do about Andrew's bookstore, which I sold, but mostly I stayed at home with my cats, all of whom were now allowed to sleep with me, on that suddenly too-wide bed.

Pink at that time chose to get under the covers with me. In a peremptory way she would tap at my cheek or my forehead, demanding to be taken in. This would happen several times in the course of the night, which was not a great help to my already fragile pattern of sleep, but it never occurred to me to deny her. And I was always too embarrassed to mention this to my doctor, when I complained of lack of sleep.

And then after several years I met Slater, at a well-meaning friend's house. Although as I have said I did not much like him at first, I was struck by his nice dark red hair, and by his extreme directness; Andrew had a tendency to be vague, it was sometimes hard to get at just what he meant. Not so with Slater, who was very clear—immediately clear about the fact that he liked me a lot, and wanted us to spend time together. And so we became somewhat involved, Slater and I, despite certain temperamental obstacles, including the fact that he does not much like cats.

And eventually we began to plan a trip to Hawaii, where Slater had business to see to.

Pink as an old cat slept more and more, and her high-assed strut showed sometimes a slight arthritic creak. Her voice got appreciably louder; no longer a littlest announcer, her statements were loud and clear (I have to admit, it was not the most attractive sound). It seems possible that she was getting a little deaf. When I took her to the vet, a sympathetic, tall and handsome young Japanese woman, she always said, "She sure doesn't look her age—" at which both Pink and I preened.

The vet, Dr. Ino, greatly admired the stripes below Pink's neck, on her breast, which looked like intricate necklaces. I admired them too (and so had Andrew).

Needless to say, the cats were perfectly trained to the sandbox, and very dainty in their habits. But at a certain point I began to notice small accidents around the house, from time to time. Especially when I had been away for a day or two. It seemed a punishment, cat turds in some dark corner. But it was hard to fix responsibility, and I decided to blame all three—and to take various measures like the installation of an upstairs sandbox, which helped. I did think that Pink was getting a little old for all those stairs.

Since she was an old cat I sometimes, though rarely, thought of the fact that Pink would die. Of course she would, eventually— although at times (bad times: the weeks and months around Andrew's illness and death) I melodramatically announced (more or less to myself) that Pink's death would be the one thing I could not bear. "Pink has promised to outlive me," I told several friends, and almost believed.

At times I even felt that we were the same person-cat, that we somehow inhabited each other. In a way I still do feel that—if I did not her loss would be truly unbearable.

I worried about her when I went away on trips. I would always come home, come into my house with some little apprehension that she might not be there. She was usually the last of the three cats to appear in the kitchen, where I stood confused among baggage, mail and phone messages. I would greet Black and Brown, and then begin to call her, "Pink, Pink?"—until, very diffident and proud, she would stroll unhurriedly toward me, and I would sweep her up into my arms with foolish cries of relief, and of love. *Ah, my darling old Pink.*

As I have said, Slater did not particularly like cats; he had nothing against them, really, just a general indifference. He eventually developed a fondness for Brown, believing that she liked him too, but actually Brown is a whore among cats; she will purr and rub up against anyone who might feed her. Whereas Pink was always discriminating, in every way, and fussy. Slater complained that one of the cats deposited small turds on the bathmat in the room where he sometimes showered, and I am afraid that this was indeed old Pink, both angry and becoming incontinent.

One night at dinner at my house, when Slater and I, alone, were admiring my view of the bay and of romantic San Francisco, all those lights, we were also talking about our trip to Hawaii. Making plans. He had been there before and was enthusiastic.

Then the phone rang, and it was Lucy, daughter of Zoe, who told me that her mother had died the day before, in Santa Barbara. "Her doctor said it was amazing she'd lived so long. All those years of booze."

"I guess. But, Lucy, it's so sad, I'm so sorry."

"I know." A pause. "I'd love to see you sometime. How's old Pink?"

"Oh, Pink's fine," I lied.

Coming back to the table, I explained as best I could about Zoe Pinkerton, how we got Pink. I played it all down, knowing his feelings about cats. But I thought he would like the multiple insemination part, and he did—as had Andrew. (It is startling when two such dissimilar men, Andrew, the somewhat dreamy book person, and Slater, the practical man, get so turned on by the same dumb joke.)

"So strange that we're going to Poipu," I told Slater. "Zoe always talked about Poipu." As I said this I knew it was not the sort of coincidence that Slater would find remarkable.

"I'm afraid it's changed a lot," he said, quite missing the point. "The early developers have probably knocked hell out of it. The greedy competition."

So much for mysterious ways.

Two days before we were to go to Hawaii, in the morning Pink seemed disoriented, unsure when she was in her sandbox, her feeding place. Also, she clearly had some bad intestinal disorder. She was very sick, but still in a way it seemed cruel to take her to the vet, whom I somehow knew could do nothing for her. However, at last I saw no alternative.

She (Dr. Ino, the admirable vet) found a large hard mass in Pink's stomach, almost certainly cancer. Inoperable. "I just can't reverse what's wrong with her," the doctor told me, with great sadness. And succinctness: I saw what she meant. I was so terribly torn, though: should I bring Pink home for a few more days, whatever was left to her—although she was so miserable, so embarrassed at her own condition?

I chose not to do that (although I still wonder, I still am torn). And I still cannot think of the last moments of Pink. Whose death I chose.

I wept on and off for a couple of days. I called some close friends who would have wanted to know about Pink, I thought; they were all most supportively kind (most of my best friends love cats).

And then it was time to leave for Hawaii.

Sometimes, during those days of packing and then flying to Hawaii, I thought it odd that Pink was not more constantly on my mind, even odd that I did not weep more than I did. Now, though, looking back on that trip and its various aftermaths, I see that in fact I was thinking about Pink all that time, that she was totally in charge, as she always had been.

We stayed in a pretty condominium complex, two-story white buildings with porches and decks, and everywhere sweeping green lawns, and flowers. A low wall of rocks, a small coarsely sanded beach, and the vast and billowing sea.

Ours was a second-floor unit, with a nice wide balcony for sunset drinks, or daytime sunning. And, looking down from that balcony one night, our first, I saw the people in the building next door, out on the grass beside what must have been their kitchen, *feeding their cats*. They must have brought along these cats, two supple gray Siamese, and were giving them their supper. I chose not to mention this to Slater, I thought I could imagine his reaction, but in the days after that, every time we walked past that building I slowed my pace and looked carefully for the cats, and a couple of times I saw them. Such pretty cats, and very friendly, for Siamese. Imagine: traveling to Hawaii with your cats—though I was not at all sure that I would have wanted Black and Brown along, nice as they are, and pretty.

Another cat event (there were four in all) came as we drove from Lihue back to Poipu, going very slowly over those very sedate tree- and flower-lined streets, with their decorous, spare houses. Suddenly I felt—we felt—a sort of thump, and Slater, looking startled, slowed down even further and looked back.

"Lord God, that was a cat," he said.

"A cat?"

"He ran right out into the car. And then ran back."

"Are you sure? she's all right?"

"Absolutely. Got a good scare though." Slater chuckled.

But you might have killed that cat, I did not say. And for a moment I wondered if he actually had, and lied, saying the cat was okay. However Slater would never lie to spare my feelings, I am quite sure of that.

The third cat happening took place as we drove down a winding, very steep mountain road (we had been up to see the mammoth gorges cut into the island, near its western edge). On either side of the road there was thick green jungular growth—and suddenly, there among the vines and shrubs I saw a small yellow cat staring out, her ears lowered. Frightened. Eyes begging.

Slater saw her too and even he observed, "Good Lord, people dumping off animals to starve. It's awful."

"You're sure she doesn't live out there? a wilderness cat?"

"I don't think so." Honest Slater.

We did not talk then or later about going back to rescue that cat—not until the next day when he asked me what I would like to do and I said, "I'd like to go back for that cat." He assumed I was joking, and I guess I mostly was. There were too many obvious reasons not to save that particular cat, including the difficulty of finding her again. But I remembered her face, I can see it still, that expression of much-resented dependence. It was a way that even Pink looked, very occasionally.

Wherever we drove, through small neat impoverished "native" settlements (blocks of houses that Slater and his cohorts planned to buy, and demolish, to replace with fancy condos), with their lavish flowers all restrained into tidy beds, I kept looking at the yards, and under the houses. I wanted to see a cat, or some cats (I wanted to see Pink again). Realizing what I was doing, I continued to do it, to strain for the sight of a cat.

The fourth and final cat event took place as we walked home from dinner one night, in the flower-scented, corny-romantic Hawaiian darkness. To our left was the surging black sea; and to our right large tamed white shrubbery, and a hotel swimming pool, glistening blackly under feeble yellow floodlights. And then quite suddenly, from nowhere, a small cat appeared in our path, shyly and uncertainly arching her back against a bush. A black cat with some yellow tortoise markings, a long thin curve of a tail.

"He looks just like your Pink, doesn't he." Slater actually said this, and I suppose he believed it to be true.

"What—Pink? But her tail—Jesus, didn't you even see my cat?"

I'm afraid I went on in this vein, sporadically, for several days. But it did seem so incredible, not remembering Pink, my elegantly striped, my tailless wonder. (It is also true that I was purposely using this lapse, as one will, in a poor connection.)

I dreaded going home with no Pink to call out to, as I came in the door. And the actuality was nearly as bad as my imaginings of it: Black and Brown, lazy and affectionate, glad to see me. And no Pink, with her scolding *hauteur*, her long delayed yielding to my blandishments.

I had no good pictures of Pink, and to explain this odd fact I have to admit that I am very bad about snapshots; I have never devised a really good way of storing and keeping them, and tend rather to enclose any interesting ones in letters to people who might like them, to whom they would have some meaning. And to shove the others into drawers, among old letters and other unclassifiable mementos.

I began then to scour my house for Pink pictures, looking everywhere. In an album (Andrew and I put together a couple of albums, early on) I found a great many pictures of Pink as a tiny, tall-eared brand-new kitten, stalking across a padded window seat, hiding behind an oversized Boston fern—among all the other pictures from those days: Zoe Pinkerton, happy and smoking a long cigarette and almost drunk, wearing outrageous colors, on the deck of her house. And Andrew and I, young and very happy, silly, snapped by someone at a party. Andrew in his bookstore, horn-rimmed and quirky. Andrew uncharacteristically working in our garden. Andrew all over the place.

But no middle-year or recent pictures of Pink. I had in fact (I then remembered) sent the most recent shots of Pink to Zoe; it must have been just before she (Zoe) died, with a silly note about old survivors, something like that. It occurred to me to get in touch with Lucy, Zoe's daughter, to see if those pictures had turned up among Zoe's "effects," but knowing the chaos in which Zoe had always lived (and doubtless died) I decided that this would be tactless, unnecessary trouble. And I gave up looking for pictures.

Slater called yesterday to say that he is going back to Hawaii, a sudden trip. Business. I imagine that he is about to finish the ruination of all that was left of Zoe's islands. He certainly did not suggest that I come along, nor did he speak specifically of our getting together again, and I rather think that he, like me, has begun to wonder what we were doing together in the first place. It does seem to me that I was drawn to him for a very suspicious reason, his lack of resemblance to Andrew: why ever should I seek out the opposite of a person I truly loved?

I do look forward to some time alone now. I will think about Pink—I always feel her presence in my house, everywhere. Pink, stalking and severe, ears high. Pink, in my lap, raising her head with some small soft thing to say.

And maybe, since Black and Brown are getting fairly old now too, I will think about getting another new young cat. Maybe, with luck, a small gray partially Manx, with no tail at all, and beautiful necklaces.

ANGELA CARTER

Puss in Boots

Figaro here; Figaro there, I tell you! Figaro upstairs, Figaro down-stairs and—oh, my goodness me, this little Figaro can slip into my lady's chamber smart as you like at any time whatsoever that he takes the fancy for, don't you know, he's a cat of the world, cos-mopolitan, sophisticated; he can tell when a furry friend is the Mis-sis's best company. For what lady in all the world could say no to the passionate yet toujours discret advances of a fine marmalade cat? (Unless it be her eyes incontinently overflow at the slightest whiff of fur, which happened once, as you shall hear.)

A tom, sirs, a ginger tom and proud of it. Proud of his fine, white shirtfront that dazzles harmoniously against his orange and tangerine tessellations (oh! what a fiery suit of lights have I); proud of his bird-entrancing eye and more than military whiskers; proud, to a fault, some say, of his fine, musical voice. All the windows in the square fly open when I break into impromptu song at the spectacle of the moon above Bergamo. If the poor players in the square, the sullen rout of ragged trash that haunts the provinces, are rewarded with a hail of pennies when they set up their makeshift stage and start their raucous choruses, then how much more liberally do the citizens deluge me with pails of the freshest water, vegetables hardly spoiled and, occasionally, slippers, shoes and boots.

Do you see these fine, high, shining leather boots of mine? A young cavalry officer made me the tribute of, first one; then, after I celebrate his generosity with a fresh obbligato, the moon no fuller than my heart—whoops! I nimbly spring aside—down comes the other. Their high heels will click like castanets when Puss takes his promenade upon the tiles, for my song recalls flamenco, all cats have a Spanish tinge although Puss himself elegantly lubricates his virile, muscular, native Bergamasque with French, since that is the only language in which you can purr.

"Merrrrrrrrrci!"

Instanter I draw my new boots on over the natty white stockings that terminate my hinder legs. That young man, observing with curiosity by moonlight the use to which I put his footwear, calls out: "Hey, Puss! Puss, there!"

"At your service, sir!"

"Up to my balcony, young Puss!"

He leans out, in his nightshirt, offering encouragement as I swing succinctly up the facade, forepaws on a curly cherub's pate, hindpaws on a stucco wreath, bring them up to meet your forepaws while, first paw forward, hup! onto the stone nymph's tit; left paw down a bit, the satyr's bum should do the trick. Nothing to it, once you know how; rococo's no problem. Acrobatics? Born to them; Puss can perform a back somersault whilst holding aloft a glass of vino in his right paw and *never spill a drop.*

But, to my shame, the famous death-defying triple somersault en plein air, that is, in middle air, that is, unsupported and without a safety net, I, Puss, have never yet attempted though often I have dashingly brought off the double tour, to the applause of all.

"You strike me as a cat of parts," says this young man when I'm arrived at his window sill. I made him a handsome genuflection, rump out, tail up, head down, to facilitate his friendly chuck under my chin; and, as involuntary free gift, my natural, my habitual smile.

For all cats have this particularity, each and every one, from the meanest alley sneaker to the proudest, whitest she that ever graced a pontiff's pillow—we have our smiles, as it were, painted on. Those small, cool, quiet Mona Lisa smiles that smile we must, no matter whether it's been fun or it's been not. So all cats have a politician's air; we smile and smile and so they think we're villains. But, I note, this young man is something of a smiler hisself.

"A sandwich," he offers. "And, perhaps, a snifter of brandy."

His lodgings are poor, though he's handsome enough, and even en déshabillé, nightcap and all, there's a neat, smart, dandified air about him. Here is one who knows what's what, thinks I; a man who keeps up appearances in the bedchamber can never embarrass you out of it. And excellent beef sandwiches; I relish a lean slice of roast beef and early learned a taste for spirits, since I started life as a wineshop cat, hunting cellar rats for my keep, before the world sharpened my wits enough to let me live by them.

And the upshot of this midnight interview? I'm engaged, on the spot, as Sir's valet: valet de chambre and, from time to time, his body servant, for when funds are running low, as they must do for every gallant officer when the pickings fall off, he pawns the quilt, doesn't he. Then faithful Puss curls up on his chest to keep him warm at nights. And if he don't like me to knead his nipples, which, out of the purest affection and the desire—ouch! he says—to test the retractability of my claws, I do in moments of absence of mind, then what other valet could slip into a young girl's sacred privacy and deliver her a billet-doux at the very moment when she's reading her prayer book with her sainted mother? A task I once or twice perform for him, to his infinite gratitude.

And, as you will hear, brought him at last to the best of fortunes for us all.

So Puss got his post at the same time as his boots and I dare say the Master and I have much in common, for he's proud as the devil, touchy as tin tacks, lecherous as licorice and, though I say it as loves him, as quick-witted a rascal as ever put on clean linen.

When times were hard, I'd pilfer the market for breakfast—a herring, an orange, a loaf; we never went hungry. Puss served him well in the gaming salons, too, for a cat may move from lap to lap with impunity and cast his eye over any hand of cards. A cat can jump on the dice—he can't resist to see it roll! poor thing, mistook it for a bird; and after I've been, limp-spined, stiff-legged, playing the silly buggers, scooped up to be chastised, who can remember how the dice fell in the first place?

And we had, besides, less . . . gentlemanly means of maintenance when they closed the tables to us, as, churlishly, they sometimes did. I'd perform my little Spanish dance while he went round with his hat: *olé!* But he only put my loyalty and affection to the test of his humiliation when the cupboard was as bare as his backside; after, in fact, he'd sunk so low as to pawn his drawers.

So all went right as ninepence and you never saw such boon companions as Puss and his master; until the man must needs go fall in love.

"Head over heels, Puss."

I went about my ablutions, tonguing my arsehole with the impeccable hygienic integrity of cats, one leg stuck in the air like a ham bone; I choose to remain silent. Love? What has my rakish master, for whom I've jumped through the window of every brothel in the city, besides haunting the virginal back garden of the convent and God knows what other goatish errands, to do with the tender passion?

"And she a princess in a tower. Remote and shining as Aldebaran. Chained to a dolt and dragon-guarded."

I withdrew my head from my privates and fixed him with my most satiric smile; I dare him warble on in *that* strain.

"All cats are cynics," he opines, quailing beneath my yellow glare.

It is the hazard of it draws him, see.

There is a lady sits in a window for one hour and one hour only, at the tenderest time of dusk. You can scarcely see her features, the curtains almost hide her; shrouded like a holy image, she looks out at the piazza as the shops shut up, the stalls go down, the night comes on. And that is all the world she ever sees. Never a girl in all Bergamo so secluded except, on Sundays, they let her go to Mass, bundled up in black, with a veil on. And then she is the company of an aged hag, her keeper, who grumps along grim as a prison dinner.

How did he see that secret face? Who else but Puss revealed it?

Back we come from the tables so late, so very late at night, we found, to our emergent surprise, that all at once it was early in the morning. His pockets were heavy with silver and both our guts sweetly a-gurgle with champagne. Lady Luck had sat with us; what fine spirits were we in! Winter and cold weather. The pious trot to church already with little lanterns through the chill fog as we go ungodly rolling home.

See, a black barque, like a state funeral; and Puss takes it into his bubbly-addled brain to board her. Tacking obliquely to her side, I rub my marmalade pate against her shin; how could any duenna, be she never so stern, take offense at such attentions to her charge-ling from a little cat? (As it turns out, this one—*Attishooo!*—does.) A white hand fragrant as Arabia descends from the black cloak and reciprocally rubs behind his ears at just the ecstatic spot. Puss lets rip a roaring purr, rears briefly on his high-heeled boots; jig with joy and pirouette with glee—she laughs to see and draws her veil aside. Puss glimpses high above, as it were, an alabaster lamp lit behind my dawn's first flush: her face.

And she smiling.

For a moment, just that moment, you would have thought it was May morning.

"Come along! Come! Don't dawdle over the nasty beast!" snaps the old hag, with the one tooth in her mouth, and warts; she sneezes.

The veil comes down; so cold it is, and dark, again.

It was not I alone who saw her; with that smile he swears she stole his heart.

Love.

I've sat inscrutably by and washed my face and sparkling dickey with my clever paw while he made the beast with two backs with every harlot in the city, besides a number of good wives, dutiful daughters, rosy country girls come to sell celery and endive on the corner, and the chambermaid who strips the bed, what's more. The mayor's wife, even, shed her diamond earrings for him and the wife of the notary unshuffled her petticoats, and if I could, I would blush to remember how her daughter shook out her flaxen plaits and jumped in bed between them, and she not sixteen years old. But never the word "love" has fallen from his lips, nor in nor out of any of these transports, until my master saw the wife of Signor Pante-leone as she went walking out to Mass, and she lifted up her veil, though not for him.

And now he is half sick with it and will go to the tables no more for lack of heart and never even pats the bustling rump of the cham-bermaid in his new-found, maudlin celibacy, so we get our slops left festering for days and the sheets filthy and the wench goes banging about bad-temperedly with her broom enough to fetch the plaster off the walls.

I'll swear he lives for Sunday morning, though never before was he a religious man. Saturday nights, he bathes himself punctiliously, even, I'm glad to see, washes behind his ears, perfumes himself, presses his uniform so you'd think he had a right to wear it. So much in love he very rarely panders to the pleasures even of Onan, as he lies tossing on his couch, for he cannot sleep for fear he miss the summoning bell. Then out into the cold morning, harking after that black, vague shape, hapless fisherman for this sealed oyster with such a pearl in it. He creeps behind her across the square; how can so amorous bear to be so inconspicuous? And yet he must; though, sometimes, the old hag sneezes and says she swears there is a cat about.

He will insinuate himself into the pew behind milady and some-times contrive to touch the hem of her garment, when they all kneel, and never a thought to his orisons; she is the divinity he's come to worship. Then sits silent, in a dream, till bedtime; what pleasure is his company for me?

He won't eat, either. I brought him a fine pigeon from the inn kitchen, fresh off the spit, parfumé avec tarragon, but he wouldn't touch it, so I crunched it up, bones and all. Performing, as ever after meals, my meditative toilette, I pondered, thus: one, he is in a fair way to ruining us both by neglecting his business; two, love is desire sustained by unfulfillment. If I lead him to her bedchamber and there he takes his fill of her lily-white, he'll be right as rain in two shakes and next day tricks as usual.

Then Master and his Puss will soon be solvent once again.

Which, at the moment, very much not, sir.

This Signor Panteleone employs, his only servant but the hag, a kitchen cat, a sleek, spry tabby whom I accost. Grasping the slack of her neck firmly between my teeth, I gave her the customary tribute of a few firm thrusts of my striped loins, and when she got her breath back, she assured me in the friendliest fashion the old man was a fool and a miser who kept herself on short commons for the sake of the mousing and the young lady a soft-hearted creature who smuggled breast of chicken and sometimes, when the hag-dragon-governess napped at midday, snatched this pretty kitty out of the hearth and into her bedroom to play with reels of silk and run after trailed handkerchiefs, when she and she had as much fun to-gether as two Cinderellas at an all-girls' ball.

Poor, lonely lady, married so young to an old dodderer with his bald pate and his goggle eyes and his limp, his avarice, his gore belly, his rheumaticks, and his flag hangs all the time at half-mast indeed; and jealous as he is impotent, tabby declares—he'd put a stop to all the rutting in the world, if he had his way, just to certify his young wife don't get from another what she can't get from him.

"Then shall we hatch a plot to antler him, my precious?"

Nothing loath, she tells me the best time for this accomplishment should be the one day in all the week he forsakes his wife and his counting house to ride off into the country to extort most grasping rents from starveling tenant farmers. And she's left all alone then, behind so many bolts and bars you wouldn't believe; all alone—but for the hag!

Aha! This hag turns out to be the biggest snag; an iron-plated, copper-bottomed, sworn man-hater of some sixty bitter winters who—as ill luck would have it—shatters, clatters, erupts into par-oxysms of the *sneeze* at the very glimpse of a cat's whisker. No chance of Puss worming his winsome way into *that* one's affections, nor for my tabby, neither! But, oh, my dear, I say; see how my

---

ingenuity rises to this challenge. . . . So we resume the sweetest part of our conversation in the dusty convenience of the coal hole and she promises me, last she can do, to see the fair, hitherto inaccessible one gets a letter safe if I slip it to her, and slip it to her forthwith I do, though somewhat discommoded by my boots.

He spent three hours over his letter, did my master, as long as it takes me to lick the coal dust off my dickey. He tears up half a quire of paper, splays five pen nibs with the force of his adoration: "Look not for any peace, my heart; having become a slave to this beauty's tyranny, dazzled am I by this sun's rays and my torments cannot be assuaged." *That's* not the high road to the rumpling of the bedcovers; she's got *one* ninny between them already!

"Speak from the heart," I finally exhort. "And all good women have a missionary streak, sir; convince her her orifice will be your salvation and she's yours."

"When I want your advice, Puss, I'll ask for it," he says, all at once hoity-toity. But at last he manages to pen ten pages: a rake, a profligate, a cardshaper, a cashiered officer well on the way to rack and ruin when first he saw, as if it were a glimpse of grace, her face . . . his angel, his good angel, who will lead him from perdition.

Oh, what a masterpiece he penned!

"Such tears she wept at his addresses!" says my tabby friend. " 'Oh, Tabs,' she sobs—for she calls me Tabs—'I never meant to wreak such havoc with a pure heart when I smiled to see a booted cat!' And put his paper next to her heart and swore it was a good soul that sent her his vows and she was too much in love with virtue to withstand him. If, she adds, for she's a sensible girl, he's neither old as the hills nor ugly as sin, that is."

An admirable little note the lady's sent him in return, per Figaro here and there; she adopts a responsive yet uncompromising tone. For, says she, how can she usefully discuss his passion further without a glimpse of his person?

He kisses her letter once, twice, a thousand times; she must and will see me! I shall serenade her this very evening!

So when dusk falls, off we trot to the piazza, he with an old guitar he pawned his sword to buy and most, if I may say so, outlandishly rigged out in some kind of vagabond mountebank's outfit he bartered his gold-braided waistcoat with poor Pierrot braying in the square for, moonstruck zany, lovelorn loon he was himself, and even plastered his face with flour to make it white, poor fool, and so ram home his heartsick state.

There she is, the evening star with the clouds around her; but such a creaking of carts in the square, such a clatter and crash as they dismantle the stalls, such an ululation of ballad singers and oration of nostrum peddlers and perturbation of errand boys that though he wails out his heart to her: "Oh, my beloved!" why she, all in a dream, sits with her gaze in the middle distance, where there's a crescent moon stuck on the sky behind the cathedral pretty as a painted stage, and so is she.

Does she hear him?

Not a grace note.

Does she see him?

Never a glance.

"Up you go, Puss; tell her to look my way!"

If rococo's a piece of cake, that chaste, tasteful, early Palladian stumped many a better cat than I in its time. Agility's not in it, when it comes to Palladian; daring alone will carry the day, and though the first story's graced with a hefty caryatid whose bulbous loincloth and tremendous pects facilitate the first ascent, the Doric column on her head proves a horse of a different color, I can tell you. Had I not seen my precious Tabby crouched in the gutter above me keening encouragement, I, even I, might never have braved that flying, upward leap that brought me, as if Harlequin himself on wires, in one bound to her window sill.

"Dear God!" the lady says, and jumps. I see she, too—ah, sentimental thing!—clutches a well-thumbed letter. "Puss in boots!"

I bow to her with a courtly flourish. What luck to hear no sniff or sneeze; where's hag? A sudden flux sped her to the privy—not a moment to lose.

"Cast your eye below," I hiss. "Him you know of lurks below, in white with the big hat, ready to sing you an evening ditty."

The bedroom door creaks open then, and whee! through the air Puss goes; discretion is the better part. And for both their sweet sakes I did it, the sight of both their bright eyes inspired me to the never-before-attempted, by me or any other cat, in boots or out of them—the death-defying triple somersault!

And a three-story drop to ground, what's more: a grand descent.

Only the merest trifle winded, I'm proud to say, I neatly land on all fours and Tabs goes wild, huzzah! But has my master witnessed my triumph? Has he, my arse. He's tuning up that old mandolin and breaks, as down I come, again into his song.

I would never have said, in the normal course of things, his voice would charm the birds out of the trees, like mine; and yet the bustle died for him, the homeward-turning costers paused in their tracks to harken, the preening street girls forgot their hard-edged smiles as they turned to him and some of the old ones wept, they did.

Tabs, up on the roof there, prick up your ears! For by its power I know my heart is in his voice.

And now the lady lowers her eyes to him and smiles, as once she smiled at me.

Then, bang! a stern hand pulls the shutters to. And it was as if all the violets in all the baskets of all the flower sellers drooped and faded at once; and spring stopped dead in its tracks and might, this time, not come at all; and the bustle and the business of the square, that had so magically quieted for his song, now rose up again with the harsh clamor of the loss of love.

And we trudge drearily off to dirty sheets and a mean supper of bread and cheese, all I can steal him, but at least the poor soul manifests a hearty appetite now she knows he's in the world and not the ugliest of mortals; for the first time since that fateful morning, sleeps sound. But sleep comes hard to Puss tonight. He takes a midnight stroll across the square, soon comfortably discusses a choice morsel of salt cod his tabby friend found among the ashes on the hearth before our converse turns to other matters.

"Rats!" she says. "And take your boots off, you uncouth bugger; those three-inch heels wreak havoc with the soft flesh of my underbelly!"

When we'd recovered ourselves a little, I ask her what she means by those "rats" of hers and she proposes her scheme to me. How my master must pose as a *ratcatcher* and I, his ambulant marmalade rattrap. How we will then go kill the rats that ravage milady's bedchamber, the day the old fool goes to fetch his rents, and she can have her will of the lad at leisure, for if there is one thing the hag fears more than a cat, it is a rat, and she'll cower in a cupboard till the last rat is off the premises before she comes out. Oh, this tabby one, sharp as a tack is she! I congratulate her ingenuity with a few affectionate cuffs round the head and home again, for breakfast, ubiquitous Puss, here, there and everywhere, who's your Figaro?

Master applauds the rat ploy; but as to the rats themselves, how are they to arrive in the house in the first place? he queries.

"Nothing easier, sir; my accomplice, a witty soubrette who lives among the cinders, dedicated as she is to the young lady's happiness, will personally strew a large number of dead and dying rats she has herself collected about the bedroom of the said ingénue's duenna, and, most particularly, that of the said ingénue herself. This to be done tomorrow morning, as soon as Sir Pantaloon rides out to fetch his rents. By good fortune, down in the square, plying for hire, a ratcatcher! Since our hag cannot abide either a rat or a cat, it falls to milady to escort the ratcatcher, none other than yourself, sir, and his intrepid hunter, myself, to the site of the infestation.

"Once you're in her bedroom, sir, if *you* don't know what to do, then I can't help you."

"Keep your foul thoughts to yourself, Puss."

Some things, I see, are sacrosanct from humor.

Sure enough, prompt at five in the bleak next morning, I observe with my own eyes the lovely lady's lubberly husband hump off on his horse like a sack of potatoes to rake in his dues. We're ready with our sign: SIGNOR FURIOSO, THE LIVING DEATH OF RATS; and in the leathers he's borrowed from the porter I hardly recognize him myself, not with the false mustache. He coaxes the chambermaid with a few kisses—poor, deceived girl! love knows no shame—and so we install ourselves under a certain shuttered window with the great pile of traps she's lent us, the sign of our profession, Puss perched atop them bearing the humble yet determined look of a sworn enemy of vermin.

We've not waited more than fifteen minutes—and just as well, so many rat-plagued Bergamots approach us already and are not easily dissuaded from employing us—when the front door flies open on a lusty scream. The hag, aghast, flings her arms round flinching Furioso; how fortuitous to find him! But at the whiff of me, she's sneezing so valiantly, her eyes awash, the vertical gutters of her nostrils aswill with snot, she barely can depict the scenes inside, rattus domesticus dead in her bed and all; and worse! in the Missis's room.

So Signor Furioso and his questing Puss are ushered into the very sanctuary of the goddess, our presence announced by a fanfare from her keeper on the noseharp. *Attishooo!!!*

Sweet and pleasant in a morning gown of loose linen, our ingénue jumps at the tattoo of my boot heels but recovers instantly, and the wheezing, hawking hag is in no state to sniffle more than: "Ain't I seen that cat before?"

"Not a chance," says my master. "Why, he's come but yesterday with me from Milano."

So she has to make do with that.

My Tabs has lined the very stairs with rats; she's made a morgue of the hag's room but something more lively of the lady's. For some of her prey she's very cleverly not killed but crippled; a big black beastie weaves its way towards us over the turkey carpet. Puss, pounce! Between screaming and sneezing, the hag's in a fine state, I can tell you, though milady exhibits a most praiseworthy and collected presence of mind, being, I guess, a young woman of no small grasp so, perhaps, she has a sniff of the plot already.

My master goes down hands and knees under the bed.

"My God!" he cries. "There's the biggest hole, here in the wainscoting, I ever saw in all my professional career! And there's an army of black rats gathering behind it, ready to storm through! To arms!"

But for all her terror, the hag's loath to leave the Master and me alone to deal with the rats; she casts her eye on a silver-backed hairbrush, a coral rosary, twitters, hovers, screeches, mutters until milady assures her, amidst scenes of rising pandemonium:

"I shall stay here myself and see that Signor Furioso doesn't make off with my trinkets. You go and recover yourself with an infusion of friar's balsam and don't come back until I call."

The hag departs; quick as a flash, la belle turns the key in the door on her and softly laughs, the naughty one.

Dusting the slut fluff from his knees, Signor Furioso now stands slowly upright; swiftly, he removes his false mustache, for no element of the farcical must mar this first, delirious encounter of these lovers, must it? (Poor soul, how his hands tremble!)

Accustomed as I am to the splendid, feline nakedness of my kind, that offers no concealment of that soul made manifest in the flesh of lovers, I am always a little moved by the poignant reticence with which humanity shyly hesitates to divest itself of its clutter of concealing rags in the presence of desire. So, first, these two smile a little, as if to say: "How strange to meet you here!" uncertain of a loving welcome still. And do I deceive myself, or do I see a tear a-twinkle in the corner of his eye? But who is it steps towards the other first? Why she; women, I think, are, of the two sexes, the more keenly tuned to the sweet music of their bodies. (A penny for my foul thoughts, indeed! Does she, that wise, grave personage in the negligee, think you've staged this grand charade merely in order to kiss her hand?) But then—oh, what a pretty blush!—steps back; now it's his turn to take two steps forward in the saraband of Eros.

I could wish, though, they'd dance a little faster; the hag will soon recover from her spasms and shall she find them in flagrante?

His hand, then, trembling, upon her bosom; hers, initially more hesitant, sequentially more purposeful, upon his breeches. Then their strange trance breaks; that sentimental havering done, I never saw two fall to it with such appetite. As if the whirlwind got into their fingers, they strip each other bare in a twinkling and she falls back on the bed, shows him the target, he displays the dart, scores an instant bull's-eye. Bravo! Never can that old bed have shook with such a storm before. And their sweet, choked mutterings, poor things: "I never . . ." "My darling . . ." "More . . ." And etc, etc. Enough to melt the thorniest heart.

He rises up on his elbows once and gasps at me: "Mimic the murder of the rats, Puss! Mask the music of Venus with the clamor of Diana!"

A-hunting we shall go! Loyal to the last, I play catch-as-catch-can with Tab's dead rats, giving the dying the coup de grace and baying with resonant vigor to drown the extravagant screeches that break forth from that (who would have suspected?) more passionate young woman as she comes off in fine style. (Full marks, Master.)

At that, the old hag comes battering at the door. What's going on? Whyfor the racket? And the door rattles on its hinges.

"Peace!" cries Signor Furioso. "Haven't I just now blocked the great hole?"

But milady's in no hurry to don her smock again; she takes her lovely time about it, so full of pleasure gratified her languorous limbs you'd think her very navel smiled. She pecks my master prettily thank you on the cheek, wets the gum on his false mustache with the tip of her strawberry tongue and sticks it back on his upper lip for him, then lets her wardress into the scene of the faux carnage with the most modest and irreproachable air in the world.

"See! Puss has slaughtered all the rats."

I rush, purring proud, to greet the hag; instantly, her eyes o'erflow.

"Why the bedclothes so disordered?" she squeaks, not quite blinded, yet, by phlegm and chosen for her post from all the other applicants on account of her suspicious mind, even (oh, dutiful) when in grande peur des rats.

"Puss had a mighty battle with the biggest beast you ever saw upon this very bed; can't you see the bloodstains on the sheets? And now, what do we owe you, Signor Furioso, for this singular service?"

"A hundred ducats," says I, quick as a flash, for I know my

master, left to himself, would, like an honorable fool, take nothing.

"That's the entire household expenses for a month!" wails avarice's well-chosen accomplice.

"And worth every penny! For those rats would have eaten us out of house and home." I see the glimmerings of sturdy backbone in this little lady. "Go, pay them from your private savings that I know of, that you've skimmed off the housekeeping."

Muttering and moaning, but nothing for it except do as she is bid; and the furious sir and I take off a laundry basket full of dead rats as souvenir—we drop it, plop! in the nearest sewer. And sit down to one dinner honestly paid for, for a wonder.

But the young fool is off his feed again. Pushes his plate aside, laughs, weeps, buries his head in his hands and, time and time again, goes to the window to stare at the shutters behind which his sweetheart scrubs the blood away and my dear Tabs rests from her supreme exertions. He sits, for a while, and scribbles; rips the page in four, hurls it aside. I spear a falling fragment with a claw. Dear God, he's took to writing poetry.

"I must and will have her forever," he exclaims.

I see my plan has come to nothing. Satisfaction has not satisfied him; that soul they both saw in one another's bodies has such insatiable hunger no single meal could ever appease it. I fall to the toilette of my hinder parts, my favorite stance when contemplating the ways of the world.

"How can I live without her?"

You did so for twenty-seven years, sir, and never missed her for a moment.

"I'm burning with the fever of love!"

Then we're spared the expense of fires.

"I shall steal her away from her husband to live with me."

"What do you propose to live on, sir?"

"Kisses," he said distractedly. "Embraces."

"Well, you won't grow fat on that, sir; though *she* will. And then, more mouths to feed."

"I'm sick and tired of your foul-mouthed barbs, Puss," he snaps. And yet my heart is moved, for now he speaks the plain, clear, foolish rhetoric of love and who is there cunning enough to help him to happiness but I? Scheme, loyal Puss, scheme!

My wash completed, I step out across the square to visit that charming she who's wormed her way directly into my own hitherto untrammeled heart with her sharp wits and her pretty ways. She exhibits warm emotion to see me; and oh! what news she has to tell me! News of a rapt and personal nature, that turns my mind to thoughts of the future, and, yes, domestic plans of most familial nature. She's saved me a pig's trotter, a whole, entire pig's trotter the Missis smuggled to her with a wink. A feast! Masticating, I muse.

"Recapitulate," I suggest, "the daily motions of Sir Pantaloon when he's at home."

They set the cathedral clock by him, so rigid and so regular his habits. Up at the crack, he meagerly breakfasts off yesterday's crusts and a cup of cold water, to spare the expense of heating it up. Down to his counting house, counting out his money, until a bowl of well-watered gruel at midday. The afternoon he devotes to usury, bank-rupting, here, a small tradesman, there, a weeping widow, for fun and profit. Dinner's luxurious, at four: soup, with a bit of rancid beef or a tough bird in it—he's an arrangement with the butcher, takes unsold stock off his hands in return for a shut mouth about a pie that had a finger in it. From four-thirty until five-thirty, he unlocks the shutters and lets his wife look out—oh, don't I know!—while hag sits beside her to make sure she doesn't smile. (Oh, that blessed flux, those precious loose minutes that set the game in motion!)

And while she breathes the air of evening, why, he checks up on his chest of gems, his bales of silk, all those treasures he loves too much to share with daylight, and if he wastes a candle when he so indulges himself, why, any man is entitled to one little extravagance. Another draught of Adam's ale healthfully concludes the day; up he tucks besides Missis, and since she is his prize possession, consents to finger her a little. He palpitates her hide and slaps her flanks: "What a good bargain!" Alack, can do no more, not wishing to prof-ligate his natural essence. And so drifts off to sinless slumber amid the prospects of tomorrow's gold.

"How rich is he?"

"Croesus."

"Enough to keep two loving couples?"

"Sumptuous."

Early in the uncandled morning, groping to the privy bleared with sleep, were the old man to place his foot upon the subfusc yet volatile fur of a shadow-camouflaged young tabby cat—

"You read my thoughts, my love."

I say to my master: "Now, you get yourself a doctor's gown, impedimenta all complete, or I'm done with you."

"What's this, Puss?"

"Do as I say and never mind the reason! The less you know of why, the better."

So he expends a few of the hag's ducats on a black gown with a white collar and his skullcap and his black bag and, under my direction, makes himself another sign that announces, with all due pomposity, how he is Il Famed Dottore: *Aches cured, pains prevented, bones set, graduate of Bologna, physician extraordinary.* He demands to know, is she to play the invalid to give him further access to her bedroom?

"I'll clasp her in my arms and jump out of the window; we, too, shall both perform the triple somersault of love."

"You just mind your own business, sir, and let me mind it for you after my own fashion."

Another raw and misty morning! Here in the hills, will the weather ever change? So bleak it is, and dreary; but there he stands, grave as a sermon in his black gown, and half the market people come with coughs and boils and broken heads and I dispense the plasters and the vials of colored water I'd forethoughtfully stowed in his bag, he too agitato to sell for himself. (And who knows, might we not have stumbled on a profitable profession for future pursuit, if my present plans miscarry?)

Until dawn shoots his little yet how flaming arrow past the cathedral on which the clock strikes six. At the last stroke, that famous door flies open once again and—*eeeeeeeeeeeeech!* the hag lets rip.

"Oh, Doctor, oh, Doctor, come quick as you can; our good man's taken a sorry tumble!"

And weeping fit to float a smack, she is, so doesn't see the doctor's apprentice is most colorfully and completely furred and whiskered.

The old booby's flat out at the foot of the stair, his head at an acute angle that might turn chronic and a big bunch of keys, still, gripped in his right hand as if they were the keys to heaven, marked: *Wanted on voyage.* And Missis, in her wrap, bends over him with a pretty air of concern.

"A fall—" she begins when she sees the doctor, but stops short when she sees your servant, Puss, looking as suitably down-in-the-mouth as his chronic smile will let him, humping his master's stock in trade and hawing like a sawbones. "You again," she says, and can't forbear to giggle. But the dragon's too blubbered to hear.

My master puts his ear to the old man's chest and shakes his head dolefully; then takes the mirror from his pocket and puts it to the old man's mouth. Not a breath clouds it. Oh, sad! Oh, sorrowful!

"Dead, is he?" sobs the hag. "Broke his neck, has he?"

And she slyly makes a little grab for the keys, in spite of her well-orchestrated distress; but Missis slaps her hand and she gives over.

"Let's get him to a softer bed," says Master.

He ups the corpse, carries it aloft to the room we know full well, bumps Pantaloon down, twitches an eyelid, taps a kneecap, feels a pulse.

"Dead as a doornail," he pronounces. "It's not a doctor you want; it's an undertaker."

Missis has a handkerchief very dutifully and correctly to her eyes.

"You just run along and get one," she says to hag. "And then I'll read the will. Because don't think he's forgotten you, thou faithful servant. Oh, my goodness, no."

So off goes hag; you never saw a woman of her accumulated Christmases sprint so fast. As soon as they are left alone, no trifling this time; they're at it, hammer and tongs, down on the carpet since the bed is occupé. Up and down, up and down, his arse; in and out, in and out, her legs. Then she heaves him up and throws him on his back, her turn at the grind now, and you'd think she'll never stop.

Toujours discret, Puss occupies himself in unfastening the shutters and throwing the windows open to the beautiful beginnings of morning, in whose lively yet fragrant air his sensitive nostrils catch the first and vernal hint of spring. In a few moments, my dear friend joins me. I notice already—or is it only my fond imagination?—a charming new *portliness* in her gait, hitherto so elastic, so spring-heeled. And there we sit upon the window sill, like the two genii and protectors of the house; ah, Puss, your rambling days are over. I shall become a hearth-rug cat, a fat and cozy cushion cat, sing to the moon no more, settle at last amid the sedentary joys of a domesticity we two, she and I, have so richly earned.

Their cries of rapture rouse me from this pleasant reverie.

The hag chooses, naturellement, this tender if outrageous moment to return with the undertaker in his chiffoned topper, plus a brace of mutes black as beetles, glum as bailiffs, bearing the elm box between them to take the corpse away in. But they cheer up something wonderful at the unexpected spectacle before them and he and she conclude their amorous interlude amidst roars of approbation and torrents of applause.

But what a racket the hag makes! Police, murder, thieves! Until the Master chucks her purseful of gold back again, for a gratuity.

(Meanwhile, I note that sensible young woman, mother naked as she is, has yet the presence of mind to catch hold of her husband's key ring and sharply tug it from his sere, cold grip. Once she's got the keys secure, she's in charge of all.)

"Now, no more of your nonsense!" she snaps to hag. "If I hereby give you the sack, you'll get a handsome gift to go along with you, for now"—flourishing the keys—"I am a rich widow and here"—indicating to all my bare yet blissful master—"is the young man who'll be my second husband."

When the governess found Signor Panteleone had indeed remembered her in his will, left her a keepsake of the cup he drank his morning water from, she made not a squeak more, pocketed a fat sum with thanks and, sneezing, took herself off with no more cries of "murder," neither. The old buffoon briskly bundled in his coffin and buried; Master comes into a great fortune and Missis rounding out already and they as happy as pigs in plunk.

But my Tabs beat her to it, since cats don't take much time about engendering; three fine, new-minted ginger kittens, all complete with snowy socks and shirtfronts, tumble in the cream and tangle Missis's knitting and put a smile on every face, not just their mother's and proud father's, for Tabs and I smile all day long and, these days, we put our hearts in it.

So may all your wives, if you need them, be rich and pretty; and all your husbands, if you want them, be young and virile; and all your cats as wily, perspicacious and resourceful as:

PUSS IN BOOTS.

URSULA K. LE GUIN

Schrödinger's Cat

As things appear to be coming to some sort of climax, I have withdrawn to this place. It is cooler here, and nothing moves fast.

On the way here I met a married couple who were coming apart. She had pretty well gone to pieces, but he seemed, at first glance, quite hearty. While he was telling me that he had no hormones of any kind, she pulled herself together and, by supporting her head in the crook of her right knee and hopping on the toes of the right foot, approached us shouting, "Well what's *wrong* with a person trying to express themselves?" The left leg, the arms, and the trunk, which had remained lying in the heap, twitched and jerked in sympathy. "Great legs," the husband pointed out, looking at the slim ankle. "My wife has great legs."

A cat has arrived, interrupting my narrative. It is a striped yellow tom with white chest and paws. He has long whiskers and yellow eyes. I never noticed before that cats had whiskers above their eyes; is that normal? There is no way to tell. As he has gone to sleep on my knee, I shall proceed.

Where?

Nowhere, evidently. Yet the impulse to narrate remains. Many things are not worth doing, but almost anything is worth telling. In any case, I have a severe congenital case of *Ethica laboris puritanica*, or Adam's Disease. It is incurable except by total decapitation. I even like to dream when asleep, and to try and recall my dreams: it assures me that I haven't wasted seven or eight hours just lying there. Now here I am, lying, here. Hard at it.

Well, the couple I was telling you about finally broke up. The pieces of him trotted around bouncing and cheeping, like little chicks, but she was finally reduced to nothing but a mass of nerves: rather like fine chicken wire, in fact, but hopelessly tangled.

So I came on, placing one foot carefully in front of the other, and grieving. This grief is with me still. I fear it is part of me, like foot or loin or eye, or may even be myself: for I seem to have no other self, nothing further, nothing that lies outside the borders of grief.

Yet I don't know what I grieve for: my wife? my husband? my children, or myself? I can't remember. Most dreams are forgotten, try as one will to remember. Yet later music strikes the note, and the harmonic rings along the mandolin strings of the mind, and we find tears in our eyes. Some note keeps playing that makes me want to cry; but what for? I am not certain.

The yellow cat, who may have belonged to the couple that broke up, is dreaming. His paws twitch now and then, and once he makes a small, suppressed remark with his mouth shut. I wonder what a cat dreams of, and to whom he was speaking just then. Cats seldom waste words. They are quiet beasts. They keep their counsel, they reflect. They reflect all day, and at night their eyes reflect. Overbred Siamese cats may be as noisy as little dogs, and then people say, "They're talking," but the noise is farther from speech than is the deep silence of the hound or the tabby. All this cat can say is meow, but maybe in his silences he will suggest to me what it is that I have lost, what I am grieving for. I have a feeling that he knows. That's why he came here. Cats look out for Number One.

It was getting awfully hot. I mean, you could touch less and less. The stove burners, for instance. Now I know that stove burners always used to get hot; that was their final cause, they existed in order to get hot. But they began to get hot without having been turned on. Electric units or gas rings, there they'd be when you came into the kitchen for breakfast, all four of them glaring away, the air above them shaking like clear jelly with the heat waves. It did no good to turn them off, because they weren't on in the first place. Besides, the knobs and dials were also hot, uncomfortable to the touch.

Some people tried hard to cool them off. The favorite technique was to turn them on. It worked sometimes, but you could not count on it. Others investigated the phenomenon, tried to get at the root of it, the cause. They were probably the most frightened ones, but man is most human at his most frightened. In the face of the hot stove burners they acted with exemplary coolness. They studied, they observed. They were like the fellow in Michelangelo's *Last Judgment*, who has clapped his hands over his face in horror as the devils drag him down to Hell—but only over one eye. The other eye is busy looking. It's all he can do, but he does it. He observes. Indeed, one wonders if Hell would exist, if he did not look at it. However, neither he, nor the people I am talking about, had enough time left to do much about it. And then finally of course there were the people who did not try to do or think anything about it at all.

When the water came out of the cold-water taps hot one morning, however, even people who had blamed it all on the Democrats began to feel a more profound unease. Before long, forks and pencils and wrenches were too hot to handle without gloves; and cars were really terrible. It was like opening the door of an oven going full blast, to open the door of your car. And by then, other people almost scorched your fingers off. A kiss was like a branding iron. Your child's hair flowed along your hand like fire.

Here, as I said, it is cooler; and, as a matter of fact, this animal is cool. A real cool cat. No wonder it's pleasant to pet his fur. Also he moves slowly, at least for the most part, which is all the slowness one can reasonably expect of a cat. He hasn't that frenetic quality most creatures acquired—all they did was ZAP and gone. They lacked presence. I suppose birds always tended to be that way, but even the hummingbird used to halt for a second in the very center of his metabolic frenzy, and hang, still as a hub, present, above the fuchsias—then gone again, but you knew something was there besides the blurring brightness. But it got so that even robins and pigeons, the heavy impudent birds, were a blur; and as for swallows, they cracked the sound barrier. You knew of swallows only by the small, curved sonic booms that looped about the eaves of old houses in the evening.

Worms shot like subway trains through the dirt of gardens, among the writhing roots of roses.

You could scarcely lay a hand on children, by then: too fast to catch, too hot to hold. They grew up before your eyes.

But then, maybe that's always been true.

I was interrupted by the cat, who woke and said meow once, then jumped down from my lap and leaned against my legs diligently.

This is a cat who knows how to get fed. He also knows how to jump. There was a lazy fluidity to his leap, as if gravity affected him less than it does other creatures. As a matter of fact there were some localised cases, just before I left, of the failure of gravity; but this quality in the cat's leap was something quite else. I am not yet in such a state of confusion that I can be alarmed by grace. Indeed, I found it reassuring. While I was opening a can of sardines, a person arrived.

Hearing the knock, I thought it might be the mailman. I miss mail very much, so I hurried to the door and said, "Is it the mail?"

A voice replied, "Yah!" I opened the door. He came in, almost pushing me aside in his haste. He dumped down an enormous knapsack he had been carrying, straightened up, massaged his shoulders, and said, "Wow!"

"How did you get here?"

He stared at me and repeated, "How?"

At this my thoughts concerning human and animal speech recurred to me, and I decided that this was probably not a man, but a small dog. (Large dogs seldom go yah, wow, how, unless it is appropriate to do so.)

"Come on, fella," I coaxed him. "Come, come on, that's a boy, good doggie!" I opened a can of pork and beans for him at once, for he looked half starved. He ate voraciously, gulping and lapping. When it was gone he said "Wow!" several times. I was just about to scratch him behind the ears when he stiffened, his hackles bristling, and growled deep in his throat. He had noticed the cat.

The cat had noticed him some time before, without interest, and was now sitting on a copy of *The Well-Tempered Clavier* washing sardine oil off its whiskers.

"Wow!" the dog, whom I had thought of calling Rover, barked. "Wow! Do you know what that is? *That's Schrödinger's cat!*"

"No it's not, not any more; it's my cat," I said, unreasonably offended.

"Oh, well, Schrödinger's dead, of course, but it's his cat. I've seen hundreds of pictures of it. Erwin Schrödinger, the great physicist, you know. Oh, wow! To think of finding it here!"

The cat looked coldly at him for a moment, and began to wash its left shoulder with negligent energy. An almost religious expression had come into Rover's face. "It was meant," he said in a low, impressive tone. "Yah. It was *meant*. It can't be a mere coincidence.

It's too improbable. Me, with the box; you, with the cat; to meet—here—now." He looked up at me, his eyes shining with happy fervor. "Isn't it wonderful?" he said. "I'll get the box set up right away." And he started to tear open his huge knapsack.

While the cat washed its front paws, Rover unpacked. While the cat washed its tail and belly, regions hard to reach gracefully, Rover put together what he had unpacked, a complex task. When he and the cat finished their operations simultaneously and looked at me, I was impressed. They had come out even, to the very second. Indeed it seemed that something more than chance was involved. I hoped it was not myself.

"What's that?" I asked, pointing to a protuberance on the outside of the box. I did not ask what the box was as it was quite clearly a box.

"The gun," Rover said with excited pride.

"The gun?"

"To shoot the cat."

"To shoot the cat?"

"Or to *not shoot* the cat. Depending on the photon."

"The photon?"

"Yah! It's Schrödinger's great Gedankenexperiment. You see, there's a little emitter here. At Zero Time, five seconds after the lid of the box is closed, it will emit one photon. The photon will strike a half-silvered mirror. The quantum mechanical probability of the photon passing through the mirror is exactly one half, isn't it? So! If the photon passes through, the trigger will be activated and the gun will fire. If the photon is deflected, the trigger will not be activated and the gun will not fire. Now, you put the cat in. The cat is in the box. You close the lid. You go away! You stay away! What happens?" Rover's eyes were bright.

"The cat gets hungry?"

"The cat gets shot—or not shot," he said, seizing my arm, though not, fortunately, in his teeth. "But the gun is silent, perfectly silent. The box is soundproof. There is no way to know whether or not the cat has been shot, until you lift the lid of the box. There is *no* way! Do you see how central this is to the whole of quantum theory? Before Zero Time the whole system, on the quantum level or on our level, is nice and simple. But after Zero Time the whole system can be represented only by a linear combination of two waves. We cannot predict the behavior of the photon, and thus, once it has behaved, we cannot predict the state of the system it has determined. We cannot predict it! God plays dice with the world! So it is beautifully demonstrated that if you desire certainty, any certainty, you must create it yourself!"

"How?"

"By lifting the lid of the box, of course," Rover said, looking at me with sudden disappointment, perhaps a touch of suspicion, like a Baptist who finds he has been talking church matters not to another Baptist as he thought, but a Methodist, or even, God forbid, an Episcopalian. "To find out whether the cat is dead or not."

"Do you mean," I said carefully, "that until you lift the lid of the box, the cat has neither been shot nor not been shot?"

"Yah!" Rover said, radiant with relief, welcoming me back to the fold. "Or maybe, you know, both."

"But why does opening the box and looking reduce the system back to one probability, either live cat or dead cat? Why don't we get included in the system when we lift the lid of the box?"

There was a pause. "How?" Rover barked, distrustfully.

"Well, we would involve ourselves in the system, you see, the superposition of two waves. There's no reason why it should only exist *inside* an open box, is there? So when we came to look, there we would be, you and I, both looking at a live cat, and both looking at a dead cat. You see?"

A dark cloud lowered on Rover's eyes and brow. He barked twice in a subdued, harsh voice, and walked away. With his back turned to me he said in a firm, sad tone, "You must not complicate the issue. It is complicated enough."

"Are you sure?"

He nodded. Turning, he spoke pleadingly. "Listen. It's all we have—the box. Truly it is. The box. And the cat. And they're here. The box, the cat, at last. Put the cat in the box. Will you? Will you let me put the cat in the box?"

"No," I said, shocked.

"Please. Please. Just for a minute. Just for half a minute! Please let me put the cat in the box!"

"Why?"

"I can't stand this terrible uncertainty," he said, and burst into tears.

I stood some while indecisive. Though I felt sorry for the poor son of a bitch, I was about to tell him, gently, No; when a curious thing happened. The cat walked over to the box, sniffed around it, lifted his tail and sprayed a corner to mark his territory, and then lightly, with that marvelous fluid ease, leapt into it. His yellow tail just flicked the edge of the lid as he jumped, and it closed, falling into place with a soft, decisive click.

"The cat is in the box," I said.

"The cat is in the box," Rover repeated in a whisper, falling to his knees. "Oh, wow. Oh, wow. Oh, wow."

There was silence then: deep silence. We both gazed, I afoot, Rover kneeling, at the box. No sound. Nothing happened. Nothing would happen. Nothing would ever happen, until we lifted the lid of the box.

"Like Pandora," I said in a weak whisper. I could not quite recall Pandora's legend. She had let all the plagues and evils out of the box, of course, but there had been something else, too. After all the devils were let loose, something quite different, quite unexpected, had been left. What had it been? Hope? A dead cat? I could not remember.

Impatience welled up in me. I turned on Rover, glaring. He returned the look with expressive brown eyes. You can't tell me dogs haven't got souls.

"Just exactly what are you trying to prove?" I demanded.

"That the cat will be dead, or not dead," he murmured submissively. "Certainty. All I want is certainty. To know for *sure* that God *does* play dice with the world."

I looked at him for a while with fascinated incredulity. "Whether he does, or doesn't," I said, "do you think he's going to leave you a note about it in the box?" I went to the box, and with a rather dramatic gesture, flung the lid back. Rover staggered up from his knees, gasping, to look. The cat was, of course, not there.

Rover neither barked, nor fainted, nor cursed, nor wept. He really took it very well.

"Where is the cat?" he asked at last.

"Where is the box?"

"Here."

"Where's here?"

"Here is now."

"We used to think so," I said, "but really we should use larger boxes."

He gazed about him in mute bewilderment, and did not flinch even when the roof of the house was lifted off just like the lid of a box, letting in the unconscionable, inordinate light of the stars. He had just time to breathe, "Oh, wow!"

I have identified the note that keeps sounding. I checked it on the mandolin before the glue melted. It is the note A, the one that drove the composer Schumann mad. It is a beautiful, clear tone, much clearer now that the stars are visible. I shall miss the cat. I wonder if he found what it was we lost?

FRANCINE PROSE

Amateur Voodoo

Philip asks for paper, crayons and tape, and papers his bedroom walls with drawings of cats. He's trying to work magic, to bring his cat back home. It's been four days since he and his parents returned from Cape Cod to find Geronimo gone. Philip and Frank and Jenny took turns calling the cat, and then, when it got dark, Philip sat on the front steps with a flashlight and an open cat food can.

"Amateur voodoo," says Frank. Basically Frank approves; some part of him even thinks it might work. In that way he and Philip are different from Jenny, who, from the start, assumed the cat was gone for good.

Philip hasn't mentioned Geronimo since that first night, and even when he takes Jenny upstairs to see his room, she senses that he still doesn't want to talk about it. He has used maybe fifty sheets from the reams of Xerox paper they buy him. Every picture is different. Cat close-ups and long shots, cats that are all whiskers and others doing things like riding bikes. Later, Frank says, "He's got his room done like Lourdes," but Jenny has had another kind of flash: those little Mexican statues of skeletons playing volleyball, riding bikes, doing just what Philip's cats are, and with similar crazy smiles.

Both of them think this is basically good, this evidence in Philip of loyalty and love. Jenny just wonders: good for whom? On their vacation, Philip, who is six, fell in love with a fifteen-year-old girl. Cheryl's parents were renting the house next door; there were no other kids around. She and Philip would go to the beach. Jenny and Frank weren't surprised—Philip is better company than most adults.

Free babysitting, they thought. But then a sixteen-year-old boy showed up and Cheryl went off with him. Philip said he was sleepy and wouldn't come out of his room, and they realized that it had been—in every way but one, they hoped—just like an adult love. It shadowed everything for a day or so until Philip cheered up. Things must be in proportion if Philip is working harder to get back his cat than he did to get back Cheryl, though maybe it just seems to him more possible.

Already this cat has had a fairly complicated history. Philip got him in May, as a kitten. A friend found him on her lawn, a passing car must have left him there. Well, not a friend, exactly; a woman named Ada whom Frank was in love with for two very terrible months. That was four years ago. At that time, Jenny had felt certain that she and Frank couldn't go on; now she is shocked by how much she has—or mostly has—forgotten. Ada has half-moved back into Boston, they rarely see her. They hadn't seen her at all this spring till the pond—directly across the road from her driveway—was blown up.

Pedersen's pond was where everyone used to go. When they first moved to New Hampshire, ten years ago, the pond was where they found each other, couple by couple and one by one. They swam there as young people with bodies pretty enough for skinny-dipping, then as mothers bringing their children to play, even after some of them could have afforded to put in ponds of their own. It had never been safe—no lifeguard, slippery banks—but they were careful. Sometimes swimmers had to be dragged in to shore; Frank used to ride with the rescue squad, and several times he was called out there to make sure some drunken teenager was okay. But no one ever really got hurt, no one ever drowned.

This year Pedersen's insurance carrier scared him about liability. He dynamited the pond at five A.M., with a crew he'd brought in from North Conway.

Word got out, and everyone made a kind of pilgrimage. Even Frank and Jenny, who hadn't swam there in several summers, felt they had to see. It looked like the set of a big-budget war movie. Uprooted spruces lay ten feet from the ragged holes they'd come out of; the blasting had destroyed a large section of the woods. You'd have thought a former pond would be mucky, but the water had drained away fast. There was just a scarred empty flat space where the deep part used to be. Everything was dried out; the leaves looked ripped and brown with dust—grimy, like unwashed cars. Philip had mixed feelings about the pond; he'd grown a little afraid of the water, while most of his friends had already learned to swim. But Philip, too, seemed stunned.

Then they saw Ada walking across the road. Even in her bare feet, Ada always seemed to be wearing high heels. She was carrying something against her shoulder, a taffy-colored kitten. As she got closer, Jenny and Frank found it easiest to look at the cat. Ada looked down at it too; then everyone focused on Philip, who was staring at the kitten. He graced Ada with his shy, six-year-old James Dean smile. "Hey," he said. "Nice cat."

"Someone drop him off on my lawn," Ada said. Ada is Czech, but everyone who meets her thinks she is French. She has been in this country fifteen years, but holds on to her accent and her own sense of English grammar and word order.

It took Jenny a moment to figure out that she was talking about how she'd gotten the cat. Frank understood right away.

"Take it," said Ada. "Please. It and the baby, already they know each other. Maybe from some other life."

Philip kept silent and let himself be called a baby. Jenny and Frank took turns saying, "We can't." Then almost in unison, they said, "Well, why not?" and everyone started to laugh. Ada said, "Come in. Think about it. Have tea."

Jenny said, "Thanks, we can't." She said, "I mean, about tea. It's all right. We'll take the cat."

They talked for a few more moments. Jenny asked about Jan, Ada's husband, who is a surgeon and rarely comes out from Boston, about Milan and Eva, their nearly grown children; everyone was fine. Ada asked about the winter: had it been bad?

"We survived," Philip said.

"What winter?" said Jenny. "I can't remember."

No one mentioned Pedersen's pond.

On the way home, Jenny said, "I'll bet we wouldn't have taken the cat if we hadn't just seen what they did to the pond. We needed to make some gesture in the face of that."

Frank said, "That cat is one lucky duck." If anyone else had given them the kitten, he thought, in a week or two he would call to report on its progress. He didn't think he call would Ada.

They had all enjoyed feeling big—adult, sensible, forgiving. Leaving Ada's, Jenny had said, "I'm glad it worked out." She meant the instant and clearly mutual affection between Philip and the cat. That Jenny would permit him to take a cat from Ada showed how much time has passed. It would have *meant* something to refuse.

Philip named the cat. When it was tiny, he used to throw it up in the air and yell, "Geronimo!" He never threw it hard. Only once Jenny saw the kitten stumbling off looking dazed, and Philip snatched it up and kissed it and said, "I'm sorry." Philip often talked to the cat. He would sit the cat up in his lap when he watched his favorite TV shows, and he'd tell it, more or less, what was happening.

What makes Jenny feel pessimistic now is a note from the high school kid they paid to feed Geronimo while they were gone. The note said, "No cat since Tuesday. I called and called." Philip—who is learning to read—can't decipher that reckless high school scrawl, and Jenny doesn't tell him. Frank says, "The cat'll be back." They've all grown fond of Geronimo. They want to believe Frank is right.

The cat has been gone eight days—not four, as Philip believes —when Philip papers his room with drawings of cats, and Frank asks Jenny to come with him to the neighbor. That either of them should suggest this is a sign of how much is at stake.

In the five years since the new house went up on the land bordering theirs, they have talked to the neighbor just twice; once, when the foundation was being put in, they asked if it couldn't be dug somewhere else—anywhere on the neighbor's fifty acres where they wouldn't see it from their kitchen window; and once, across a table at a friend's dinner party, when they really had no choice.

At first there was much ill will—they wouldn't acknowledge the neighbor on the road, pretended not to see him in the store or the bank. But that only increased his importance, his claim on their lives, so now they nod and wave. And when Jenny looks out of her kitchen window his house doesn't register, is not there, is hidden behind some psychic equivalent of an optical blindspot.

The neighbor (they never speak or think of him as anything but "the neighbor") is a biologist. They tried to see this as a comfort— it could have been a rod-and-gun club next door—until he partly filled in the wetland behind his house to alleviate a drainage problem; herons used to wade there, and in spring, huge flocks of geese would stop on their way to wherever.

The neighbor had a wife when he moved here. Her name was Mercedes. For a while the wind used to carry the sound of them yelling. She was gone by the time of that dinner party—moved to New York, said the gossip. Jenny has often thought that all the resentment they'd focused on the neighbor's house must have had its effect. In fact it's probably true that their real estate feud didn't help his domestic life. If things were as bad as they sounded, his wife probably took their side.

The neighbor's cat, a glossy, gray-and-white male, has always felt free to walk on Frank and Jenny's lawn. At first it made Jenny shudder, like a possum or a woodchuck, something you wouldn't kill but you didn't have to like. But finally she and Frank had to admit: it was a pretty cat. It seems possible that at some lonely dinner hour Geronimo went to eat with the neighbor's cat, though they tell themselves that Geronimo would be home by now, wouldn't stay there when they'd come back.

They wait until Philip is in day camp. If what's happened is what Jenny secretly suspects—that the neighbor has run the cat over in his driveway—they would like to predigest the news and tell Philip themselves.

The neighbor answers the door in tennis shorts and a T-shirt. If it were anyone else, Jenny would think he had a handsome, well-cared-for body, but in this case she thinks: imagine, a guy living alone and keeping his shorts and T-shirts so white.

Jenny makes Frank let *her* talk; she is less likely, she says, to let all the events of those first few months make the most casual question tense and malignant with strain. She says, "Listen, have you seen a little, taffy-colored cat?"

The neighbor claps his hand over his mouth. He says, "Oh my God, that was yours?" He says the cat was around. He says it was fighting with his cat, and besides, he couldn't feed another cat, and just at that moment the gray-and-white cat shows up, as if it knows they are discussing it. The neighbor says he's sorry, he took the little cat and drove it down the road and left it in a field at the very bottom of Cider Hill Road. He thought it could catch mice there.

Frank and Jenny look at each other and roll their eyes. Otherwise, they feel eerily calm. Frank says, "You must be joking." Jenny says, "That was our cat." Her voice sounds thin and slightly whiny, like Philip protesting some irrevocable adult decision. Jenny says, "That's amazing." The neighbor says, "I'm sorry, I'm really, really sorry." Neither Frank nor Jenny say anything to that. With shrugs and neutral gestures expressing something halfway between "Don't be" and "You should be," they turn and leave. The neighbor calls after them, "Hey, man, I'm really sorry."

Frank says, "Can you believe he told us? If *I* did that I would *never* have told. I would have said, 'What cat? I didn't see any cat.'"

"You wouldn't have done it," says Jenny.

They are home drinking coffee when Jenny finally says, "Of course the truly strange thing is that he should have dropped it off on Cider Hill Road." That is where Ada lives, where they got Geronimo in the first place, although the field the neighbor means is miles from Ada's house. "Does he know Ada?"

"I doubt it," says Frank.

"Oh, I don't know," Jenny says. "Maybe that cat just wasn't meant to be our cat. Maybe we should leave it."

"It's Philip's cat," says Frank.

Frank says he'll go to Cider Hill and look for the cat. He'll go after Philip comes home from camp, this evening, after dinner. He'll take Philip with him. Jenny thinks it is wrong to take a child on a wild goose chase like that, but to say that would be to admit all the differences in how she and Frank see the world. "I'll go with you," she says.

Later, as they are getting into the car, Philip says, "Wouldn't it be weird if the cat turned up at Ada's?" Of course they are all thinking that. Philip knows only that Ada is a fairly distant family friend. It irritates Jenny that her son should just say Ada's name as if it were perfectly normal.

Frank is driving, and as they turn up Cider Hill Road, Jenny has one of those moments of clarity and prescience: she is positive that the cat is at Ada's. For an instant it crosses her mind that the neighbor knows Ada, knows their histories, that this is at once their retribution and his revenge. But it all seems unlikely—hardly anyone knew about Ada and Frank; even if the neighbor knew everything —whose cat it was and where it came from and all they had gone through—he wasn't the type to even let himself consider revenge.

They stop at the first house on the road, nearest the field the neighbor described. Frank knows the old couple who live there from the rescue squad. He sends Philip up to the door, and Philip comes back beaming. "They saw him," says Philip, and points further on down the road.

From what they can tell, the cat has made its way along the road, dining at a different home every night. Everyone seems to have been struck by its winning personality. Jenny counts the houses, the nights the cat's been gone, and remembers the counting games she played as a child: how far in advance you could see you'd be "out." The cat is at Ada's, there's no doubt in her mind, but still for the sake of form they keep stopping at houses, tracing the cat's progressive dinner up the hill.

Ada lives in a white frame eyebrow colonial up a long drive surrounded by trees; when you get out of the car in the clearing in front of the house, you feel you are being watched. It makes Jenny wonder who would drop off a cat back here. Though Ada says some outrageous things, but she has never actually lied.

Three cats play in front of the house, but Geronimo isn't among them. Frank, Jenny and Philip walk up the steps; it's Philip who knocks on the door. No one answers, but Geronimo appears at the window, pressing his face on the glass. Philip jumps up to meet him. Frank steps up and knocks. No one answers. Frank says, "We can't just go in and get it." Philip says, "Isn't it strange that it's here?"

"*Strange* is the word," says his father.

Finally Ada appears. She is wearing a beautiful antique silk kimono. Her hair is down on her forehead, and she pushes it back with her hand. "I am just sleeping," she says. "Jan and the children are in Boston." But Philip has already pushed by her and is hugging the cat.

"How the cat came here?" Ada says.

Frank seems on the point of telling the story, but something stops him. He is afraid his voice will betray him when he says, as he almost has to: What a coincidence. Instead he looks at Jenny, who tells the story quickly, emphasizing the neighbor's villainy. Ada makes clicking sounds and says, "How terrible. How awful. Oh, what a terrible man." There is a silence. Then Ada says, "Him you never liked. I come home, I don't know why the cat is here. I think it don't work out with you, and maybe you drop her here when I am gone."

"We wouldn't do that," Jenny says.

There's another pause, and Ada sighs. "Well, it could have been sad but is happy. And now you have to come in."

Ada steps aside to let Frank and Jenny pass. They follow her into the kitchen. Ada's kimono, and Ada herself, make it impossible not to notice the body under the silk. Frank is struck—as if for the first time—by how much civilization depends on not seeing certain things and pretending others never occurred. Jenny notices, too, and tries not to see. The only way she survived that time and forgave and kept going was by refusing to let certain pictures enter her head. She and Frank sit down across from each other at the pine kitchen table.

"This time we drink to the cat," Ada says. "We drink to it staying home with you where it belongs." She takes out three delicate shot glasses with deep blue rims and plunks them on the table with a bottle of vodka from the freezer. She and Frank and Jenny clink glasses and drink. No one looks at anyone else. Ada says, "You have been again to the pond?"

Frank says, "What a mess." And suddenly Jenny is surprised by a strange feeling: she's glad that the pond is gone. But why should that surprise her? The night everything started between Frank and Ada, Jenny had been in Boston, visiting a friend, and when she got back everyone in the grocery was talking about the drunken teenage kid the rescue squad saved from drowning in Pedersen's pond. But Frank hadn't told her, hadn't mentioned it, and when she asked him, he looked guilty and said, "What kid?" She had seen Frank and Ada talking at parties; it had made her unhappy. And right then she knew—just as she knew today that the cat would be back at Ada's—she knew that Frank had gone over to Ada's when he got through at the pond.

Suddenly Jenny feels panicked. She wants to get Philip and Frank and get out. She feels she cannot stand it that the memory of that night is something that Frank and Ada share, and it is different from hers. What she does not know, or want to know, is this:

That night, when Ada opened her door and saw Frank, she burst into tears. When at last she stopped crying and pacing and smoking cigarettes, she told him that she had wanted to see him so badly, she had been almost hoping that something would happen at the pond, that he would have to go there and he would be so close to her house, and he would know she wanted to see him, he would have felt it, and that night he would stop by. When she had heard the sirens and cars, she couldn't help thinking she'd caused it. But still she prayed Frank would come. Frank said she couldn't have caused it. And besides, the kid was all right.

There is a long silence. No one seems able to speak. They finish their vodka and Ada pours another round. Then Ada says, "Look. The sky." Outside the clouds have turned lavender. Ada and Frank and Jenny gaze fixedly out the window; it is something that's easy to stare at with more interest than they feel.

Suddenly a voice says, very clearly, "Did you miss me?" And all three of them turn, a little fast, a bit startled—as if they don't know that it's Philip, murmuring to his cat.

Part Eight

Contemporary Poets on Cats

STEPHEN DUNN

Cleanliness

My cat in a patch of sun
   on the floor, my cat
to whom everything is natural,

puts a little spit on her paws
   and touches herself clean.
Pussy: an epithet, insulting.

Or redeemed, a lover's word
   when only the vulgar
is equal to our wild good humor.

My pussycat in a patch of sun
   licking away
all that's accumulated . . .

Cleanliness, if only we believed,
   without guilt,
in the tongue's intelligence

and the wisdom of genitals,
   wouldn't that erase
a few dirty words? He sucks,

for example. She sucks. How lovely
   as words of praise.
Now my cat, spit-clean,

in a crouch, tail going,
   she's seen
something she wants

and what lover of cats
   wouldn't admire
how perfectly she's made for this?

REGINALD GIBBONS

Hoppy

Ancientest of cats, truest
model of decrepitude,
you shamble and push your own
sloppy shape across the room,
nosing the floor in your slow
unhappy step-by-step, and
with dollops of baby food
splashed around your whiskers, on
chin, on snout, and in one scarred
ear, don't you think it's gotten
crappy, this life, now the years
have slipped by, old Counselor?
You mop the rug with your tail,
you slap a tired paw against
the door, and turn dim yellow
eyes, flecked with a weariness
of having seen so much, back
over your jutting shoulder
to the faces that study
the exquisite mishap or
the dopey luck that has left
it to you—of all the world's
mopes and most unlikely wise,
prophets and poets—to stop
the bored chatter of these frail
merely human types and top
all their tiny, much boasted

perseverances with your
pained, apocalyptic glance.

DANIEL HALPERN

Sisterhood

There's a gray cat who's not allowed into the house
where our cat for twenty years has been the one cat.

There's a storm working over the low mountains,
building with a stillness of air and light

over the nearest peaks. And soon the rain,
the full storm gets under way, thunder and light,

the passing thickness of air, the sudden rush
of wind, and the sheet of rain spraying the valley.

The gray cat presses against the door frame, and we sit
down to dinner, our cat in the third chair, the stew

done right and placed on the table, the wine poured.
The evening survives the storm and we walk out for a look

at what's left. A moon finally free, a hostage
sprung from a Jihad of clouds breaking up. The wet grass

regains its starch from this afternoon's wet heat,
and the gray cat emerges from under the porch steps,

dry but intense, charging our legs and getting over
in the language of cats her wish to enter our lives.

In the window, mirroring the table lamp, our cat,
shrewd, disappointed, and accusatory, studies us.

She's hurt and shows no apparent sympathy for a sister
left to the cold of the outside world. We're not surprised,

she's an indoor cat, her claws clipped, her movements
suited to the angles of furniture, the surface of rugs.

She will stand before her bowl of food and demand our best,
a gourmet cat when hungry: squab, fillet, hearts of chicken.

ANTHONY HECHT

Divination by a Cat

Fence walker, balancer, your devil-may-care
Astounds the workman teetering on his girder
Whom gravity and the pavement want to murder,
   But with eight lives to spare
Who would lack courage? From his jungle-gym
He lowers, thin as a hair, the strand of fear
To plumb the seventy stories under him,
   And for his firm intent
The spirit level of the inner ear
   Is his chief instrument.

But you are classic, striking the S-curve
In a half-gainer from some eminence,
And with Athenian equipoise and sense
   To qualify your nerve,
End up unerringly upon your feet.
O this is Greek to all of us. I dare
Construe your figure for our human fate,
   And like the Pythoness

Decoding viscera, anoint the air
   With emblematic guess.

You are the lesser Tiger, yet the night
Blazes with the combustion of your eye,
And we, in our imperfect symmetry,
   Combining double sight,
Can see mirrored in your chatoyant gaze
Our fire, slight, diminished. If the first
Intensity return of that white blaze
   To run our bodies through,
Might it not burn us? If the fire burst,
   Will it not barbecue?

Cat, you are meat for study. All our youth
Shall vanish, like your literary kin,
Dwindle into a disembodied grin;
   And if we want the truth,
Why, we must cram for it, gather your drift,
Like that odd family trudging from St. Ives.
Be Plutarch to our ignorance; your gift
   Compares Athens to Rome,
And the collected tails of all your lives
   Shall drive the moral home.

EDWARD HIRSCH

Wild Gratitude

Tonight when I knelt down next to our cat, Zooey,
And put my fingers into her clean cat's mouth,
And rubbed her swollen belly that will never know kittens,
And watched her wriggle onto her side, pawing the air,
And listened to her solemn little squeals of delight,

I was thinking about the poet, Christopher Smart,
Who wanted to kneel down and pray without ceasing
In every one of the splintered London streets,

And was locked away in the madhouse at St. Luke's
With his sad religious mania, and his wild gratitude,
And his grave prayers for the other lunatics,
And his great love for his speckled cat, Jeoffry.
All day today—August 13, 1983—I remembered how
Christopher Smart blessed this same day in August, 1759,
For its calm bravery and ordinary good conscience.

This was the day that he blessed the Postmaster General
"And all conveyancers of letters" for their warm humanity,
And the gardeners for their private benevolence
And intricate knowledge of the language of flowers,
And the milkmen for their universal human kindness.
This morning I understood that he loved to hear—
As I have heard—the soft clink of milk bottles
On the rickety stairs in the early morning,

And how terrible it must have seemed
When even this small pleasure was denied him.
But it wasn't until tonight when I knelt down
And slipped my hand into Zooey's waggling mouth
That I remembered how he'd called Jeoffry "the servant
Of the Living God duly and daily serving Him,"
And for the first time understood what it meant.
Because it wasn't until I saw my own cat
Whine and roll over on her fluffy back
That I realized how gratefully he had watched
Jeoffry fetch and carry his wooden cork
Across the grass in the wet garden, patiently
Jumping over a high stick, calmly sharpening
His claws on the woodpile, rubbing his nose
Against the nose of another cat, stretching, or
Slowly stalking his traditional enemy, the mouse,
A rodent, "a creature of great personal valour,"
And then dallying so much that his enemy escaped.

And only then did I understand
It is Jeoffry—and every creature like him—
Who can teach us how to praise—purring
In their own language,
Wreathing themselves in the living fire.

JOHN HOLLANDER

Kitty and Bug

```
        I        a
      cat       who
      coated    in   a
      dense     shadow
      which   I   cast
      along      myself
        absorb     the
        light    you
        gaze   at   me
        with   can   yet
        look   at   a   king
        and   not   be   seen
        to   be   seeing   any
      more     than     himself
    a     motionless     seer
    sovereign    of    gray
    mirrored          invisibly
  in    the    seeing    glass
  of   air   Whatever   I   am
  seeing   is   part   of   me
  As   you   see   me   now   my
  vision   is   wrapped   in
  two     green     hypotheses
    darkness          blossoming
    in   two   unseen   eyes
      which   pretend   to   be
      intent   on   a   spot   of                    bug
      upon
      the
      rug
    Who
    can
      see
          how
            eye
              can
      know
```

TED HUGHES

Esther's Tomcat

Daylong this tomcat lies stretched flat
As an old rough mat, no mouth and no eyes,
Continual wars and wives are what
Have tattered his ears and battered his head.

Like a bundle of old rope and iron
Sleeps till blue dusk. Then reappear
His eyes, green as ringstones: he yawns wide red,
Fangs fine as a lady's needle and bright.

A tomcat sprang at a mounted knight,
Locked round his neck like a trap of hooks
While the knight rode fighting its clawing and bite.
After hundreds of years the stain's there

On the stone where he fell, dead of the tom:
That was at Barnborough. The tomcat still
Grallochs odd dogs on the quiet,
Will take the head clean off your simple pullet,

Is unkillable. From the dog's fury,
From gunshot fired point-blank he brings
His skin whole, and whole
From owlish moons of bekittenings

Among ashcans. He leaps and lightly
Walks upon sleep, his mind on the moon.
Nightly over the round world of men,
Over the roofs go his eyes and outcry.

GALWAY KINNELL

The Cat

The first thing that happened
was that somebody borrowed the Jeep,
drove fifty feet, went off the road.
The cat may have stuck a tire iron
or baseball bat into the steering wheel.
I don't know if it did or didn't.
I do know—I don't dare say it aloud—
when the cat is around something goes wrong.
Why doesn't our host forewarn us? Well,
he tries. He gives each guest on arrival
a list of instructions about the cat.
I never was able to read mine,
for the cat was watching when I got it,
so I stuck it in my pocket to read later,
but the cat saw, leapt at me, nearly
knocked me down, clawed at the pocket,
would have ripped my clothes off
if I had not handed it over.
The guest book contains the name
of the young woman who was my friend,
who brought me here in the first place,
who is the reason I have come back,
to find out what became of her.
But no one would tell me anything.
Except tonight, my final evening,
at dinner, the host says, "There is
someone . . . someone . . . a woman . . .
in your life . . ." I know he means her,
but why the present tense? "Whom you have in . . ."
The next word sounds like "blurrarree"
but it could be "slavery." "Well, yes,"
I say. "Yes, but where is the cat?"
"It is an awful thing you are doing,"

he goes on. "Quite awful." "But who?"
I protest. "What are you talking about?"
"The cat," he says. "When you lock her up
she becomes dangerous." "The cat?
What cat?" I remember the kitten I saved
out of the burlap sack when I was seven,
I was fathering or mothering her, my father
or mother said, "Stop smothering it."
Suddenly an electric force grabs my feet.
I see it has seized the host too—
he is standing up, his hands are flopping
at his sides. "What is it?" I whisper.
"I'm washing the dishes," he says.
"O my God," I think.
"I'm washing the dishes," he repeats.
I realize he is trying to get the cat to believe
he is not in a seizure but washing the dishes.
If either of us lets on about the seizure
I know for certain the cat will kill us both.

JOHN L'HEUREUX

The Thing About Cats

Cats hang out with witches quite a lot;
that's not it.

The thing about cats is
they're always looking at you.
Especially when you're asleep.

Some cats pretend they're not looking
until you're not looking.
They are not to be trusted.

Some cats scowl because they're wearing
imitation fur. They feel inferior.

Some other cats look at you straight on
so that you can't drink your drink
or make love
              but keep thinking
that cat's looking at me straight on.

But all cats do the same:
they look at you
                and you look out
and in.

A cat is not a conscience; I'm not
saying that.

What I'm saying is
                why are they looking?

WILLIAM MATTHEWS

The Cat

While you read
the sleepmoth begins
to circle your eyes
and then—
a hail of claws
lands the cat
in your lap.
The little motor
in his throat
is how a cat says
Me. He rasps the soft
file of his tongue

along the inside
of your wrist.
He licks himself.
He's building
a pebble of fur
in his stomach.
And now he pulls
his body in a circle
around the fire of sleep.

This is the wet
sweater with legs
that shakes in
from the rain,
split-ear the sex burglar,
Fish-breath, Wind-
minion, paw-poker
of dust
tumbleweeds,
the cat that kisses
with the wet
flame of his tongue
each of your eyelids
as if sealing
a letter.

One afternoon
napping under the light-
ladder
let down by the window,
there are two of them:
cat and cat-
shadow, sleep.

One night you lay your book
down like the clothes
your mother wanted
you to wear tomorrow.
You yawn.
The cat exhales a moon.
Opening a moon,

---

you dream of cats.
One of them strokes you
the wrong way. Still,
you sleep well.

This is the same cat
Plunder.
This is the old cat
Milk-whiskers.
This is the cat
eating one of its lives.
This is the first cat
Fire-fur.
This is the next cat
St. Sorrow.
This is the cat with its claws
furled, like sleep's flag.
This is the lust cat
trying to sleep with its shadow.
This is the only cat
I have ever loved.
This cat has written
in tongue-ink
the poem you are reading now,
the poem scratching
at the gate of silence,
the poem
that forgives
itself
for its used-up lives,
the poem
of the cat waking,
running a long shudder
through his body,
stretching again,
following the moist bell
of his nose
into the world
again.

ROGER McGOUGH

My cat and i

Girls are simply the prettiest things
My cat and i believe
And we're always saddened
When it's time for them to leave

We watch them titivating
(that often takes a while)
And though they keep us waiting
My cat & i just smile

We like to see them to the door
Say how sad it couldn't last
Then my cat and I go back inside
And talk about the past.

HOWARD MOSS

Catnip and Dogwood

A cat's quite different from a dog
And you name it differently, too;
A library cat might be Catalogue,
And a Siamese, Fu Manchu.
Dogs usually have humdrum names
Like Molly, Blacky, Biff, and James.

Cats eat catnip excitedly,
Get drunk and jump around,
But a dog can sniff at a dogwood tree,
And sniff and sniff quite diligently,
Sit down and never budge—
And be as smug and sober as a judge.

ROBERT PHILLIPS

Poem for Pekoe

Our lives were only half gone
when she had used up

all her nine. Time came
upon her like a sledgehammer:

her insides dropped, she
waddled like a duck,

her belly ballooned,
not with child—she'd

never kittened, early on
was "fixed." Her belly

carried cancer and stones,
her muscles too flaccid

ever to tighten again.
Her bowels moved wherever,

she who had been so
extremely fastidious.

The vet said she had
only days, not months.

But the alertness!
The grandmotherly face!

We hoped. Then she couldn't
eat. You tried everything.

She became a wire sculpture.
Still we couldn't stand

to "put to sleep"
a life that'd been family

for fourteen years—traveling
to Austria, France, Italy,

uncomplaining in her carrying
case. I was away

the day you had to
have them do it.

When I called I said,
"What's new?"—then heard.

And though our two new cats
are handsome, I cannot

stroke them long. They
never stay in my lap

as if to say they know.

BIN RAMKE

The Cats of Balthus

We must bear witness to something.
At the Château de Chassy, near Autun,
Balthus Klossowski de Rola eats breakfast
under the green eye of Mitsou, Angora.

In the painter's eye girls forever
sprawl like morning sun among the hassocks
and fainting-sofas. They drink tea
the color of sunrise and as bitter.

At the Château de Chassy the sun
tries hard to be nameless in spite
of the painter's eye and will
to tame it, drape it across the proper chair.

But he will not tame the cats,
and only pretends to name them
for the neighbors' sake. They drape
where they like, leave their marks

on the muslin, chew through the doilies
the shape of white suns; they leave
their film of hair thickening
on the furniture. They sprawl.

We would like to look at the girls
doomed to adolescence, to see them
through the wide windows he offers us
as if we, on the way home late,

the evening's carouse given way
to gray sunrise, were caught by the slight

movement of girls in the house; as if
we stand in the shrubbery to look

then notice ourselves noticed
by the cat, its green eye narrowing
as if we both stare at the jungled coast
of wilderness and wanton desire.

PATTIANN ROGERS

Without Violence

That cat who comes during sleep, quiet
On his cushioned claws, without violence,
Who enters the house with a low warm rattle
In his throat; that cat who has been said
To crawl into a baby's crib without brushing
The bars, to knit his paws on the pale
Flannel of the infant's nightdress, to settle
In sleep chin to chin with the dear one
And softly steal the child's breath
Without malice, as easily as pulling
A silk scarf completely through a gold ring;

The same cat who has been known to nudge
Through castle doors, to part tent flaps,
To creep to the breasts of brave men,
Ease between their blankets, to stretch
Full length on the satin bodices of lovely
Women, to nuzzle their cheeks with his great
Feline mane; it was that cat who leaped last night
Through the west window of father's bedroom,
Who chose to knead his night's rest on my father's
Shoulder, who slept well, breathing deeply,
Leaving just before dawn to saunter toward

The north, his magnificent tail and rump
Swaying with a listless and gorgeous grace.

MAY SWENSON

Cat & the Weather

Cat takes a look at the weather.
Snow.
Puts a paw on the sill.
His perch is piled, is a pillow.

Shape of his pad appears.
Will it dig? No.
Not like sand.
Like his fur almost.

But licked, not liked.
Too cold.
Insects are flying, fainting down.
He'll try

to bat one against the pane.
They have no body and no buzz.
And now his feet are wet;
it's a puzzle.

Shakes each leg,
then shakes his skin
to get the white flies off.
Looks for his tail,

tells it to come on in
by the radiator.

World's turned queer
somehow. All white,

no smell. Well, here
inside it's still familiar.
He'll go to sleep until
it puts itself right.

JOHN UPDIKE

Touch of Spring

Thin wind winds off the water,
earth lies locked in dead snow,
but sun slants in under the yew hedge,
and the ground there is bare,
with some green blades there,
and my cat knows,
sharpening her claws on the flesh-pink wood.

THEODORE WEISS

Pleasure, Pleasure

And watching Hoppy curled up
in my lap, the way he goes
purring under my hand into sleep,
this watching is a pleasure.

A pleasure too Renée
in the next room practicing
the violin, going over the same
tracks again and again, trying

the notes like doors
to stores more and more open
for business, like stars lighting
up some Persian night asleep

under the skin of day.
Is a pleasure and a pleasure
this friend and that, a light
of one color and another,

not only to read
by as the world takes shape,
the sea rolled over like Hoppy
in a rapture of churning,

but a light
that is also the thing lit,
the world in its juicy, joyous
particulars. And outside the day

in each leaf now
is lighting, each leaf by its own
lights, maple first, then sumac,
inspired but responding

as it must. Already
the year is more than half way
here, to be followed by snow,
at first hesitant midair,

going up and then,
to go farther, down in a very
ecstasy of windy cold. Pleasure,
pleasure and the darkest light.

Part Nine

ITALO CALVINO

The Tale of the Cats

A woman had a daughter and a stepdaughter, and she treated the stepdaughter like a servant. One day she sent her out to pick chicory. The girl walked and walked, but instead of chicory she found a cauliflower, a nice big cauliflower. She tugged and tugged, and when the plant finally came up, it left a hole the size of a well in the earth. There was a ladder, and she climbed down it.

She found a house full of cats, all very busy. One of them was doing the wash, another drawing water from a well, another sewing, another cleaning house, another baking bread. The girl took a broom from one cat and helped with the sweeping, from another she took soiled linen and helped with the washing; then she helped draw water from the well, and also helped a cat put loaves of bread into the oven.

At noon, out came a large kitty, the mamma of all the cats, and rang the bell. "Ding-a-ling! Ding-a-ling! Whoever has worked, come and eat! Whoever hasn't worked, come and look on!"

The cats replied, "Mamma, every one of us worked, but this maiden worked more than we did."

"Good girl!" said the cat. "Come and eat with us." The two sat down to the table, the girl in the middle of the cats, and Mamma Cat served her meat, macaroni, and roast chicken; but she offered her children only beans. It made the maiden unhappy, however, to be the only one eating and, noticing the cats were hungry, she shared with them everything Mamma Cat gave her. When they got up, the girl cleared the table, washed the cats' plates, swept the room, and put everything in order. Then she said to Mamma Cat, "Dear cat, I must now be on my way, or my mother will scold me."

"One moment, my daughter," replied the cat. "I want to give you something." Downstairs was a large storeroom stacked on one side with silk goods, from dresses to pumps, and on the other side with homemade things like skirts, blouses, aprons, cotton handkerchiefs, and cowhide shoes. The cat said, "Pick out what you want."

The poor girl, who was barefooted and dressed in rags, replied, "Give me a homemade dress, a pair of cowhide shoes, and a neckerchief."

"No," answered the cat, "you were good to my little ones, and I shall give you a nice present." She picked out the finest silk gown, a large and delicately worked handkerchief, and a pair of satin slippers. She dressed her and said, "Now when you go out, you will see a few little holes in the wall. Push your fingers into them, then look up."

When she went out, the girl thrust her fingers into those holes and drew them out ringed with the most beautiful rings you ever saw. She lifted her head, and a star fell on her brow. Then she went home adorned like a bride.

Her stepmother asked, "And who gave you all this finery?"

"Mamma, I met up with some little cats that I helped with their chores, and they gave me a few presents." She told how it had all come about. Mother could hardly wait to send her own idle daughter out next day, saying to her, "Go, daughter dear, so you too will be blessed like your sister."

"I don't want to," she replied, ill-mannered girl that she was. "I don't feel like walking. It's cold, and I'm going to stay by the fire."

But her mother took a stick and drove her out. A good way away the lazy creature found the cauliflower, pulled it up, and went down to the cats' dwelling. The first one she saw got its tail pulled, the second one its ears, the third one had its whiskers snatched out, the one sewing had its needle unthreaded, the one drawing water had its bucket overturned. In short, she worried the life out of them all morning, and how they did meow!

At noon, out came Mamma Cat with the bell. "Ding-a-ling! Ding-a-ling! Whoever has worked, come and eat! Whoever hasn't worked, come and look on!"

"Mamma," said the cats, "we wanted to work, but this girl pulled us by the tail and tormented the life out of us, so we got nothing done!"

"All right," replied Mamma Cat, "let's move up to the table." She offered the girl a barley cake soaked in vinegar, and her little ones macaroni and meat. But throughout the meal the girl filched food from the cats. When they got up from the table, heedless of clearing away the dishes or cleaning up, she said to Mamma Cat, "Give me the stuff now you gave my sister."

So Mamma Cat showed her into the storeroom and asked her what she wanted. "That dress there, the nicest! Those pumps with the highest heels!"

"All right," replied the cat, "undress and put on these greasy woolen togs and these hobnailed shoes worn down completely at the heels." She tied a ragged neckerchief around her and dismissed her, saying, "Off with you, and when you go out, stick your fingers in the holes and look up."

The girl went out, thrust her fingers into the holes, and countless worms wrapped around them. The harder she tried to free her fingers, the tighter the worms gripped them. She looked up, and a blood sausage fell on her face and hung over her mouth, and she had to nibble it constantly so it would get no longer. When she arrived home in that attire, uglier than a witch, her mother was so angry she died. And from eating blood sausage day in, day out, the girl died too. But the good and industrious stepsister married a handsome youth.

—Retold by Italo Calvino. Translated from the Italian by George Martin

THE BROTHERS GRIMM

Cat and Mouse in Partnership

A certain cat had made the acquaintance of a mouse, and had said so much to her about the great love and friendship she felt for her, that at length the mouse agreed that they should live and keep house together. "But we must make a provision for winter, or else we shall suffer from hunger," said the cat; "and you, little mouse, cannot venture everywhere, or you will be caught in a trap some day." The good advice was followed, and a pot of fat was bought, but they did not know where to put it. At length, after much consideration, the cat said: "I know no place where it will be better stored up than in the church, for no one dares take anything away from there. We will set it beneath the altar, and not touch it until we are really in need of it." So the pot was placed in safety, but it was not long before the cat had a great yearning for it, and said to the mouse: "I want to tell you something, little mouse; my cousin has brought a little son into the world, and has asked me to be godmother; he is white with brown spots, and I am to hold him over the font at the christening. Let me go out to-day, and you look after the house by yourself." "Yes, yes," answered the mouse, "by all means go, and if you get anything very good to eat, think of me, I should like a drop of sweet red christening wine myself." All this, however, was untrue; the cat had no cousin, and had not been asked to be godmother. She went straight to the church, stole to the pot of fat, began to lick at it, and licked the top of the fat off. Then she took a walk upon the roofs of the town, looked out for opportunities, and then stretched herself in the sun, and licked her lips whenever she thought of the pot of fat, and not until it was evening did she return home. "Well, here you are again," said the mouse, "no doubt you have had a merry day." "All went off well," answered the cat. "What name did they give the child?" "Top off!" said the cat quite coolly. "Top off!" cried the mouse, "that is a very odd and uncommon name, is it a usual one in your family?" "What does that matter," said the cat, "it is no worse than Crumb-stealer, as your god-children are called."

Before long the cat was seized by another fit of yearning. She said to the mouse: "You must do me a favor, and once more manage the house for a day alone. I am again asked to be godmother, and, as the child has a white ring round its neck, I cannot refuse." The good mouse consented, but the cat crept behind the town walls to the church, and devoured half the pot of fat. "Nothing ever seems so good as what one keeps to oneself," said she, and was quite satisfied with her day's work. When she went home the mouse inquired: "And what was this child christened?" "Half-done," answered the cat. "Half-done! What are you saying? I never heard the name in my life, I'll wager anything it is not in the calendar!"

The cat's mouth soon began to water for some more licking. "All good things go in threes," said she, "I am asked to stand godmother again. The child is quite black, only it has white paws, but with that exception, it has not a single white hair on its whole body; this only happens once every few years, you will let me go, won't you?" "Top-off! Half-done!" answered the mouse, "they are such odd names, they make me very thoughtful." "You sit at home," said the cat, "in your dark-grey fur coat and long tail, and are filled with fancies, that's because you do not go out in the daytime." During the cat's absence the mouse cleaned the house, and put it in order, but the greedy cat entirely emptied the pot of fat. "When everything is eaten up one has some peace," said she to herself, and well filled and fat she did not return home till night. The mouse at once asked what name had been given to the third child. "It will not please you more than the others," said the cat. "He is called All-gone." "All-gone," cried the mouse, "that is the most suspicious name of all! I have never seen it in print. All-gone; what can that mean?" and she shook her head, curled herself up, and lay down to sleep.

From this time forth no one invited the cat to be godmother, but when the winter had come and there was no longer anything to be found outside, the mouse thought of their provision, and said: "Come, cat, we will go to our pot of fat which we have stored up for ourselves—we shall enjoy that." "Yes," answered the cat, "you will enjoy it as much as you would enjoy sticking that dainty tongue of yours out of the window." They set out on their way, but when they arrived, the pot of fat certainly was still in its place, but it was empty. "Alas!" said the mouse, "now I see what has happened, now it comes to light! You a true friend! You have devoured all when you were standing godmother. First top off, then half done, then—" "Will you hold your tongue," cried the cat, "one word more, and I will eat you too." "All gone" was already on the poor mouse's lips; scarcely had she spoken it before the cat sprang on her, seized her, and swallowed her down. Verily, that is the way of the world.

AESOP

Four Fables

VENUS AND THE CAT

In ancient times there lived a beautiful cat who fell in love with a young man. Naturally, the young man did not return the cat's affections, so she besought Venus, the goddess of love and beauty, for help. The goddess, taking compassion on her plight, changed her into a fair damsel.

No sooner had the young man set eyes on the maiden than he became enamored of her beauty and in due time led her home as his bride. One evening a short time later, as the young couple were sitting in their chamber, the notion came to Venus to discover whether in changing the cat's form she had also changed her nature. So she set down a mouse before the beautiful damsel. The girl, reverting completely to her former character, started from her seat and pounced upon the mouse as if she would eat it on the spot, while her husband watched her in dismay.

The goddess, provoked by such clear evidence that the girl had revealed her true nature, turned her into a cat again.

Application: WHAT IS BRED IN THE BONE WILL
NEVER BE ABSENT IN THE FLESH.

THE HEN AND THE CAT

All the barnyard knew that the hen was indisposed. So one day the cat decided to pay her a visit of condolence. Creeping up to her nest the cat in his most sympathetic voice said: "How are you, my dear friend? I was so sorry to hear of your illness. Isn't there something that I can bring you to cheer you up and to help you feel like yourself again?"

"Thank you," said the hen. "Please be good enough to leave me in peace, and I have no fear but I shall soon be well."

Application: UNINVITED GUESTS ARE OFTEN MOST
WELCOME WHEN THEY ARE GONE.

THE CAT AND THE FOX

A fox was boasting to a cat one day about how clever he was. "Why, I have a whole bag of tricks," he bragged. "For instance, I know of at least a hundred different ways of escaping my enemies, the dogs."

"How remarkable," said the cat. "As for me, I have only one trick, though I usually make it work. I wish you could teach me some of yours."

"Well, sometime when I have nothing else to do," said the fox, "I might teach you one or two of my easier ones."

Just at that moment they heard the yelping of a pack of hounds. They were coming straight toward the spot where the cat and the fox stood. Like a flash the cat scampered up a tree and disappeared in the foliage. "This is the trick I told you about," she called down to the fox. "It's my only one. Which trick are you going to use?"

The fox sat there trying to decide which of his many tricks he was going to employ. Nearer and nearer came the hounds. When it was quite too late, the fox decided to run for it. But even before he started the dogs were upon him, and that was the end of the fox, bagful of tricks and all!

Application: ONE GOOD PLAN THAT WORKS IS BETTER
THAN A HUNDRED DOUBTFUL ONES.

THE CAT AND THE MICE

A cat, grown feeble with age, and no longer able to hunt for mice as she was wont to do, sat in the sun and bethought herself how she might entice them within reach of her paws.

The idea came to her that if she would suspend herself by the hind legs from a peg in the closet wall, the mice, believing her to be dead, no longer would be afraid of her. So, at great pains and with the assistance of a torn pillow case she was able to carry out her plan.

But before the mice could approach within range of the innocent-looking paws a wise old gaffer-mouse whispered to his friends: "Keep your distance, my friends. Many a bag have I seen in my day, but never one with a cat's head at the bottom of it."

Then turning to the uncomfortable feline, he said: "Hang there, good madam, as long as you please, but I would not trust myself within reach of you though you were stuffed with straw."

Application: HE WHO IS ONCE DECEIVED IS DOUBLY
CAUTIOUS.

RUDYARD KIPLING

The Cat That Walked by Himself

Hear and attend and listen; for this befell and behappened and became and was, O my Best Beloved, when the Tame animals were wild. The Dog was wild, and the Horse was wild, and the Cow was wild, and the Sheep was wild, and the Pig was wild—as wild as wild could be—and they walked in the Wet Wild Woods by their wild lones. But the wildest of all the wild animals was the Cat. He walked by himself, and all places were alike to him.

Of course the Man was wild too. He was dreadfully wild. He didn't even begin to be tame till he met the Woman, and she told him that she did not like living in his wild ways. She picked out a nice dry Cave, instead of a heap of wet leaves, to lie down in; and she strewed clean sand on the floor; and she lit a nice fire of wood at the back of the Cave; and she hung a dried wild-horse skin, tail-down, across the opening of the Cave; and she said, "Wipe your feet, dear, when you come in, and now we'll keep house."

That night, Best Beloved, they ate wild sheep roasted on the hot stones, and flavored with wild garlic and wild pepper; and wild duck stuffed with wild rice and wild fenugreek and wild coriander; and marrow-bones of wild oxen; and wild cherries, and wild grenadillas. Then the Man went to sleep in front of the fire ever so happy; but the Woman sat up, combing her hair. She took the bone of the shoulder of mutton—the big fat blade-bone—and she looked at the wonderful marks on it, and she threw more wood on the fire, and she made a Magic. She made the First Singing Magic in the world.

Out in the Wet Wild Woods all the wild animals gathered together where they could see the light of the fire a long way off, and they wondered what it meant.

Then Wild Horse stamped with his wild foot and said, "O my Friends and O my Enemies, why have the Man and the Woman made that great light in that great Cave, and what harm will it do us?"

Wild Dog lifted up his wild nose and smelled the smell of roast mutton, and said, "I will go up and see and look, and say; for I think it is good. Cat, come with me."

"Nenni!" said the Cat. "I am the Cat who walks by himself, and all places are alike to me. I will not come."

"Then we can never be friends again," said Wild Dog, and he trotted off to the Cave. But when he had gone a little way the Cat said to himself, "All places are alike to me. Why should I not go too and see and look and come away at my own liking." So he slipped after Wild Dog softly, very softly, and hid himself where he could hear everything.

When Wild Dog reached the mouth of the Cave he lifted up the dried horse-skin with his nose and sniffed the beautiful smell of the roast mutton, and the Woman, looking at the blade-bone, heard him, and laughed, and said, "Here comes the first. Wild Thing out of the Wild Woods, what do you want?"

Wild Dog said, "O my Enemy and Wife of my Enemy, what is this that smells so good in the Wild Woods?"

Then the Woman picked up a roasted mutton-bone and threw it to Wild Dog, and said, "Wild Thing out of the Wild Woods, taste and try." Wild Dog gnawed the bone, and it was more delicious than anything he had ever tasted, and he said, "O my Enemy and Wife of my Enemy, give me another."

The Woman said, "Wild Thing out of the Wild Woods, help my Man to hunt through the day and guard this Cave at night, and I will give you as many roast bones as you need."

"Ah!" said the Cat, listening. "This is a very wise Woman, but she is not so wise as I am."

Wild Dog crawled into the Cave and laid his head on the Woman's lap, and said, "O my Friend and Wife of my Friend, I will help your Man to hunt through the day, and at night I will guard your Cave."

"Ah!" said the Cat, listening. "That is a very foolish Dog." And he went back through the Wet Wild Woods waving his wild tail, and walking by his wild lone. But he never told anybody.

When the Man waked up he said, "What is Wild Dog doing here?" And the Woman said, "His name is not Wild Dog any more but the

First Friend, because he will be our friend for always and always and always. Take him with you when you go hunting."

Next night the Woman cut great green armfuls of fresh grass from the water-meadows, and dried it before the fire, so that it smelt like new-mown hay, and she sat at the mouth of the Cave and plaited a halter out of horse-hide, and she looked at the shoulder of mutton-bone—at the big broad blade-bone—and she made a Magic. She made the Second Singing Magic in the world.

Out in the Wild Woods all the wild animals wondered what had happened to Wild Dog, and at last Wild Horse stamped with his foot and said, "I will go and see and say why Wild Dog has not returned. Cat, come with me."

"Nenni!" said the Cat. "I am the Cat who walks by himself, and all places are alike to me. I will not come." But all the same he followed Wild Horse softly, very softly, and hid himself where he could hear everything.

When the Woman heard Wild Horse tripping and stumbling on his long mane, she laughed and said, "Here comes the second. Wild Thing out of the Wild Woods, what do you want?"

Wild Horse said, "O my Enemy and Wife of my Enemy, where is Wild Dog?"

The Woman laughed, and picked up the blade-bone and looked at it, and said, "Wild Thing out of the Wild Woods, you did not come here for Wild Dog, but for the sake of this good grass."

And Wild Horse, tripping and stumbling on his long mane, said, "That is true; give it me to eat."

The Woman said, "Wild Thing out of the Wild Woods, bend your wild head and wear what I give you, and you shall eat the wonderful grass three times a day."

"Ah," said the Cat, listening, "this is a clever Woman, but she is not so clever as I am."

Wild Horse bent his wild head, and the Woman slipped the plaited hide halter over it, and Wild Horse breathed on the Woman's feet and said, "O my Mistress, and Wife of my Master, I will be your servant for the sake of the wonderful grass."

"Ah," said the Cat, listening, "that is a very foolish Horse." And he went back through the Wet Wild Woods, waving his wild tail and walking by his wild lone. But he never told anybody.

When the Man and the Dog came back from hunting, the Man said, "What is Wild Horse doing here?" And the Woman said, "His name is not Wild Horse any more, but the First Servant, because he will carry us from place to place for always and always and always. Ride on his back when you go hunting."

Next day, holding her wild head high that her wild horns should not catch in the wild trees, Wild Cow came up to the Cave, and the Cat followed, and hid himself just the same as before; and everything happened just the same as before; and the Cat said the same things as before, and when Wild Cow had promised to give her milk to the Woman every day in exchange for the wonderful grass, the Cat went back through the Wet Wild Woods waving his wild tail and walking by his wild lone, just the same as before. But he never told anybody. And when the Man and the Horse and the Dog came home from hunting and asked the same questions same as before, the Woman said, "Her name is not Wild Cow any more, but the Giver of Good Food. She will give us the warm white milk for always and always and always, and I will take care of her while you and the First Friend and the First Servant go hunting."

Next day the Cat waited to see if any other Wild Thing would go up to the Cave, but no one moved in the Wet Wild Woods, so the Cat walked there by himself; and he saw the Woman milking the Cow, and he saw the light of the fire in the Cave, and he smelt the smell of the warm white milk.

Cat said, "O my Enemy and Wife of my Enemy, where did Wild Cow go?"

The Woman laughed and said, "Wild Thing out of the Wild Woods, go back to the Woods again, for I have braided up my hair, and I have put away the magic blade-bone, and we have no more need of either friends or servants in our Cave."

Cat said, "I am not a friend, and I am not a servant. I am the Cat who walks by himself, and I wish to come into your cave."

Woman said, "Then why did you not come with First Friend on the first night?"

Cat grew very angry and said, "Has Wild Dog told tales of me?"

Then the Woman laughed and said, "You are the Cat who walks by himself, and all places are alike to you. You are neither a friend nor a servant. You have said it yourself. Go away and walk by yourself in all places alike."

Then Cat pretended to be sorry and said, "Must I never come into the Cave? Must I never sit by the warm fire? Must I never drink the warm white milk? You are very wise and very beautiful. You should not be cruel even to a Cat."

Woman said, "I knew I was wise, but I did not know I was

beautiful. So I will make a bargain with you. If ever I say one word in your praise you may come into the Cave."

"And if you say two words in my praise?" said the Cat.

"I never shall," said the Woman, "but if I say two words in your praise, you may sit by the fire in the Cave."

"And if you say three words?" said the Cat.

"I never shall," said the Woman, "but if I say three words in your praise, you may drink the warm white milk three times a day for always and always and always."

Then the Cat arched his back and said, "Now let the Curtain at the mouth of the Cave, and the Fire at the back of the Cave, and the Milk-pots that stand beside the Fire, remember what my Enemy and the Wife of my Enemy has said." And he went away through the Wet Wild Woods waving his wild tail and walking by his wild lone.

That night when the Man and the Horse and the Dog came home from hunting, the Woman did not tell them of the bargain that she had made with the Cat, because she was afraid that they might not like it.

Cat went far and far away and hid himself in the Wet Wild Woods by his wild lone for a long time till the Woman forgot all about him. Only the Bat—the little upside-down Bat—that hung inside the Cave, knew where Cat hid; and every evening Bat would fly to Cat with news of what was happening.

One evening Bat said, "There is a Baby in the Cave. He is new and pink and fat and small, and the Woman is very fond of him."

"Ah," said the Cat, listening, "but what is the Baby fond of?"

"He is fond of things that are soft and tickle," said the Bat. "He is fond of warm things to hold in his arms when he goes to sleep. He is fond of being played with. He is fond of all those things."

"Ah," said the Cat, listening, "then my time has come."

Next night Cat walked through the Wet Wild Woods and hid very near the Cave till morning-time, and Man and Dog and Horse went hunting. The Woman was busy cooking that morning, and the Baby cried and interrupted. So she carried him outside the Cave and gave him a handful of pebbles to play with. But still the Baby cried.

Then the Cat put out his paddy paw and patted the Baby on the cheek, and it cooed; and the Cat rubbed against its fat knees and tickled it under its fat chin with his tail. And the Baby laughed and the Woman heard him and smiled.

Then the Bat—the little upside-down Bat—that hung in the mouth of the Cave said, "O my Hostess and Wife of my Host and Mother of my Host's Son, a Wild Thing from the Wild Woods is most beautifully playing with your Baby."

"A blessing on that Wild Thing whoever he may be," said the Woman, straightening her back, "for I was a busy woman this morning and he has done me a service."

The very minute and second, Best Beloved, the dried horse-skin Curtain that was stretched tail-down at the mouth of the Cave fell down—*woosh!*—because it remembered the bargain she had made with the Cat, and when the Woman went to pick it up—lo and behold!—the Cat was sitting quite comfy inside the Cave.

"O my Enemy and Wife of my Enemy and Mother of my Enemy," said the Cat, "it is I: for you have spoken a word in my praise, and now I can sit within the Cave for always and always and always. But still I am the Cat who walks by himself, and all places are alike to me."

The Woman was very angry, and shut her lips tight and took up her spinning-wheel and began to spin.

But the Baby cried because the Cat had gone away, and the Woman could not hush it, for it struggled and kicked and grew black in the face.

"O my Enemy and Wife of my Enemy and Mother of my Enemy," said the Cat, "take a strand of the wire that you are spinning and tie it to your spinning-whorl and drag it along the floor, and I will show you a Magic that shall make your Baby laugh as loudly as he is now crying."

"I will do so," said the Woman, "because I am at my wits' end; but I will not thank you for it."

She tied the thread to the little clay spindle-whorl and drew it across the floor, and the Cat ran after it and patted it with his paws and rolled head over heels, and tossed it backward over his shoulder and chased it between his hind-legs and pretended to lose it, and pounced down upon it again, till the Baby laughed as loudly as it had been crying, and scrambled after the Cat and frolicked all over the Cave till it grew tired and settled down to sleep with the Cat in its arms.

"Now," said the Cat, "I will sing the Baby a song that shall keep him asleep for an hour." And he began to purr, loud and low, low and loud, till the Baby fell fast asleep. The Woman smiled as she looked down upon the two of them and said, "That was wonderfully done. No question but you are very clever, O Cat."

That very minute and second, Best Beloved, the smoke of the fire at the back of the Cave came down in clouds from the roof—*puff!*—because it remembered the bargain she had made with the Cat, and when it had cleared away—lo and behold!—the Cat was sitting quite comfy close to the fire.

"O my Enemy and Wife of my Enemy and Mother of my Enemy," said the Cat, "it is I, for you have spoken a second word in my praise, and now I can sit by the warm fire at the back of the Cave for always and always and always. But still I am the Cat who walks by himself, and all places are alike to me."

Then the Woman was very very angry, and let down her hair and put more wood on the fire and brought out the broad blade-bone of the shoulder of mutton and began to make a Magic that should prevent her from saying a third word in praise of the Cat. It was not a Singing Magic, Best Beloved, it was a Still Magic; and by and by the Cave grew so still that a little wee-wee mouse crept out of a corner and ran across the floor.

"O my Enemy and Wife of my Enemy and Mother of my Enemy," said the Cat, "is that little mouse part of your magic?"

"Ouh! Chee! No indeed!" said the Woman, and she dropped the blade-bone and jumped upon the footstool in front of the fire and braided up her hair very quick for fear that the mouse should run up it.

"Ah," said the Cat, watching, "then the mouse will do me no harm if I eat it?"

"No," said the Woman, braiding up her hair, "eat it quickly and I will ever be grateful to you."

Cat made one jump and caught the little mouse, and the Woman said, "A hundred thanks. Even the First Friend is not quick enough to catch little mice as you have done. You must be very wise."

That very moment and second, O Best Beloved, the Milk-pot that stood by the fire cracked in two pieces—*ffft*—because it remembered the bargain she had made with the Cat, and when the Woman jumped down from the footstool—lo and behold!—the Cat was lapping up the warm white milk that lay in one of the broken pieces.

"O my Enemy and Wife of my Enemy and Mother of my Enemy," said the Cat, "it is I; for you have spoken three words in my praise, and now I can drink the warm white milk three times a day for always and always and always. But *still* I am the Cat who walks by himself, and all places are alike to me."

Then the Woman laughed and set the Cat a bowl of the warm white milk and said, "O Cat, you are as clever as a man, but remember that your bargain was not made with the Man or the Dog, and I do not know what they will do when they come home."

"What is that to me?" said the Cat. "If I have my place in the Cave by the fire and my warm white milk three times a day I do not care what the Man or the Dog can do."

That evening when the Man and the Dog came into the Cave, the Woman told them all the story of the bargain while the Cat sat by the fire and smiled. Then the Man said, "Yes, but he has not made a bargain with *me* or with all proper Men after me." Then he took off his two leather boots and he took up his little stone axe (that makes three) and he fetched a piece of wood and a hatchet (that is five altogether), and he set them out in a row and he said, "Now we will make *our* bargain. If you do not catch mice when you are in the Cave for always and always and always, I will throw these five things at you whenever I see you, and so shall all proper Men do after me."

"Ah," said the Woman, listening, "this is a very clever Cat, but he is not so clever as my Man."

The Cat counted the five things (and they looked very knobby) and he said, "I will catch mice when I am in the Cave for always and always and always; but *still* I am the Cat who walks by himself, and all places are alike to me."

"Not when I am near," said the Man. "If you had not said that last I would have put all these things away for always and always and always; but I am now going to throw my two boots and my little stone axe (that makes three) at you whenever I meet you. And so shall all proper Men do after me!"

Then the Dog said, "Wait a minute. He has not made a bargain with *me* or with all proper Dogs after me." And he showed his teeth and said, "If you are not kind to the Baby while I am in the Cave for always and always and always, I will hunt you till I catch you, and when I catch you I will bite you. And so shall all proper Dogs do after me."

"Ah," said the Woman, listening, "this is a very clever Cat, but he is not so clever as the Dog."

Cat counted the Dog's teeth (and they looked very pointed) and he said, "I will be kind to the Baby while I am in the Cave, as long as he does not pull my tail too hard, for always and always and always. But *still* I am the Cat that walks by himself, and all places are alike to me."

"Not when I am near," said the Dog. "If you had not said that last I would have shut my mouth for always and always and always; but *now* I am going to hunt you up a tree whenever I meet you. And so shall all proper Dogs do after me."

Then the Man threw his two boots and his little stone axe (that makes three) at the Cat, and the Cat ran out of the Cave, and the Dog chased him up a tree; and from that day to this, Best Beloved, three proper Men out of five will always throw things at a Cat whenever they meet him, and all proper Dogs will chase him up a tree. But the Cat keeps his side of the bargain too. He will kill mice and he will be kind to Babies when he is in the house, just as long as they do not pull his tail too hard. But when he has done that, and between times, and when the moon gets up and night comes, he is the Cat that walks by himself, and all places are alike to him. Then he goes out to the Wet Wild Woods or up the Wet Wild Trees or on the Wet Wild Roofs, waving his tail and walking by his wild lone.

LEWIS CARROLL

[The Cheshire-Cat]

For a minute or two she stood looking at the house, and wondering what to do next, when suddenly a footman in livery came running out of the wood—(she considered him to be a footman because he was in livery: otherwise, judging by his face only, she would have called him a fish)—and rapped loudly at the door with his knuckles. It was opened by another footman in livery, with a round face, and large eyes like a frog; and both footmen, Alice noticed, had powdered hair that curled all over their heads. She felt very curious to know what it was all about, and crept a little way out of the wood to listen.

The Fish-Footman began by producing from under his arm a great letter, nearly as large as himself, and this he handed over to the other, saying, in a solemn tone, "For the Duchess. An invitation from the Queen to play croquet." The Frog-Footman repeated, in the same solemn tone, only changing the order of the words a little, "From the Queen. An invitation for the Duchess to play croquet."

Then they both bowed, and their curls got entangled together.

Alice laughed so much at this, that she had to run back into the wood for fear of their hearing her; and, when she next peeped out, the Fish-Footman was gone, and the other was sitting on the ground near the door, staring stupidly up into the sky.

Alice went timidly up to the door, and knocked.

"There's no sort of use in knocking," said the Footman, "and that for two reasons. First, because I'm on the same side of the door as you are: secondly, because they're making such a noise inside, no one could possibly hear you." And certainly there *was* a most extraordinary noise going on within—a constant howling and sneezing, and every now and then a great crash, as if a dish or kettle had been broken to pieces.

"Please, then," said Alice, "how am I to get in?"

"There might be some sense in your knocking," the Footman went on, without attending to her, "if we had the door between us. For instance, if you were *inside*, you might knock, and I could let you out, you know." He was looking up into the sky all the time he was speaking, and this Alice thought decidedly uncivil. "But perhaps he ca'n't help it," she said to herself; "his eyes are so *very* nearly at the top of his head. But at any rate he might answer questions.—How am I to get in?" she repeated, aloud.

"I shall sit here," the Footman remarked, "till to-morrow——"

At this moment the door of the house opened, and a large plate came skimming out, straight at the Footman's head: it just grazed his nose, and broke to pieces against one of the trees behind him.

"——or next day, maybe," the Footman continued in the same tone, exactly as if nothing had happened.

"How am I to get in?" asked Alice again, in a louder tone.

"*Are* you to get in at all?" said the Footman. "That's the first question, you know."

It was, no doubt: only Alice did not like to be told so. "It's really dreadful," she muttered to herself, "the way all the creatures argue. It's enough to drive one crazy!"

The Footman seemed to think this a good opportunity for repeating his remark, with variations. "I shall sit here," he said, "on and off, for days and days."

"But what am *I* to do?" said Alice.

"Anything you like," said the Footman, and began whistling.

"Oh, there's no use in talking to him," said Alice desperately: "he's perfectly idiotic!" And she opened the door and went in.

The door led right into a large kitchen, which was full of smoke from one end to the other: the Duchess was sitting on a three-legged stool in the middle, nursing a baby: the cook was leaning over the fire, stirring a large cauldron which seemed to be full of soup.

"There's certainly too much pepper in that soup!" Alice said to herself, as well as she could for sneezing.

There was certainly too much of it in the *air*. Even the Duchess sneezed occasionally; and as for the baby, it was sneezing and howling alternately without a moment's pause. The only two creatures in the kitchen, that did *not* sneeze, were the cook, and a large cat, which was lying on the hearth and grinning from ear to ear.

"Please would you tell me," said Alice, a little timidly, for she was not quite sure whether it was good manners for her to speak first, "why your cat grins like that?"

"It's a Cheshire-Cat," said the Duchess, "and that's why. Pig!"

She said the last word with such sudden violence that Alice quite jumped; but she saw in another moment that it was addressed to the baby, and not to her, so she took courage, and went on again:—

"I didn't know that Cheshire-Cats always grinned; in fact, I didn't know that cats *could* grin."

"They all can," said the Duchess; "and most of 'em do."

"I don't know of any that do," Alice said very politely, feeling quite pleased to have got into a conversation.

"You don't know much," said the Duchess; "and that's a fact."

Alice did not at all like the tone of this remark, and thought it would be as well to introduce some other subject of conversation. While she was trying to fix on one, the cook took the cauldron of soup off the fire, and at once set to work throwing everything within her reach at the Duchess and the baby—the fire-irons came first; then followed a shower of sauce-pans, plates, and dishes. The Duchess took no notice of them even when they hit her; and the baby was howling so much already, that it was quite impossible to say whether the blows hurt it or not.

"Oh, *please* mind what you're doing!" cried Alice, jumping up and down in an agony of terror. "Oh, there goes his *precious* nose!" as an unusually large saucepan flew close by it, and very nearly carried it off.

"If everybody minded their own business," the Duchess said, in a hoarse growl, "the world would go round a deal faster than it does."

"Which would *not* be an advantage," said Alice, who felt very glad to get an opportunity of showing off a little of her knowledge. "Just think what work it would make with the day and night! You see the earth takes twenty-four hours to turn round on its axis——"

"Talking of axes," said the Duchess, "chop off her head!"

Alice glanced rather anxiously at the cook, to see if she meant to take the hint; but the cook was busily stirring the soup, and seemed not to be listening, so she went on again: "Twenty-four hours, I *think*; or is it twelve? I——"

"Oh, don't bother *me*!" said the Duchess. "I never could abide figures!" And with that she began nursing her child again, singing a sort of lullaby to it as she did so, and giving it a violent shake at the end of every line:—

"Speak roughly to your little boy,
And beat him when he sneezes:
He only does it to annoy,
Because he knows it teases."

CHORUS

(in which the cook and the baby joined):—
"Wow! wow! wow!"

While the Duchess sang the second verse of the song, she kept tossing the baby violently up and down, and the poor little thing howled so, that Alice could hardly hear the words:—

"I speak severely to my boy,
I beat him when he sneezes;
For he can thoroughly enjoy
The pepper when he pleases!"

CHORUS

"Wow! wow! wow!"

"Here! You may nurse it a bit, if you like!" the Duchess said to Alice, flinging the baby at her as she spoke. "I must go and get ready to play croquet with the Queen," and she hurried out of the room. The cook threw a frying-pan after her as she went, but it just missed her.

Alice caught the baby with some difficulty, as it was a queer-shaped little creature, and held out its arms and legs in all directions, "just like a star-fish," thought Alice. The poor little thing was snorting like a steam-engine when she caught it, and kept doubling itself up and straightening itself out again, so that altogether, for the first minute or two, it was as much as she could do to hold it.

As soon as she had made out the proper way of nursing it (which was to twist it up into a sort of knot, and then keep tight hold of its right ear and left foot, so as to prevent its undoing itself), she carried it out into the open air. "If I don't take this child away with me," thought Alice, "they're sure to kill it in a day or two. Wouldn't it be murder to leave it behind?" She said the last words out loud, and the little thing grunted in reply (it had left off sneezing by this time). "Don't grunt," said Alice; "that's not at all a proper way of expressing yourself."

The baby grunted again, and Alice looked very anxiously into its face to see what was the matter with it. There could be no doubt that it had a *very* turn-up nose, much more like a snout than a real nose: also its eyes were getting extremely small for a baby: altogether Alice did not like the look of the thing at all. "But perhaps it was only sobbing," she thought, and looked into its eyes again, to see if there were any tears.

No, there were no tears. "If you're going to turn into a pig, my dear," said Alice, seriously, "I'll have nothing more to do with you. Mind now!" The poor little thing sobbed again (or grunted, it was impossible to say which), and they went on for some while in silence.

Alice was just beginning to think to herself, "Now, what am I to do with this creature, when I get it home?" when it grunted again, so violently, that she looked down into its face in some alarm. This time there could be *no* mistake about it: it was neither more nor less than a pig, and she felt that it would be quite absurd for her to carry it any further.

So she set the little creature down, and felt quite relieved to see it trot away quietly into the wood. "If it had grown up," she said to herself, "it would have made a dreadfully ugly child: but it makes rather a handsome pig, I think." And she began thinking over other children she knew, who might do very well as pigs, and was just saying to herself "if one only knew the right way to change them——" when she was a little startled by seeing the Cheshire-Cat sitting on a bough of a tree a few yards off.

The Cat only grinned when it saw Alice. It looked good-natured, she thought: still it had *very* long claws and a great many teeth, so she felt that it ought to be treated with respect.

"Cheshire-Puss," she began, rather timidly, as she did not at all know whether it would like the name: however, it only grinned a little wider. "Come, it's pleased so far," thought Alice, and she went on. "Would you tell me, please, which way I ought to go from here?"

"That depends a good deal on where you want to get to," said the Cat.

"I don't much care where——" said Alice.

"Then it doesn't matter which way you go," said the Cat.

"——so long as I get *somewhere*," Alice added as an explanation.

"Oh, you're sure to do that," said the Cat, "if you only walk long enough."

Alice felt that this could not be denied, so she tried another question. "What sort of people live about here?"

"In *that* direction," the Cat said, waving its right paw round, "lives a Hatter: and in *that* direction," waving the other paw, "lives a March Hare. Visit either you like: they're both mad."

"But I don't want to go among mad people," Alice remarked.

"Oh, you ca'n't help that," said the Cat: "we're all mad here. I'm mad. You're mad."

"How do you know I'm mad?" said Alice.

"You must be," said the Cat, "or you wouldn't have come here."

Alice didn't think that proved it at all: however, she went on: "And how do you know that you're mad?"

"To begin with," said the Cat, "a dog's not mad. You grant that?"

"I suppose so," said Alice.

"Well, then," the Cat went on, "you see a dog growls when it's angry, and wags its tail when it's pleased. Now *I* growl when I'm pleased, and wag my tail when I'm angry. Therefore I'm mad."

"*I* call it purring, not growling," said Alice.

"Call it what you like," said the Cat. "Do you play croquet with the Queen to-day?"

"I should like it very much," said Alice, "but I haven't been invited yet."

"You'll see me there," said the Cat, and vanished.

Alice was not much surprised at this, she was getting so well used to queer things happening. While she was still looking at the place where it had been, it suddenly appeared again.

"By-the-bye, what became of the baby?" said the Cat. "I'd nearly forgotten to ask."

"It turned into a pig," Alice answered very quietly, just as if the Cat had come back in a natural way.

"I thought it would," said the Cat, and vanished again.

Alice waited a little, half expecting to see it again, but it did not appear, and after a minute or two she walked on in the direction in which the March Hare was said to live. "I've seen hatters before," she said to herself: "the March Hare will be much the most interesting, and perhaps, as this is May, it wo'n't be raving mad—at least not so mad as it was in March." As she said this she looked up, and there was the Cat again, sitting on a branch of a tree.

"Did you say 'pig,' or 'fig'?" said the Cat.

"I said 'pig'," replied Alice; "and I wish you wouldn't keep appearing and vanishing so suddenly: you make one quite giddy!"

"All right," said the Cat; and this time it vanished quite slowly, beginning with the end of the tail, and ending with the grin, which remained some time after the rest of it had gone.

"Well! I've often seen a cat without a grin," thought Alice; "but a grin without a cat! It's the most curious thing I ever saw in all my life!"

She had not gone much farther before she came in sight of the house of the March Hare: she thought it must be the right house, because the chimneys were shaped like ears and the roof was thatched with fur. It was so large a house, that she did not like to go nearer till she had nibbled some more of the left-hand bit of mushroom, and raised herself to about two feet high: even then she walked up towards it rather timidly, saying to herself "Suppose it should be raving mad after all! I almost wish I'd gone to see the Hatter instead!"

AMBROSE BIERCE

Cat and King

A cat was looking at a King, as permitted by the proverb.

"Well," said the monarch, observing her inspection of the royal person, "how do you like me?"

"I can imagine a King," said the Cat, "whom I should like better."

"For example?"

"The King of Mice."

The sovereign was so pleased with the wit of the reply that he gave her permission to scratch his Prime Minister's eyes out.

AMBROSE BIERCE

Cat and Youth

A cat fell in love with a handsome Young Man and entreated Venus to change her into a woman.

"I should think," said Venus, "you might make so trifling a change without bothering me. However, be a woman."

Afterward, wishing to see if the change were complete, Venus caused a mouse to approach, whereupon the woman shrieked and made such a show of herself that the Young Man would not marry her.

AMBROSE BIERCE

John Mortonson's Funeral *

John Mortonson was dead: his lines in "the tragedy of 'Man'" had all been spoken and he had left the stage.

The body rested in a fine mahogany coffin fitted with a plate of glass. All arrangements for the funeral had been so well attended to that had the deceased known he would doubtless have approved. The face, as it showed under the glass, was not disagreeable to look upon: it bore a faint smile, and as the death had been painless, had not been distorted beyond the repairing power of the undertaker. At two o'clock of the afternoon the friends were to assemble to pay their last tribute of respect to one who had no further need of friends and respect. The surviving members of the family came severally every few minutes to the casket and wept above the placid features beneath the glass. This did them no good; it did no good to John Mortonson; but in the presence of death reason and philosophy are silent.

As the hour of two approached the friends began to arrive and after offering such consolation to the stricken relatives as the proprieties of the occasion required, solemnly seated themselves about the room with an augmented consciousness of their importance in the scheme funereal. Then the minister came, and in that overshadowing presence the lesser lights went into eclipse. His entrance was followed by that of the widow, whose lamentations filled the

* Rough notes of this tale were found among the papers of the late Leigh Bierce. It is printed here with such revision only as the author might himself have made in transcription.

room. She approached the casket and after leaning her face against the cold glass for a moment was gently led to a seat near her daughter. Mournfully and low the man of God began his eulogy of the dead, and his doleful voice, mingled with the sobbing which it was its purpose to stimulate and sustain, rose and fell, seemed to come and go, like the sound of a sullen sea. The gloomy day grew darker as he spoke; a curtain of cloud underspread the sky and a few drops of rain fell audibly. It seemed as if all nature were weeping for John Mortonson.

When the minister had finished his eulogy with prayer a hymn was sung and the pallbearers took their places beside the bier. As the last notes of the hymn died away the widow ran to the coffin, cast herself upon it and sobbed hysterically. Gradually, however, she yielded to dissuasion, becoming more composed; and as the minister was in the act of leading her away her eyes sought the face of the dead beneath the glass. She threw up her arms and with a shriek fell backward insensible.

The mourners sprang forward to the coffin, the friends followed, and as the clock on the mantel solemnly struck three all were staring down upon the face of John Mortonson, deceased.

They turned away, sick and faint. One man, trying in his terror to escape the awful sight, stumbled against the coffin so heavily as to knock away one of its frail supports. The coffin fell to the floor, the glass was shattered to bits by the concussion.

From the opening crawled John Mortonson's cat, which lazily leapt to the floor, sat up, tranquilly wiped its crimson muzzle with a forepaw, then walked with dignity from the room.

AMBROSE BIERCE

A Cargo of Cat

On the 16th day of June, 1874, the ship *Mary Jane* sailed from Malta, heavily laden with cat. This cargo gave us a good deal of trouble. It was not in bales, but had been dumped into the hold loose. Captain Doble, who had once commanded a ship that carried coals, said he had found that plan the best. When the hold was full of cat the hatch was battened down and we felt good. Unfortunately the mate, thinking the cats would be thirsty, introduced a hose into one of the hatches and pumped in a considerable quantity of water, and the cats of the lower levels were all drowned.

You have seen a dead cat in a pond: you remember its circumference at the waist. Water multiplies the magnitude of a dead cat by ten. On the first day out, it was observed that the ship was much strained. She was three feet wider than usual and as much as ten feet shorter. The convexity of her deck was visibly augmented fore and aft, but she turned up at both ends. Her rudder was clean out of water and she would answer the helm only when running directly against a strong breeze: the rudder, when perverted to one side, would rub against the wind and slew her around; and then she wouldn't steer any more. Owing to the curvature of the keel, the masts came together at the top, and a sailor who had gone up the foremast got bewildered, came down the mizzenmast, looked out over the stern at the receding shores of Malta and shouted: "Land, ho!" The ship's fastenings were all giving way; the water on each side was lashed into foam by the tempest of flying bolts that she shed at every pulsation of the cargo. She was quietly wrecking herself without assistance from wind or wave, by the sheer internal energy of feline expansion.

I went to the skipper about it. He was in his favorite position, sitting on the deck, supporting his back against the binnacle, making a V of his legs, and smoking.

"Captain Doble," I said, respectfully touching my hat, which was really not worthy of respect, "this floating palace is afflicted with curvature of the spine and is likewise greatly swollen."

Without raising his eyes he courteously acknowledged my presence by knocking the ashes from his pipe.

"Permit me, Captain," I said, with simple dignity, "to repeat that this ship is much swollen."

"If that is true," said the gallant mariner, reaching for his tobacco pouch, "I think it would be as well to swab her down with liniment. There's a bottle of it in my cabin. Better suggest it to the mate."

"But, Captain, there is no time for empirical treatment; some of the planks at the water line have started."

The skipper rose and looked out over the stern, toward the land; he fixed his eyes on the foaming wake; he gazed into the water to starboard and to port. Then he said:

"My friend, the whole darned thing has started."

Sadly and silently I turned from that obdurate man and walked forward. Suddenly "there was a burst of thunder sound!" The hatch that had held down the cargo was flung whirling into space and sailed in the air like a blown leaf. Pushing upward through the hatchway was a smooth, square column of cat. Grandly and impressively it grew—slowly, serenely, majestically it rose toward the welkin, the relaxing keel parting the mastheads to give it a fair chance. I have stood at Naples and seen Vesuvius painting the town red—from Catania have marked afar, upon the flanks of Ætna, the lava's awful pursuit of the astonished rooster and the despairing pig. The fiery flow from Kilauea's crater, thrusting itself into the forests and licking the entire country clean, is as familiar to me as my mother-tongue. I have seen glaciers, a thousand years old and quite bald, heading for a valley full of tourists at the rate of an inch a month. I have seen a saturated solution of mining camp going down a mountain river, to make a sociable call on the valley farmers. I have stood behind a tree on the battle-field and seen a compact square mile of armed men moving with irresistible momentum to the rear. Whenever anything grand in magnitude or motion is billed to appear I commonly manage to beat my way into the show, and in reporting it I am a man of unscrupulous veracity; but I have seldom observed anything like that solid gray column of Maltese cat!

It is unnecessary to explain, I suppose, that each individual grimalkin in the outfit, with that readiness of resource which distinguishes the species, had grappled with tooth and nail as many others as it could hook on to. This preserved the formation. It made the column so stiff that when the ship rolled (and the *Mary Jane* was a devil to roll) it swayed from side to side like a mast, and the Mate said if it grew much taller he would have to order it cut away or it would capsize us.

Some of the sailors went to work at the pumps, but these discharged nothing but fur. Captain Doble raised his eyes from his toes and shouted: "Let go the anchor!" but being assured that nobody was touching it, apologized and resumed his revery. The chaplain said if there were no objections he would like to offer up a prayer, and a gambler from Chicago, producing a pack of cards, proposed to throw round for the first jack. The parson's plan was adopted, and as he uttered the final "amen," the cats struck up a hymn.

All the living ones were now above deck, and every mother's son of them sang. Each had a pretty fair voice, but no ear. Nearly all their notes in the upper register were more or less cracked and disobedient. The remarkable thing about the voices was their range. In that crowd were cats of seventeen octaves, and the average could not have been less than twelve.

Number of cats, as per invoice	127,000
Estimated number dead swellers	6,000
Total songsters	121,000
Average number octaves per cat	12
Total octaves	1,452,000

It was a great concert. It lasted three days and nights, or, counting each night as seven days, twenty-four days altogether, and we could not go below for provisions. At the end of that time the cook came for'd shaking up some beans in a hat, and holding a large knife.

"Shipmates," said he, "we have done all that mortals can do. Let us now draw lots."

We were blindfolded in turn, and drew, but just as the cook was forcing the fatal black bean upon the fattest man, the concert closed with a suddenness that waked the man on the lookout. A moment later every grimalkin relaxed his hold on his neighbors, the column lost its cohesion and, with 121,000 dull, sickening thuds that beat as one, the whole business fell to the deck. Then with a wild farewell wail that feline host sprang spitting into the sea and struck out southward for the African shore!

The southern extension of Italy, as every schoolboy knows, resembles in shape an enormous boot. We had drifted within sight of it. The cats in the fabric had spied it, and their alert imaginations were instantly affected with a lively sense of the size, weight and probable momentum of its flung boot-jack.

W. H. HUDSON

A Friendly Rat

Most of our animals, also many creeping things, such as our "wilde wormes in woods," common toads, natterjacks, newts, and lizards, and stranger still, many insects, have been tamed and kept as pets.

Badgers, otters, foxes, hares, and voles are easily dealt with; but that any person should desire to fondle so prickly a creature as a hedgehog, or so diabolical a mammalian as the bloodthirsty, flat-headed little weasel, seems very odd. Spiders, too, are uncomfortable pets; you can't caress them as you could a dormouse; the most you can do is to provide your spider with a clear glass bottle to live in, and teach him to come out in response to a musical sound, drawn from a banjo or fiddle, to take a fly from your fingers and go back again to its bottle.

An acquaintance of the writer is partial to adders as pets, and he handles them as freely as the schoolboy does his innocuous ring-snake; Mr. Benjamin Kidd once gave us a delightful account of his pet humble-bees, who used to fly about his room, and come at call to be fed, and who manifested an almost painful interest in his coat buttons, examining them every day as if anxious to find out their true significance. Then there was my old friend, Miss Hopley, the writer on reptiles, who died recently, aged ninety-nine years, who tamed newts, but whose favorite pet was a slow-worm. She was never tired of expatiating on its lovable qualities. One finds Viscount Grey's pet squirrels more engaging, for these are wild squirrels in a wood in Northumberland, who quickly find out when he is at home and make their way to the house, scale the walls, and invade the library; then, jumping upon his writing-table, are rewarded with nuts, which they take from his hand. Another Northumbrian friend of the writer keeps, or kept, a pet cormorant, and finds him no less greedy in the domestic than in the wild state. After catching and swallowing fish all the morning in a neighboring river, he wings his way home at meal-times, screaming to be fed, and ready to devour all the meat and pudding he can get.

The list of strange creatures might be extended indefinitely, even fishes included; but who has ever heard of a tame pet rat? Not the small white, pink-eyed variety, artificially bred, which one may buy at any dealers, but a common brown rat, *Mus decumanus*, one of the commonest wild animals in England and certainly the most disliked. Yet this wonder has been witnessed recently in the village of Lelant, in West Cornwall. Here is the strange story, which is rather sad and at the same time a little funny.

This was not a case of "wild nature won by kindness"; the rat simply thrust itself and its friendship on the woman of the cottage: and she, being childless and much alone in her kitchen and living-room, was not displeased at its visits: on the contrary, she fed it; in return the rat grew more and more friendly and familiar towards her, and the more familiar it grew, the more she liked the rat. The trouble was, she possessed a cat, a nice, gentle animal not often at home, but it was dreadful to think of what might happen at any moment should pussy walk in when her visitor was with her. Then, one day, pussy did walk in when the rat was present, purring loudly, her tail held stiffly up, showing that she was in her usual sweet temper. On catching sight of the rat, she appeared to know intuitively that it was there as a privileged guest, while the rat on its part seemed to know, also by intuition, that it had nothing to fear. At all events these two quickly became friends and were evidently pleased to be together, as they now spent most of the time in the room, and would drink milk from the same saucer, and sleep bunched up together, and were extremely intimate.

By-and-by the rat began to busy herself making a nest in a corner of the kitchen under a cupboard, and it became evident that there would soon be an increase in the rat population. She now spent her time running about and gathering little straws, feathers, string, and anything of the kind she could pick up, also stealing or begging for strips of cotton, or bits of wool and thread from the work-basket. Now it happened that her friend was one of those cats with huge tufts of soft hair on the two sides of her face; a cat of that type, which is not uncommon, has a quaint resemblance to a mid-Victorian gentleman with a pair of magnificent side-whiskers of a silky softness covering both cheeks and flowing down like a double beard. The rat suddenly discovered that this hair was just what she wanted to add a cushion-like lining to her nest, so that her naked pink little ratlings should be born into the softest of all possible worlds. At once she started plucking out the hairs, and the cat, taking it for a new kind of game, but a little too rough to please her, tried for a while to keep her head out of reach and to throw the rat off. But she wouldn't be thrown off, and as she persisted in flying back and jumping at the cat's face and plucking the hairs, the cat quite lost her temper and administered a blow with her claws unsheathed.

The rat fled to her refuge to lick her wounds, and was no doubt as much astonished at the sudden change in her friend's disposition as the cat had been at the rat's new way of showing her playfulness. The result was that when, after attending to her scratches, she started upon her task of gathering soft materials, she left the cat severely alone. They were no longer friends; they simply ignored one another's presence in the room. The little ones, numbering about a dozen, presently came to light and were quietly removed by the woman's husband, who didn't mind his missis keeping a rat, but drew the line at one.

The rat quickly recovered from her loss and was the same nice affectionate little thing she had always been to her mistress; then a fresh wonder came to light—cat and rat were fast friends once more! This happy state of things lasted a few weeks; but, as we know, the rat was married, though her lord and master never appeared on the scene, indeed, he was not wanted; and very soon it became plain to see that more little rats were coming. The rat is an exceedingly prolific creature; she can give a month's start to a rabbit and beat her at the end by about forty points.

Then came the building of the nest in the same old corner, and when it got to the last stage and the rat was busily running about in search of soft materials for the lining, she once more made the discovery that those beautiful tufts of hair on her friend's face were just what she wanted, and once more she set vigorously to work pulling the hairs out. Again, as on the former occasion, the cat tried to keep her friend off, hitting her right and left with her soft pads, and spitting a little, just to show that she didn't like it. But the rat was determined to have the hairs, and the more she was thrown off the more bent was she on getting them, until the breaking-point was reached and puss, in a sudden rage, let fly, dealing blow after blow with lightning rapidity and with all the claws out. The rat, shrieking with pain and terror, rushed out of the room and was never seen again, to the lasting grief of her mistress. But its memory will long remain like a fragrance in the cottage—perhaps the only cottage in all this land where kindly feelings for the rat are cherished.

LAFCADIO HEARN

The Little Red Kitten

The kitten would have looked like a small red lion, but that its ears were positively enormous,—making the head like one of those little demons sculptured in mediæval stonework which have wings instead of ears. It ate beefsteak and cockroaches, caterpillars and fish, chicken and butterflies, mosquito-hawks and roast mutton, hash and tumble-bugs, beetles and pigs' feet, crabs and spiders, moths and poached eggs, oysters and earthworms, ham and mice, rats and rice pudding,—until its belly became a realization of Noah's Ark. On this diet it soon acquired strength to whip all the ancient cats in the neighborhood, and also to take under its protection a pretty little salmon-colored cat of the same sex, which was too weak to defend itself and had been unmercifully mauled every night before the tawny sister enforced reform in the shady yard of the old Creole house. The red kitten was not very big, but was very solid and more agile than a monkey. Its flaming emerald eyes were always watching, and its enormous ears always on the alert; and woe to the cat who dared approach the weak little sister with hostile intentions. The two always slept together—the little speckled one resting its head upon the body of its protector; and the red kitten licked its companion every day like a mother washing her baby. Wherever the red kitten went the speckled kitten followed; they hunted all kinds of creeping things together, and even formed a criminal partnership in kitten stealing. One day they were forcibly separated; the red kitten being locked up in the closet under the stairs to keep it out of mischief during dinner hours, as it had evinced an insolent determination to steal a stuffed crab from the plate of Madame R. Thus temporarily deprived of its guide, philosopher, and friend, the speckled kitten unfortunately wandered under a rocking-chair violently agitated by a heavy gentleman who was reading the "Bee"; and with a sharp little cry of agony it gave up its gentle ghost. Everybody stopped eating; and there was a general outburst of indignation and sorrow. The heavy gentleman got very red in the face, and said he had not intended to do it. "Tonnerre d'une pipe;—nom d'un petit bonhomme!"—he might have been a little more careful! . . . An hour later the red kitten was vainly seeking its speckled companion—all ears and eyes. It uttered strange little cries, and vainly waited for the customary reply. Then it commenced to look everywhere—upstairs, downstairs, on the galleries, in the corners, among the shrubbery, never supposing in its innocent mind that a little speckled body was lying far away upon a heap of garbage and ashes. Then it became very silent; purring when offered food, but eating nothing. . . . At last a sudden thought seemed to strike it. It had never seen the great world which rumbled beyond the archway of the old courtyard; perhaps its little sister had wandered out there. So it would go and seek her. For the first time it wandered beyond the archway and saw the big world it had never seen before—miles of houses and myriads of people and great cotton-floats thundering by, and great wicked dogs which murder kittens. But the little red one crept along beside the houses in the narrow strip of shadow, sometimes trembling when the big wagons rolled past, and sometimes hiding in doorways when it saw a dog, but still bravely seeking the lost sister. . . . It came to a great wide street—five times wider than the narrow street before the old Creole house; and the sun was so hot, so hot. The little creature was so tired and hungry, too. Perhaps somebody would help it to find the way. But nobody seemed to notice the red kitten, with its funny ears and great bright eyes. It opened its little pink mouth and cried; but nobody stopped. It could not understand that. Whenever it had cried that way at home, somebody had come to pet it. Suddenly a fire-engine came roaring up the street, and a great crowd of people were running after it. Then the kitten got very, very frightened; and tried to run out of the way, but its poor little brain was so confused and there was so much noise and shouting. . . . Next morning two little bodies lay side by side on the ashes—miles away from the old Creole house. The little tawny kitten had found its speckled sister.

Part Ten

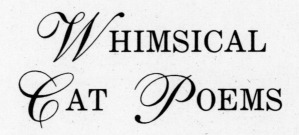

Whimsical Cat Poems

EDWARD LEAR

The Owl and the Pussy-cat

The Owl and the Pussy-cat went to sea
  In a beautiful pea-green boat,
They took some honey, and plenty of money,
  Wrapped up in a five-pound note.
The Owl looked up to the stars above,
  And sang to a small guitar,
"O lovely Pussy! O Pussy, my love,
  What a beautiful Pussy you are,
      You are,
      You are!
  What a beautiful Pussy you are!"

Pussy said to the Owl, "You elegant fowl!
  How charmingly sweet you sing!
O let us be married! too long have we tarried:
  But what shall we do for a ring!"
They sailed away, for a year and a day,
  To the land where the Bong-tree grows,
And there in a wood a Piggy-wig stood
  With a ring at the end of his nose,
      His nose,
      His nose,
  With a ring at the end of his nose.

"Dear Pig, are you willing to sell for one shilling
  Your ring?" Said the Piggy, "I will."
So they took it away, and were married next day
  By the Turkey who lives on the hill.
They dined on mince, and slices of quince,
  Which they ate with a runcible spoon;
And hand in hand, on the edge of the sand,
  They danced by the light of the moon,

The moon,
The moon,
They danced by the light of the moon.

ANONYMOUS

Two Nursery Rhymes

"Pussy-cat, Pussy-cat,
    Where have you been?"
"I've been to London,
    To look at the Queen."
"Pussy-cat, Pussy-cat,
    What did you do there?"
"I frightened a little mouse
    Under her chair."

* * *

There was a wee bit mousikie,
    That lived in Gilberaty, O;
It couldna get a bite o' cheese,
    For cheety-poussie-catty, O.

It said unto the cheesikie,
    "Oh, fain wad I be at ye, O,
If it were na for the cruel paws
    O' cheety-poussie-catty, O."

LA FONTAINE

The Old Cat and the Young Mouse

A mouse—young, inexperienced—
Thought he could pit his wit against
A wise old cat, Raminagrobis' kin.
   "Mercy, I pray," the mite commenced,
   Pleading his case to save his skin.
   "Mouse that I am, it must be clear
   I make but little difference here.
Surely my hosts—Madame, Monsieur, *et al.*—
   Won't starve for what I eat, indeed!
   A grain of wheat is all I need;
Why, with a nut I'd be a butterball!
   Besides, sir, I'm still much too small.
Save me to feed your children when I'm grown."
Replied the cat in condescending tone:
"You might as well be talking to the wall!
   My, how you err! To ask a cat
To spare you! And a wise, old one at that!
   You must think I'm a dunderhead!
Well, you can go harangue the Fates on high,
Children indeed! Don't worry, they'll be fed.
   Now, rules are rules: come down and die."
And so he did. *Requiescat!*

         In brief,
The moral of the tale I've been presenting?
Youth, sure it must prevail, must come to grief:
   Old age is cold and unrelenting.

       —Translated from the French by Norman R. Shapiro

AMBROSE BIERCE

The Vain Cat

Remarked a Tortoise to a Cat:
"Your speed's a thing to marvel at!
I saw you as you flitted by,
And wished I were one-half so spry."
The Cat said, humbly: "Why, indeed
I was not showing then my speed—
That was a poor performance." Then
She said exultantly (as when
The condor feels his bosom thrill
Remembering Chimborazo's hill,
and how he soared so high above,
It looked a valley, he a dove):
" 'Twould fire your very carapace
To see me with a dog in chase!"
Its snout in any kind of swill,
Pride, like a pig, will suck its fill.

VACHEL LINDSAY

The Mysterious Cat

I saw a proud, mysterious cat,
I saw a proud, mysterious cat,
Too proud to catch a mouse or rat—
Mew, mew, mew.

But catnip she would eat, and purr,
But catnip she would eat, and purr,

And goldfish she did much prefer—
Mew, mew, mew.

I saw a cat—'twas but a dream,
I saw a cat—'twas but a dream,
Who scorned the slave that brought her cream—
Mew, mew, mew.

Unless the slave were dressed in style,
Unless the slave were dressed in style,
And knelt before her all the while—
Mew, mew, mew.

Did you ever hear of a thing like that?
Did you ever hear of a thing like that?
Did you ever hear of a thing like that?
Oh, what a proud mysterious cat.
Oh, what a proud mysterious cat.
Oh, what a proud mysterious cat.
Mew . . . mew . . . mew.

DON MARQUIS

from

archy & mehitabel

the song of mehitabel

this is the song of mehitabel
of mehitabel the alley cat
as i wrote you before boss
mehitabel is a believer
in the pythagorean
theory of the transmigration
of the soul and she claims
that formerly her spirit
was incarnated in the body

of cleopatra
that was a long time ago
and one must not be
surprised if mehitabel
has forgotten some of her
more regal manners

i have had my ups and downs
but wotthehell wotthehell
yesterday sceptres and crowns
fried oysters and velvet gowns
and today i herd with bums
but wotthehell wotthehell
i wake the world from sleep
as i caper and sing and leap
when i sing my wild free tune
wotthehell wotthehell
under the blear eyed moon
i am pelted with cast off shoon
but wotthehell wotthehell

do you think that i would change
my present freedom to range
for a castle or moated grange
wotthehell wotthehell
cage me and i d go frantic
my life is so romantic
capricious and corybantic
and i m toujours gai toujours gai

i know that i am bound
for a journey down the sound
in the midst of a refuse mound
but wotthehell wotthehell
oh i should worry and fret
death and i will coquette
there s a dance in the old dame yet
toujours gai toujours gai

i once was an innocent kit
wotthehell wotthehell

with a ribbon my neck to fit
and bells tied onto it
o wotthehell wotthehell
but a maltese cat came by
with a come hither look in his eye
and a song that soared to the sky
and wotthehell wotthehell
and i followed adown the street
the pad of his rhythmical feet
o permit me again to repeat
wotthehell wotthehell

my youth i shall never forget
but there s nothing i really regret
wotthehell wotthehell
there s a dance in the old dame yet
toujours gai toujours gai

the things that i had not ought to
i do because i ve gotto
wotthehell wotthehell
and i end with my favorite motto
toujours gai toujours gai

boss sometimes i think
that our friend mehitabel
is a trifle too gay

mehitabel and her kittens

well boss
mehitabel the cat
has reappeared in her old
haunts with a
flock of kittens
three of them this time

archy she said to me
yesterday
the life of a female
artist is continually

hampered what in hell
have i done to deserve
all these kittens

i look back on my life
and it seems to me to be
just one damned kitten
after another
i am a dancer archy
and my only prayer
is to be allowed
to give my best to my art
but just as i feel
that i am succeeding
in my life work
along comes another batch
of these damned kittens
it is not archy
that i am shy on mother love
god knows i care for
the sweet little things
curse them
but am i never to be allowed
to live my own life
i have purposely avoided
matrimony in the interests
of the higher life
but i might just
as well have been a domestic
slave for all the freedom
i have gained
i hope none of them
gets run over by
an automobile
my heart would bleed
if anything happened
to them and i found it out
but it isn t fair archy
it isn t fair
these damned tom cats have all
the fun and freedom

if i was like some of these
green eyed feline vamps i know
i would simply walk out on the
bunch of them and
let them shift for themselves
but i am not that kind
archy i am full of mother love
my kindness has always
been my curse
a tender heart is the cross i bear
self sacrifice always and forever
is my motto damn them
i will make a home
for the sweet innocent
little things
unless of course providence
in his wisdom should remove
them they are living
just now in an abandoned
garbage can just behind
a made over stable in greenwich
village and if it rained
into the can before i could
get back and rescue them
i am afraid the little
dears might drown
it makes me shudder just
to think of it
of course if i were a family cat
they would probably
be drowned anyhow
sometimes i think
the kinder thing would be
for me to carry the
sweet little things
over to the river
and drop them in myself
but a mother s love archy
is so unreasonable
something always prevents me
these terrible

conflicts are always
presenting themselves
to the artist
the eternal struggle
between art and life archy
is something fierce
yes something fierce
my what a dramatic
life i have lived
one moment up the next
moment down again
but always gay archy always gay
and always the lady too
in spite of hell . . .

Part Eleven

THE TRUTH ABOUT CATS

PIERRE LOTI

Dogs and Cats

PROLOGUE

Cats are possessed of a shy, retiring nature, cajoling, haughty, and capricious, difficult to fathom. They reveal themselves only to certain favored individuals, and are repelled by the faintest suggestion of insult or even by the most trifling deception.

They are quite as intelligent as dogs, and are devoid of the yielding obsequiousness, the ridiculous sense of importance, and the revolting coarseness of these latter animals. Cats are dainty patricians, whereas dogs, whatever their social status, retain a *parvenu's* lack of cleanliness, and are irredeemably vulgar.

A CAT

A cat is watching me. . . . He is close at hand, on the table, and thrusts forward his dimly thoughtful little head, into which some unwonted flash of intelligence has evidently just entered. Whilst servants or visitors have been on the spot, he has scornfully kept out of the way, under an armchair, for no other person than myself is allowed to stroke his invariably immaculate coat. But no sooner does he perceive that I am alone than he comes and sits in front of me, suddenly assuming one of those expressive looks that are seen from time to time in such enigmatical, contemplative animals as belong to the same genus as himself. His yellow eyes look up at me, wide open, the pupils dilated by a mental effort to interrogate and attempt to understand: "Who are you, after all?" he asks. "Why do

I trust you? Of what importance are you in the world? What are you thinking and doing here?"

In our ignorance of things, our inability to know anything, how amazing—perhaps terrifying—if we could but see into the curious depths of those eyes and fathom the *unknowable* within the little brain hidden away there! Ah! if only for a moment we could put ourselves in its place and afterwards remember, what an instantaneous and definite solution—though no doubt terrifying enough—we might obtain of the perplexing problems of life and eternity! Are these familiar animals our inferiors and far removed from us, or are they terribly near to us? Is the dark veil which conceals from them the cause and end of life more dense than that stretched before our own eyes? . . . No, never will it be our privilege to solve the secret of those little wheedling heads, which allow themselves so lovingly to be held and stroked, almost crushed, in our hands. . . .

And now he is about to sleep, maybe to dream, on this table at which I am writing; he settles down as close to me as possible, after stretching out his paw towards me two or three times, looking at me as though craving permission to leap on to my knees. And there he lies, his head daintily resting on my arm, as though to say: "Since you will not have me altogether, permit this at least, for I shall not disturb you if I remain so."

How mysterious is the *affection* of animals! It denotes something lofty, something superior in those natures about which we know so little.

And how well I can understand Mohammed, who, in response to the chant of the *muezzin* summoning him to prayers, cut off with a pair of scissors the hem of his cloak before rising to his feet, for fear of disturbing his cat, which had settled down thereon to sleep.

ANOTHER CAT

Quite a little puss, a grey kitten three or four months old, striped like a tiger, besides being spotted, his tail ring-streaked like a panther's, belly and muzzle white, and the end of his nose quite pink. He made his appearance one morning,—Heaven alone knows where he sprang from!—a pitiable sight, lean and wretched-looking. Within a very short time he recovered, and for the past fortnight has been my most devoted companion.

To-day we have had a strong equinoctial gale, sudden and irresistible, bending the trees, dashing the sand along in maddening whirls, and lashing the sea into fury.

My grey kitten was in the garden, terrified by the deafening noise and the rush of the wind; he dashes into the house, just as a mighty gust comes through the doorway, accompanied by a quantity of fallen leaves and twigs. There is the utmost excitement throughout the house as the wind from the open sea beats upon it: the servants hasten to the badly-jointed windows to stop the sudden downpour of rain from making its way within; finally, they decide to close the shutters of those windows that overlook the sea, leaving me in semi-darkness. The little grey puss has made up his mind to take refuge in my arms, and is now stretching himself on my knees, with a friendly purring sound, having changed into a soft, velvety thing which I might crush between my fingers if I wished.

Little velvety thing, tiny being come to birth so recently, a conglomeration of atoms which six months ago was neither formed nor even thought of, but floated about in some pre-existent state of nothingness—a nothingness more absolute and mysterious than that which follows death. . . . How strange, when one thinks of it, that he already has such genteel notions of appearance, that he is so reserved and clean—above all, that he experiences the essentially human desire of some friendly presence when the great blind, awe-inspiring forces of Destruction are let loose.

Whilst wind and sea are furiously raging outside, I stroke the dainty soft paw he has trustingly left in my hands, between which I could easily crush it. Through the velvety fur I can feel, or rather guess at, a little flesh, frail tendons, and bones: exactly what constitutes my own human limbs, so near akin to those of the feline order. Moreover, like myself, he has eyes and ears, a nose and a mouth; which statement—one, by the way, that M. de la Palisse would have been capable of making, this I quite acknowledge—now leads me to remark how similar is the model upon which both he and I are alike fashioned, how resourceless Nature seems in varying her methods, in producing something different. Besides, this same Nature, reputed to be so inventive, so inexhaustibly diverse, must always have had recourse to this system, the only one she has thought out for the evolving of moving and thinking beings in numberless planets. . . . Then, in that dim light caused by the closed shutters and the great overhanging clouds, in the aimless roar and crash of unthinking matter around us, I suddenly become conscious that there exists between me and this little being, son and grandson of a cat, a strong link of brotherhood: both of us owing our physical life to an almost identical arrangement of the elements of which we are made up; and afterwards, both alike destined to yield up our bodies to the same dust.

TWO CATS MEET

A white-and-yellow cat is lying close to the edge of a house-top; he is not asleep, nor has he the slightest intention of sleeping. In obedience to the contemplative instincts of his race, he has there taken up his post, and is engaged in idle reverie as he looks down, from time to time, on the distant surroundings.

Suddenly, at the corner of a neighboring gable, a pair of erect ears are seen issuing from behind a chimney, then a pair of alert eyes, followed by an entire head: another cat! . . . This one is quite black; he makes his silent appearance with all the precaution of a Red Indian. He perceives the first cat from behind, and immediately stops short to reflect; then, in a series of counter-movements, very carefully planned, he steals nearer, advancing his velvety paws one after the other with ever-increasing caution.

All the same, the yellow-coated day-dreamer is conscious of the other's approach, and suddenly turns his head: ears completely drooping, the faint outline of a grimace on his lips, an imperceptible preparing of claws beneath his soft furry skin. . . .

And now the visitor starts, with back erect, though he continues to come forward, and pretends to assume once more his attitude of profound calm, whilst the first-comer, without rising, steadily keeps his green eyes fixed on him the whole time.

Evidently these two cats are slightly acquainted, and have already a certain esteem for each other; were it not so, a duel would be inevitable, and fur would soon be flying.

The black continues to approach with the same skilful, sidelong movements, the same prolonged pauses; then, when he has come to within a couple of feet of his yellow friend, he sits down and looks upwards as though to say: "You see, my intentions are perfectly honorable; I, too, wish to admire this fine landscape, that's all I have come for."

Thereupon the other turns away his eyes and fixes his gaze on the distant scene, as a sign that he understands and has lost all sense of mistrust; seeing which, the new-comer stretches himself out in his turn, but with what slow, measured movements as he advances one silky paw after another! . . .

A few more glances are again exchanged; their eyes half close as though in a friendly smile, and finally, now that the pact of mutual confidence has been definitely signed, the two thinkers, paying no further attention to each other, speedily become absorbed in a blissful state of dreamy contemplation.

EPILOGUE

Finally, as regards the canine tribe, it cannot be denied that there are good dogs, very good dogs; dogs that look up at you with the most lovable eyes. Personally, I must confess that I have felt considerable esteem and affection for some of them. All the same, I share the opinion of the Orientals, who rather despise the dog as being tainted with filthy instincts, whilst they respect and fear the cat as a sort of little sphinx.

—Translated from the French by Fred Rothwell

PIERRE LOTI

The Lives of Two Cats

MOUMOUTTE BLANCHE

I had been long without a cat when Moumoutte Blanche was brought to me. She lay, a tiny ball of white fur, on the red carpet, and I lifted her up very gently with both hands, so that she might be reassured, and say to herself after the manner of kittens: "This is a man who understands how to hold me, who is a friend, and whose caresses I can venture to receive with condescension!" Such a pretty little cat as she was, her baby eyes yellow and gleaming, her tiny nose rose pink, her fur deep and soft, warm to the touch, and beautifully clean. A patch of black on her forehead looked like a coquettish little bonnet, another on her shoulders, like a cape; her tail was black, her throat and paws whiter than swan's down. She weighed nothing, this bundle of nerves, of snowy fur, of subtle and infinite caprice.

After a time she grew to love us, as a cat loves, with no docility, but with an unalterable and touching constancy, which well deserves that I should hold her memory dear. In the spring, when the pale March sun warmed the chilly earth, she had the ever-repeated delight of watching Suleïma, the tortoise, her friend and fellow guest, crawl down the garden paths. In the lovely May weather she grew bold and restless, wearying of her austere surroundings, and escaping more than once to wander over the neighboring roofs. In the summer time she was languid as a Creole, drowsing for hours on the wall beneath the honeysuckle and roses, or sunning herself on the white stones between the pots of flowering cactus. Exquisitely and fastidiously neat, sedate in manner, an aristocrat to the tips of her little claws, she so hated other cats that the advent of a visitor put all her serenity to flight. In her own domain she suffered no intrusion. If over the garden wall two little ears were raised, two little eyes peeped furtively, if a rustling in the branches, a trembling of the ivy leaves awakened her suspicion, her fur bristled, and she sprang like a young Fury at the stranger. Nothing could restrain her, and presently we, the listeners, would hear the sound of scuffling, a fall, and lamentable cries. On the whole, an independent and somewhat lawless cat; but affectionate and caressing, eager to roam, and still more glad to return to us when her vagabond excursions were over.

Moumoutte Blanche was five years old, in the flower of her beauty, and I had grown attached to her as a member of the family and a household god, when, from the Gulf of Pekin, three thousand leagues away, there came one who was destined to be her inseparable friend, the strange, bizarre, humbly born little cat, Moumoutte Chinoise.

MOUMOUTTE CHINOISE

I remember the day when the Chinese cat and I established friendly relations. It was a melancholy afternoon in September. The first fogs of autumn were brooding over the cold, unquiet waters. We were sailing eastward, and the ship creaked plaintively as she slid into the hollows of the sea. I sat writing in the obscurity of my cabin, which grew darker and darker as the green waves washed over my closed port-hole.

Suddenly a little form came stealing out of the shadows. It drew nearer, stealthily and hesitatingly. There was an oriental grace in its fashion of holding one paw suspended in air, as though uncertain where to place it next. It looked at me with anxious interrogation.

"What does the cat want?" I said to myself. "She has had her dinner. She is not hungry. What is it she is after?"

As though to answer me, *la Chinoise* crept closer and closer, until she was at my feet. Then sitting upright, and curling her tail about her, she uttered a gentle little cry, looking straight into my eyes which seemed to hold some message she could read. She understood that I was a thinking creature, capable of pity, accessible to a mute prayer, and that my eyes were mirrors in which her troubled soul must study my good or bad designs. It is terrifying to think how near an animal is to us when it can realize such things.

For the first time I looked attentively at the little visitor who for two weeks had shared my lodgings. She was tawny as a wild hare, and striped like a tiger. Her face and neck were white. Certainly an ugly and a miserable cat; but her very ugliness had in it something strange and appealing, something which contrasted pleasantly with the comely cats of France. Her movements were stealthy and sinuous, her great ears stood erect, her tail was long and ragged, her eyes alone were beautiful, the deep golden eyes of the East, restless and full of expression.

While I watched her, I carelessly laid my hand on her head, and stroked the yellow fur. It was not mere physical pleasure she felt in the caress, but a sense of protection, of sympathy in her abandonment. It was for this she had crept from her hiding-place; it was for this, and not for food and drink, that she had come, wistful and terrified, to beg. Her little cat soul implored some company, some friendship in a lonely world.

Where had she learned this need, poor outcast, never before touched by a kindly hand, never the object of affection, unless, indeed, the paternal junk held some forlorn Chinese child, as joyless, as famished, as friendless as herself; a child who, perishing perchance in that miserable abode, would leave no more trace of its incomplete existence than she had done.

At last one small paw was lifted, oh, so delicately, so discreetly, and after a long, anxious look, Moumoutte, believing the time had now come for venturing all things, took heart of grace, and leaped upon my knee.

There she curled herself, but with tact and reserve, seeming to make her little body as light as possible, a mere featherweight, and never taking her eyes from my face. She stayed a long time, inconveniencing me greatly; but I lacked the courage to put her down, as I should have done had she been pretty and gay. Nervously aware of my least movement, she watched me intently, not as though fearing I would do her harm,—she was too intelligent to think me capable of such a thing,—but as though to ask, "Are you sure I do not weary or offend you?" Then her disquietude softened into cajolery, and her eyes, lifted to mine, said with charming distinctness: "On this autumn evening, so dreary to the soul of a cat, since we two are isolated in this unquiet abode, and lost amid infinite dangers, let us bestow upon each other a little of that mysterious something which sweetens misery and quiets death, which is called affection, and which expresses itself from time to time in a caress."

THE TWO CATS

The spring was clear and beautiful, the air loud with the song of birds, and to Moumoutte Chinoise, reared in suffocating darkness, the bright sunshine, the soft winds, and the presence of other cats were both a mystery and a delight. She explored the garden from end to end, smelling the young blades of grass, and the tiny leaves that came shooting up from the warm earth. All that was so familiar to us was to her new and strange; and Moumoutte Blanche, once the sole ruler of this lovely place, shared with her its endless wonders.

The borders of the miniature lake pleased *la Chinoise* best of all. She picked her careful way through the grass, which grew taller day by day; she crawled on her belly, as though tracking down her quarry; she hid behind the lilliputian rocks, and crouched under the ivy, for all the world like a little tiger in a jungle. I amused myself by watching her slow progress, her frequent pauses, her bewilderment; and, whenever she caught me looking at her, she turned and faced me, immovable as a statue, with one paw delicately held in air. Her droll yellow eyes fixed upon my face said as plainly as words could do: "You will permit me to continue my stroll? See how lightly and carefully I walk. And don't you think that everything here is very pretty? These paths, and these strange little green things which smell so good? And then those other objects I see above me, which are called the sun, the moon, the stars. How different it is from our old lodgings, and how well off we are, you and I, in this country."

. . . .

In the winter our cats became our fireside guests, our constant companions, sharing with us, not only the warmth and flicker of the flames, but the vague melancholy of our twilight reveries, and our unfathomable dreams. This, too, is the time of their greatest beauty. At the first approach of cold weather, Moumoutte Chinoise patched up the holes in her ragged coat, and Moumoutte Blanche adorned herself with an imposing cravat, a snow white boa, which framed her little face like some vast Medicean ruff. The friendship of the two cats for each other grew stronger in such close companionship. In the depth of an armchair, or on their cushions before the fire, they slept for days together, rolled up into one big furry ball, without visible head or tail.

It was Moumoutte Chinoise who perseveringly courted this comfortable warmth. When, after a short and chilly run in the garden, she found her friend sleeping by the fire, she would steal up to her very softly, and with as much caution as if she were stalking a mouse. Moumoutte Blanche, always nervous, pettish, and averse to being disturbed, would sometimes resent the intrusion, and give her a gentle slap by way of remonstrance. It was never returned. *La Chinoise* would merely lift her little paw with a mocking gesture, looking at me meanwhile out of the tails of her eyes, as though to say: "She has a difficult temper, hasn't she; but you know I never take her seriously." Then with gentle determination she would nestle resolutely by Blanche's side, and bury her head in the soft white fur. Her glance of drowsy triumph expressed the fulness of her content. "This is what I was after," it said, "and here I am."

—Translated from the French by Fred Rothwell

GUY DE MAUPASSANT

On Cats

Seated on a bench, the other day at my door, in the full sunlight, with a cluster of anemones in flower before me, I read a book recently published, an honest book, something uncommon and charming,— "The Cooper" by George Duval. A large white cat that belonged to the gardener jumped upon my lap, and by the shock closed the book, which I placed at my side in order to caress the animal.

The weather was warm; a faint suggestive odor of new flowers was in the air, and at times came little cool breezes from the great white summits that I could see in the distance. But the sun was hot and sharp, and the day was one of those that stir the earth, make it alive, break open the seed in order to animate the sleeping germs, and cleave the buds so that the young leaves may spring forth. The cat rolled itself on my knees, lying on its back, its paws in the air, with claws protruding, then receding. The little creature showed its pointed teeth beneath its lips, and its green eyes gleamed in the half-closed slit of its eyelids. I caressed and rubbed the soft, nervous animal, supple as a piece of silk, smooth, warm, delicious, dangerous. She purred with satisfaction, yet was quite ready to scratch, for a cat loves to scratch as well as to be petted. She held out her neck and rolled again, and when I took my hand from her, she raised herself and pushed her head against my lifted hand.

I made her nervous, and she made me nervous also, for, although I like cats in a certain way, I detest them at the same time,—those animals so charming and so treacherous. It gives me pleasure to fondle them, to rub under my hand their silky fur that sometimes crackles, to feel their warmth through this fine and exquisite covering. Nothing is softer, nothing gives to the skin a sensation more delicate, more refined, more rare, than the warm, living coat of a cat. But this living coat also communicates to me, through the ends of my fingers, a strange and ferocious desire to strangle the animal I am caressing. I feel in her the desire she has to bite and scratch me. I feel it,—that same desire, as if it were an electric current communicated from her to me. I run my fingers through the soft fur and the current passes through my nerves from my finger-tips to my heart, even to my brain; it tingles throughout my being and causes me to shut my teeth hard.

And if the animal begins to bite and scratch me, I seize her by the neck, I give her a turn and throw her far from me, as I would throw a stone from a sling, so quickly and so brutally that she never has time to revenge herself.

I remember that when I was a child I loved cats, yet I had even then that strange desire to strangle them with my little hands; and one day at the end of the garden, at the beginning of the woods, I perceived suddenly something gray rolling in the high grass. I went to see what it was, and found a cat caught in a snare, strangling, suffocating, dying. It rolled, tore up the ground with its claws, bounded, fell inert, then began again, and its hoarse, rapid breathing made a noise like a pump, a frightful noise which I hear yet. I could have taken a spade and cut the snare, I could have gone to find the servant or tell my father. No, I did not move, and with beating heart I watched it die with a trembling and cruel joy. It was a cat! If it had been a dog, I would rather have cut the copper wire with my teeth than let it suffer a second more. When the cat was quite dead, but yet warm, I went to feel of it and pull its tail!

These little creatures are delicious, notwithstanding, delicious above all, because in caressing them, while they are rubbing against our skin, purring and rolling on us, looking at us with their yellow eyes which seem never to see us, we realize the insecurity of their tenderness, the perfidious selfishness of their pleasure.

Some women, also, give us that sensation,—women who are charming, tender, with clear yet false eyes, who have chosen us entirely for their gratification. Near them, when they open their arms and offer their lips, when a man folds them to his heart with bounding pulses, when he tastes the joy of their delicate caress, he realizes well that he holds a perfidious, tricky cat, with claws and fangs, an enemy in love, who will bite him when she is tired of kisses.

Many of the poets have loved cats. Baudelaire has sung of them divinely.

I had one day the strange sensation of having inhabited the enchanted palace of the White Cat, a magic castle where reigned one of those undulant, mysterious, troubling animals, the only one, perhaps, of all living creatures that one never hears walk.

This adventure occurred last year on this same shore of the Mediterranean. At Nice there was atrocious heat, and I asked myself as to whether there was not, somewhere in the mountains above us, a fresh valley where one might find a breath of fresh air.

Thorence was recommended to me, and I wished to see it immediately. To get there I had first to go to Grasse, the town of perfumes, concerning which I shall write some day, and tell how the essences and quintessences of flowers are manufactured there, costing up to two thousand francs the liter. I passed the night in an old hotel of the town, a poor kind of inn, where the quality of the food was as doubtful as the cleanliness of the rooms. I went on my way in the morning.

The road went straight up into the mountains, following the deep ravines, which were overshadowed by sterile peaks, pointed and savage. I thought that my advisers had recommended to me a very extraordinary kind of summer excursion, and I was almost on the point of returning to Nice the same day, when I saw suddenly before me, on a mountain which appeared to close the entrance to the entire valley, an immense and picturesque ruined castle, showing towers and broken walls, of a strange architecture, in profile against the sky. It proved to be an ancient castle that had belonged to the Templars, who, in bygone days, had governed this country of Thorence.

I made a detour of this mountain, and suddenly discovered a long, green valley, fresh and reposeful. Upon its level were meadows, running waters, and willows; and on its sides grew tall pine-trees. In front of the ruins, on the other side of the valley, but standing lower, was an inhabited castle, called the Castle of the Four Towers, which was built about the year 1530. One could not see any trace of the Renaissance period, however. It was a strong and massive square structure, apparently possessing tremendous powers of resistance, and it was supported by four defensive towers, as its name would indicate.

I had a letter of introduction to the owner of this manor, who would not permit me to go to the hotel. The whole valley is one of the most charming spots in summer that one could dream of. I wandered about there until evening, and after dinner I went to the apartment that had been reserved for me. I first passed through a sort of sitting-room, the walls of which were covered by old Cordova leather; then I went through another room, where, by the light of my candle, I noticed rapidly, in passing, several old portraits of ladies—those paintings of which Théophile Gautier has written.

I entered the room where my bed was, and looked around me. The walls were hung with antique tapestries, where one saw rose-colored donjons in blue landscapes, and great fantastic birds sitting under foliage of precious stones! My dressing-room was in one of the towers. The windows wide on the inside and narrowed to a mere slit on the outside, going through the entire thickness of the walls, were, in reality, nothing but loopholes, through which one might kill an approaching enemy.

I shut my door, went to bed, and slept. Presently I dreamed; usually one dreams a little of something that has passed during the day. I seemed to be traveling; I entered an inn, where I saw at a table before the fire a servant in complete livery, and a mason,—a strange association which did not astonish me. These people spoke of Victor Hugo, who had just died, and I took part in their conversation. At last I went to bed in a room, the door of which I could not shut; and suddenly, I saw the servant and the mason, armed with sabers, coming softly toward my bed.

I awoke at once, and a few moments passed before I could recollect where I was. Then I recalled quickly my arrival of the day before at Thorence, the occurrences of the evening, and my pleasant reception by the owner. I was just about to close my eyes, when I saw distinctly in the darkness, in the middle of my room, at about the height of a man's head, two fiery eyes watching me.

I seized a match, and while striking it I heard a noise, a light, soft noise, like the sound of a wet rag thrown on the floor, but after I had lighted the candle I saw nothing but a tall table in the middle of the room. I rose, went through both apartments, looked under the bed and into the closets, and found nothing. I thought then that perhaps I had continued dreaming after I was awake, and so I went to sleep again, but not without trouble.

I dreamed again. This time I traveled once more, but in the Orient, in the country that I love. I arrived at the house of a Turk, who lived in the middle of a desert. He was a superb Turk,—not an

Arab, but a Turk, fat, friendly, and charming. He was dressed in Turkish attire, with a turban on his head, and a whole shopful of silk on his back,—a real Turk of the Théâtre Français, who made me compliments while offering me sweetmeats, sitting on a voluptuous divan.

Then a little black boy took me to a room—all my dreams ended in this fashion in those days! It was a perfumed room decorated in sky blue, with skins of wild beasts on the floor, and before the fire,—the idea of fire pursued me even in the desert,—on a low chair, was a woman, lightly clothed, who was waiting for me. She was of the purest Oriental type, with stars tattooed on her cheeks and forehead and chin; she had immense eyes, a beautiful form, and slightly brown skin,—a warm and exciting skin.

She looked at me, and I thought: "This is what I understand to be the true meaning of the word hospitality. In our stupid and prudish northern countries, with their hateful mawkishness of ideas, and silly notions of morality, a man would never receive a stranger in this fashion."

I went up to the woman and spoke to her, but she replied only by signs, not knowing a word of my language, which the Turk, her master, understood so well. All the happier that she would be silent, I took her by the hand and led her toward my couch, where I placed myself by her side. . . .

But one always awakens at those moments! So I opened my eyes and was not greatly surprised to feel beneath my hand something soft and warm, which I caressed lovingly. Then, my mind clearing, I recognized that it was a cat, a big cat rolled up against my cheek, sleeping there with confidence. I left it there and composed myself to sleep once more. When daylight appeared he was gone; and I really thought I had dreamed he had been with me; for I could not understand how he could have come in and gone out, as my door was locked.

When I related my dream and my adventure to my agreeable host (not the whole of it!) he began to laugh, and said: "He came in through his own door," and raising a curtain, he showed me a little round hole in the wall. I learned then that the old habitations of this country have long narrow runways through the walls, which go from the cellar to the garret, from the servants' rooms to the rooms of the *seigneur*, and these passages render the cat king and master of the interior of the house. He goes where it pleases him, visits his domain at his pleasure, sleeps in all the beds, sees all, hears all, knows all the secrets, all the habits, all the shames of the house. Everywhere he is at home, the animal that moves without noise, the silent prowler, the nocturnal rover of the hollowed walls. And I thought of Baudelaire.

HERODOTUS

The Cat of Egypt

The number of domestic animals in Egypt is very great, and would be still greater, were it not for what befalls the cats. As the females, when they have kittened, no longer seek the company of the males, these last, to obtain once more their companionship, practice a curious artifice. They seize the kittens, carry them off, and kill them; but do not eat them afterwards. Upon this, the females, being deprived of their young, and longing to supply their place, seek the males once more, since they are particularly fond of their offspring.

On every occasion of a fire in Egypt, the strangest prodigy occurs with the cats. The inhabitants allow the fire to rage as it pleases, while they stand about at intervals and watch these animals, which, slipping by the men, or else leaping over them, rush headlong into the flames. When this happens, the Egyptians are in deep affliction. If a cat dies in a private house by a natural death, all the inmates of the house shave their eyebrows. The dead cats are taken to the city of Bubastis, where they are embalmed, after which they are buried in certain sacred repositories.

——Translated by George Rawlinson, M.A.

MONTAIGNE

My Cat

When my cat and I entertain each other with mutual antics, as playing with a garter, who knows but that I make more sport for her than she makes for me? Shall I conclude her to be simple that has her time to begin or to refuse to play, as freely as I have mine. Nay, who knows but that it is a defect of my not understanding her language (for doubtless cats can talk and reason with one another) that we agree no better; and who knows but that she pities me for being no wiser than to play with her; and laughs, and censures my folly in making sport for her, when we two play together.

JAMES BOSWELL

Hodge

I shall never forget the indulgence with which Dr. Johnson treated Hodge, his cat, for whom he himself used to go out and buy oysters, lest the servants, having that trouble, should take a dislike to the poor creature. I am unluckily one of those who have an antipathy to a cat, so that I am uneasy when I am in the room with one; and I own I frequently suffered a good deal from the presence of this same Hodge. I recollect him one day scrambling up Dr. Johnson's breast, apparently with much satisfaction, while my friend, smiling and half whistling, rubbed down his back, and pulled him by the tail; and when I observed he was a fine cat, saying, "Why, yes, sir, but I have had cats whom I liked better than this"; and then, as if perceiving Hodge to be out of countenance, adding, "but he is a very fine cat, a very fine cat indeed."

This reminds me of the ludicrous account which he gave Mr. Langton of the despicable state of a young gentleman of good family: "Sir, when I heard of him last, he was running about town, shooting cats." And then, in a sort of kindly reverie, he bethought himself of his own favorite cat, and said, "But Hodge shan't be shot; no, no, Hodge shall not be shot."

CHATEAUBRIAND

An Appreciation

TO M. DE MARCELLUS

I value in the cat the independent and almost ungrateful spirit which prevents her from attaching herself to any one, the indifference with which she passes from the salon to the housetop. When we caress her, she stretches herself and arches her back responsively; but this is because she feels an agreeable sensation, not because she takes a silly satisfaction, like the dog, in faithfully loving a thankless master. The cat lives alone, has no need of society, obeys only when she pleases, pretends to sleep that she may see the more clearly, and scratches everything on which she can lay her paw.

SIR WALTER SCOTT

Hinse of Hinsefeld

TO JOANNA BAILLIE

I have added a romantic inmate to my family,—a large bloodhound, allowed to be the finest dog of the kind in Scotland, perfectly gentle, affectionate, good-natured, and the darling of all the children. He is between the deer-greyhound and mastiff, with a shaggy mane like a lion, and always sits beside me at dinner, his head as high as the back of my chair; yet it will gratify you to know that a favorite cat keeps him in the greatest possible order, insists upon all rights of precedence, and scratches with impunity the nose of an animal who would make no bones of a wolf, and pulls down a red deer without fear or difficulty. I heard my friend set up some most piteous howls (and I assure you the noise was no joke), all occasioned by his fear of passing Puss, who had stationed himself on the stairs.

THOMAS GRAY

A Letter of Condolence

TO HORACE WALPOLE

As one ought to be particularly careful to avoid blunders in a compliment of condolence, it would be a sensible satisfaction to me (before I testify my sorrow, and the sincere part I take in your misfortune) to know for certain who it is I lament. I knew Zara and Selima (Selima was it, or Fatima?), or rather I knew them both together; for I cannot justly say which was which. Then as to your handsome Cat, the name you distinguish her by, I am no less at a loss, as well knowing one's handsome cat is always the cat one likes best; or if one be alive and the other dead, it is usually the latter that is the handsomest. Besides, if the point were never so clear, I hope you do not think me so ill-bred or so imprudent as to forfeit all my interest in the survivor. Oh, no! I would rather seem to mistake, and imagine to be sure it must be the tabby one that has met with this sad accident. . . . I feel (as you have done long since) that I have very little to say, at least in prose. Somebody will be the better for it; I do not mean you, but your Cat, *feue* Mademoiselle Sélime, whom I am about to immortalize for one week or fortnight.

ROBERT SOUTHEY

In Memoriam

TO GROSVENOR C. BEDFORD

Alas, Grosvenor, this day died poor old Rumpel, after as long and happy a life as cat could wish for, if cats form wishes on that subject. His full titles were:—

"The most Noble the Archduke Rumpelstiltzchen, Marquis Macbum, Earl Tomlemagne, Baron Raticide, Waowhler, and Skaratch."

There should be a court mourning in Catland, and if the Dragon[1] wear a black ribbon round his neck, or a band of crape, *a la militaire*, on one of his fore legs, it will be but a becoming mark of respect.

As we have no catacombs here, he is to be decently interred in the orchard, and catmint planted on his grave. Poor creature, it is well that he has thus come to his end, since he had grown to be an object of pity. I believe we are, each and all, servants included, more sorry for his loss, or rather more affected by it, than any one of us would like to confess.

I should not have written to you at present, had it not been to notify you of this event.

[1] Bedford's cat.

RAINER MARIA RILKE

The Cats of Balthus

Who understands cats? Do you think you do? As far as I'm concerned, their existence has never struck me as more than a fairly risky hypothesis.

If animals are going to belong to our world, they have to come partway into it, agreeing to tolerate to some extent our way of life; if not, whether it's out of hostility or fear, their way of relating will be to measure the distance between us and them.

Think of dogs: their relationship to us is so confidential and full of admiration that some of them seem to have abandoned their most ancient canine traditions to worship our customs and even our mistakes. And that's what makes them tragic and noble. Their decision to let us in forces them to live, so to speak, at the boundaries of their nature, constantly overstepping them with their humanized expressions and sentimental snouts.

But what attitude do cats have?—Cats are cats, and theirs is a cat world from one end to the other. They watch us, you say? But does anyone know if they condescend to hold even for a second our meaningless images at the backs of their eyes? Is their staring simply a kind of opposition, a magic refusal of eyes that have no room for us?—It's true that some of us let ourselves be moved by their cuddly, electrical caress. But they only need to recall how their favorite animal's strange, abrupt loss of attention often put an end to expressions of emotion they thought were reciprocated. And it's those same ones, privileged to be allowed near, who have been denied and rejected many times and, even as they pressed the mysteriously indifferent creature to their bodies, felt themselves stopped at the entrance to that world inhabited exclusively by cats, where they live in the midst of events none of us can even guess at.

Was man ever a contemporary?—I doubt it. And I assure you that sometimes at dusk the neighbor's cat leaps across my path, either unconscious of me or proving to the astonished world of things that I don't even exist.

Do you think I'm wrong to involve you in these reflections, all in the name of leading you up to the story my dear friend Balthus is going to tell you? Granted, he drew it without using words, but by and large his pictures should tell you what you need to know. So why should I repeat them in another form? I'd rather add what has not been said. Let me summarize the story:

Balthus (I think he was ten years old at the time) finds a cat at the Château de Nyon, which you are no doubt familiar with. He is allowed to take him, and off he goes on a trip with his trembling little find. By boat to Geneva, by streetcar to Molard. He introduces his new companion to home life, domesticating, spoiling and treasuring him. "Mitsou" joyfully goes along with the rules and regulations, sometimes breaking the monotony of the house with a playful, ingenious trick. Do you think the fact that his master attaches an annoying leash when he walks him is overdoing it? He does it because he's wary of all the fantasies lurking in the heart of his loving but unknown and adventurous tomcat. However, he's wrong. Even a dangerous move is made without a problem, and the unpredictable little creature adapts to his new surroundings with amused obedience. Then suddenly he disappears. The house is in an uproar; but, thank God, this time it's not serious: they find Mitsou out on the lawn and Balthus, far from scolding the deserter, installs him on the kindly radiator. I guess you can savor, as I do, the rich feeling that follows such anguish. Alas! it's no more than a respite. Sometimes Christmas is too seductive. You eat cake without counting the cost. You get sick, and you go to bed. Mitsou, bothered by your overly long sleep, runs away instead of waking you up. What commotion! Fortunately, Balthus has recovered enough to get right into the search for the runaway. He begins by crawling under his bed: nothing there. Doesn't he look really brave all alone in the cellar with his candle, a symbol of the search that he takes everywhere, into the garden, out in the street: nothing! Look at his solitary little figure: who abandoned him? A cat?—Will his father's recent sketch of Mitsou comfort him? No, there was a sense of foreboding in it, and the loss permanent and inevitable began God only knows when! He comes back inside. He cries, showing you his tears with both hands:

Look carefully at them.

That's the whole story. The artist told it better than I could. So what's left for me to say? Very little.

Finding a thing is always fun, because a moment before it didn't exist. But finding a cat: that's incredible! Because, let's admit it, that cat does not enter your life completely as, for example, one plaything or another would. While it's yours now, it's still somewhat apart, and that will always add up to:

life + a cat,

which, I assure you, is a huge total.

To lose a thing is very sad. You need to imagine it's in poor condition, that wherever it is it's broken or has ended up rotting away. But to lose a cat: No! that's not allowed. No one ever has. How can you lose a cat, a living thing, a live creature, a life? But you can lose a life: that's death!

Right, that's death.

Finding. Losing. Have you considered carefully what loss involves? It's not simply the negation of that generous moment that fulfilled an expectation you yourself weren't aware you had. For between that moment and the loss there is always what we call—awkwardly enough, I admit—possession.

Now loss, as cruel as it is, has no effect on possession. If you like, it ends it or affirms it. But at bottom it's just a second acquisition, this time completely internal, with a different intensity.

And you experienced this, Balthus. No longer seeing Mitsou, you began to see him more.

Is he still alive? He lives on in you who, having delighted in his carefree kittenish gaiety, were obliged to express it through the labors of your sorrow.

And thus, a year later I found you grown and comforted.

But for those who will always see you only at the end of your book, I wrote the first—somewhat fanciful—part of this preface. So

I could tell them at the end: "Don't worry: I'm here. So is Balthus. Our world is still intact.

There are no cats."

Chäteau de Berg-am-Irchel
November 1920

—Translated from the German by William Kulik

WILLIAM FAULKNER

From *The Reivers*
Cats

. . . he neither toils nor spins, he is a parasite on you but he does not love you; he would die, cease to exist, vanish from the earth (I mean, in his so-called domestic form) but so far he has not had to. (There is the fable, Chinese I think, literary I am sure: of a period on earth when the dominant creatures were cats: who after ages of trying to cope with the anguishes of mortality—famine, plague, war, injustice, folly, greed—in a word, civilized government—convened a congress of the wisest cat philosophers to see if anything could be done: who after long deliberation agreed that the dilemma, the problems themselves were insoluble and the only practical solution was to give it up, relinquish, abdicate, by selecting from among the lesser creatures a species, race optimistic enough to believe that the mortal predicament could be solved and ignorant enough never to learn better. Which is why the cat lives with you, is completely dependent on you for food and shelter but lifts no paw for you and loves you not; in a word, why your cat looks at you the way it does.)

BENJAMIN FRANKLIN

An Humble Petition Presented to Madame Helve'tius by Her Cats

We shall not endeavour to defend ourselves equally from devouring as many sparrows, blackbirds, and thrushes, as we can possibly catch. But here we have to plead in extenuation, that our most cruel enemies, your Abbés themselves, are incessantly complaining of the ravages made by these birds among the cherries and other fruit. The Sieur Abbé Morellet, in particular, is always thundering the most violent anathemas against the blackbirds and thrushes, for plundering your vines, which they do with as little mercy as he himself. To us, however, most illustrious Lady, it appears that the grapes may just as well be eaten by *blackbirds* as by *Abbés*, and that our warfare against the winged plunderers will be fruitless, if you encourage other biped and featherless pilferers, who make ten times more havoc.

We know that we are also accused of eating nightingales, who never plunder, and sing, as they say, most enchantingly. It is indeed possible that we may now and then have gratified our palates with a delicious morsel in this way, but we can assure you that it was in utter ignorance of your affection for the species; and that, resembling sparrows in their plumage, we, who make no pretensions to being connoisseurs in music, could not distinguish the song of the one from that of the other, and therefore supposed ourselves regaling only on sparrows. A cat belonging to M. Piccini has assured us, that they who only know how to *mew*, cannot be any judges of the art of singing; and on this we rest for our justification. However, we will henceforward exert our utmost endeavours to distinguish the *Gluck-ists*, who are, as we are informed, the sparrows, from the *Piccinists*, who are the nightingales. We only intreat of you to pardon the inadvertence into which we may possibly fall, if, in roving after nests, we may sometimes fall upon a brood of *Piccinists*, who, being then destitute of plumage, and not having learnt to sing, will have no mark by which to distinguish them.

ADLAI STEVENSON

The Roaming Cat

STATE OF ILLINOIS
EXECUTIVE DEPARTMENT
Springfield, April 23, 1949

To the Honorable, the Members of the Senate of the 66th General Assembly:

I herewith return, without my approval, Senate Bill No. 93 entitled "An Act to Provide Protection to Insectivorous Birds by Restraining Cats." This is the so-called "Cat Bill." I veto and withhold my approval from this Bill for the following reasons:

It would impose fines on owners or keepers who permitted their cats to run at large off their premises. It would permit any person to capture, or call upon the police to pick up and imprison, cats at large. . . . This legislation has been introduced in the past several sessions of the Legislature, and it has, over the years, been the source of much comment—not all of which has been in a serious vein. . . . I cannot believe there is a widespread public demand for this law or that it could, as a practical matter, be enforced.

Furthermore, I cannot agree that it should be the declared public policy of Illinois that a cat visiting a neighbor's yard or crossing the highway is a public nuisance. It is in the nature of cats to do a certain amount of unescorted roaming. . . . Also consider the owner's dilemma: To escort a cat abroad on a leash is against the nature of the cat, and to permit it to venture forth for exercise unattended into a night of new dangers is against the nature of the owner. Moreover, cats perform useful service, particularly in rural areas, in combating rodents—work they necessarily perform alone and without regard for property lines. . . .

The problem of cat *versus* bird is as old as time. If we attempt to resolve it by legislation who knows but what we may be called upon to take sides as well in the age-old problem of dog *versus* cat, bird *versus* bird, or even bird *versus* worm. In my opinion, the State of Illinois and its local governing bodies already have enough to do without trying to control feline delinquency.

For these reasons, and not because I love birds the less or cats the more, I veto and withhold my approval from Senate Bill No. 93.

Respectfully,
Adlai E. Stevenson, Governor

ROY BLOUNT, JR.

Dogs Vis-à-Vis Cats

Which is the better pet, a cat or a dog?

Well, which is the better fruit, an apple or an orange?

Of dogs, in my time, I have had Sailor, Brownie, Bobby, Smokey, Butch, Snoopy (before "Peanuts"), Tubby, Sam, Chipper, Owen, Peggy, Ned, Sadie, Mollie and Pie. Of cats, I have had Stranger, Lulu, Angel, Emmy, Piedmont, Haile, Bale, Snope and Eloise. And Peggy's eight puppies and Eloise's two batches of kittens.

Down through the years, those hairy little entities have been parts of my life, nearly as intimate to me as my ankles. I have predominantly fond thoughts about every one of them, except possibly Smokey, who used to get lost and have to be bailed out of the pound all the time.

In the presence of all those names, I hate to generalize. Emmy acted a lot like a dog, and Tubby hung around happily with cats. You can't lump your pets together by their species any more than you can your friends by their professions. (I have known English professors who acted like people in the shrimping business.) But I'll tell you one thing. A cat can't smile. Or won't.

A dog will smile. Romp with your dog for a while and he or she will beam. Light up. You tell me the expression on that dog's face is not a smile. A mule or a monkey or a porpoise will sort of grin, but a dog is the only animal that will *smile*.

I'm not saying a cat won't joke. One morning I came downstairs to find a whole, perfect, upright rabbit's head on the floor. It looked as though a rabbit had stuck its head up through the floor to take a look around. Only the head wasn't moving.

"Waughh!" was my first reaction. Then I realized that a perky-looking disembodied rabbit's head on the floor was Snope's or Eloise's idea of a joke. Neither of them would own up to it in any way, of course. Neither of them smiled. I love cats but . . . But I am always saying, "I love cats, but . . ."

A dog will make eye contact. A cat will, too, but a cat's eyes don't even look entirely warm-blooded to me, whereas a dog's eyes look human except less guarded. A dog will look at you as if to say, "What do you want me to do for you? I'll do anything for you." Whether a dog *can* in fact, do anything for you if you don't have sheep (I never have) is another matter. The dog is *willing*.

A cat will do something for you: a cat will mouse. But I'm not sure that a house free of mice is better off than a house free of kitty litter. (I hate kitty litter. Have you ever been washing your hands and had your wet bar of soap fall into the kitty litter? Or your toothbrush? In the morning?) And a cat that mouses will also gerbil, parakeet, and rabbit. Furthermore, a cat will not do any of these things because you want him to.

I say that from experience and observation. I say it in the face of recent comments by Dr. Michael W. Fox, the scientific director of the Humane Society of the U.S. Fox maintains that he knows of cats that switch on lights, cats that flush the toilet, cats that press the lever of an electric can opener, and one cat that "knocks the telephone off the hook when it rings, listens to the receiver and meows into the mouthpiece." He cites another cat that would only take a pill "after its owner told it the pill was important to take."

Okay. Okay. After its owner told it the pill was *important to the cat.* You won't find a cat that will do something because it means a great deal to the owner.

When a cat makes eye contact with a person, the cat's expression says, "So?" There is little that a person can say in response to this expression. Cats have not forgotten that they were worshiped by the ancient Egyptians. It went to their heads. A cat's eyes know what a cat's eyes know.

Dogs' eyes twinkle, well up, express yearning. Which may be why cats are fast overtaking dogs in popularity in American homes. Taking care of cats is less of a problem than taking care of dogs, and cats are less demanding *emotionally*. A dog will smile, and a dog will also look at you as if you have been abusing him because you have not kneaded the place where his ears join onto his head in the last ten minutes. "Is it something I did?" the dog's eyes ask. "Haven't

I been a good enough dog to you? God knows you know I love you. Why don't you want to go out into the woods and watch me chase squirrels? You're breaking—I'm not *accusing* you. I know you must have a reason, but I'm just saying—you're breaking my heart." Having a dog in the home is too much like having a person. Having a cat in the home is not enough like having a person.

Robert Graves once said that he wrote novels for the money he needed to live so he could write poetry. His books or prose, he said, were the show dogs he raised to support his cat. I guess a cat is sort of like a poem. A cat is relatively short. A cat is only subtly demonstrative. To be sure, you can curl up with a good cat, but that doesn't mean you *understand* the cat. A dog is like Dickens.

ACKNOWLEDGMENTS

"The China Cat" by Walter de la Mare is reprinted by permission of The Literary Trustees of Walter de la Mare and The Society of Authors as their representative.

"Peter" by Marianne Moore. Reprinted with permission of Macmillan Publishing Company from *Collected Poems of Marianne Moore*. Copyright © 1935 by Marianne Moore; renewed 1963 by Marianne Moore and T. S. Eliot.

"Sad Memories" reprinted from *The English Poems of Charles Calverly* by Charles Calverly, Leicester University Press, 1974, by permission of the publishers. All rights reserved.

"Lullaby for the Cat" from *The Complete Poems: 1927–1979* by Elizabeth Bishop. Copyright © 1979, 1983 by Alice Helen Methfessel. Reprinted by permission of Farrar, Straus & Giroux, Inc.

"The Cats" reprinted from *The Collected Poems of Weldon Kees* by Weldon Kees, edited by Donald Justice, by permission of the University of Nebraska Press. Copyright © 1975 by the University of Nebraska Press.

"The Happy Cat" from *The Complete Poems* by Randall Jarrell. Copyright © 1941, renewal copyright © 1968, 1969 by Mrs. Randall Jarrell. Reprinted by permission of Farrar, Straus & Giroux, Inc.

"Poem" from *The Collected Poems of William Carlos Williams, 1909–1939, vol. I* by William Carlos Williams. Copyright 1938 by New Directions Publishing Corporation. Reprinted by permission of New Directions Publishing Corp.

"Mrs. Bond's Cats" copyright © 1973, 1974 by James Herriot. From the book *All Things Bright and Beautiful* and reprinted with permission from St. Martin's Press, Inc., New York, N.Y.

"Death of a Favorite" by J. F. Powers first appeared in *The New Yorker*. Copyright © 1950 by J. F. Powers. Used with permission of the author.

"The Best Bed" by Sylvia Townsend Warner from *The Salutation*, Viking Press, 1932. Reprinted by permission of the Executors of the Estate of Sylvia Townsend Warner and Chatto & Windus Publishers.

"I Am a Cat" by Soseki Natsume, English translation by Katsue Shibata and Motonari Kai, published 1968 by Kenkyusha Ltd., Tokyo, Japan.

"The Black Cat" from *The Selected Poetry of Rainer Maria Rilke* by Rainer Maria Rilke, translated by Stephen Mitchell. Copyright © 1982 by Stephen Mitchell. Reprinted by permission of Random House, Inc.

"Cat," "The Cat," and "Cats" from *Les Fleurs du Mal* by Charles Baudelaire, translated by Richard Howard. Translation copyright © 1983 by Richard Howard. Reprinted by permission of David R. Godine, publisher.

"Woman and Cat" by Paul Verlaine from *Paul Verlaine: Selected Poems*, translated and edited by C. F. MacIntyre. Copyright © 1948 The Regents of the University of California.

"White Cats" by Paul Valéry. From *The Collected Works in English by Paul Valéry, Vol. I—The Poems*, translated by David Paul. Copyright © 1971 by Princeton University Press.

"The Cats of Saint Nicholas" by George Seferis. © 1989 by Edmund Keeley and Philip Sherrard. From *George Seferis: Collected Poems*, Revised Edition, Princeton University Press, 1993.

"The Cat" from *Selected Poems of Pablo Neruda*, translated by Ben Belitt. English translation copyright © 1961, 1989 by Ben Belitt. Used by permission of Grove Press, Inc.

"The White Cat" by Joyce Carol Oates first appeared in *A Matter of Crime* published by Harcourt Brace Jovanovich. Copyright © 1987 by Joyce Carol Oates.

"The Islands" by Alice Adams. Copyright © 1991 by Alice Adams. Used with permission of the author.

"Puss in Boots" by Angela Carter. From *The Bloody Chamber* by Angela Carter. Copyright © 1979 (Harper & Row). Used with permission of Rogers, Coleridge & White Ltd.

"Schrödinger's Cat" by Ursula K. Le Guin. Copyright © 1974 by Ursula K. Le Guin. First appeared in *Universe 5*. Reprinted by permission of the author and the author's agent, Virginia Kidd.

"Amateur Voodoo" by Francine Prose. Reprinted by permission of Georges Borchardt, Inc., for the author. Copyright © 1989 by Francine Prose. First published in *Boulevard*.

"Cleanliness" is reprinted from *Between Angels, Poems by Stephen Dunn*, by permission of W. W. Norton & Company, Inc. Copyright © 1989 by Stephen Dunn.

"Hoppy" from *The Ruined Motel*. Copyright © 1981 by Reginald Gibbons.

"Sisterhood" by Dan Halpern. From a larger poem entitled "Infidelities" published in *Foreign Neon* by Daniel Halpern, Knopf. Copyright © 1991, Daniel Halpern.

"Divination by a Cat" from *A Summoning of Stones*. Copyright © 1948 by Anthony Hecht. Used by permission of the author.

"Wild Gratitude" from *Wild Gratitude* by Edward Hirsch. Copyright © 1985 by Edward Hirsch. Reprinted by permission of Alfred A. Knopf, Inc.

"Kitty and Bug" from *Harp Lake* by John Hollander. Copyright © 1988 by John Hollander. Reprinted by permission of Alfred A. Knopf, Inc.

"Esther's Tomcat" from *New Selected Poems* by Ted Hughes. Copyright © 1960 by Ted Hughes. Reprinted by permission of HarperCollins Publishers.

"The Cat" from *When One Has Lived a Long Time Alone* by Galway Kinnell. Copyright © 1990 by Galway Kinnell. Reprinted by permission of Alfred A. Knopf, Inc.

"The Thing About Cats" by John L'Heureux, from *No Place For Hiding*, Doubleday, 1971. Copyright © 1971 by John L'Heureux. Used with permission of the author.

"The Cat" by William Matthews. Copyright © 1972. Reprinted by permission of the author.

"My Cat and i" by Roger McGough, reprinted by permission of the Peters Fraser & Dunlop Group Ltd.

"Catnip and Dogwood" by Howard Moss. Used with the permission of the Estate of Howard Moss.

"Poem for Pekoe" by Robert Phillips. Copyright © 1981, 1984 by Robert Phillips. Reprinted by permission of the author.

"The Cats of Balthus" from *The Language Student* by Bin Ramke, published by Louisiana State University Press. Copyright © 1986 by Bin Ramke. Reprinted by permission of the author.

"Without Violence" from *The Expectations of Light*. Copyright © 1981 by Pattiann Rogers. Reprinted by permission of the author.

"Cat & the Weather" by May Swenson © 1963, renewed 1991. Used with permission of The Literary Estate of May Swenson.

"Touch of Spring" from *Tossing and Turning* by John Updike. Copyright © 1977 by John Updike. Reprinted by permission of Alfred A. Knopf, Inc.

"Pleasure, Pleasure" from *Princeton One Autumn Afternoon: Collected Poems of Theodore Weiss*, published by Macmillan. Copyright © Theodore Weiss, 1988. Reprinted by permission of the author.

"The Tale of the Cats" from *Italian Folktales* by Italo Calvino, copyright © 1956 by Giulio Einaudi editore, s.p.a.; English translation copyright © 1980 by Harcourt Brace Jovanovich, Inc. Reprinted by permission of the publisher.

Use of "The Cat That Walked by Himself" from *Just So Stories* by Rudyard Kipling granted by the publisher, Bantam Doubleday Dell Publishing Group, Inc.

"A Friendly Rat" from *The Book of a Naturalist* by W. H. Hudson. Copyright © 1968. Reprinted by permission of AMS Press, Inc.

"the song of mehitabel," "mehitabel and her kittens" from *archy & mehitabel* by Don Marquis. Copyright 1927 by Doubleday, a division of Bantam Doubleday Dell Publishing Group, Inc. Used by permission of Doubleday, a division of Bantam Doubleday Dell Publishing Group, Inc.

Excerpt from *The Reivers* by William Faulkner. Copyright © 1962 by William Faulkner. Used by permission of the publisher, Random House, Inc.

"Dogs Vis-a-Vis Cats" from *Now, Where Were We* by Roy Blount, Jr. Copyright © 1978, 1984, 1985, 1986, 1987, 1988, 1989 by Roy Blount, Jr. Reprinted by permission of Villard Books, a division of Random House, Inc.